The Masseuse

The Masseuse

SIERRA KINCADE

HEAT | NEW YORK

THE BERKLEY PUBLISHING GROUP
Published by the Penguin Group
Penguin Group (USA) LLC
375 Hudson Street, New York, New York 10014

USA • Canada • UK • Ireland • Australia • New Zealand • India • South Africa • China

penguin.com

A Penguin Random House Company

This book is an original publication of The Berkley Publishing Group.

Library of Congress Cataloging-in-Publication Data

Kincade, Sierra.
The masseuse / Sierra Kincade. — Heat trade paperback edition.
pages cm
ISBN 978-0-425-27799-7 (paperback)
1. Masseurs—Fiction.   2. Billionaires—Fiction.   I. Title.
PS3611.I564M36 2014
813'.6—dc23   2014021078

PUBLISHING HISTORY
Heat trade paperback edition / December 2014

PRINTED IN THE UNITED STATES OF AMERICA

10 9 8 7 6 5 4 3 2 1

For Jason, who gave me a real-life love story

ACKNOWLEDGMENTS

This story was so fun to write. From the moment the characters popped up in my head, I knew I was in for wild ride. Thank you to the following people for joining me, leading me, and laughing with me on this incredible journey:

My agents Danielle Egan-Miller, Joanna MacKenzie, and Abby Saul. Thank you for making this happen. Thank you for all the giggles, the encouragement, and the brainstorming sessions on creative . . . ahem . . . positions and colorful synonyms. You guys are truly the best.

My editor, Leis Pederson, and the whole team at Berkley who have embraced and supported this girl and her naughty book.

My husband, who laughed when he read this, and said, "You can't even say half these words out loud!" I love you, and every day I'm grateful for our life together.

Three of the greatest beta-reading friends a girl could ask for: Courtney the lawyer, who only once told me during the course of this trilogy that I couldn't just make up whatever laws I wanted (and then very gently corrected my legal liberties from there on out); Deanna, who has been there every time I needed pity-party ice cream; and Katie, who believed this story was more than my just-for-fun venture that I'd penned between changing diapers. I am lucky to have you all.

And finally, thank you, reader. I hope you enjoy Alec and Anna as much as I have.

One

I chewed the straw sticking out of the plastic lid of my fountain Coke and inspected the sandstone wall, draped with ivy and fragrant white jasmine that curved around the street. It was 4:55 p.m., still over a half hour before my appointment. Typically I showed up a *little* early to get a feel for the place and set up, but on a first meeting, especially with a client like this, I wasn't about to be late.

Maxim Stein was the richest man I'd probably ever get my hands on. When his assistant had called my personal cell phone to make the appointment, I'd done my research.

He came from old money, as my dad would have said. An international string of hotels and island resorts. Some professional sports teams scattered throughout the world. When his father died, he branched out into aviation—private jets, specifically. He was now the sole owner of Force, a company that manufactured custom airplanes for an exclusive international clientele. *Forbes* magazine had called him "a Force to be reckoned with." Too bad he was fifty and on wife number three.

Twice I'd driven past the guard station, just to make sure I had the address right. I'd never been there, but had lived in Tampa just long enough to know Davis Island was a mile above my pay grade. When I'd told my friend Amy about where I was heading, her eyebrows had disappeared beneath her curtain of platinum blonde bangs. Now I could see why.

With its extravagant bayside mansions and gated communities, Davis Island was a hidden refuge close enough to downtown to be accessible, but far enough away to feel like its own world. And it was a world I'd never experienced before—each multimillion-dollar house I'd passed seemed to come with its own gardener trimming the hedges, a security station at the end of its driveway, and a shiny black SUV with tinted windows. My little red Kia was going to get a complex if we stayed out on the street much longer.

The A/C was probably draining my gas tank, but I didn't care. It was better than showing up drenched in sweat. I pointed all the vents in my direction and thought about how Baltimore, where I'd lived last, was probably covered in snow by now.

February in Florida was awesome.

Besides the constant buzzing of a lawn mower behind one of these mystery walls, the neighborhood was quiet. With a few minutes to spare, I rested my head back against the seat and closed my eyes.

And was scared half to death when a hard knock came at the passenger-side window.

"Shit!" I grabbed the cup I'd dropped on my lap and stuffed it into the holder before any Coke could spill.

A man was looking through the window at me. My throat tightened; I hadn't even heard him approach. He stood and walked around the back of the car, placing one hand on the trunk like the damn thing belonged to him. As subtly as I could, I pressed the automatic lock button.

You couldn't be raised by a cop and not end up at least a little cautious.

The man reappeared on my side and tapped again on the window with his knuckle. With the sun behind him, his face was shadowed, but I could tell he was wearing dark glasses that matched his black slacks and button-up shirt. From my vantage point he looked tall, over six feet.

And built. The way he filled out his shirt didn't escape me. Lean, hard muscles stretched across his chest and shoulders had me wondering what he looked like beneath the thin, pressed fabric.

I cracked the window.

He chuckled and slid one finger slowly over the glass edge. "Is this supposed to stop me from getting in?"

I retrieved the mace spray from the pocket in the driver-side door and flashed it where he could see.

"No, but this should."

He laughed a little louder, a deep, smooth sound that made my skin tingle, and then he leaned down, hands resting on top of the car.

We were face-to-face through the glass, and for one drawn-out moment, all I could do was stare. Unruly waves of coffee-colored hair framed an angular jaw that was lined with dark stubble. His nose was the slightest bit crooked, like he'd broken it once, and though his sunglasses hid his eyes, I could feel the heat of his gaze holding me in place. He might have been younger than thirty, but there was a confidence and intensity in the way he moved that seemed older.

He was sexy in an *I-don't-give-a-fuck* kind of way.

I was unable to look away from his mouth, curved in a teasing smirk, or from his full lower lip that I had the sudden urge to bite. I could imagine that mouth pressed against my shoulder, following the line of my collar and then lowering. Just the thought of it made my breath catch.

"Maybe this window's thicker than I thought," he said, giving the glass a little flick.

"What?" I gripped the wheel and tore my gaze away to look straight ahead. I didn't know what had gotten into me. Men, even undeniably attractive men like this one, didn't normally get me going like that. Clearly it had been a while since I'd gotten any.

"I asked if you were lost." He was smirking again, and I nearly groaned. I'd been so caught up staring that I'd missed what he said.

Across the street, a woman walked her two Maltese. She was probably double his age with a pile of white curls on her head, and was shamelessly staring at his ass as he leaned over my car. He must have heard the dogs yapping, but he didn't even flinch. It was like he knew she was looking and either didn't care or was so used to being gawked at, it didn't even faze him.

Probably the latter.

"No," I said quickly. "I was just . . ." I pointed down the road, feeling the blush rise in my cheeks. "I have an appointment with someone."

"In the street."

Apparently he thought he was funny.

"No," I said. "In their home." Not that I needed to explain this to a stranger.

His tongue glided over that bottom lip, and I had to press my thighs together to stifle the sudden need burning low in my belly. He was gorgeous—mesmerizingly so. Never had I had such a reaction to someone before. Usually I was the one making others squirm.

His voice lowered. "When's your next opening?"

"You don't even know what I do," I said suggestively. He wanted to play? Fine. Bring it on.

He kept running his first finger over the top of the window, making me wonder just what else those hands were capable of.

"You're right," he said. "But I bet it's bad." The growl in his voice sent a heated shiver through me. I rolled down the window another six inches.

"Why would you say that?" I licked my lips.

He leaned closer, like he was about to tell me a secret, and I scooted to the edge of my seat.

"You're parked in a no-parking zone," he whispered.

Oh.

His hand left the window to point at the street sign parallel to my spot. Some cop's kid I was; I hadn't even noticed it. With that, he tapped the hood of my car and stood. Whatever chemistry I'd sensed building between us snapped in half.

Who was this guy? Part of the neighborhood watch or something? I fell back in the seat, deflated.

"Right."

I turned the key in the ignition, and the series of clicks from the engine immediately reminded me that the car was already on. Perfect. I checked to see if he'd noticed, and of course he had. His grin stretched wider.

I gave him a little wave. "Thanks."

He took a step back as I put the car in drive and eased off the curb. He must have lived in one of the houses in this neighborhood. I was probably blocking his giant SUV from pulling out of his hand-laid cobblestone driveway through some hidden Batman gate.

Thanks? I asked myself, the sound of his laughter fading behind me. *Nice one, Anna.*

Still, I couldn't help but admire his build in my rearview mirror—long legs; broad, sculpted shoulders. He stood with his arms crossed over his chest right where I'd left him in the middle of the street like he could stop traffic. Hell, he probably could. Maybe he was captain of the neighborhood watch, but he was seriously hot. I was almost sorry when he disappeared from view as I rounded the corner.

Two

pulled into the driveway I'd scouted earlier, and stopped at the guard station just before a tall wrought-iron gate. A guy with a buzz cut in a black suit jacket, way too heavy for today's temperature, stepped out, making note of my license plate. I cleared my throat and sat a little taller, remembering that Mr. Stein's assistant, Ms. Rowe, had said I would have to check in out front.

I rolled the window all the way down, and was hit by a blast of humidity and the sweet jasmine fragrance from the white flowers hanging over the gate. I caught a glimpse of myself in the side mirror—I hadn't even reapplied my lipstick. Neighborhood Watch had seriously thrown me off. I consciously tried to push him from my mind, but my body still buzzed from the smooth sound of his voice accusing me of being bad.

If I wasn't already booked, I might have turned around and showed him just how bad I could be.

No, it was better this way. He was arrogant, probably used to women bending over backward and doing whatever he wanted, just because he was so damn sexy. I didn't mess around with men like that. I needed the upper hand, to call the shots. Anything else was too risky.

The guard approached my window.

"Hi, I'm Anna Rossi. I have a five thirty appointment with Mr. Stein." I made a conscious effort to sound professional; people didn't always take women in my line of work seriously.

The guard looked at me for the first time—his close-set eyes immediately dipped to my cleavage. I pulled up the collar of my black cotton V-neck subtly, used to people looking but not always welcoming the attention. I was a natural C cup, and curvy enough to draw a few stares. He gave a little snort, and I felt my mouth pull into a thin line.

"The masseuse."

"Yes." I forced a smile. This guy had a serious creep factor. It probably served him well in his position guarding this fortress of a house.

"Mr. Stein's assistant is expecting you. You can park in the lot by the gazebo and ask for Ms. Rowe."

The lot by the gazebo? How many lots were there?

"Great, thank you." I pulled forward as the gate slowly opened to reveal a stone fountain, spraying water fifteen feet into the air. The driveway circled around it, taking me past one lot lined with the required black SUV and two tiny two-seater sports cars—bumblebee yellow and candy-apple red—and a slick Harley.

My mouth fell open as I passed the house. Carved from beige sandstone and surrounded by slender palm trees stretching all the way to the roof, it looked like something that belonged in the Mediterranean rather than the United States. Two white marble pillars framed the Venetian doors and held up a second-story balcony where ivy and bright purple flowers cascaded over the ledge. Ceiling fans spun lazily over the porch and the windows were round and made of bright blue glass.

I eased past the gazebo, a quaint wooden seating area between what I assumed was a guest lot and the main residence. Six empty spots waited for me and I chose to park right in the middle, facing a wall of lush greenery.

Quickly I pulled down my visor mirror and reapplied my lipstick. I had naturally bronze skin, but the Florida sun had made it even darker; Amy had completely changed my color pallette at the salon where we both worked since I'd moved here. My smoky eye shadow had held up in the heat, and my dark, wavy hair was still somewhat tame, despite the humidity. Apart from the lipstick, I looked pretty good.

When I stepped out of the car, I felt as if I'd entered some remote area of the world. None of the noises from the street could be heard, even the wall leading to the guard station was hidden behind the landscaping.

A little giggle built inside of me. Even if Mr. Stein didn't like what I had to offer—and I was sure he would because I was good at my job—this was going to be one to remember.

Just as I popped the trunk open, an older man in a gray suit, complete with tails, appeared beside me. With a quiet nod, he motioned toward the back of my car.

"Do you need assistance, Ms. Rossi?" He was eyeing the portable table, folded in half within its black carrying case. It took up most of the room in the back of my car, even with the seats folded down.

"No," I said, making a mental note to tell Amy about the butler. "I'm used to hauling this stuff around. Thanks, though."

"I insist," he said as I hauled the table out by its nylon handle. With a shrug, I passed it to him, feeling guilty when he bowed sideways to lift the strap over his narrow shoulder.

With a heave, I grabbed my matching black duffle and knock-off Coach purse and followed Jeeves toward the house.

"Thank you," I said, waiting for an opportune moment to take back the table without wounding his pride.

"Of course, Ms. Rossi," he said, and swung his leg awkwardly to accommodate the heavy load.

"How long have you worked for Mr. Stein?" I asked as we followed the stone path past the gazebo. Sweat was beginning to bead on his brow, and I felt the urge to make conversation to take the focus off the obvious fact that he had bitten off more than he could chew.

"Some time, I suppose."

I was fairly certain he was trying to be cryptic, not just struggling for breath.

"This is my first time here," I said. "My name's Anna."

"Yes, Ms. Rossi."

"And your name?"

"Here we are," interrupted Jeeves. We'd climbed the front steps of the building and stepped through the double doors into the main foyer. It was a house straight from the movies: Dark marble floors, surrounding an indoor pond filled with koi, were textured by tiles of carved wood. On the opposite side of the expansive entryway was a wall of glass, and though I was twenty feet away, I could see the pool with its stone waterfall and the bay behind it.

"Wow."

"Breathtaking, isn't it?"

I turned to find that Jeeves had vanished just as silently as he'd come and been replaced by a woman in her late thirties with a severe brunette bob and a killer French manicure. A phone earpiece hung from the collar of her snug red wrap dress. She made me more than a little self-conscious of my black yoga pants and matching T-shirt.

"You must be Ms. Rossi." She shook hands like a woman who was used to doing business with men. "You came highly recommended from my stylist, Derrick."

Derrick was the manager at Rave salon, where I worked during the day. He had assured me this would be a good connection, convincing me to break my usual rule of meeting the client at the spa first.

"Anna, please," I said. "And you must be Ms. Rowe."

"I am," she said, making it clear I wouldn't be using her first name. This didn't bother me; Derrick had mentioned she was a little tightly wound. "Mr. Stein is still in a meeting, so if you'll follow me upstairs, I'll show you where you can set up."

"Sounds great." I was ready to get started. No wonder Mr. Stein needed a massage; I was stressed and I'd been here only five minutes.

Ms. Rowe departed without looking back, gliding across the floor in her red pumps as silently as she'd arrived. I picked up the table, crossed the strap over my chest, and followed her up the dizzying steps to the loft.

We passed an open seating area and a bar, and entered a wide hallway lined with antique mirrors and decadently framed oil paintings of landscapes. Track lighting on the ceiling highlighted each piece of art. I sucked in my breath, trying not to bang into anything with all my cargo.

"You'll be meeting Mr. Stein here," she said, exiting through a door at the end of the hallway onto a veranda, where we were greeted by the blue waters of the bay and the afternoon sun lowering in the pink sky. I dropped the fifty-pound table case to stretch my back, and walked to the railing, breathing in the sweet scents from the flowers hanging in red pots from the ledge and the chlorine from the pool below. Cool air misted in from the revolving ceiling fans, making the temperature comfortable.

"What I wouldn't give for a view like this," I murmured.

Ms. Rowe snorted. "You should see the house in Naples."

"Naples, Florida?" I asked with a grin.

"No," she said, clearly not a fan of sarcasm. "Italy. The Steins have six homes."

At the mention of Maxim Stein's wife, I turned. "Will Mrs. Stein be around this evening?" I was hoping to take her on as a client as well.

"Mrs. Stein stays at the flat in New York."

From the sound of it, Mr. Stein didn't join her there.

"There is a sink in the washroom just inside, and an iPod dock here if you need music." She pointed to a beige box embedded into the wall.

I nodded. If I'd known that I wouldn't have dragged my portable system from the car.

"Anything else you need?"

"Just a body."

She smiled tightly. "You will, of course, be compensated for staying late."

"That's not what I meant," I said, feeling a little guilty for cracking jokes. "Please tell Mr. Stein to take his time. I can be here as late as he needs."

It wasn't exactly true. I had my second date with Randall at nine, but I wasn't too worried about canceling. He was cute enough, but he didn't exactly do it for me.

Not like I was sure Neighborhood Watch could.

Ms. Rowe had judgment in her eyes. It was almost like she was reading my mind.

"Now, if you'll just sign this." She handed me a clipboard, and I felt my brows lift in surprise. "It's standard for all of Mr. Stein's employees, domestic or otherwise."

"Domestic or otherwise," I repeated, scanning the form. Is that what I was? A domestic employee? No one had told me I'd be signing anything besides maybe a tax form, and looking over the items on the list, I could see why.

"Um," I said. "I'm not going to steal any of his things."

There were a dozen more items equally as offensive, almost laughable. I guess they had all made the list for a reason, but I was still shocked to see that I couldn't pick any plants without written permission from the landscaping crew or take photographs of any of the art.

She placed a hand on her bony hip. "You can have your lawyer review it, but I assure you . . ."

"No," I said, reading through the rest of the list and signing on the dotted line. Ms. Rowe had offered $300 for this hour, three times my usual house-call rate, and I wasn't about to blow it. "It's fine. But if you'd like to contact my references, they can assure you I'm professional."

"I already have, and they already have." She snatched back the clipboard as soon as I was done. "I'm glad you understand."

The earpiece hanging around her neck lit up blue, and she placed it in her ear.

"Mr. Stein will be up as soon as he's done. Make yourself comfortable. His meetings have been known to run long." She said the last words through her teeth, obviously annoyed.

I sighed as she closed the door behind her, glad she was gone.

"Somebody needs to get laid," I said to myself, realizing I wasn't in much better shape after the way I'd reacted to Neighborhood Watch outside. Then, resolving to enjoy this beautiful house and a big fat paycheck, I started setting out my supplies.

The table, a gift I'd bought myself after I'd finished massage school, was the Cadillac of tables—big, plush, and expensive. When I'd decided I wanted to do work in people's homes, I'd taken the plunge and made the purchase. It was worth every penny; more than one client had told me it was softer than their bed.

After that, I laid out my oil and three bottled aromatherapy scents for Mr. Stein to choose from. Lavender, cinnamon, and sandalwood. I preferred the last—it was soothing; I even had sandalwood-scented shampoo—but few clients chose it. I could almost guarantee Mr. Stein would choose cinnamon. Men usually did. It made them think of sex.

It made me think of Christmas, but whatever. I wasn't a guy.

After setting up my iPod and laying out the sheets, I filled a silver basin with water from the washroom and set a towel and a bamboo box of salt scrub for Mr. Stein's foot treatment beside it. People generally felt pampered by the extra service, but the truth was, I preferred knowing their feet wouldn't stink like four-day-old socks when I went to rub them.

Mr. Stein had yet to make an entrance when I'd finished. For a while I admired the view, awed by the setting sun and the explosion of pink and orange lighting the horizon, but as the sun disappeared, I went to check the watch I'd left in my purse—6:10 p.m. He was forty minutes late.

Curiosity getting the better of me, I walked the length of the veranda, coming to a descending staircase at the far end. I glanced over my shoulder, but there was still no sign of my client, and since exploring wasn't explicitly forbidden in the contract I'd signed, I made my way down.

Maybe it was because the grounds were so quiet, but I found myself trying to keep each step silent—not hard to do in the leopard-print ballet slippers I was wearing. When I reached the bottom, I followed the stone steps to an adjacent cottage, fashioned in the same open, airy Mediterranean style as the house. I listened for movement from upstairs, and hearing nothing, I moved a little closer, spotting an entrance cut through the house to a deck over the bay.

"Just a quick look," I told myself, feeling a little reckless.

I walked through a small courtyard with another smaller stone fountain, straight out to the deck, taking in one last view of the sunset. Behind me, long white linen curtains blew in the breeze, and below, the water lapped against the pier. The place was truly incredible. I could only imagine what some of Mr. Stein's other houses were like.

I was just about to turn back when I heard something behind me: the distinct, rhythmic slapping of skin on skin, and a woman's throaty moan.

Three

"*Harder,*" she ordered.

I ducked without thinking.

"Yes," she said. "Like that. Don't slow down!"

The slapping sound quickened and was accompanied by her cries of pleasure.

I swore silently. What had I been thinking, coming down here? This wasn't my house. I hadn't even met the owner yet. And now I'd just blindly walked into someone's fuckpad. There was no way I was making it out of this one without getting caught.

I hid behind the wall like some teenager trying to sneak out her bedroom window, and leaned out around the corner to see if my exit was clear.

The courtyard was no longer empty. A woman with red hair, completely naked and angled away from me, was bent over, gripping the smooth white stone of the fountain while a man in only a white collared shirt rammed into her from behind. Just past them, the door of a room had been flung open, and scattered across the ground were articles of clothing.

The tempo increased. *Slap, slap, slap, slap.*

I ducked back around the corner, trying to unsee the man's clenched white ass, and the woman's hard, fake breasts that barely moved as he fucked her. I was sure they hadn't seen me, or at least if they had, they didn't care, because he began to grunt, and she began to shriek, and as strange and wrong as it was, it made me hot as hell.

For just a flash, I imagined myself bent over that fountain, but instead of this guy, it was Neighborhood Watch and his hard body behind me. His hands gripping my hips. His teeth nipping my ear while his hard cock speared into me over and over.

"Goddammit, I said harder," demanded the woman.

I snapped out of my trance and searched for a way out. The man had to be Maxim Stein. Who else would be having sex out in the open on this property? I'd caught a glimpse of his silver hair—I recognized that from the pictures I'd seen of him online. The woman was clearly not his wife, though. Maxim's wife was petite, blonde, and in her midfifties, not nearly ten years younger with red hair. Besides, according to Ms. Rowe, Mrs. Stein was in New York.

I blew out a tight breath. I was probably going to get arrested. Or sued. There went my massage license. There went my three hundred bucks for rent.

To my left near the end of the deck was a door, and I crawled toward it, praying it was unlocked and that it would lead me out of there unnoticed. Rising to my knees, I tried the handle. Apparently I was luckier than I thought. The door pulled outward with just a slight whine, and I crawled within, checking carefully first to make sure the room was empty.

It was an office; an antique mahogany desk sat in the center of the room, backed by a wall of bookcases filled with hardcovers and trinkets. I made my way across the room to another door, but this one was unfortunately locked.

"Shit." I was going to have to wait it out. Hopefully, when

they finished, which should be soon, I could sneak back to the veranda and wait for Mr. Stein.

If Ms. Rowe hadn't already come searching for me.

I padded quietly over the plush carpet, glancing over the contents on the desk. There was a slim leather file case and a pile of papers, spread over the glass top. It looked like the design of an engine. I couldn't help but be intrigued. My father liked to rebuild car engines, so I was used to seeing schematics like this from time to time. The layout of this one was obviously different—I assumed the design was for a plane engine, not a car, since that was the business behind Maxim's considerable wealth—but they were similar nonetheless. The bottom of each document was stamped with a narrow emerald leaf, standing out in contrast to the black and white designs, and the words *GREEN FUSION*.

They were still going at it outside, so I made my way to the shelves to look at the framed pictures. It was definitely Maxim Stein in the courtyard. Maybe I hadn't seen his face, but I could tell from his hair and build that the man I saw and the man holding a fat silver perch on a fishing boat in this photo were one and the same.

There were other pictures here as well. Maxim receiving awards. Maxim giving speeches.

Maxim with his arm around the shoulders of a handsome man half his age with dark chocolate hair and a cocky little smirk.

Neighborhood Watch.

I moved closer to the photograph, careful not to touch it. The man I'd met in the street was pictured wearing a black leather jacket, looking away as though being called by someone. He was younger, maybe twenty-one or twenty-two, with shorter hair but more scruff on his jaw. Though he was still undeniably sexy, there was a tightness around his eyes, a wariness he was trying to hide with that grin. It wasn't obvious, at least not to a beaming Maxim, but I could see it. The mark of someone who was waiting for the other shoe to drop—a look you disguised so that no one asked why. I'd perfected that cover. It was how I'd survived for as long as I could remember.

It looked like they were on a college campus somewhere. Maxim was probably a donor there.

I spun as the locked door clicked, and then slid inward. My chest tightened. I nearly considered running back outside, but held my ground, knowing running would just make it worse. I was so busted.

Then, as if I'd conjured him with my thoughts, I found myself face-to-face with the very man I'd been lusting over since my arrival.

"I should have pegged you as someone who liked to watch," he said, that smooth voice rich with sensuality.

He wasn't wearing his sunglasses now. His eyes were dark blue like the bay, and just as intense as I'd imagined. I was pinned to the spot by his gaze, cheeks heating from being caught, skin growing damp from the hard look of his body. My eyes dropped to the open collar of his white dress shirt. The lines of his throat collided with a swell of muscle that disappeared beneath the pressed fabric. Just the top of his collarbone was revealed, and my fingers itched to trace it, to spread his shirt open so I could see what would surely be the impressive physique beneath.

I wasn't the only one enjoying the view. He devoured me with his eyes, leaving me feeling naked and wanting. His thumb tapped against his thigh, the only betrayal of his composed facade. The tension in the room became so thick I could barely breathe. Surely he had to feel it sizzling between us.

He moved closer, steps fluid like a jungle cat, and sat on the edge of the desk, an arm's length away. At five foot four I wasn't short, but even though he was seated, I had to look up to him. He made no sign that he could hear the sounds of sex just outside, but I could. I'd never been more uncomfortable, embarrassed, or turned on.

He crossed his arms over his muscular chest, knees spread,

and because I was suddenly envisioning myself kneeling between them, I stepped back, tearing away from the pull he had on me.

"What are you doing here?" I managed.

His mouth turned up in a grin. He had a dimple on one side that was somehow cute and erotic at the same time. The shadows of worry I'd seen in the picture were hidden now. Maybe he'd exorcised those demons. If they were anything like mine, I doubted it. Experiences that gave you a look like that marked you for life.

Not that I presumed to know anything about him.

He tilted his head, as if trying to read my mind.

"I was just about to ask you the same thing."

I tried to concentrate on his words, but outside, the woman began a series of staccato cries, matching each thrust.

"Yes," she cried. "Yes! I'm coming. Don't stop!"

"I got a little lost," I said.

"I see."

He glanced to the paperwork on the desk, a frown flashing quickly across his face. It made me nervous.

"What were you looking for in here, Anna?" His voice had hardened.

My brows lifted. He knew my name. It shouldn't have stirred up the butterflies inside me—he was Mr. Stein's security, or bodyguard maybe. He'd probably known who I was since he had approached me on the street.

"I was just trying to get out of the way," I said truthfully.

His eyes narrowed. "To hide."

"That's right."

I felt a chill cut through the room. That wary look in his eyes returned, just for one unmistakable moment. The sudden urge to smooth the lines between his brows with my thumbs took me by surprise.

"I wasn't here to steal anything, if that's what you're thinking," I said.

"Why would I think that?"

I placed my hands on my hips, feeling the defensiveness creep up inside me.

"I signed the papers. No stealing. No picking the flowers. No feeding the fish."

He gave a little snort and relaxed again, turning the papers facedown on the desk. I wondered what was so important that he was trying to hide—I could care less about engine designs, plane or otherwise—but I reminded myself that one didn't become a millionaire without being a little bit paranoid.

I cleared my throat. "Are you his son?" It occurred to me how twisted this was if it were true. At sixteen, I'd walked in on my parents in bed, and all two seconds were enough to leave permanent scars.

He shook his head. "I work for him."

That was a little better, but not much.

He stood and, before he could get too close, I backed into the bookshelf. The pictures rattled, and I spun to hold them in place before any fell.

He stepped closer. I could feel his body behind me. Fighting the image of us naked, I turned slowly, my throat dry.

"What do you do, exactly?" I asked weakly. He was close enough to touch. I kept my hands down at my sides, fearful I would forget myself if I touched him, aware that my breasts, heaving with each breath, were just inches from his chest.

Part of me couldn't believe this was happening. He'd gone from hot to cold to hot again in seconds. I should have told him to back off, but either I couldn't or I didn't want to.

"A little of this, a little of that." He smelled so masculine; the kind of scent that made me want to rip his clothes off and rub against him.

I was losing my mind.

"That's cryptic," I said, focusing on the desk behind him. "How did you find me?"

He stepped even closer, and my breath caught. Slowly, our

bodies aligned, chest to chest, his cock, hard and heavy, against my stomach. His mouth was inches from mine. My nipples were so tight they were painful as they rubbed against the clothing between our bodies.

"What are you doing?" I asked breathlessly.

He shifted, and I nearly groaned from the friction.

"It makes you hot, doesn't it? Listening to other people fuck."

The way he said it brought an intense ache between my thighs.

"I . . ." I couldn't admit the truth, could I? I'd never been in a situation like this before.

"Or is that what you want?" he continued, all traces of his grin gone. "Being taken like that, out where anyone might see you?"

No one had ever said such dirty things to me before. I should have been offended, but it just made me want him more. His arms lifted, caging me in as he gripped a shelf behind me.

"I wouldn't share you, not even like that." His lip skimmed my ear. "Your body, your sounds, they'd be all mine."

I sagged against the bookcase, feeling my knees begin to wobble. Who was this man, talking to me like this? It felt like something out of a dream. The kind where I woke up wet and empty, with the sheets twisted around my sweating body.

He glanced up, just for a second, and retrieved something from the top shelf. Backing away slowly, he held out the object for me to see. A small video camera. My suspicions were confirmed; he wasn't just head of the neighborhood watch, he was Mr. Stein's security.

That was twice he'd made me feel like an idiot. It was beginning to get on my nerves. I stepped away, out of the hold he had on me. My breath came a little easier with the distance, but not much.

"Let me get this straight. You're following me, and probably those two as well," I tilted my head toward the courtyard, where Maxim gave a hoarse shout, "and *I'm* the voyeur." I could feel his eyes on my back.

"Yes, but I get paid to watch."

"Doesn't make you any less of a pervert." I pulled my hair over one shoulder to give him a clear look of my back and waist, and was pleased when I heard him draw in a quick breath.

"Never said I wasn't a pervert," he said. "Maybe we can explore that some time."

We were both stalled by a sudden silence in the adjoining courtyard. I turned.

"Maybe," I said. "If you can get me out of here."

He moved to the door where he'd entered. "Follow me, Anna."

He placed one finger on his lips, and I followed him in silence through a bedroom, where more clothes were tossed on a four-poster, and through a side door that went around the back of the cottage. From there we walked quickly to the staircase I had come down earlier, and I cut ahead of him in my hurry to get to the top. I stopped after a few steps when I heard he wasn't following.

"Looks like you know where you're going," he said, grasping the side railings with both hands, blocking my way back down. His shirtsleeves were rolled up to the elbow, and the way his forearms flexed had me dying to see what his biceps looked like underneath.

"Thank you." I bit my lip, aware of how his eyes lowered to my mouth as I did so. "I wonder if you might be kind enough to forget what happened back there."

He gave a low chuckle, and the sound went straight to my core. If I didn't get away from him soon, I was going to end up jumping him right here on the stairs.

"It's our little secret."

I gave him a grateful nod. "I owe you."

"Careful," he warned. "I'll hold you to that."

What I would give to find out what that entailed.

He turned to leave, and I admired his perfectly shaped back-side for all of three seconds before I heard the buzz of a security camera turning over my head. I don't know how I'd missed it before, but I couldn't say I was altogether too sorry now.

It wasn't until I returned to the top of the stairs that I realized I hadn't even asked his name.

Four

Maxim Stein arrived on the veranda exactly fifteen minutes later, wearing a terry-cloth robe and leather sandals. The pictures in the cottage study had paled in comparison to reality; there was a cool confidence in the way he carried himself that couldn't be captured on camera. His jaw was clean-shaven and set, his gaze appraising. His silver hair was combed back and damp—maybe that meant he'd washed off following his romp with the redhead, but I doubted it. Power, wealth, and status seemed to ooze off him. As he approached, I was surprised he wasn't much more than four or five inches taller than me—he carried himself like someone who was used to looking down on others.

I found myself shrinking, unable to look him in the eye. All I could think of were his bare legs and grunts of pleasure as he had plowed into his demanding redheaded mistress from behind. When it was clear he didn't know I'd caught him, I exhaled, but remained jittery from all that had just happened.

"The masseuse, I presume," he said in a flat voice, already removing the robe from his shoulders.

"Anna." I offered my hand, but he had made his way to the table and was kicking off his sandals.

I cleared my throat, feeling my jaw twitch. Something told me I wasn't about to get an apology for his late arrival—not that I deserved one. Any thought I'd had of asking him the name of his bodyguard vaporized.

"Please have a seat on the table," I told him. "I'd like to begin our session with a foot scrub, if that's all right."

"Is that included in the price?"

I nearly choked. According to Forbes, Mr. Stein was worth 3.8 billion dollars. If I charged for a foot scrub, which I didn't, I was pretty sure he could afford it. I doubted he even knew how much he was paying for today's service anyway.

"Of course," I said with my best smile. I kneeled before him as he sat down, and moved the water under his pedicured toes. He fished a smartphone out of his pocket and began to scroll through his messages, barely even glancing down as I prepared the salt scrub.

"I just finished working out and didn't have a chance to shower," he said as I moved one foot into the basin of warm water. "I hope you don't mind."

Right. I forced myself not to look up, aware of the smell of sex now wafting off him as the breeze changed. I nearly gagged; I may have been turned on before, but that had disappeared with Neighborhood Watch.

I finished quickly and offered Maxim the scents to choose from. He chose cinnamon. Of course.

When I got back to my car, I was $400 richer and had three messages waiting on my cell phone; two from Amy asking if I'd been kidnapped by rich people, and one from my dad. I called him first, my paycheck celebration momentarily put on pause by the tiredness in his voice.

"Well, if it isn't my favorite daughter," he said, answering after the first ring.

"Only daughter."

"That doesn't make you any less my favorite," he pointed out. "What are you doing out so late?"

His handsome face came to mind: green eyes, fair skin, freckles. Big saucer glasses that he wore at the end of the day after he took his contacts out. We looked nothing like each other, a fact that had often drawn stares in my youth. But even though we weren't related by blood, that didn't make him any less my father.

I made the final turn out of Davis Island and climbed onto the freeway that would take me to my apartment in Ybor City, right in the heart of the historic district.

"First, it's only eight thirty," I told him. "Second, I had a client."

"First," he replied, mirroring my tone, "your curfew's eight. And second, I don't like you going out to people's houses so late at night."

I smiled. "My curfew hasn't been eight since I was in middle school. I'm twenty-seven, in case you forgot."

"Stop growing up," he said. "I've had about enough of that."

His voice fell at the end; we'd reached the boundary of his good mood.

"Yes, sir." I cleared my voice. "So what'd you do today?" I'd talked to him every day this week. It was a hard one; we'd lost my adoptive mother four years ago to breast cancer. This was their anniversary week. They would have been married thirty-six years.

The sting was gone, though the ache remained. But as much as I missed her, I knew it was so much harder for him. She'd been his whole world.

"I had Tuesday breakfast," he said, and I was flooded with double-decker-pancake nostalgia, the special at Manny's Diner where we'd spent every Tuesday morning of my youth.

Cincinnati—the place I called home, thanks to my dad—felt a long way away all of a sudden.

He sighed. "And then I went to see my girl."

I pulled into my parking garage and killed the engine. I couldn't get out of my car yet; my body felt too heavy. The thought of going out on a date tonight with Randall seemed like an enormous amount of work.

"Yeah?" I could picture my dad going to her grave with a bundle of yellow roses—her favorite—and a bottle of wine. He would sit beside her like he always did, telling her about what he'd done that day, filling her in on any new updates about me, until he ran out of things to say. Then he'd sit in the silence just because he wanted to be close to her.

I couldn't imagine anyone loving me the way he loved her.

"Maybe . . . Dad, maybe you should try going out."

He groaned. "The guys have talked me into joining the bowling league. Can you believe that? Thirty years on the force I managed to avoid that crap, and the minute I retire, they talk me into it. Soon I'll be fat and bald and eating donuts every morning."

I sincerely doubted it. My dad's strawberry blond hair may have been a bit more blond than strawberry these days, but he still ran three miles every morning, something he had done as long as I could remember. Though he was afraid of becoming a classic cop cliché, anyone who knew him could have told you he wasn't really going to give up the job completely. It was too much a part of who he was.

"Good," I said, glad he was doing something with friends. He hadn't done much socially since Mom died. "But you know what I meant."

There was a pause on the line. "I had my time, Anna. Your mom, she was my sweetheart. You don't get that twice in one life. I was lucky to get it at all."

My heart hurt. "I just don't like the thought of you being lonely."

"I'm not lonely," he retorted. "I've got Mug."

Mug was his Great Dane, the biggest lap dog I'd ever seen.

"I'll come home soon," I told him. I'd already scheduled a follow-up with Mr. Stein next week. A month of this, and I'd definitely have the money for plane fare.

"All right." His tone lightened. "Mug won't be happy, though. He's already taken over your room. You'll have to sleep on the couch."

"Love you, Dad."

"Love you, Anna."

I nearly called Randall and told him I wasn't in the mood, but after talking to my dad, I wasn't sure I wanted to be alone either.

I'd texted to tell him I'd be late, but when I met Randall at Pho, a Vietnamese fusion restaurant downtown, he was already waiting at the table, mouth tight with impatience. It looked like he'd already ordered and finished an appetizer when I sat down across from him.

He looked up from his cell phone, surprised. I guess he hadn't seen me come in.

Randall was handsome and he knew it. With his semi-ridiculous dirty blond hair swept across his forehead and dark lashes, he looked more like an ex–boy-band member than a psychologist. He had just the right amount of stubble, which no doubt he'd planned, and wore a beige sweater to complement his brown eyes.

We'd been out only once before, a setup by Amy. On that first date he'd informed me he was in the top one percent of educated Americans, and one of the youngest psychologists in the state with his own private practice. He certainly wasn't modest, but Amy had convinced me that was just the nerves talking.

"Sorry I'm late," I said. "A client ran over."

He finished typing something before replying, and I ordered a glass of red wine, trying not to focus on the fact that this was the second man today who'd chosen to look at his cell phone rather than me when I was talking.

"Thanks, just had to finish that e-mail," he said, placing the phone in his pocket. "Wow. You look nice."

Nice wasn't exactly what I'd been going for in the black skirt, knee-high boots, and turquoise halter top, but from the look on his face I could tell the word didn't convey what he really thought. He was trying hard not to stare at my cleavage.

Normally I would have been pleased to have him right where I wanted him, but the lust in his eyes barely roused the butterflies in my stomach. Probably just hunger, combined with the call from my dad and thoughts of my mom.

I needed a distraction.

A distraction with penetrating blue eyes, chiseled shoulders, and a dirty mouth.

I'd thought of Mr. Stein's sexy security guard when I'd picked out my outfit. Originally I'd planned on wearing a bright pink button-up blouse and silver flats, but when I'd thought of those eyes, I'd changed course to something less conventional—an impulse buy I'd picked up last month that I had planned to hand over to a much sassier Amy.

"What's good here?" I asked, perusing the menu.

"The spring rolls are good," he said. "Or the shaking beef. That's what I had."

I glanced at his plate, which had yet to be cleared. "You already ate dinner?"

He swiped his hair out of his eyes. "Yes, but don't feel like you have to hurry on my account. My last patient canceled, so I got here a little early."

Miffed, I leaned back in my chair, noting that the butterflies were beginning to growl. They had their diva moments.

"I'll just get some spring rolls then," I said, shifting gears. "So what's new with Dr. Randall?"

A lot, apparently, was new with Randall. He told me all about his week, his practice, the new insurance billing program that was gouging him, his depressed housewives and alcoholic retirees who'd thought that Florida was going to be everything they'd dreamed it would be—beaches, sunsets, perpetual vacation—only to find it was just like anywhere else but with palm trees and a really hot summer.

I didn't mind his nonstop chatter; it was better than talking about what was going on with me.

When I'd finished my second glass of wine, the spring rolls, and a bowl of pho, he finally paused for breath.

"I'm boring you," he said. "I spend so much time listening at work, sometimes it's nice to have someone else do it for a change."

"Your practice sounds fascinating," I said, watching as he again shoved back his hair. I wanted to shove back Neighborhood Watch's hair. I wanted to grip it with both hands as he kissed me, sliding his tongue between my lips and grinding his hips against mine.

"There are a lot of people out there who are hurting." He sat forward in his chair. "How about you?"

I felt my spine zip up straight. Randall the date had changed; the tone of his voice softer, more empathetic, his brows furrowed with concern. He was Dr. Randall now, looking for my vulnerabilities.

"I'm sorry?" I had to force my shoulders to relax.

"You have a background in the field, don't you? I thought that's what Amy said."

Of course, that's what he meant. Relieved to avoid a glimpse into the troubled past of Anna Rossi, I picked up my chopsticks, set them down again. I knew Amy had told him about my last line of work; it was why she'd set us up in the first place. It was just a matter of time before one of us brought it up.

"Sort of," I acknowledged. "Nothing like your practice."

"Ah, minimization," he said, entertained. "The favorite cognitive distortion of all nice people."

I snickered. "I'm not that nice, believe me."

He waited. Or rather, used therapeutic silence—a technique I'd learned in college—to let me work through my thoughts. The idea was that it could make even the most stubborn people share.

"Social work," I said, giving in. "That was a long time ago." Maybe he wasn't that bad of a psychologist after all.

"Oh." His brows flattened as he leaned back in his seat. "Social work. The society of bleeding hearts. What did you do, stamp welfare checks?" He laughed like this was some sort of inside joke.

"Not exactly," I said stiffly.

He leaned forward, elbows on the table. His fingertips found my hands and began to trail lightly over them.

"That was rude," he acknowledged without an apology. "I got my Ph.D. so I wouldn't have to do the dirty work. You're a better person than I am, Anna."

A better person wouldn't have let her personal life leak all over her professional life. A better person wouldn't have quit.

"I don't know about that," I said. "There were a lot of kids I couldn't help." Strange that after all this time I could still see their faces and feel like a failure.

"You can't save everyone." He made a face. "All those crack babies and abusive parents fighting over custody. Sounds like a nightmare. No wonder you burned out."

He made the same assumption most people did—that child protective services was only about snatching babies out of bad homes, not about bringing families back together, and that I couldn't stand the heat. The truth was, that kind of work hit too close to home, but I wasn't about to open that can of worms here and now.

I subtly pulled my hands away and waved to the waiter for the check. It was almost eleven, and the place was going to be closing soon. One of the downfalls of being a masseuse was a lot of late hours. Psychologists also set their own schedules, and as Randall informed me, he enjoyed sleeping in and seeing clients in the afternoon and evening.

We could have worked. If I'd felt something.

"Well," I said. "Nothing lasts forever."

"One check or two?" interrupted the waiter, a cute artsy guy around eighteen.

"Two," said Randall without looking up.

The water raised a brow at me.

"Two checks would be perfect," I said.

Having known I was going to have a glass of wine, I'd taken the trolley to Channelside and walked the rest of the way. It was late, and downtown was fairly quiet on weeknights, so I decided to wait for a cab.

I turned to say good-bye, ready to cut ties, when Randall invaded my personal space and kissed me.

For one flash of a moment I wavered and considered taking him to bed. Randall would be a good lover, if maybe a little self-ish. He had a nice body—one hardened by treadmills and free weights and personal trainers, no doubt. He'd keep me from thinking about my family and, best of all, he'd be easy to push out the door in the morning.

But I couldn't shake the memory of another man's body press-ing mine up against a bookcase. I couldn't get those piercing eyes or his voice out of my head. I couldn't stop thinking about what he would feel like, driving into me as I scratched my nails down his back.

Randall seemed like a poor substitute, and it wasn't fair to lead him on.

Too late to fully escape, I turned, and his lips found the corner of mine. They were waxy with Chapstick and stuck a little as I tried to pull away. His eyes were already closed, and my nose itched a little from the overpowering smell of his cologne.

The butterflies in my belly yawned. They made a big, dra-matic show of it.

"I like a woman with curves," he said, giving my hips a little squeeze. "More to hold on to."

Translation: You're not skinny, but you have nice boobs.

Carefully, I placed my hands on his chest and eased back. I may not have been a Calvin Klein model, but I'd be damned if I didn't look good filling out a size eight.

"Why don't you let me give you a ride home?" Randall wove his fingers together behind my lower back, latching me in place. "Better yet, why don't you come over?"

I pulled away, placing a hand on his forearm. "I think it's better I didn't."

The poor guy looked genuinely confused by this.

"Did I misinterpret what was happening here?"

"If you thought this would end in me spending the night, then yes," I said.

"Oh, come on," he said, reaching again to push the hair out of his eyes. I couldn't believe Amy had agreed to give him that terrible haircut. "When you put on that outfit, you didn't think you'd be spending the night too?"

My gaze narrowed. I had been thinking about spending the night with someone, just not him.

"Don't make this ugly," I said.

"What?" he asked, and then threw his shoulders back. "You know what, forget it. Have a great night. I should have offered a tip if I wanted a happy ending."

"A tip?" I asked, hip cocked out. "You didn't even buy me dinner."

The light from the restaurant revealed the color rising in his cheeks.

"And spare me the masseuse jokes," I added. "I've heard them all before."

I left him standing in front of his white Lexus, nervously glancing around to make sure no one was within earshot.

Fueled by annoyance, I walked quickly, the heels of my boots clicking over the sidewalk. The occasional car passed, but there weren't any cabs nearby. Pho wasn't in the restaurant district—this area was mostly dedicated to business, so after work hours, it tended to empty out. I crossed the street, making my way toward the Taco Bus and the police station. There was always someone in need of a cab there.

I was glad I hadn't succumbed to loneliness and brought Randall home. He was a pompous ass, only interested in himself—which is exactly why I'd liked him on the first date. I usually preferred guys who didn't ask any questions. I didn't want Randall digging around in my baggage, but at the same time it bothered me that he hadn't really tried. It was a double standard I'd struggled with my whole life: I wanted someone to know me, but I wouldn't let them get close enough to do it. It wasn't worth it in the long run. You ended up alone, hurt, sitting on a grave by yourself drinking wine.

It was better this way. I'd been thrown off by all the stuff with my dad and the grief he lived with every day for his soul mate. The last thing I needed was Randall trying to fill the void.

Frowning, I passed the station and all the cop cars parked in the lot. Before he made detective, my dad used to take me to school in his cruiser. All the buttons and lights and sirens inside fascinated me, even when I was fifteen and having a cop in your family was the absolute worst. It always reminded me of the first night I'd ridden with him—I'd been eight years old, tired, scared, and starving, but hopeful too. Sometimes the first time you meet someone you know they're going to change your life, and that's the way I felt about Officer Rossi, the man who would later become my father.

As I came to the police station, I changed my mind about the cab. The night was cool, and it felt better to walk. With each step, my bad date and overthinking faded behind me, and once again I found my mind returning to Neighborhood Watch, and the incomprehensible, almost uncontrollable need I'd felt in his presence.

I couldn't believe I didn't know his real name, and I hadn't given him my number, not that he would have called anyway. He probably had a hundred women waiting for the chance to jump into bed with him. Maybe I wasn't looking for anything serious, but I also didn't want to be a notch on someone's belt. I got the feeling Neighborhood Watch was a serious playboy, and I could count the number of guys I'd slept with on two hands.

I kept to the well-lit streets, heading straight for the Channelside area. A Lightning hockey game was just letting out at the downtown arena, and as I approached the hordes of fans in blue emptying into the street, I felt a shiver work down my spine. I glanced behind me, but apart from a few homeless men, there was no movement.

Hugging my clutch to my chest, I hurried on, still glancing around. Someone was following me, I was sure of it. I removed the Mace from my wallet and held it in my fist, remembering all the self-defense classes my dad had made me take before I left for college.

Only, instead of feeling scared, I was flushed. My breasts were heavy and aching, and each step brought the slightest bit of friction to my oversensitive sex. It was like someone was watching me, checking me out, *wanting* me. I could feel the stranger's eyes roaming over my exposed skin, and I fought the urge to slow down and reveal a little bit more, a crazy impulse that went against everything I'd ever learned.

When I crossed the intersection into the crowd, I stopped and turned in a full circle, but I couldn't see anyone. It was probably just my overactive imagination.

Giving up on my search, I jogged to catch the red trolley at the corner and climbed aboard. The compartment was packed with men and women in oversize hockey jerseys celebrating the Lightning's victory. Drunk as some of them were, I was safer here than I had been on the street. I probably should have taken a cab, but at least I wasn't alone now.

The trolley dropped me off near my apartment in an old cigar factory converted into restaurants, studio flats, and condos. Before entering the building, I checked behind me one last time to make sure I wasn't being followed. This part of the city was just beginning to come to life—music from the clubs down the street was already pounding, and a group of men across the street whistled at three cross-dressing strippers who blew them kisses. What a surprise the boys were in for when they realized what was hidden beneath those miniskirts. It was Ybor City at its best.

I climbed the steps to the second floor, hit hard by the strong aroma of Chinese food from the take-out restaurant below my studio apartment. The location—which always smelled of lo mein and sounded like a team of toddlers had broken out the pots and pans—was how I'd gotten the place so cheap.

The space was small, but it was mine, and for now I liked it. It was the sixth place I'd lived in within seven years and would do until the itch to move on struck me again. I liked to think of each new destination as a check mark on my explore-the-world bucket list.

I threw my purse on the flowery three-legged stool I'd picked up at a yard sale and locked the dead bolt behind me. One room may not have seemed very big, but it was enough for me. The tiny bathroom and closet were off to the left, while the '70s-era pea-green kitchen sat opposite, taking the right corner of the room. The far window overlooked Seventh Avenue, with its pretty strings of twinkling lights draped between the old streetlamps. The bottom floor of the old immigrant hospital across the street had been converted to a steak house, but the second story was still empty, so I didn't bother closing the curtains over the bay window as I took off my shirt and threw it on the bed. The black low-set frame from IKEA may have been cheap, but I'd sprung for the softest sheets I could find, and a plush purple comforter that made me feel like royalty.

Slipping off the skirt, I looked out the window, knowing those on the street couldn't see me in my yellow lace strapless bra and matching boy short panties. I wanted someone to see me, though, and as my hands slid down my body of their own accord I thought of him. I imagined his strong arms around my waist, lifting me up, spreading me, his thick cock sliding deep inside while I screamed his name. I thought of my hands fisting his dark hair, and his mouth on my neck. I turned, and leaned back against the glass, feeling the way it would press against my skin as he fucked me.

My hand slid down the front of my panties, finding my slit sensitive and slippery, and when I came, it was with a whimper, not a scream.

Five

It was a long, restless night. I barely slept, and when I did, my dreams were haunted by a man with wavy hair and wild blue eyes, pressing my knees apart and planting hot, wet kisses up my thighs. But every time he got close to my center, I woke up, aching and edgy and too hot, even after I'd shucked my nightie and thrown my comforter to the floor.

It was an obsession. A crazy fantasy that would never come true. I didn't know why Mr. Stein's security guard had had such an effect on me, but it was unhealthy. I couldn't even concentrate long enough to make coffee, and it was an automatic coffeemaker.

I settled for pushing the love seat in the center of my apartment aside, turning my iPod to classic Aerosmith, and powering through an hour of yoga. It was worth it: After five sun salutations and a cold shower, I'd burned up most of my angst and was feeling considerably more in control.

A little mascara, eyeliner, and my new cosmetic fave—a dark red lipstick called Siren—and I was out the door. I didn't bother doing my hair; one of the perks of working at a salon was there were plenty of people there to do it for you, so I left it down to dry in the Tampa heat.

I stopped at Javaz, a coffee shop around the corner from my apartment and five blocks from the salon, Rave, and stepped through the wall of air-conditioning to treat myself to twenty-four ounces of caffeinated heaven.

Bob Dylan was playing from the speakers as I got into line, and the aroma of roasting beans immediately perked me up. I checked my cell—four texts from Amy, ending with WTF ARE YOU DEAD?—and a list of my booked appointment times from the receptionist at the salon. I sent a quick text back to Amy that I'd see her in a few with a peace offering of her favorite iced green tea, and stepped to the front of the line, where a barista, in his thirties with a stocking cap and a braided goatee, took my order.

"Good morning, my love."

"Hey, Kevin," I said, smirking at his customary declaration. "The usual, plus an iced green tea for Amy."

"Got it." He wrote my drinks on the large white paper cups in a green marker.

"No charge," he told me as I reached for my wallet.

I lifted my eyes. "Huh?"

"That guy over there took care of it when you came in." He pointed to the seats in the back corner, but a woman in a sage maxidress was blocking my view.

"You have a secret admirer." He looked a little annoyed.

"Well, awesome, I guess." I shoved a five in the tip jar and made my way to the back to thank my mysterious do-gooder, but the woman in the dress was clearly trying to make conversation with him. I wondered how many drinks he'd bought people this morning.

"So if you're not doing anything for dinner . . ." she was saying.

"Excuse me," he interrupted. His voice curled around me like warm velvet. Neighborhood Watch.

The woman, a perky brunette with a jangly necklace, stepped aside. When our eyes met, her cheeks grew rosy.

"Lucky you," she said, taking a sip from her drink before heading for the door.

He rose from the soft chair like some sort of Greek god, dark hair curling at the tips, gaze more penetrating than it had been even in my dreams. He wore a black suit that had been tailored to fit his broad shoulders and lean waist to perfection, with a white dress shirt left unbuttoned at the collar. When he stood, his slacks moved in such a way that offered only a hint of the long muscles beneath and made me curious as to just how well-endowed he actually was.

"Anna."

The word from his mouth made my breath hitch; his voice was mesmerizing. It conjured images of him hovering over me, growling my name against my neck.

The space between us crackled with electricity; I felt it humming in my blood, making my body sensitive and damp. Fearful I would drop the two drinks I was holding, I set them down on the table beside me and tried to pull myself together.

"If it isn't the neighborhood watch," I said, scarcely more than a whisper.

His lips quirked, and I wanted to lick them. The butterflies in my belly were going haywire.

"What do you mean?"

I blinked, trying to break the spell. "I don't know your name."

"Alec Flynn." He moved closer, and his hand rose to my long, wet hair, twisting the ends around his fingers.

"Did you just get out of the shower?"

I nodded, unable to move.

His eyes darkened, like storm clouds over the ocean. I could feel my temperature rising and the tension building inside me, the muscles I'd just stretched out growing taut again.

"It's bad enough you're wearing those pants," he said, referring to the black tights I'd tucked inside my knee-high boots. "Now I'm thinking of you naked *and* wet."

"Is that a problem?" Seeing the desire in his face made me bold.

"Depends on how long you're going to make me wait to see you that way."

I swallowed, and reminded myself I knew nothing about him.

"You seem awfully sure of where this is going," I told him.

"And you're not?" His hand left my hair, trailing down my side before coming to rest on my hip. Heat streaked through the thin fabric of my flowing black peasant top, making me shudder. He must have felt my reaction because he moved close enough for his lips to skim my ear.

"You kept me up last night, Anna. I know you thought of me, too."

I froze, memories flashing bright in my mind of the glass window against my back and my fingers sliding over places I wanted him to touch. He couldn't have seen me; no one from the street could see up to the second floor. I'd checked it several times. It was nothing more than a cocky assumption, but I couldn't help but feel transparent.

Suddenly I became aware of our surroundings—the coffee shop, the people watching us, the barista with the goatee glaring from his position at the cash register. I took a step back, pulling my hair over one shoulder.

"Do you live nearby?" I asked. "I haven't seen you here before."

He breathed in deeply, pushing his hands into his pockets. He didn't have a drink; maybe he'd already finished it.

"Just here for business."

"A little of this and a little of that," I said, remembering what he'd told me the previous day in the study.

"Right."

"It's too bad," I said. "I was going to say we should have coffee sometime. Now I've got to go to work."

"At Rave?"

I felt my brows pull together. "How did you . . . ?"

"I asked around," he said with a devious glint in his eyes. Then conceded. "Ms. Rowe."

So he had been thinking about me. I felt the power shift back to my corner.

"Well," I said, fighting the urge to grab him by the lapels and drag him back to my apartment. "I guess if you know where I work, you can make that appointment we discussed."

He tilted his head. "I will. You owe me, remember?"

I bit my lip; yesterday's run-in with Maxim Stein and his red-headed mistress seemed more like a dream than reality.

"I do." I picked up my drinks. "Thanks for the coffee."

I could feel his gaze on my back until I was out the door and across the street. Maybe I let my hips sway a little more than normal, but I didn't giggle until I was sure Javaz was out of sight.

Rave was sandwiched between an Irish pub and a tattoo parlor, neither of which were that busy at ten o'clock in the morning. Still strutting, I breezed through the glass doors, passing the salon's manager, Derrick, at the front desk with a little wave, and making my way past the decadently framed mirrors and hair-washing stations to the styling chairs. There were only a couple of people in this morning—Rave did most of its business in the early afternoon and evening hours.

A rail-thin girl in a black velvet tuxedo jacket, shorts, and torn fishnets replaced a broom against the wall and stalked toward me. With white-blonde hair, cut asymmetrically, and purple eye shadow, Amy was the definition of edgy. Here at Rave, she fit right in.

"You . . ." she snarled as I plopped myself into her chair. I held the tea out before me like a shield to avoid the full extent of her wrath.

She growled like a puppy and lifted the cup to her mouth. "You got laid. Good, it's about time."

"What?" I hid my smile in my vanilla latte, taking a long, scalding sip. I didn't mind the hot coffee in hot weather. The hotter, the better.

"Oh, don't even pretend you didn't. I can see it all over your face, you smug little floozy."

"I didn't." I laughed.

She rolled her eyes, set down her tea on the tray with her blow-dryer and other tools, and spun me around to face the mirror. Without discussion, she began piecing my hair, clipping it up, and making her mental preparations of just how she would dress up her favorite doll today.

"It was the doctor, wasn't it?" Her mouth fell open. "Dr. Randall!"

"Dr. Boy Band? Yeah, *no*." I made a face. "And honestly, what were you thinking giving him that haircut?"

She stifled a laugh. "He asked for it."

"He asked to look like the only thirty-year-old cast member of the Mickey Mouse Club? Please."

"He brought in a picture."

I closed my eyes. Amy hated it when people brought in pictures of the hairstyles they wanted. According to her, they never were a good fit for the person's face or personality.

"Oh, come on," she said. "You liked him after the first date."

When I was reasonably buzzed, and the bar where we'd met was too loud to hear him talk about himself.

"He was an ass," I raised my voice to talk over the dryer as Amy began to straighten my hair. "He ate dinner before I even showed up, and then, when I told him I wasn't going home with him, he made a pathetic masseuse joke."

"I make masseuse jokes," Amy said. "Dr. Randall was supposed to be a fling."

"Speaking of masseuse jokes . . ." Derrick strode up from the front desk, tablet in hand. With dark, flawless skin and a body perfected by hours at the gym, Derrick was two parts business, one part glam. Today he was showcasing the new smoky eyeliner we'd gotten in last week. If I was being honest, it looked a lot better on him than it had on me.

I raised my cup. "Here we go . . ."

"Mr. Herman is your eleven o'clock."

I groaned and slumped in the chair. Melvin Herman was a lonely accountant who scheduled a little too regularly and had to be reminded more than once about the sexual-harassment policy. He was harmless, but exhausting.

Amy began to chuckle.

"Hasn't he been banned yet?" she asked.

"He signed a client-conduct form," said Derrick with a grimace. "He agreed to stop asking you out on dates and knows that he can only see you for scheduled appointments during regular business hours. You'll tell me if he gets sassy?"

I could hardly imagine Melvin "getting sassy." The guy was forty-five, six feet tall, and a hundred and thirty pounds soaking wet. I doubted he even really knew what I looked like—every time he got a massage, he took off his telescope-lens glasses.

"Yes, sir," I said.

"Good." Derrick flashed a smile of perfect teeth as he made his way back to the front of the shop.

"Since all seems hopeless with the good doctor, I suppose you could always take Melvin out for a spin," Amy grinned.

"What is your obsession with my sex life?"

"Just lookin' out," she said.

Amy was always "just lookin' out." We'd gone to high school together in Cincinnati. At fourteen, she'd been wild and untamable, angry over her dad leaving her mom, and her brother getting killed overseas. And I'd been a loner, too wary to trust anyone. Somewhere between a sampling of boys and booze, we evened each other out. She was the first real friend I'd ever had. The only one, really.

After senior year, we'd gone our separate ways: me on my quest to see the world, her to Florida with the twenty-one-year-old guitar player who was just trying to "find himself" in her pants. We'd kept in touch, and when things had gone stale in Baltimore, I'd come down to Tampa to nurse her through a divorce from the lying, cheating husband who'd left her with nothing but a beautiful little girl.

Amy was the one who'd gotten me the job and my apartment.

"Maybe," she said, trading the blow-dryer for a flatiron, "I just want you to stick around for longer than two months." Her gaze didn't stray from my hair.

"Baltimore was eight." It was a weak argument. Her wanting me close felt good, but it also made me sad. Part of me wanted to put down roots somewhere, anywhere, but it seemed like the ground beneath was always too hard.

"And Atlanta was six. And Austin was two."

"*Three*. You know, I had to sign a conduct form of my own last night," I said, changing the subject.

"At the big shot's house? Do tell."

I launched into a full description of what had happened at Maxim Stein's, beginning with my first run-in with Alec. When I got to the part where I walked in on Maxim and his mistress, the flatiron Amy had been using fell to the floor.

"You're full of shit," she said.

I hushed her. "I swear."

"They didn't see you?"

I told her how I hid in a room until I'd been rescued by Alec, and then proceeded with the appointment as if nothing had happened.

Amy shook her head, nose scrunched up like it always did when she was worried about something.

"*And*"—I held up my coffee—"he showed up out of the blue at Javaz this morning and bought us drinks."

"Out of the blue," she said. "Yeah, right. He showed up because he wanted to see you."

The thought of his fingers teasing my hair and his warm hand on my waist made my skin feel sensitive. I had wondered if he'd arranged to run into me, but it seemed too good to be true.

"You're really into him," Amy noticed.

"It's probably nothing," I said, trying not to get my hopes up.

"Are you kidding?" She finished pulling the top strands of hair back in a silver clip. "He'd be crazy not to like you. I just worry about those house calls. I seriously could have kicked your ass for not texting me back last night."

"I'm sorry." I meant it. She was a good friend—the best.

"I know. Just be careful, all right? It's different when you're on someone else's turf. You never know what you're going to walk in on."

We both giggled. But though she sounded like my dad, she was right. They both were.

"I'll text you as soon as I'm done with my appointments, I promise."

"Anna," called Derrick from the front. "Your eleven o'clock is here."

Six

Melvin Herman lay facedown on the massage table, covered by a sheet. The lights were low, and the sound of waterfalls piped in through the speakers. After our last visit, when he'd shared that he'd been dreaming about me on my knees before him, I'd informed him that we would no longer be doing the complimentary foot scrub.

He rose up on his elbows so that he could look at me, a red ring from the face pillow on his pasty cheeks.

"I just want to apologize again for my behavior last time, Anna. I was out of line."

"I accepted your apology earlier," I told him, gently pushing him back down on the adjustable headrest. "And I accepted your apology last session for the time before that." I didn't want to be rude, but it was important to set boundaries in a field where you slid your hands over someone's greasy body.

"It's just difficult to think straight, you being so beautiful and—"

"Melvin, we've talked about this. You can't say things like that if you want to stay." I removed my hands from his deltoids and waited for him to get himself under control.

"You're right, you're right. I'm sorry. I'll just lie here."

"Relax."

"I'm relaxed."

In the quiet, I worked my way down from his shoulders to his lower back and he let out a low groan. Most clients did this, so I didn't stop, but Melvin's leash was getting shorter by the second. I'd made it to his right hamstring when he spoke again.

"I'm so appreciative of all everyone does here." His voice was muffled by the face pillow. "Tax season has me so stressed. I really look forward to these appointments."

"I'll pass that along," I said, knowing full well I was the only person he saw here.

"I brought a box of chocolates—for everyone. Since everyone does such a good job. I thought maybe you *all* might enjoy them."

It took a lot of will power to hold back my sigh. After the flowers he'd sent last month, I was sure Derrick had made it clear he couldn't bring gifts.

"That's very thoughtful," I said. "You didn't have to do that."

"But I wanted to," he said.

I reached over him for the edge of the sheet, careful not to touch him with my body any more than necessary.

"I'm going to lift this up," I told him. "Go ahead and roll onto your back and scoot down for me."

He did, and when I put the sheet down, I blinked in surprise at his very obvious erection. Melvin Herman pitched quite a tent.

"Melvin," I warned.

"*Hmm?*" He grinned sleepily.

"*Melvin.*" This time I was more direct. "I'm going to leave the room. I'd like you to get your things and go, please."

Melvin sat up quickly, noticing, as if for the first time, what might have accounted for the sudden change.

"Oh," he said. "Oh, dear."

"Oh, dear is right," I said on my way out. I made my way quickly toward the break room. Only once I was inside with the door firmly shut behind me did I shake off the creeps and wash the cinnamon-infused oil off my hands. He wasn't the first male client to get hard during a massage; it happened occasionally. But I wasn't about to put up with it from a man who had such a difficult time with the word *no*.

I'd have to tell Derrick that Melvin had indeed gotten sassy with me, but I wanted to give him the chance to leave with some dignity first. I reached into the cubby marked with my name in glittery letters, and pulled my cell out of my purse.

There was one text, from a local number I didn't recognize.

Ready to collect on that favor.

Alec.

My body hummed to life. Ten different images of what he might mean—ranging from dinner to sweaty, sheet-fisting sex—flashed through my mind.

He must have gotten my cell number from Ms. Rowe—she had been the one to call me first to make the appointment for her employer. The fact that he'd not only asked about me but gotten my number sent a little jolt through my veins.

What did you have in mind? I texted back.

I waited a minute, pacing around the break room. Another minute passed.

Out in the hallway, a door closed quietly, and I could hear footsteps padding quickly toward the exit to the salon floor. Melvin was leaving, which meant I needed to get out to the front to talk to Derrick.

Reluctantly, I put the phone back in my purse, but just as I was turning, I heard it vibrate again.

Payback.

Payback? What did that mean?

For what? I typed. He responded immediately.

Being a tease.

I smirked.

I don't know what you're talking about.

Thirty seconds passed, in which I started to wonder if I'd said something stupid and blown it. When my phone buzzed, I quickly read the new message.

You're doing it again.

I chewed my bottom lip, debating what to say next.

So do something about it.

I bounced on my heels, hoping I hadn't taken it too far and come off as slutty.

I plan to.

I swallowed, my throat suddenly dry. What was I doing? I barely knew anything about Alec. Intuition said he was dangerous, but not unsafe. A little flirting was probably harmless, but I did have a cop for a father.

You should know I never kiss on the first date, I typed.

Would my words end this, whatever *this* was?

We'll see.

I laughed, then cupped my hand over my mouth. As much as I didn't want to, I had to wrap this up.

Got to go.

I want to see you. A second later another text came through. Tonight.

I frowned. Tonight I had a session with June Esposito, a sixty-year-old woman with chronic pain caused by lupus. If she hadn't been the sweetest woman in the world, I would have considered canceling.

I have a session. After?

Just say where and when.

I shot off the name of a Cuban restaurant near Mrs. Esposito's house that I knew was open late and told him I would be there at eight thirty. I could hardly stand waiting that long. It had been a long time since I was this excited about a date. Mentally I was already sorting through my closet trying to pick something to wear. And it was a good thing I worked at a salon—I'd recently waxed.

Not that I planned on bringing him home tonight. I had my standards.

But if anyone could make me break the rules, it was him.

"He did not." Amy was doubled over with laughter while I relayed what had happened with Melvin to her and Derrick. "Was he hung like a horse? The skinny ones always are."

"*Ew*. And yes. Dammit." I hid my face shamefully in my hands.

Derrick put an arm over my shoulder. "Sorry you were scandalized."

"Me, too."

"I'll put a note in the system and send him a letter," he said. "He won't be permitted back on the premises. I do need you to fill out an incident report."

"Sure," I said, dropping my arms. "Of course."

As Derrick went to retrieve the paperwork, I asked Amy if she'd seen Melvin leave.

"No," she shook her head. "He must have gone through the back. My eleven thirty canceled, so I was helping out up front."

The back of the building led to an alley that led back to the main street on the opposite side of the tattoo parlor. The thought of Melvin, nerdy and dejected, back there with the inked-up smokers and the stray chickens that roamed the Ybor streets made me feel a little guilty.

"He'll be all right," Amy said, reading my mind.

I leaned closer. "Alec texted. We're going out tonight."

Her brows lifted. "That was quick."

I flipped my hair over my shoulder. "What can I say? I'm on fire today."

She jabbed me in the ribs before her face turned serious. "What are you wearing? You shaved, right? Are your toenails done?"

"I don't know," I said. "Yes. And I think they're okay. Julie just did them a couple weeks ago."

"Come on." Amy took my hand, dragging me toward the pedicure chairs. "We've got work to do."

By the time I'd reached June Esposito's house in North Tampa my legs were smooth, my hair was redone with soft curls, and my toes were dark red to match my lipstick. I wore black leggings and my customary black cotton shirt to the appointment, but had brought a hip-hugging emerald tank to change into afterward.

I parked the red Kia in the driveway and carried my bulky supplies to the front door of the small ranch-style home. Mrs. Esposito, a frail Mexican woman, answered on the third knock, hobbling back to give me space to set up in her living room. The walls were covered with pictures of her children and new grandchildren, and a delicious scent was coming from the kitchen.

"What is that?" I asked. "It smells incredible."

"Tamales," she said. "My mother's secret recipe. It's my son's birthday tomorrow."

"Well, happy birthday to him," I said.

"I will send you with some. For your date."

I grinned as I began to unfold the heavy table.

"What makes you think I have a date?"

"You have sexy hair," she said with a little giggle. "And the look of a woman in love."

"I don't know about that. I've only just met him."

"Well," she said. "You have the look. I will make tamales for your wedding."

I laughed. "Sounds perfect."

When I'd laid out the sheets, I helped her up, easing her down slowly to a prone position. She was doing worse than last week; her joints were stiff and she winced with each move.

"How's the pain today, June?"

Her wrinkled hand, still bearing the wedding ring from a man who'd died ten years ago, squeezed my forearm lightly.

"Better now that you're here."

It was easy to let my mind wander while I worked through June's shoulders, neck, and lower back. Thoughts of Alec made my mouth water. I'd reread the texts he'd sent half a dozen times, and prepped like a girl going to the prom. Every time I thought about what might happen afterward, my body responded. I wanted him, more than I'd ever wanted anyone. The intensity of my desire frightened me a little. I was used to keeping men at a distance, emotionally if not physically, but the way Alec had invaded my mind with barely a touch already had me reeling.

I needed to turn the tables, get back on my feet. I planned to do that tonight. He thought I was in for a little payback? Game on. By the time I was done with him, he'd be wrapped around my finger.

I pulled into the parking lot of the restaurant, fixed my lipstick in the visor mirror, and walked inside.

I looked hot. I felt good.

Alec Flynn was mine.

The host was a stocky man in his fifties. He took me to a table for two where I had a clear view of the door. I ordered some of their homemade lemonade, waiting until Alec arrived to order a cocktail, and texted Amy to tell her I was at the restaurant.

Give him your panties under the table, she texted back. I saw that in a movie once. Totally sexy.

I laughed and sent her a Good night, then set my phone down.

The excitement turned to nerves as I finished my drink. I checked my phone. Fifteen minutes late. I leaned back in my chair, crossed my arms, tried to ignore that familiar feeling creeping up the back of my neck.

I'd practiced being alone in college, sitting in restaurants, movie theaters, allowing the panic to wash over me until all that remained was numbness. Now I could stand to wait, but not without some anxiety. And it increased with each minute that passed, each refill of my water glass, each time the server asked if there wasn't something he could bring out while I waited.

Not coming.

He's not coming.

He was coming. He was just running behind. He was into me; I hadn't made it up. I read through the texts we'd sent each other earlier in the day, making sure the restaurant information and time had been delivered.

It had been delivered and received.

Twenty minutes passed.

Twenty-five.

I couldn't help it. I was eight years old, sitting in a restaurant, waiting for her to come back. I told the manager she was coming, but he said he was calling someone anyway. It didn't matter if it was twenty years ago or yesterday, abandonment felt the same.

My cell buzzed.

Something came up. Have to reschedule. Sorry for the late notice.

"Shit," I said under my breath.

Seven

I didn't text him back. Maybe it was petty, but I didn't care. It wasn't just him I was pissed at—it was me, too. I'd built him up too much in my head, set my expectations too high. Painting my nails, hanging on his messages—I'd acted like a little girl.

This was what happened when you got too close to people. They disappointed you.

The next day, after checking in with my dad about his pitiful bowling game, I went to work, bypassing the coffee shop just in case Alec was there. Whatever, or whoever, had kept him so busy last night had apparently taken up most of his morning, too. He had my number, but I didn't hear from him.

My first two sessions at Rave were new clients—a prenatal massage with a woman in her second trimester, and a marathon runner who was rehabbing a torn hamstring. Both of them were delightful and signed up for follow-up sessions.

I had finished remaking the table and was taking the dirty sheets to the laundry room when Amy popped in. Her hair was in pigtails this morning, and she was wearing a slinky black dress with a low neckline that exposed her nonexistent cleavage. Boobs or not, she was sizzling.

"Either it was so good you're speechless, or it was so bad you're hiding under someone else's laundry." She crossed her arms and leaned against the wall. "Whatever the case, you're avoiding me and that, my minxy little friend, is unacceptable."

I wasn't avoiding her; she hadn't been here when I'd arrived this morning. Although if things had gone well, I probably would have called, or snuck out between sessions to tell her about it.

I threw the wet sheets into the dryer.

"Neither," I said. "It didn't happen."

Her arms dropped to her sides. "What do you mean? You were at the restaurant when you texted me."

"Yes, but he wasn't. He didn't show."

"Oh." She shuffled through the sea of dirty sheets on the floor between us and threw her arms around me. "Oh, I'm so sorry, Anna."

I rested my head on her shoulder and sighed. There were only a handful of people who were aware of what I'd been through in my childhood, and she was one of them. Amy knew just how painful it was for me to be stood up.

"It's okay," I lied. I'd spent the night watching movies curled up on my couch because I couldn't sleep. Today I was exhausted, but at least I'd traded feeling hurt for being pissed. Anger was so much easier to deal with.

"It's not. Let's slash his tires."

A laugh bubbled up inside of me. "I don't even know what kind of car he drives."

"Then we'll egg his house."

"What are we, fifteen?" I pulled back. "And anyway, I don't know where he lives."

She kept her hands on my arms, rubbing up and down. As terrible as I felt, I was so glad to have her here. If I'd been living anywhere else, I would have dealt with this alone.

"I can't believe he didn't even call. What a prick."

"He sent a text," I said. "Half hour late. *Sorry for the late notice, let's reschedule.* Something like that."

"Well, that's something." At the look on my face, she scowled. "But not enough. I still hate him."

"Good."

She picked up a clean sheet out of the wicker basket and helped me fold.

"Come over tonight. We'll have ice cream and throw darts at pictures of my ex."

I smirked. Amy's divorce had hurt her pride more than anything else. Once she'd fallen in and out of love more than anyone I'd ever met, but that was before she'd been burned.

"Sounds perfect," I told her.

"Anna, are you back here?" Derrick slipped through the door. When he saw the look on my face, he stuck out his lower lip. "Oh, no, boy drama?"

"How did you guess?" I started the dryer and poured the lavender-scented detergent into the washing machine.

"Believe me," he said, placing a fist on one cocked hip. "I know boy drama. And I'm about to add onto it. You've got a delivery up front. The card doesn't say Melvin Herman, but I made the delivery guy stick around just in case you want to send it back."

I slumped. "Great. Probably an apology for my four-star salute yesterday."

"What is it? Flowers?" Amy clapped her hands. "Don't send them back!"

"Probably chocolate," I mumbled. "He mentioned something about that."

"Wrong and wrong," said Derrick, leading us to the front desk where two cups of coffee from Javaz sat in a cardboard holder.

My stomach clenched.

"Uh-oh," I heard Amy whisper beside me.

Kevin leaned against the counter, looking starkly out of place in his baggy hemp shorts and coffee-stained undershirt. He twirled his finger around his long goatee, peering at the interior of the salon like something might jump out and bite him.

"Hey, Kevin," I said.

"Hello, my love!" He visibly relaxed. "I've never seen where you work. It's frightening. Lots of sharp things."

"They're called scissors." Amy plucked the card off the tray, read it, and then handed it to me.

Anna, sorry for last night. Won't happen again.

"You're right," I said. "It won't."

"He didn't even sign his name," said Amy, already sipping her green tea through the straw. "How presumptuous. At least he got my drink right."

"Amy! Put it down. We're sending it back."

She pouted.

"Sorry, Anna," said Kevin. "'Fraid I can't do that. Once it's made, it's made."

"Well, I don't want it," I said. "You drink it."

"You sure?" he asked.

Derrick was looking down at the trash can where I'd crumpled and thrown the note. "Is it from Melvin?"

"Yes," I said to Kevin. "No," I told Derrick. "It's from someone else."

Kevin picked up the large coffee and drained half of it in one impressive gulp. I cringed a little watching him. His throat had to be scalding.

"He's groveling," Amy said. "Do we still hate him?"

"Yes." I left the three of them at the front desk and made my way back to the break room, still steamed at Alec for standing me up and doubly steamed that he'd thought a cup of coffee would fix it. I snatched my phone out of my purse and wasn't surprised to see a message.

Coffee okay?

I texted back, Wouldn't know. Sent it back.

I didn't see if he responded. I turned off my phone, threw it in my cubby, and went to welcome my next appointment.

The three appointments that followed were not my best work. I was distracted, finishing early, spending too long on the right leg and then rushing through the left. Rookie mistakes. My two o'clock had to remind me twice that the pressure was too strong. I felt it afterward as I stretched my sore hands. There was a reason you didn't see many sixty-year-old masseuses; their careers were always stunted by carpal tunnel syndrome or arthritis.

But for now, my work made me happy. Usually.

Despite my frustration, I did feel calmer after the massages. It was impossible not to let the soothing music and low lights mellow you. By the time I walked my third client back out to the front to pay, I was almost back to myself.

"Anna."

My shoulders rose, tense, even as something warm stirred deep in my belly. Just the sound of his voice made my knees weak. I kept my eyes trained on the receptionist as she rang up my client's ticket, but I could feel Alec behind me, feel his gaze lowering down my body.

"Remember to drink water throughout the day," I told Maryanne Jenkins, a referral from another of my clients. She rubbed the red semicircle on her forehead from the face pillow with the heel of her hand, and fluffed her gray bangs. "It will help flush the toxins released by your muscles from today's session."

"Sure," she said. "Yes. Whatever you say." She laughed. "You're my new favorite person, you know that, right?"

Most people said some variation of this when we were done, even if I knew it wasn't as good a session as it could have been.

I patted her back gently. "I'm glad you enjoyed it."

I waited until she was out the door before turning around.

Alec Flynn was undeniably gorgeous. In a royal blue button-up that complemented the dark heat of his eyes, and jeans that were slim enough to cup his ample package, I couldn't help but stare. It was impossible to look at him and not think of sex—hot, sweaty, wild sex.

Clinging to memories of how I'd felt sitting alone last night, I pulled back my shoulders and marched across the small waiting area dedicated to the spa clients.

"Damn," he said appreciatively. "Are those thigh-highs?"

I smoothed down the front of my black skirt, wondering if he had X-ray vision; I was wearing a garter belt, but it was well hidden. It was part of the fuck-you-I'm-still-hot wardrobe I'd chosen after a night of feeling like crap. On top, I was wearing a black lace tank over a camisole. It was classy, but still sexy, and from the look on his face, he liked what he saw.

Too bad for him.

"What are you doing here?" I smiled sweetly.

He inhaled audibly. "Right now, admiring the view."

"Yeah?" I batted my eyelashes. "Wondering what's under the hood?"

"You read my mind."

The strain in his voice made those tendrils of need tighten into a hot knot inside of me. God, I wanted to make him growl my name in that voice. I wanted him to throw me on a bed and push inside me like he couldn't wait a moment longer. His dark hair was hanging down over his ears, and my hands itched to weave through it and yank his mouth down to mine.

He'd screwed us both when he'd stood me up.

We were barely maintaining the limits of professional distance—a little too close for close talkers, but not close enough for our bodies to touch.

"I'm wearing red satin panties," I whispered. And to make my point, I pulled open my collar slightly to reveal the matching bra strap.

As if out of his control, he reached for the skin I exposed. His lips parted.

"The fabric's so thin I can barely feel it," I said.

My hand slid down, skimming my breast on the way to rest on my hip. No one else could see it but him, and I reveled when his jaw twitched.

"It's like I'm naked, and no one knows but you and me."

He leaned forward.

I stepped back and covered my shoulder.

"Oops," I said. Score one for Anna.

"You're teasing again." His voice was low, dangerous.

I crossed my arms over my chest. "You should have seen what I was wearing last night."

His brows rose. His hand fell.

"Good-bye, Alec," I said. "As you can see, I'm busy today."

The receptionist, a pixie-like girl with short red hair who was finishing her cosmetology license, appeared beside me with a glass of cucumber-infused water.

"Mr. Flynn, I see you've met Anna. She'll see you back for your session now."

My mouth fell open.

Alec grinned.

Eight

"In my defense, you did say to make an appointment."

Alec followed me through the door into the dimly lit hallway. The music changed to the sounds of rain—relaxing for just about everyone in the world but me.

I *had* told him that. Before last night.

"I have the right to refuse service to any client," I informed him, walking stiffly.

"But you won't."

I stopped and turned slowly to face him. "Oh, and why is that?"

"Because you want to hear my apology for missing our dinner in person," he said, and the low light casting shadows over him made me that much hotter. I couldn't look him in the face; he was like some sort of male siren, luring me in just to hang me out to dry. I had to be careful.

"And," he continued, "you want to know how I'm going to make it up to you."

Dammit all to hell. I wasn't forgiving him—I told myself I wasn't hurt enough to want an apology anyway—but the possibility of amends was intriguing.

We entered the room I'd prepped while Maryanne Jenkins was getting dressed. At the time I'd been expecting a new client, someone who'd made an appointment earlier this morning, but I'd been distracted and hadn't thought to check the name.

Alec eased back against the table, which was distracting enough because it looked too much like a bed with the sheets and blankets. I closed the door softly and leaned against the wall, giving myself enough distance to think.

"You could start with what happened last night," I prompted.

His head tilted slightly. "When the boss calls, I have to answer. That's the way it works." There was an edge to his voice—maybe sarcasm, maybe something else.

"Like a dog." I gave myself another point.

"Ouch." Amusement flickered across his face. "I deserved that."

I hummed my agreement.

For a moment he was quiet, studying me, and as the seconds ticked by, I felt as though my skin had turned to glass and he could see every secret I'd carefully hidden inside.

"I hurt you," he said.

He rubbed his knuckles across his chin, a scowl on his face. The wariness I'd seen in the picture in Mr. Stein's office returned to his eyes.

"I'm sorry," he added, and I could feel it—a brick in the wall around my heart crumbling. He sounded so genuine I couldn't help but believe him.

"I'm a big girl, I'll get over it." I tried to sound tough, but the mood had shifted from tense to fragile. I didn't know what to do; I didn't let men make me feel vulnerable. He shouldn't have anyway. He was on my turf, he was asking for *my* forgiveness.

He pushed off the table and closed the space between us. With the wall firm against my back there was nowhere to go, not that I could have moved anyway—my heels felt rooted to the floor. His fingertips skimmed down my cheek, and though it felt good and the butterflies in my belly spazzed out like they'd been drinking a little too much caffeine, I turned my head away. I didn't know what it meant that I could accept his dirty words but not his kindness. Something was wrong with me.

I panicked.

"Just undress to the level of your comfort and lie facedown on the table." The line was so practiced it came out without a second thought.

With that, I escaped into the hallway, closing the door behind me. I needed to breathe, to get myself under control. This man could turn me on with a look, then bring out my most vindictive side. He'd invaded my thoughts and made me lose control over my body, and I knew practically nothing about him.

"Ohmigod, is that him?" Amy pounced from the laundry room where she'd been lying in wait for my break.

"*Shh!* Yes."

"What's he doing here?" She was staring at the door like if she tried hard enough, she might see through it.

"Apologizing. And getting a massage, I guess. I don't know." It dawned on me that he was probably taking off his clothes. He could be naked *right now*, and I would be lathering his perfect body with oil and rubbing my hands all over him.

How I was going to get through this without getting fired for sexual harassment was beyond me.

"Let me get this straight," she planted her fists on her narrow hips. "He's apologizing, but *you're* giving *him* a massage."

I breathed in slowly, exhaled. We were both staring at the door.

"He's hot, Anna."

"I know, Amy."

"No, Anna. He's *hot* hot. Like, molten-lava hot. Like unearthly hot. Like . . ."

"Yes, I get it. I've seen him."

"All of him?" She shook her head in disbelief. "I'd like to see all of him, if you know what I'm saying."

I flexed my fingers and stretched my hands. Even if this wasn't how Alec had intended to spend this time, I was going to proceed as though he had. He needed to see he couldn't throw me, and since he quite obviously had, I didn't know what else to do but play it cool.

"I have to go in," I told her.

Straightening my spine, I reminded myself I was strong, independent, and, most important, in control.

"Good luck." She stayed while I cracked the door, trying to peer inside until I shooed her away. With a pout on her face, she backpedaled down the hallway and slipped through the door to the waiting room.

I waited until she was gone before stepping back into the room. I hadn't known what to expect, and in those seconds before I saw him, my imagination had gone wild. Visions of him lying on his chest, his bare back exposed for my tingling fingers, followed by him lying on his back, naked and hard as a rock, filled my mind.

What I didn't expect was to see him still fully dressed, peering at my supplies on the granite countertop.

I blew out the breath I'd been holding.

"What is this?" He held up a small amber bottle.

So much for staying steady. When he turned, and his gaze found mine, I practically melted.

"They're essential oils," I said, motioning to the matching bottles behind the black marble sink. "You pick the scent that you like best, and I mix it in the oil for the massage."

"This one, specifically," he said.

I approached, and took the small glass bottle, uncorked it, and breathed it in.

"Sandalwood," I said. "It's supposed to be calming." Unless inhaled in concentrated doses, when it became an aphrodisiac. I wasn't going to tell him that, though. The small, dim space was already brimming with sexual tension.

"It smells like you." He slid closer and leaned down, the tip of his nose running down the wildly pulsing vein in my neck. "I can't get it out of my head."

He backed me into the counter, hands on either side, and eased his body against mine. He was so warm, even through the layers of our clothing, and his muscular chest rubbed my nipples to peaks. I nearly groaned from the pressure of his heavy cock against my belly. My breath came out in a shudder.

"Is this what you want?" I tried to focus, but it was quickly becoming impossible. "The oil, I mean. Is that what you'd like me to use on you?" I set the bottle down on the counter before I dropped it.

He pulled back and smiled wickedly. "Always with the teasing."

Unexpectedly, he lowered and cupped the back of my legs with his strong hands. In one fluid motion, he lifted me up to straddle his hips. From this position, the soft parts of me found his hardness, and the friction alone was enough to bring me close to orgasm. I gasped, unable to hide the reaction as the blood rushed to my cheeks and the dampness flooded between my legs. My calves flexed around him and I grabbed his shoulders, eliciting a hiss through his teeth.

My skirt bunched around my waist as he turned and set me on the end of the table. When he stepped back, I had to bite back the groan of frustration. I was on fire, my breasts heavy and sensitive. If he didn't kiss me soon, I would die.

He removed one of the black patent-leather ankle boots I was wearing. Not the wisest choice for working on your feet, but they matched my outfit, and today I'd dressed to kick ass. As he removed the other shoe, that well-laid plan crashed through the floorboards.

"What are you doing?" I whispered as his fingers skimmed over the bare strip of skin between my rumpled skirt and the straps of my garter belt. He unhooked both of the fastenings with a flick of his fingers. One smooth, practiced move. He'd done this before.

My gaze shot to the door. I was at work. I couldn't do this.

But one of his fingers slipping beneath the top of my thigh-high made me forget everything but him.

He eased it down, fingers grazing the inside of my leg and tickling the sensitive skin behind my knee. When he got to my calf, he stopped, and began again on the other side.

"I told you," he said, and I trembled as his fingertips came close to my sex. "I'm making it up to you."

Embarrassment flushed through me. My desire was obvious, and I was making no attempt to cover myself up.

He knelt, his head even with my throbbing clit. Gently, he pulled the nylons free and left them in a puddle on the floor. My chest was rising and falling, my heart beating wildly. I held absolutely still, scared he would do what I thought he was about to do, but at the same time petrified that he wouldn't.

He rocked back on his heels, and took one foot in his hands.

"I'm giving you a foot rub."

The air whooshed out of my lungs. Oh. A foot rub. Of course. Automatically, I went to cover up my exposed hips.

"Don't." The word was hard, a command, and I froze at the sound of it. "Leave your skirt up. I want to see you."

Slowly, I moved my hands back behind me, and rested on straight arms.

He began to knead my arches, working to the balls of my feet and then my heels. He had talent, I couldn't deny it. In seconds, I was practically putty in his hands. I hadn't realized how sore my feet were until he'd begun.

Minutes passed, and his silence began to make me nervous. Did he have a foot fetish? Was this something he did to get off? Or was this truly just for me? Still, the feel of his hands working my sore muscles was incredible. I didn't want him to stop.

"Do you accept my apology?" he finally asked. There was something endearing about this sexy man kneeling on the floor, touching me this way.

I nodded, still unable to speak. When he went to the other side, I sagged, my head tilting back. But when his tongue slid up my instep, I sat bolt upright. He kept kneading as though he'd done nothing different, but the move sent bolts of electricity straight up my legs into my core. Instantly, the ache became a throb; it was almost painful that he wasn't touching me where I needed him most. For one crazed moment, I considered doing it myself. One rub, that was all it would take to push me over the edge, I was sure of it.

"Good," he said. "Because you still owe me."

As I looked down my body into his eyes, I knew he intended to fuck me. Right here. Right now.

I shook with anticipation and trepidation. A tiny part of me was aware of the people in the adjoining rooms, of my coworkers and friends on the other side of the salon. The doors didn't lock, and though the music was on, the walls weren't soundproof. But the rest of me needed him to finish this, to take me now before I lost my mind completely. The feeling was completely foreign; I never gave up control when it came to sex. Sometimes I pretended to, sometimes I even came close, but until this moment I'd never needed anything so badly that I'd let my guard down enough to take it.

He kissed my ankle, then my calf, his tongue drawing a slow circle on the inside of my knee. He pulled me closer to the edge of the table, and my hips began to churn and move of their own accord. I couldn't wait much longer.

"Hurry," I whispered.

He stopped, and pulled away.

I blinked down at him.

"I have a full hour," he informed me. "I intend to use it."

An hour? I wasn't going to last thirty more seconds the way this was going.

He started again, fingertips tracing up my thighs and higher to my panties. Tender kisses covering the inner surface of my thighs. He made me feel wanted, worshipped, even *loved,* though I knew that couldn't be right. Love was not something I expected to feel with men I brought to bed.

But I hadn't brought him to bed. We weren't even on a bed.

With a jerk, he thrust my legs open, leaving me straddling his face, just inches away. All concerns evacuated from my mind. My legs hung down, unable to reach the floor, puppets to his placement. His touch grew soft again, skimming the backs of my calves. He licked a straight line up my inner thigh, stopping just short of the mark, and then nipped the flesh with his teeth.

I groaned, fisting the now crumpled sheets, unable to look away from his exquisite torture.

"Are you going to tell me to stop?" He pulled back, staring up into my eyes.

Was he joking? I shook my head, back in that terrible cycling dream where he backed away every time he got close to giving me the intimate touch I so craved.

"Good," he said. "Because I've wanted to do this since the moment I first saw you."

He bit me lightly again, and I gasped.

"So do it."

"Patience," he cooed. "I'm going to take care of you."

My muscles were beginning to flex and shake. I couldn't hold still.

"Easy," he whispered, breath hot on my skin.

Finally, his thumb trailed over my slit, and I bucked against his touch.

"You're so wet, Anna," he growled. "I can feel how wet you

are for me. I can see it, soaking your panties." He stroked me again and I quivered. "Look how ready you are."

He drew back, licking my opposite inner thigh. Every time he got closer he backed away.

Payback. So this is what he meant.

"Please." I would have gotten on my knees and begged if he wasn't already there.

He looked up, dark eyes blazing. Very slowly he kissed my damp, aching center, right through the fabric. My sex clenched. It was the most erotic thing I'd ever seen.

"Is this what you want?" He kissed me again. "Is this what you need, Anna?"

"I need you inside me," I said, shocked by my own admission.

He pressed his lips against my panties and laughed, the rumble nearly sending me to pieces. I bit my lip hard to keep from crying out.

"Soon," he said, growing serious. "When I have more time, I'm going to fuck you just how you need. Long, and hard, and over and over. You're going to give me all of this sweet, hot body, and I'm going to take it. And just when you think we're done, I'm going to make you come again."

His words made me that much more desperate. I had never been so hot for someone before. In that moment, I would have done anything he wanted.

"But for now, you owe me this. I can't get you out of my mind, Anna. I need to see you come. I need to taste you."

I reached for my clit, unable to stop myself, and he grabbed my wrist, and moved it aside.

"This is mine right now, do you understand?"

I nodded reluctantly.

"This," he licked me through the fabric and I moaned, "is payback."

Softly, he bit at the silk, now soaked with my desire, and pulled it back. My knees snapped shut but he wedged them open with his broad shoulders. His fingers slipped within the elastic and eased down my cleft, staying on either side but not entering me.

Then he pushed aside the satin and blew. The cold air on my hot skin brought new sensitivity, and my back arched.

"So smooth," he said. "I wondered if you waxed."

I'd begun to pant. He was taking his time and killing me in the process.

"There are perks to working at a salon."

"You're beautiful." He parted my folds, exerting pressure with his thumbs as he massaged up and down. I don't know where he learned that little trick, but I had to bite the inside of my cheek to keep from screaming.

Finally, one finger pushed inside of me. It was enough to drive me right to the brink. He eased out slowly.

"So tight," he said, face taking on an almost pained expression. "I can't wait to slide my cock in you, Anna. I'm going to fill you completely."

"Yes," I whispered.

He added a second finger, twisted, and gave my clit the lightest pressure with his thumb. All the while he watched my face, watched as I fell back to my elbows and squirmed on the table. He paused only to draw my panties down my legs and leave me bare, exposed.

"Fuck, you're hot." He lowered his head to suckle one lip, then the other, tongue flicking into my slit just long enough to make me insane. So close—he was *so close* to my clit, but each time I thought he would kiss me there, his thumb returned to cover it, as if hiding it from his tongue. His lips pressed against my bare mound.

"Do you want to come now, Anna?"

"*Yes.*"

He leaned down and replaced his thumb with his mouth. One suck on my clit and I shattered, back arching, and shoved a fistful of sheets into my mouth to muffle my scream. The heat inside of me erupted, flooding fire through my veins, centering the pleasure in my nipples and cunt. I saw stars. My knees snapped shut around his head, and he pinned me down in place with his free hand.

"Again," he said.

"No . . ." I grabbed a fistful of his hair, and tried to push him back, but he'd begun to lick in long strokes, pulling me into his mouth for another suck after each one. "I can't so soon."

He didn't cease; the movement of his tongue changed to a fast flick, and already I felt the ache building inside of me again. His fingers increased their tempo, in and out, in and out, curving and rubbing upward in a way that made me groan. I squeezed my breasts to relieve some of the pressure. Then his tongue was spearing inside of me as his hands spread me wide. No one had ever done that to me before. Little scrapes of his teeth sent ripples of heat through me.

"You taste so good," he muttered between thrusts, and then returned to my clit, swirling over it.

The orgasm tore through me, unyielding spasms making my body a taut bow. I couldn't breathe. I could only feel. The blood was rushing through my ears, blocking out the soundtrack of rain coming through the speakers.

He didn't stop, and my oversensitive sex convulsed again, bringing on a third climax right on the heels of the second. His fingers continued their assault, pushing up to the palm, and I clenched around him uncontrollably.

It didn't stop. I kept coming. Writhing, bucking, kicking.

"Anna." My name brought me back.

I collapsed, my back hitting the table while my chest heaved. Sweaty hair stuck to my face. He brought me back down, fingers easing in tempo, tongue drawing slow, lazy circles around my pulsing clit. He finished with one soft, reverent kiss there, and another on my thigh before moving over me.

I tried to rise, but my arms were weak. And as I pushed myself up to a seated position, I wobbled. He caught me before I collapsed, pressing his lips to my collarbone. His arms wrapped around my waist and I clung to him weakly, letting him support my weight, and for several minutes he held me until the shaking had passed.

"Damn," he said. "I should have booked the rest of your afternoon."

I giggled, feeling completely reckless and light as a feather. "Now that I know what's in store, expect a lot more teasing."

His teeth found my earlobe, reminding me that he'd yet to kiss me.

"Payback's a bitch," he whispered into my hair, breathing deeply. His fingers traced my spine, and with his hips and still raging hard-on nestled between my thighs, the move felt more intimate than anything I'd ever experienced.

The sheets were a mess; a blanket had landed on the floor. He moved back, creating a space between us, and I lowered my hands down his chest to his belt, feeling the need to touch him.

He stopped me with a tight grimace.

"Not now," he said. "Soon though."

I liked the promise in his tone.

"I want to make you feel good, too," I said, unfamiliar with the vixen I'd suddenly transformed into.

"You did." He moved my hands to his mouth and kissed my knuckles. "I think I enjoyed that as much as you."

"I doubt it." I could see from the sheen of sweat on his forehead and the bulge in his pants that he was still painfully aroused. This surprised me; I'd never met a man who enjoyed giving oral sex so much.

The sound of rain transitioned into symphony music, bringing me back to where we were, and what we'd just done.

"I want to see you tonight," he said.

I wanted to see him, too. If this was a preview of what was to come, I wanted to leave work now.

But I had already committed to Amy. I considered canceling, but I needed a chance to cool off, to let the anticipation build again. What I was feeling for him felt too intense. I needed some time and space to make sense of it.

"Sorry, girls' night," I told him. "I'm free tomorrow."

"Tomorrow night you have an appointment with my boss."

He stepped away, and the heat departed with him. A veil of awkwardness slid between us. I smoothed my skirt, feeling the slickness between my thighs. I wasn't wearing any panties. I searched the floor, but instead caught a glimpse of red fabric peeking out of his jeans pocket.

The thought of him keeping them like some kind of trophy turned me on all over again. I retrieved my stockings and pulled them up while he straightened his shirt. He wouldn't look at me. Just seconds ago I'd felt so connected to him, but now he was distant. Cool.

I picked up the sheets.

"I thought I wasn't supposed to see Mr. Stein until next week." I asked, focusing on his words.

"And here I thought it was just me you were ignoring." He straightened the bottles on the counter, his back to me. "Ms. Rowe called. So did I."

I hesitated. "You did?"

"After you turned down my coffee, I had to get your attention somehow." He helped me retrieve the sheets and pile them on the table.

"Well, you succeeded," I said. "So tomorrow night, what time does Ms. Rowe need me?"

"Early, I think. Six. Let me have you afterward."

Let me have you. I closed my eyes for just a moment to imagine what that might mean.

Our time was drawing to a close. I had another client coming. Still, I couldn't convince myself to move any faster.

He leaned forward and pressed his lips to my forehead.

"Tomorrow night," he murmured. "We'll see if I can survive that long."

With that, he fixed his pants to make his hard-on slightly less obvious, and sauntered out the door, leaving me staring at a table I would never look at the same way again.

Nine

F our hours later, I pulled into a guest spot at Amy's apartment complex and climbed the steps to her second-floor two-bedroom home. The remainder of the workday had passed by excruciatingly slowly. Convinced someone had heard or seen something, I stayed as hidden as possible, keeping myself to laundry duty until the receptionist found me for my next appointment. I had even managed to avoid Amy, who'd left early to pick up her daughter from preschool.

I couldn't believe what I—*we*—had done. I wasn't a prude by any means; I liked to flirt, and even bring the occasional man home to share my bed. Okay, it had been a while, but that was just because I'd been getting used to the area. But despite that, I wasn't particularly adventurous in that arena. The woman who had climaxed not once, but three times, at her workplace was no one I even recognized.

That I wanted to do it again confused me even more.

Alec was right; he had called. Twice. When I turned my phone back on, I'd seen his missed calls, and listened to two voice mails. One from Ms. Rowe explaining that Mr. Stein was in the midst of a large merger right now and therefore in need of my services. She'd given the time and date—tomorrow night, just as Alec had said—and asked that I be there. Clearly she was a woman who wasn't used to hearing the word *no*.

The other voice mail had been from Randall.

"Hi Anna," he had said, his voice taking on that soft, empathetic therapist quality again. "I just wanted to apologize for my behavior last night. Please know that it was the wine speaking. I'm not that way normally. Clearly I've got some displacement issues over the stress at my work with the new billing system." He paused and cleared his throat. I could almost see him pushing back his long, golden bangs. "That's when the stress from one area of your life transfers into another."

Thank you, Dr. Randall.

He'd gone on to say he would love to make it up to me with dinner, his treat—gee, thanks—but understood if I never wanted to speak to him again. The apology sounded genuine. I almost felt sorry for him.

Almost.

I didn't have to knock on Amy's door. Before I'd raised my hand, it was flung open, and a pretty five-year-old blonde with pigtails attached herself to my leg. Dressed in a purple tutu, green T-shirt, and black leggings, she had clearly inherited her mother's sense of style.

"Paisley!" I knelt to give her a hug. She released my leg and smiled, but didn't say a word. You could tell she was smart, even though she hardly ever spoke. She was always watching.

I tickled her ribs and she erupted in giggles.

"Shit! I mean, shoot. Dammit. *Darn* it!" Amy groaned from the kitchen.

"Sounds like Mommy needs some help," I told Paisley, who nodded and led me by the hand to the kitchen.

"It's mac and cheese—I don't need any help." Amy sounded irritable. She was still rocking flashy aqua eye shadow, but was in mom clothes now—sweatpants and a T-shirt with a smear of neon orange down the center. She was scraping the remnants of a hot dog explosion off the microwave door. I'd picked up some brownies at the bakery, and dropped them off on their small dining room table.

"The cheese goes in the pot, not on your boobs," I told her, taking a seat at one of the two stools against the breakfast bar. Paisley giggled.

"Thank you so much, Miss Helpful." A bag of baby carrots came flying at my head.

"We have an orange theme tonight, I see." I began to dump them out on a plate.

"Vegetables are vegetables." She sucked in her tiny waist so she could open the refrigerator door. The kitchen was the size of most closets. Behind us, a love seat was crammed against the wall across from a small TV set. Colorful plastic toys were strewn across the beige carpet.

"Sweetheart, what do you want to drink?" Amy set three cups on the counter.

Paisley climbed down from the stool beside me and entered the kitchen.

"Uh-uh," I heard Amy say gently. "Use your words, Paisley. Milk or juice?"

A moment of silence passed, in which I busied myself carrying our bowls of mac and cheese out on the TV trays.

"Apple juice," I heard a small voice whisper.

"Good job," Amy told her. When she stood, I could see the frustration wrinkling her forehead. Paisley had been a regular chatterbox until her father had left last year.

After we ate, we snuggled on the couch under one blanket, Paisley's head on her mom's thigh, her feet up on my legs. There was comfort in routine. We watched the same movies we always watched: *The Little Mermaid* and, when that was done and Paisley was in bed, *Magic Mike*. There was nothing quite as perfect as a good friend, brownies, and male strippers to close a crazy day.

"All right, dish," said Amy. She was fast-forwarding through the boring talking scenes to get to the good stuff. "What happened with Alec?"

I sighed. This conversation had been waiting like my landlord when the rent was due; there was no way to avoid it.

"It was . . . interesting."

She rolled her eyes. "Start with his body. Did you get a good look?"

"Not really . . ." I picked at my fingernails.

"He doesn't seem like the modest type." She stopped the DVD and hit rewind when she'd overshot her mark.

"No, he certainly doesn't," I muttered. "I didn't give him a massage. He came to apologize." *And get me off.* There were a lot of things I could confess to Amy, but this was not one of them. She'd vouched for me at that job; she needed it to take care of Paisley. If Amy got in trouble because of me, I'd never forgive myself.

"Did you buy it?" she asked.

"The apology? Yes. He was pretty convincing." I shivered, remembering the feel of his hands sliding up my calves and the heat in his stare as he'd looked up at me from between my thighs.

She glanced over at me, mouth curving up. "He kissed you, didn't he?"

I shook my head, feeling my cheeks warm. "No. No, he didn't kiss me." Not on the mouth, anyway.

We lapsed into appreciative silence as Channing Tatum slid across the dance floor on his knees, ripping off his clothes for a crowd of screaming women.

"Damn, he's hot," said Amy.

Dark hair and secretive eyes flashed before my vision. Alec was hot. He was the hottest guy I'd ever seen. And he was interested in me. I felt like the choirgirl who'd been invited to prom by the quarterback. It was awesome, but I couldn't help waiting for the universe to reveal that this had been some cruel cosmic joke.

"You really like him, don't you?"

Amy's voice brought me back from the most recent fanta-syland I'd journeyed off to. "Channing? Of course."

"Sorry, he's mine. Already called him. I meant Alec, dumbass."

I hesitated. "What makes you say that?"

"Besides the fact that your answers are about as elaborate as my five-year-old's, you're frowning at the best scene in the movie," she said, and at her words my thumb pressed between my furrowed eyebrows. "He got under your skin. It's all right for people to do that, you know. Not everyone has to stay an arm's length's away."

I snuggled closer to her, dropping my head to her shoulder. "He makes me nervous."

"Yikes," she said, taking a swig from the apple juice sippy cup. "When was the last time a guy made *you* nervous?"

"Franco Bernard."

She laughed so hard she choked on her juice. "I haven't thought about him since . . . sophomore year?"

"Junior year," I corrected her.

"Oh God, wasn't he . . ."

"Yes." I giggled.

Sweet Franco, with his pretty brown eyes and curly blond hair. The French foreign exchange student had shown me the world in the back of his host mother's van. If only our love affair had been fated to last longer than three months.

"Wow." She passed me another brownie. "I almost feel sorry for you. A new guy makes me nervous every twenty-five seconds."

"And look how well that's worked out for you."

She froze. I buried my face in my hands.

"I can't believe I just said that." I peeked out at her through my fingers. "I'm so sorry. I didn't mean that. I'm such an idiot."

"No," she said. "You're right. It's okay." She sighed. "I'm al-ways in the market for a new broken heart."

I hesitated. "Danny . . ."

She crossed herself. Every time her ex was mentioned she demanded a moment of silence to exorcise the demons.

"Did he make you nervous?" I asked while she fast-forwarded to the next scene.

"Yes," she said.

"Great."

She paused the movie. "It *was* great," she said. "Things are ugly between us now, but look what he gave me." She glanced back to the room where her daughter slept soundly. "He was worth it. And if Alec makes you happy, or nervous, or *whatever*, even for a minute, he's worth it, too."

I pulled her close and took another bite of my brownie. I wasn't sure where this was going with Alec, but it didn't have to end with heartbreak. We would keep things purely physical—enjoy each other. And then when it was done, go our separate ways. That would have to be good enough. It was all I could give anyway.

The following day I didn't go into the salon, but busied myself driving across town for house calls—two ladies in one of Florida's fifty billion active senior communities, a plastic surgeon at his office, and a housebound pregnant woman carrying triplets. Seven hours and one hundred miles on the Kia later, I pulled up to the gate at Maxim Stein's estate and was buzzed through by the same creepy gate guard I'd seen last time.

The butterflies in my stomach were already doing backflips by the time I pulled into my same parking spot. We weren't meeting until later, but that didn't mean Alec wouldn't be here now. I touched up my lipstick and smoothed back my hair, then scrolled through the texts we had exchanged throughout the day about the panties he'd stolen from me yesterday at the salon.

Alec: Red demands company. Please provide tonight.

Me: I do not negotiate with thieves or perverts.

Alec: Then you'll never see Red again.

Me: I see you're not above making threats.

Alec: The only thing I plan on being above is you.

When I'd received that text, I'd been finishing my setup for the plastic surgeon. I hadn't been able to focus for an hour.

Me: Afraid it would come to this. Have taken measures to
        prevent future robbery.

Alec: How is that?

Me: If I don't wear panties, there will be nothing to steal.

In the following text silence, I'd gloated. Point for Anna. He hadn't responded until after I'd started with my last client, and as I read the most recent message, shivers alighted my skin.

Alec: Remember what happens when you tease.

There was no butler to greet me at the car today, and I was relieved not to have to witness him shouldering the weight of my table. Still, my back was killing me, and the muscles in my hands were sore. I looked forward to a day off tomorrow. Maybe in bed with Alec.

I carried my bags to the front door and rang the bell, but no one came. Surprised, I set down the massage table and tried the handle. It was open.

"Hello?" I called, not wanting to trespass. Memories of the last time I'd wandered around the property were still all too clear in my mind.

When no one came, I stepped back outside and walked along the porch, peeking through windows. Hidden by the lush green palms and landscaping, I didn't see the red Porsche careening around the fountain or the black SUV following it until they had pulled in front of the house.

The driver door of the SUV opened and Alec stepped out. In a black suit and matching sunglasses, he looked more like the sexy secret service than a personal security guard, if that's indeed what he was. My breath caught—already I could feel the pull to be near him, like a magnet, tugging me closer, even while something told me to be still. He didn't see me, and I was glad for the moment just to observe his strong, masculine shape and the way his dark, thick hair gleamed in the light. Before taking quick strides to the Porsche, he removed his glasses and pinched the bridge of his nose between his thumb and forefinger. His head tilted to the side subtly as if to stretch tense muscles in his neck.

My fingers itched to rub him down; I made a note to include that in tonight's festivities. But I also wondered what was troubling him, what had put those shadows under his eyes. I hoped he would tell me.

As I made my way back to the entrance of the house, a woman burst from the driver's side of the sports car. I had assumed Mr. Stein had been driving, and was surprised to recognize the redhead I had previously seen in the courtyard. Bent over the fountain. Naked.

Immediately my cheeks heated. I averted my eyes, swallowed, and, when I'd composed myself, greeted her with a warm smile.

She did not return it. She stormed past Alec up the stairs, her emerald skirt suit riding up her thighs with each step. She stopped in front of me, her eyes narrowed and her breasts—which I did *not* remember hardly moving while she was being pounded from behind—heaving beneath her cream-colored camisole with every breath. Despite her obvious fuming, she was quite beautiful. Blunt-cut hair angled around her heart-shaped face, and straight bangs hung over her dazzling green eyes.

"Who the hell are you?" At the snap in her tone, my shoulders rose an inch.

"Anna," I said evenly. "Mr. Stein's masseuse."

"His masseuse?" she said with a cold laugh. "Now that is *rich*."

I gritted my teeth. "From the sounds of it, you could use my services, too."

"Charlotte," Alec said from the bottom step. "This is a bad idea."

He had yet to look at me, though I was practically willing him to do so.

"Shut up, Alec." She waited in front of the door expectantly, as if willing it to open.

After a moment, Alec climbed the rest of the way and stepped between the redhead and me, placing his hand on the door.

"Excuse us," he said. The woman pushed by Alec into the foyer, and he followed with a sigh.

"Hi." My throat went dry as his chest brushed against mine, and I became acutely aware of my lack of panties, but he didn't look down and meet my eyes. He barely acknowledged that I was there.

I knew he was working, but not even a hello?

"Max!" As her voice cracked over his name, I felt a jab of sympathy. Trembling thumbs pressed to her temples. She reminded me of a cornered animal, striking out in fear.

I took one step over the threshold, unsure if I should venture farther than the front mat.

"Charlotte," Alec said again, placing his hand gently on the small of her back. I stiffened; the move suggested they were more than just acquaintances.

"Mr. Stein is unavailable." Ms. Rowe strode into the room, heels clicking across the marble floor. She was wearing a charcoal blouse and high-waisted black slacks, and held a cell phone in one hand.

"Jesus," said the redhead. "Who's he fucking now?"

"Not me," I muttered.

Ms. Rowe's gaze shot in my direction. Her mouth pinched at the corners. "Ms. Rossi. I'd forgotten you would be here this afternoon."

You just called me yesterday, I wanted to say. It surprised me that someone who seemed as organized as she did had made a scheduling error. I focused on the $300 I'd be making from this visit, not the crazy scene unfolding before my eyes or the man who'd tormented me with his tongue, now standing five feet away and ignoring me.

"Mr. Stein had to make a last-minute trip to New York. To see his *wife*." With that, Ms. Rowe faced Charlotte, hands placed on her hips and stance wide, as though she could stop a train just with her cold stare. I had to hand it to her; she could be quite the bulldog.

"We had business," said Charlotte between her teeth, and I winced, remembering just what *that* entailed. "Business I'm sure he doesn't want getting out."

It took a concentrated effort not to let the surprise show on my face. This wasn't my client's house, this was the set of a soap opera. Someone was going to yell, "Cut!" any minute, right? I should have grabbed some popcorn.

It occurred to me that Maxim Stein had flown to New York for damage control. He must have sensed that his mistress was about to expose their affair.

"Be careful making statements like that," Ms. Rowe warned her.

Alec leaned close and whispered something in Charlotte's ear. Her eyes lowered. My hands clenched.

"We'll have to reschedule, Ms. Rossi," Ms. Rowe snapped. "As you can see, we're a bit preoccupied here."

It was clear I was being dismissed. Deflated, I took a step back, but not before I heard Alec say softly to the redhead, "Come on, Charlotte. Let me take you home."

"I can't go home," she said flatly.

"Then let me buy you a drink."

Apparently our date was off. I thought of his text from when he hadn't shown at the restaurant: *Something came up*. Something with red hair? Jealousy wasn't a feeling I had much experience with, but it was rearing its ugly head now. Even if he was acting this way because of his job, I didn't appreciate the cold shoulder.

His gaze met mine, just for a second, and the chill in his eyes confirmed my suspicion. Something was going on between him and this woman, and he didn't want me to see.

I didn't know what it was. I told myself I didn't need to know, because it didn't matter. I should have trusted my instincts that he was trouble—I'd had enough of *that* to last a lifetime. Things were good right now. Uncomplicated. They needed to stay that way.

It was a shame, though. We could have had fun.

"See you around," I offered on my way out the door. He didn't say a word, and even though part of me wanted him to follow, I was relieved when he didn't. I closed the door behind me, despite the urge to watch the soap opera escalate into an episode of the *Jerry Springer Show*.

As if I hadn't had enough drama, creepy gate guard was kneeling in front of my bags when I came out on the porch. When he realized he'd been caught, he stood, and though he was only taller than me by a couple inches, he looked like some kind of body builder—too muscular in the chest, with skinny legs that didn't fill out his pants. He wasn't wearing his dark glasses anymore, and I could see his eyes now—clear blue like the sky— with blond, almost invisible lashes that matched his buzz cut.

"See something you want?" I asked, slamming the zipper to my duffle closed.

"That's a loaded question." His eyes roamed down my back and stopped on my ass. I tried to mute the sound of disgust in my throat, but was only moderately successful.

Charlotte's voice rose within.

Creepy tilted his head toward the door. "You're not staying to watch?"

"I think I've seen enough." I bent to retrieve my table, crossing the strap over my chest. Despite his obvious strength, he made no move to help, not that I'd have wanted it anyway.

The porch boards creaked as he stepped closer.

"Oh, yeah? What did you see?" His voice was steely now, demanding.

It may have been strangely primal to know Alec had seen me walk in on Maxim Stein and his mistress, but this guy was another issue entirely. The very thought of him watching me watch others have sex made my skin crawl.

"Nothing I haven't seen before." I shrugged into the strap of the duffle.

As I turned to walk away, he grabbed my wrist. Training took over, and before I took another breath, I'd twisted free and shoved him back hard.

"Whoa there," he said, hands raised in surrender. "A little touchy, don't you think?"

I moved closer to the stairs. "A girl's got to be careful these days."

"That's very true."

I swallowed. My body stilled, heartbeat on pause. Something about his tone, and the twitch in his thin lips made me think there was more to his offhand comment.

"Do we have a problem?" I asked, wanting him to know I wasn't afraid. I was trained in self-defense and wasn't a helpless little girl. Not anymore.

"Not that I know of." He smiled. "Not yet, anyway."

"I see." I reached in the duffle, blindly sweeping for my Mace.

Before I had the ability to even consider blinding him with it, he turned to go, meandering down the steps toward the front gate.

"Have a good night, Anna," he tossed over his shoulder.

What. A. Creep. I trudged down the stone path to my car. I threw my table into the trunk and my duffle into the passenger seat, and turned the key in the ignition, wondering if this fat paycheck was really worth it. There was something strange going on here. These people ranged from ice cold to crazy, with the man I still wanted right in the middle.

Maybe I wanted him, but I didn't need him. I needed simple. I needed predictable. I needed someone I could walk away from, and even now I had a feeling Alec was not that guy.

I picked up my cell phone, scrolled through the missed calls, and hit the Send key before I could change my mind.

It rang once.

"Randall? Hi, it's Anna. I think I will let you make it up to me. What are you doing now?"

Ten

I met Randall at a swanky piano bar in Hyde Park near his
office. Because I'd already planned on staying out with Alec, I
had brought a change of clothes in the car: a red slip dress that
pulled over my black camisole, and black strappy sandals. I
wriggled out of my yoga pants and combed my hair before leaving the front seat, annoyed that I had chosen not to bring underwear. But, considering the circumstances, it might have been the
right choice anyway. I had a shitload of sexual frustration to
work out, topped off with some serious irritation. Dr. Randall
was about to get lucky.

I found a seat at a tall table away from the bar and texted Amy
my change of plans. Before she could shoot back a series of questions I didn't want to answer, I slipped my phone back in my purse
and got my bearings. The lighting was dim, the music elegant, and
the clientele composed entirely of pastel-clad yuppies. I stuck out
like a gypsy in a church with my wild black hair and red dress.

Aware of the stares I was drawing, I averted my eyes out the
window. Daylight was fading and the sky had taken on an orange
hue. It would have been the perfect night to sit out at a waterside

restaurant like the one I'd planned on going to with Alec. I wondered if he was there right now with Charlotte, getting drinks.

Maybe I'd been too quick to judge him; I didn't know anything about his job and what it entailed. But then I remembered the easy way his hand had found another woman's back and how he'd completely ignored me in her presence, and I felt assured in my decision to be here.

"I'm so glad you called."

I turned in my seat to find Randall, wearing a thin, salmon-colored sweater and khakis. He grinned, a dimple appearing on his right cheek, and tossed his head back to clear the ridiculous hair from his eyes. Okay, maybe not so ridiculous. He was fairly cute when he wasn't being an ass.

"I'm glad I called, too," I said.

He sat across from me. I tried to picture him without his shirt on, but I kept seeing what I'd imagined Alec's body would look like. Rippled abs and a chiseled chest, smooth skin for my fingers to explore.

"Again, Anna, I'm sorry for the other night. It's so not like me."

I dismissed his guilt with a wave of my hand. I wasn't here to start a relationship; I was here to get this itch out of my system.

I was here to stop thinking about Alec.

Which seemed a little juvenile, now that I thought about it.

"What's on your mind?" Randall asked, making me aware of my frown.

I forced a laugh. "Nothing. I'm just hungry. It's been a busy day."

He hummed, tapping the menu with his thumb. "If we were in the office, I'd tell you that people typically deflect direct questions as a safety mechanism, but that deep down, they really want to tell you what's going on."

My smile turned genuine.

"Then it's a good thing we're not in your office," I said. "Because right now I just want to forget about my day, my week, and everything else, and relax. Is that all right with you?"

He nodded, looking relieved. "Would you like something to drink?"

"Absolutely."

Drinks were martinis, and dinner consisted of portabella mushroom sliders and a teensy, tiny spinach salad. It was delicious, but not exactly filling. The conversation was fine, though, and by the second glass of wine he had me laughing about his failed kiss on our last date.

"I panicked," he admitted. "It wasn't my best effort. If I get another chance, I promise not to ambush you."

"You may get another chance," I said. So maybe Randall didn't get my juices flowing like Alec, but that didn't mean I felt *nothing*. He was cute, and smart, and he did have a kick-ass body.

He was quiet for a moment. "Another glass of wine?"

"Are you trying to get me drunk?" I was already feeling pleasantly warm and tingly.

He looked at me through his overly long bangs. "Only drunk enough to sleep with me."

I laughed as he departed to the bar to order our drinks. Taking this chance to go to the restroom, I hopped down off the stool, grabbing the back of the chair to steady myself. If I didn't add water to my beverage list, I was going to be hating myself tomorrow.

When the room stopped tilting, I made my way to the bathroom. On the way back to my chair, I stopped at the bar to ask for a glass of water and saw Randall waiting on the other side for our drinks. He was talking to a woman in a pink fitted dress with a sweater draped over her shoulders, and he couldn't see me behind the mirrors that adorned the center island. A bottled blonde, the woman had spent her fair share of time in a tanning bed—her skin was too orange to have been tinted by the sun. She laughed at something he said, placing her hand on top of his.

His eyes lingered on where their hands touched, and after a moment he leaned forward and whispered something in her ear. A blush rose from her chest up her neck, and her smile melted. She nodded.

I hung around only a few more seconds to see him take out his cell phone and get her number. Feeling incredibly more sober, I made my way back to our table and sat down. I crossed my legs. Uncrossed them.

My date—who was supposed to be making up for being a jerk-off—was hitting on another woman no more than thirty feet away. I should have been furious. I looked down at the water the waitress brought and imagined myself throwing it in his face and then storming out. But I didn't care enough.

Still, I couldn't help but be annoyed. I picked up my purse, half convinced to make a silent escape, but figured I'd better tell him to go fuck himself first. I still had my pride after all.

I was just building up for my exit speech when another man took Randall's seat directly across from me.

Not just any man. Alec.

"Nice dress," he said curtly. "You know how I feel about you in red."

I did know. After all, he'd stolen my red panties.

I clenched the small purse on my lap. In a tight black T-shirt and jeans, he was smoldering. The thin material stretched across his chest as he leaned back. His fists knocked on the arms of the wooden chair. I tried not to stare at the muscles of his forearms that flexed with each movement, or his dark gaze, so heated it made my skin dew and my stomach quiver.

Excitement coursed through me. He was here. He'd found me. He wanted me just as much as I wanted him.

And then I remembered Charlotte.

"What are you doing here?" I asked.

"There are a few things you should know about me." His

voice was cool and sharp as a knife. "One, I don't share. Two, I don't appreciate having to search for the woman I'm seeing."

I choked. "I'm sorry, the woman you're seeing?" I leaned over the table. "So you're seeing me now? Not the redhead you just took home?"

He mirrored my posture, eyes boring straight through me. My mouth went dry.

"That," he said, "was work. If you and I are . . ."

"There is no *you and I*." I shoved back in my chair and stood up. "Especially if you stand me up or choose to ignore me when other women are around." I didn't care if people were staring; I was never coming back here anyway.

"Three," he continued. "I hate being interrupted."

I laughed coldly, stepping close enough to his seat that our knees collided. "Since you like lists so much, try this one on for size. One," I stuck up a finger. "You don't have to worry about sharing me, because I don't belong to you. Two." Another finger flew up. "I don't know how you tracked me down, but I'm on a date. With someone else. And three, I'll interrupt whoever I damn well please whenever I damn well want."

I was fuming, chest rising and falling with each breath. I'd definitely gotten too close. He smelled good enough to lick, and it took everything I had not to crawl into his lap, grab handfuls of his dark, messy hair, and crush my lips against his. The colder he was, the hotter I became.

"You're not on a date," he said, steel flashing in his eyes.

I glanced at the bar, searching for Randall's blond hair and ridiculous sweater, or even the girl he'd been flirting with.

"He's gone," Alec said. "Don't expect him to call."

The muscles between my shoulder blades tightened. "What did you do?"

Finally he rose, standing at least a foot taller than me.

"I told him if he was going to be a big boy, he shouldn't play with his Barbie dolls in public. And I let him know if he tried to contact you again, I would break his fingers."

"Who *are* you?" I said, more flattered than I cared to admit. "You can't just go around threatening strangers." Despite my intent, my anger was dissipating, and in its place came a wave of humiliation. It was bad enough Randall was working on his next prospect in my presence, but to have Alec witness it made it a hundred times worse.

"I can threaten whoever I damn well please whenever I damn well want."

I gave him a nasty look.

"I had it covered," I told him. "I didn't need your *help*."

"Oh yeah?"

"Yes." I crossed my arms. "For your information, I had a whole 'kiss my ass' speech worked out. And I was considering kicking him under the table." I smoothed back my hair. "In a way that would severely limit his ability to have children."

A grin spread across Alec's face, wiping away the irritation as if it had never been there in the first place.

"That's my girl."

"I'm *not* your girl." *Simmer down, butterflies.*

"We'll see," he said.

Cocky bastard. I smirked.

"Everything all right, Alec?" A handsome, middle-aged man in a black jacket appeared from behind me. The gold badge on his lapel stated that he was the manager.

"More than all right," Alec responded, taking out his wallet. "Can I settle up with you, Jackson? We're going to have to take off."

"Of course," said the manager. "Ms. Rossi, I hope you'll come back and see us again."

"Um . . ." Had I given him my name? I guess I had when I checked in. "Sure."

I narrowed my eyes on Alec while he paid for the meal I'd

shared with Randall. I was sure Randall would be offended by the gesture, which was precisely why I let it happen.

"Your pal, Jackson," I said as the manager walked away. "Is he how you found me here?"

"Him, and the tracking device I put in your car."

My mouth fell open. When he chuckled, I realized he was kidding and gave him a little shove. I shouldn't have touched him; his biceps were as hard as a rock, and I couldn't help but let my fingers linger. The man had incredible arms.

We stepped outside into the night. I breathed in the fresh ambrosia and let the humidity warm my bare legs and shoulders. A breeze made ripples in my skirt, sending cool air to other places I was bare, too.

Alec faced me, hands in his pockets, as if waiting for me to say something. I didn't know what he expected me to say. I'd known him less than a week, and already the roller-coaster ride was giving me whiplash.

I needed to walk away. This was too much drama, and I didn't do drama. Every time things got too complicated, I moved on, gave myself a fresh start, but I wasn't ready to move yet. I liked it here, liked my job, liked being near Amy and Paisley. Things were good. For now.

"What's the deal with Charlotte?" I asked, ignoring the instinct to get in my car and close this chapter.

A muscle beside his eye twitched.

"Forget it," I said. "It's none of my business." I turned on my heels and began walking back toward the parking garage.

"Wait." His hand found my shoulder and sent bolts of heat down my arm. I stopped; it was impossible to think clearly when he was touching me.

"Charlotte and the boss have a . . . complex relationship."

"Yeah," I said, the blush staining my cheeks. "I gathered that much. Looked like she might also have a complex relationship with you."

My hands balled into fists as I remembered his hand on the small of her back.

His mouth twitched. His hand on my arm paused.

"She doesn't. Not in the way you're thinking." He took a deep breath and his features softened. "And she won't. It's strictly professional."

My eyes lowered. It shouldn't have mattered, but it felt good for him to say so.

"What do you know about her?" he asked. His fingers brushed a strand of hair behind my ear.

"Nothing," I said, not seeing what this had to do with anything. "I'd never seen her before . . . well, *before*."

His mouth pulled tighter. "She's a little paranoid that people will figure out what she and Max are doing together. I was trying to keep you out of it today. I didn't want her to have any reason to suspect you might have seen anything. Obviously, I didn't do a very good job."

"No," I agreed. "You didn't."

Alec stepped closer. Now both hands were weaving through my hair.

"Let me make it up to you."

"You know," I said, "that's the second time a man has said that to me this week. The first one did a shitty job, and the jury's still out on you."

A low laugh rumbled from his perfect mouth.

"Careful, Anna," he warned. "When you get all fired up, it's hard for me to keep my hands off you."

I poked him in the chest. "Behave."

His arms lowered to my waist and pulled me closer. I gasped; his cock, hard and ready, brushed against my belly.

"I make no promises," he said. And somehow that felt like a promise.

Though I wanted to melt into him, I placed my hands on his

chest and took a step back. I appraised him as objectively as I could and came up with one answer: He was trouble.

But I couldn't say no to him. Not until I'd broken free from whatever this hold was he had on me.

"Fine," I conceded. "Take me somewhere to get something to eat. I'm starving."

Eleven

We took his car. I wasn't stupid enough to drive after a couple of drinks, and when I offered to split a cab, he'd called me cute and laughed at me. Five minutes later, I was in the passenger seat of his Jeep, cruising west on Highway 60, distracted by the vibrations in the seat and the seemingly subconscious way his thumb stroked the shifter when he changed gears.

He was different—just as gorgeous, oozing the same sexuality as before, but more visibly tense despite his down-to-earth car and casual clothes. The storm clouds were practically visible over his head. I knew it was safer to keep a distance, enjoy only his body until we parted ways, but I still wanted to know what he was thinking.

I turned my attention to the deep water of Tampa Bay as we merged onto the bridge that led us away from the bright lights of the city.

"I love the water at night," I said, watching the way the moonlight caught the soft swells below us. "It's beautiful, isn't it?"

His hand moved to my thigh, the touch making me ultrasensitive. I became aware of my whole body—my heated skin, the silky movement of my hair on my shoulders, the sudden tightening of my nipples. My gaze tracked up his arm to his face, and found his attention to the road unwavering.

"It is," he said.

"Did you grow up here?"

His fingers climbed an inch higher. I reminded myself to breathe.

"Here and there," he said.

I frowned at his vague answer. "You grew up here and there, and do this and that for work."

"Tell me about this dress." He changed the subject, fingertips rubbing the seam of my skirt. "Did you wear it because you knew it would make me crazy?"

His knuckles skimmed an inch higher, now just a hand's width away from my naked slit.

I'd picked it because he'd liked my red panties so much, and because I hoped it would remind him of what had happened in the room at Rave. But mostly because it made me feel sexy and powerful.

"I went out with someone else, remember?" I said. "Maybe I was trying to make him crazy."

His eye twitched. And then his hand traveled the seam of my dress toward the valley between my thighs. My fingers flexed against the sides of the leather seat.

"Baby," he growled. "He wouldn't have known what to do with you."

Alec was probably right about that. Randall may have looked fine, but I doubted he was interested in orgasmic reciprocity.

The hand inching up my legs slid beneath my skirt and climbed higher, until one finger traced the V at the apex of my thighs. He'd just realized I wasn't wearing underwear; I could see the surprise tighten his features.

"Fuck," he murmured. "You little tease."

My breath shuddered.

"I wore the dress for me," I confessed. "I left the panties off for you."

His eyes remained forward as he slowly gathered my skirt and pulled it up around my hips. The cool air against my hot skin made me squeeze my thighs together. I could already feel the moisture gathering there, making my cleft wet and slippery. I almost pushed his hand away; it didn't seem decent to be so obvious with my desire.

"So this is all it takes to get to the truth," he said, dipping his middle finger into my folds. "Interesting."

My toes curled in their sandals. I clenched my teeth together.

"What else do I need to know about this dress?" he asked, his finger rising, coated with my arousal, then slipping back down again. He wasn't going deeper; it was almost painful that he wasn't inside of me.

"What?" I managed.

"Zippers?" he asked. "Buttons? How does it come off?"

I bit my bottom lip to keep from groaning. For some reason it felt dirtier to be here in his car, driving sixty-five miles per hour down a dark road while he stroked me, than it had when his face was between my thighs. Before, he'd been almost reverent. Now I wondered if he was using me. In the part of my mind that could still think straight, I wondered if this was punishment for going out with Randall.

"Zip . . . zipper." I moaned as the heel of his hand pressed on my mound.

"What's the matter, Anna? Having trouble concentrating?"

I glanced over, but he was still staring straight ahead. If not for the muscle jumping in his jaw, I would have thought he was completely unaffected.

"Why are you doing this?" My breath was coming faster. Everything inside wound tighter and tighter, ready to snap. I could feel my pulse pounding hard in my sex.

"Can't focus. Can barely breathe. That's how I feel all the

time now," he said, glancing over at me. His eyes were so dark I could barely see the irises reflected off the glowing gauges on the dashboard. "Ever since I first saw you. I don't know what it is, but my cock is so hard I can't even fucking think straight."

His hand ground against my clit and I squirmed beneath him. I fought to keep my eyes open, but my lids were shutting against my will.

"You think I could ignore you when I feel this way?" His hand moved faster, still not inside me, but with enough friction to bring me right to the edge. "You think I could touch another woman?"

He pulled his hand away and I cried out, but this time from the loss. I was on fire for him, burning, and then suddenly cold and empty and exposed. Immediately the shame washed over me. I shoved my dress down, cheeks glowing.

He pressed hard on the brakes, swerving off the asphalt. I was jostled in the seat, still trying to make sense of what was happening.

He threw the car into park and faced me. The muscles of his neck were taut.

"I want you, Anna," he said, and the intensity in his gaze stole my breath. "And I won't share you. If you can't play that way, you need to tell me now."

I didn't want to share him either. I didn't want to think of him with Charlotte, fucking her the way I'd seen her with Maxim Stein. My need for him was intoxicating, and he was right; it did make me crazy.

"I want you," I said. "Just you."

I grabbed his face in my hands and kissed him hard. I gripped his hair just like I'd wanted to from the moment I'd first seen him. He kissed me back, head tilting, lips parting, and then his tongue thrust into my mouth in the way I wanted his cock deep inside me. I felt his groan in our kiss, and then his hand, frantically seeking the place he'd abandoned seconds earlier.

His fingers plunged inside me—first one, then two, twisting, stroking, desperate and hard against my swollen walls. The orgasm tore through me unexpectedly. I arched back, tearing my lips from his, writhing in the seat as my world exploded.

"So fucking hot." His words filtered through the rush in my ears. His mouth found my neck, feasted there with short flicks of his tongue and scrapes of his teeth.

"Spread your legs." He pushed them apart. "Keep them open. Wide. I have to see you."

His fingers fucked me faster, thumb rubbing against my clit. The slap of his hand against my damp center made me wild. I gripped his shoulders, digging my nails into his shirt.

"Alec," I groaned. "Oh God. *Alec*."

He kissed me again, his tongue battling mine in a frenzy of lust. I yanked his hair and he growled, the sound shooting straight through to my core. His hand changed position, and soon another finger was rimming the sensitive entrance to my rear.

I jerked in surprise, never having been touched there by anyone before. He sucked my bottom lip into his mouth and drew my nipple through my dress's fabric with the circular motion of his opposite palm.

"You like that," he murmured, his pinky finger easing inside. "I'm going to know everything you like soon."

The thought of him exploring my naked body made me hate his car and all the stupid layers of clothing between us. We needed to find a bed and soon.

His forefinger curved, stroking me inside. My hips slid forward to the edge of the seat. Sweat coated my skin.

"You feel like hot silk. Squeeze me tight. Just like that." My muscles flexed at his command, pushing the sensations higher. The cold distance was gone and he was with me now, driving me to climax again in his hand.

I came with a shudder, bright lights bursting behind my closed lids. The sensations pummeled me, wave upon wave of velvet heat. He stroked me faster, hissing through his teeth.

"Christ, Anna. The way you sound."

Still flying high, I shoved his hand away and tore off my sandals.

"Your pants. Take them off," I demanded.

A challenging look passed over his face. He leaned the seat down, but before he could lower his fly all the way, I was scrambling across the center console. He finished with the zipper and tugged the jeans down his hips.

"Come on," I said, willing him to go faster. "Get them off. Hurry."

I bruised my knee against the car door as I straddled his lap. My red dress bunched around my hips, too heavy and warm. His hips bucked; my wet, needy pussy separated from his straining hard-on by only the thin cotton of his boxer briefs. I moaned, desperate for more contact.

"Condom," he said between his teeth, pulling the wallet out of his back pocket. I snatched it out of his hands, feverish now. Something primal had stolen my control, made me a slave to my own hunger. Every thought was directed toward one goal: impaling myself on his cock. Riding him into oblivion. I didn't care that my head was smashed against the ceiling, or my ass was trapped between his hips and the steering wheel. I needed him inside of me immediately.

I ripped the condom package with my teeth while he shoved his jeans down. An instant later his hands were beneath my dress, sliding up my sweat-dampened stomach. They found my breasts, finally, and hurriedly shoved up the cups of my bra. His thumbs grazed over my nipples while my hips began to grind against his.

"Yes," I whimpered. "More, more, more."

"Do you feel what you're doing to me?" He thrust his hips up, rocked against my center. His face tightened into a grimace.

I pulled the condom free. He slid down his boxer briefs, now wet with my desire for him. I gasped.

"Oh," I said, unable to do anything but stare. He was large. More than large, *huge*. The head of his penis was nearly even with my belly button, the shaft, veined and thick, was rock hard.

"Oh?" A wolfish grin lifted his lips.

I exhaled in a whoosh.

"I'm not sure that'll fit."

He held it in his hand and pressed the head against my clit. I gripped his shoulders, overwhelmed for the moment by the soft stone feel of him.

He laughed dryly. "It'll fit."

I didn't care how big he was then, just as long as he put it inside me. I lowered the condom to his shaft. Later there would be time for me to touch him, feel him, put my mouth on him. But now I couldn't take my time. The need was too great, too demanding.

A knock came on the hood of the car. I screamed, jumped. My butt hit the car horn and the subsequent honk made me scream again.

A round of applause went up somewhere in the darkness. I froze.

The nastiest curse words I'd ever heard ripped from Alec's mouth as he tucked himself back inside his pants.

"Is there someone behind me?" I asked when I was able to speak.

"Yes. Goddammit."

I still didn't move. I couldn't. I could only close my eyes and wish to disappear.

"I was afraid of that," I said.

"Alec? That you?" came a voice from outside the car.

"Oh dear God." I tried to move back to my seat, but Alec held me firmly in place. His seat back rose as he jerked the lever.

Then to my shock, he rolled down the window.

I buried my face in his neck, hiding beneath my wild, sexed-up hair. I could still feel the ache in my body, now heightened by the presence of others. Thank everything holy my dress was still covering my top half.

"Hey, Mac," said Alec.

Shoot me now. They were friends.

"Just thought you'd want to know you've got an audience."

With the window open, I could hear the voices through the dark. I didn't chance lifting my head to look. I didn't even know where we were. I'd been fairly distracted when we'd stopped.

"Can't you tell them to fuck off?" asked Alec tightly.

"Hey!" called the man outside. "Fuck off, you guys! Alec and . . ."

"Anna," said Alec.

I snorted. Or sobbed. And somehow ended up swallowing a laugh.

Kill. Me. Now.

"Alec and Anna need some privacy!" called Mac.

"Then they shouldn't have pulled into a parking lot!" called someone through the distance.

"A parking lot?" I whispered. "You pulled into a parking lot?" I bit him hard on the neck.

He winced, hands squeezing around my ribs.

"You didn't seem to mind a second ago," he said.

"Well, I'll just give you two a minute," said Mac. "See you inside." The sound of his footsteps trudging over the gravel disappeared as Alec rolled his window back up.

I pulled back to look him in the face. He had the good sense to look worried.

"A fucking parking lot? Are you kidding me?"

I looked behind me, but it was only dark. If I focused, I could hear sounds beyond the still-running motor—the water lapping against the shore somewhere nearby, the quiet thrum of music.

And several male voices, now booing.

"Technically we're not in a parking lot," Alec said. "The restaurant's down the road a bit. Behind the trees." I couldn't see the lights behind the brush.

I slapped him on the shoulder. "This is the second restaurant today I can't go back to because of you."

"Believe me," said Alec. "The people that come here have seen far worse."

I narrowed my eyes, wondering if he meant he'd done this sort of thing here a lot.

"So you brought me to some kind of strip club for our first date? Nice."

He shrugged. "You said you were hungry. They have the best burgers on the Bay."

I shook my head. As much as I wanted to move back to the passenger seat and make him take me somewhere else, I didn't want to shrink off into the distance. He should know I wasn't a coward.

"And those guys cheering are all your friends."

He cringed. "Some of them. Mac's the cook. He and I go back a ways."

"You really want to stay here?" I asked.

He moved his hips, making a sigh slip from my throat. I still wanted him badly.

"What I really want is to find the nearest hotel room and fuck until we both pass out."

"That could be a while," I warned him. "I have excellent stamina."

"So do I," he said with a smile in his voice.

The mood had changed between us, from heated to playful. He was still ready, as was I, but the urgency had simmered. We could wait, at least for a little while.

"Best burgers, huh?" I asked.

His mouth found my collarbone and licked a straight line up behind my ear. I shivered.

"They're all right," he said, slipping the dress strap down over one shoulder. This time, I definitely heard the cheers.

"You better eat fast," I whispered, nipping his ear lobe. "Because it's going to be a long night."

I opened the car door and crawled over him outside. He watched me curiously, brows raised.

"Oh shit," I heard someone say in the dark. I could make out the shadows thirty feet away, but no faces. "Go. *Go.* Alec's going to kick your ass."

I tucked one foot behind me, and like I'd once seen in one of Paisley's princess movies, made my very best curtsey.

The cheers filled the night.

Twelve

It wasn't a strip club, at least. It was a bar. The kind that played the music loud and didn't boast a health rating on the tinted windows. We sat outside in plastic lawn chairs on a wooden deck decorated with neon beer signs that stretched into a dock over the water. The air smelled like grease and mosquito repellent, and the men inside playing pool swore like sailors.

It was sort of perfect.

"Is this okay?" Alec asked, returning from inside with two beers.

"It's great," I said. "It reminds me of the cop hangouts my dad used to take me to after work."

He froze, and cleared his throat before fixing his attention on the bottle. "Your dad's a cop, huh?"

I nodded. The urge to tell him more about the man I called my father was confusing; normally I didn't volunteer information about my past.

"A detective," I said. "Recently retired."

"Does he live here?"

"Cincinnati." I thought of the money I'd banked from my

first appointment with Maxim Stein. With the extra cash I'd been making from home visits, I'd be able to check in on him soon.

Alec's shoulders rose and fell with a deep breath.

"What?" I teased. "Were you afraid I'd bring you home to Sunday dinner or something?" It didn't bother me that my father's profession made him nervous. It made most people nervous.

"I'm not sure I'm the type you bring home to meet Mom and Dad," he said.

I wasn't sure what that meant—if he didn't want to be more than fuck buddies, or if he thought they'd disapprove.

My dad probably would disapprove. When my date to the senior prom picked me up, my dad was actually sitting on the porch cleaning his gun.

"Are you close to your parents?" I asked.

He looked out over the water and nursed his beer. "Close enough."

I settled back in my seat and put my bare feet up on the chair next to me. "Just out of curiosity, what isn't off-limits?"

He scratched the back of his head. "What do you mean?"

"You won't talk about your job, you won't talk about your past. I'm just wondering if there's something you can tell me about yourself?"

Clearly this guy had gotten under my skin. Normally I wouldn't have cared if he didn't want to talk about himself; I would have been happy to keep things light. But I was drawn to him in more ways than just the physical—a realization that scared me a little.

He frowned, peeling the label off the bottle. "I'm into you. Isn't that good enough?"

I felt the warmth shimmer all the way down to my toes.

"For now," I said.

Mac, a big man in his sixties with a stained white T-shirt and a Santa Claus belly, brought out the burgers himself. He had a handsome smile and kind eyes, and covered his gray hair with a worn

Marines veteran ball cap. I braced myself for the embarrassment—the last time he'd seen me, I'd been attempting to ride Alec like a rodeo bull.

"This guy giving you trouble, Anna?" he asked me as he set the heaping plates down on the rickety table. The smell of French fries made my stomach growl.

Alec smirked.

"Some," I admitted, grateful for the lack of awkwardness. "But if he gets fresh, I think I can take him."

Mac chuckled. "You let me know if you need backup. I've got a twelve gauge behind the bar."

"Noted," I said.

When Alec and I were alone again on the deck, I picked up the burger with both hands and took a bite. It was so delicious. I practically groaned. I'd almost gotten through half when I realized he had yet to dig in.

"Problem?" I asked, wiping my hands with the paper napkin.

"No," he said. "I'm impressed. I've never seen a woman eat like that."

I glanced down at the fries and the huge dripping burger and realized attacking my food like a starved lion on a Nature Channel special didn't make the best impression.

"Excuse me for not being one of your stick models," I said.

He tilted his head. "What makes you think I like stick models?"

Was he kidding? I could see him paired with an actress, or any one of the girls from the Victoria's Secret catalogue, and here he was with me—a solid hourglass figure topping out at five feet, four inches. I wasn't normally insecure about the way I looked, but I'd never been out with a man so beautiful before.

I glanced up through my lashes. "Look at you."

"What about me?"

I scoffed, and then realized he was serious.

"You're decent to look at," I said. "If you can get past the flabby gut and elephant ears."

He grinned, a look that made my heart stutter.

"You're not so bad either," he told me. "Once you get past the chicken legs and flat chest."

"And ridiculous hair." The humidity and sexcapade in his car had made my hair double the normal volume. I reached up to tie it back in a knot at the base of my neck.

"I don't mind the hair," he said. "But that mouth is going to get you in trouble."

I pursed my lips. "And why is that?"

He leaned across the table, pulling my knees between his. Slowly, his fingers skimmed behind my calves, teasing circles that moved up the backs of my thighs.

"It's very distracting." He came closer, until he was just a breath away.

"Then how come I had to kiss you first?" I asked, pulse flying.

His nose brushed against mine.

"You said you don't kiss on the first date. I was trying to be respectful."

I would have laughed if my heart wasn't caught in my throat.

"I guess some rules are made to be broken," I said.

He murmured his agreement.

It started slow, a feather-soft press of his lips on mine, but as they slanted and opened, the fire was rekindled. My eyelids drifted closed. Tendrils of heat curled in my belly as he sucked my lower lip into his mouth and traced it with his tongue. The kiss deepened as his fingers threaded through my hair, massaging my scalp. My hair tumbled free from the knot and cascaded down my back. I could feel myself drawing closer to him, melting into him as his tongue caressed mine.

"Get some, Alec!" someone called through the window.

Alec slowly pulled away, a look of annoyance on his face.

"Excuse me a second." He started to rise, but I grabbed the collar of his shirt and pulled him back down.

"He's trying to," I shouted back. "Quit interrupting!"

Laughter came from inside, and Alec chuckled.

I planted one more searing kiss on him before leaning back.

"Finish eating," he told me. "I can't keep my hands off you much longer."

I toyed with a fry while he went to work on his burger. I wasn't sure I was hungry—at least not in that way—anymore. My legs were still between his knees, and I crossed them, slowly running my ankle up his calf. Even through his jeans I could feel the muscles beneath tense.

"What time do you work tomorrow?" he asked roughly.

"Tomorrow I have the day off," I told him. "You?"

One of his perfect brows arched. "I think my schedule just cleared up."

I took a sip from the bottle, running the top of the glass back and forth across my lower lip. His jaw twitched watching me, his desire completely obvious in the tight expression on his face. I loved knowing I could turn him on so easily.

"You sure Mr. Stein won't need you?" *Or Charlotte won't need you?*

"The boss is in New York," he reminded me.

"So you don't have to work when he's not in town?"

"You ask a lot of questions," he said.

I shrugged. "I like to know who I'm getting into bed with."

"Are you sure about that?" He tapped the table with his thumb. I was making him nervous.

I wondered if his implied warning had any truth behind it. He'd told me so little about who he was—he could have been the leader of the North American cocaine industry for all I knew. Maybe I should have been taking a step back to think about things before rushing into a relationship, however shallow, with him.

"Now I've scared you," he noticed. His hands returned to my

knees. "I didn't mean to. How about this? For every one of your questions, I get one of mine."

"Sounds fair." I narrowed my eyes, trying to figure him out. "What do you do for Maxim Stein?"

He took another bite of his burger. Chewed, swallowed, chased it with beer while I waited. Now *he* was making *me* nervous.

"Whatever he needs," Alec finally answered. "Security mostly. If he needs a proxy for business deals I do that, too. The managers of various divisions in Force Enterprises report to me, and if there's a problem, I take care of it."

"You take care of it," I repeated. "Like a *body man*." I'd heard the term in a mafia movie I'd seen with my dad once. Apparently it was a legit occupation; my dad had said that even the president had one. I'd gathered that Alec was highly trusted by Maxim Stein, but it seemed he was more important than I thought.

"Exactly like a body man," he said.

"Kind of young to have all that responsibility, aren't you?"

"Is that your next question?"

I crossed my arms over my chest. "No. It falls under the same topic: the occupation of Alec Flynn."

He considered this a moment. "I'm twenty-nine. I've known the boss for fourteen years."

It made sense now why Alec was so close to the business operations, he'd probably been groomed since he was a teenager. "Was he your parents' friend or something?"

"Or something," said Alec, raising the wall between us again. "My turn. Have you been tested?"

The change of direction was jarring, but I should have known by the bulge in his pants that his mind was still on sex.

"I have, and I'm clean."

"I am as well. Are you on birth control?"

His straightforwardness was making me blush. "It's not your turn."

"My question falls under the same topic."

"Which is?"

"If I can come inside you."

My lips parted. No, I was definitely not hungry for French fries anymore. My legs parted slightly as his thumbs rose just beneath the hem of my skirt, like he could control me with just a touch.

"Because I want to," he added. The bar behind him faded; for a moment it felt as if we were the only two people in the world.

"I'm on the pill." I swallowed. "And we'll see how it goes."

He nodded, holding my gaze. The promise of what was to come crackled between us.

"Your turn," he said.

"Have you been with many women?" I shouldn't have asked; I knew the answer already. But part of me wanted to know I was different, not just a number to him. I wanted to be important. I wanted to be remembered when we went our separate ways. I already knew I wasn't going to be able to forget him.

He mulled over my words, long enough for me to wish I could have shoved them back in my mouth. My gaze dropped to my lap.

"I haven't been with anyone like you." Slowly, his hand rose to my face, and one fingertip traced my lips. "I have never wanted anything as much as I want you, Anna."

My heart hammered in my chest. Maybe it was a line, but it felt real. For tonight, I would believe him.

"Your turn," I whispered, mouth dry. I reached for my glass of water.

"What were you doing in Max's office the night we met?"

I felt my spine straighten at his direct tone. If not for the gentle way he'd begun to caress my legs again, I would have thought I was in trouble.

"Hiding," I answered stiffly. "When Mr. Stein was late to our appointment I wandered around a little. You know that. I told you."

He dismissed it with the wave of his hand. "You're up."

"What did you think I was doing in Mr. Stein's office?" I

pulled my legs back, disguising my shift in positions as a way to grab the ketchup for my fries. His question rubbed me the wrong way. How long had he wanted to ask me that? Why had he waited until this moment? It seemed suddenly like this wasn't a date at all for him, but just an extension of work.

"I don't know." He took a deep breath. "We weren't sure how you'd gotten there at first."

"We?"

"Bobby and I. You may have seen him at the front gate."

The creepy guy with buzzed hair came to mind. "Right. I had the pleasure of meeting him earlier when he was digging through my bags without permission."

"Bobby's a little more direct than I am."

His words sunk in slowly, but carried the weight of a ten-pound brick. This was all some smooth ploy to assure I would keep my mouth shut about Maxim Stein's affair—something I didn't see anyone besides his wife being interested in knowing anyway. The sting annoyed me. I didn't let other people hurt me—there were only a handful I let close enough who could. I pushed my plate back, feeling the night's chill for the first time.

"I'm beginning to think I like Bobby's way better. At least he didn't try to cover up what he wanted with dinner and sex." My voice had gone cold, just like the blood in my veins. I felt my nails dig into my palms. "I didn't snoop around or steal anything, and I certainly didn't intend on watching him and Charlotte play porno outside in broad daylight. He can go and fuck whoever he wants for all I care." I stood. "And you can go and fuck yourself. Thanks for the burger, Alec. I think I'll call a cab to take me home."

The humiliation burned my cheeks. I hated feeling stupid. As I looked at Alec, I saw the surprise on his face turn to anger. I was going to call Ms. Rowe tomorrow and tell her to find a new masseuse. The entire venture had been a giant mess from the beginning. I'd find another way to earn the money to see my dad; it just might take a little longer than I'd planned.

"Sit down," he said.

"Kiss my ass."

"Sit. Down." His tone was sharp, and before I could stop myself, I'd done just what he'd demanded. My body betrayed my convictions; my nipples had pebbled, and a new surge of moisture had dampened my inner thighs. I didn't know what had come over me, how he could make me so hot when I should have been walking away, but the power coming off of him was staggering, and the urge to please him nearly brought me to my knees.

"Don't doubt me," he said quietly, and I could feel the heat spread throughout my body. He looked like a wildcat ready to pounce—muscular, sleek, and beautiful. "I told you I want you, and if you think I'm here for any other reason, you're seriously mistaken."

I believed him. I could feel the truth in his serious gaze. He circled one of my wrists with his strong hand, careful not to squeeze too tightly as he lifted it to his chest and dragged it down his solid, muscular abs to his belt.

My breath caught.

His hand lowered, pressing my palm against his hard cock. A moan slipped from my mouth, and then my breath came faster. My clothes, light as they were, chafed my sensitive skin. The desire I felt for him overrode my anger, shoved aside my insecurities. Maybe he wanted me, but I *needed* him. It was like nothing I'd ever experienced before. Every cell existed to give him pleasure, and take it in return.

"It's time to go," he said.

I nodded.

He took my hand, holding it firmly as we walked through the loud bar in silence.

Mac waved to us from the front door. "I'll stop by the house later this week."

Alec only nodded and led me out the door to his car. He

opened my door, and shut it once I was inside. I'd begun to feel feverish; I could hardly hold still.

"My apartment is in Ybor City," I said when he'd entered the driver's side.

I wasn't sure if I could keep off of him that long.

"Touch yourself," he commanded. "But don't come."

A dark thrill trembled through me. Slowly, I pulled back my skirt. I lifted my leg and placed one bare foot on the dash, the other on his thigh, giving him a clear view even as the overhead lights dimmed. Slowly, I lowered one hand to my aching center.

Gravel sprayed from under his tires as he hit the gas.

He drove fast.

Thirteen

I could barely concentrate enough to direct Alec to my parking spot. He was out of the Jeep before I could unlatch my seat belt. I wasn't sure how he knew to climb the stairs past the Chinese restaurant to my apartment, but I was in no shape to argue. My legs were trembling, my hands clumsy. The ache in my sex had become so demanding my head was beginning to throb.

I dropped my keys on the welcome mat in the hallway. With a hard, impatient expression on his face, he stooped down to pick them up and held them out in the palm of his hand.

"That one," I said.

He opened the door.

The curtains were still open, and the streetlamps outside bathed my apartment in long shadows. I didn't care that dirty clothes were strewn over the back of the love seat in the center of the room or that my bed was unmade. My nerves were raw from the energy sizzling between us. He stepped close behind me, and his warm breath on the back of my neck sent hot shivers down my spine.

"Alec, I . . ." I didn't know what to say, or how to begin. It was like I'd never brought a man home before. Was I supposed to offer him something to drink? Make small talk?

I didn't even get a chance to flip on the lights.

He spun me around to face him, and the door closed forcefully as he pressed my body against it. His mouth found mine, and his kiss stole my breath. There was a fierce passion in the way his tongue thrust past my teeth, in the almost bruising pressure of his lips. He held my face in his hands, burying his fingers in my hair. It was as if he were starved for the taste of me. Like he couldn't get enough. Like I was the most wanted woman in the world.

His hands cuffed my wrists, a gentle, but solid prison that he moved above my head. The weight of him against me, and the intensity of his mouth made me moan. I could feel his hard length pressing against my pelvis, begging to be freed from his pants. I rose to my tiptoes as he rocked down, then pressed his hips to mine—a promise.

"Christ," he said. "You're killing me."

I was so tightly coiled, I nearly came from the friction of his movement. He swallowed my stunted cry, dragging his hands heavily down my sides to my hips. Automatically, I lifted one knee, and he grabbed the underside of my leg and ground hard against me.

"Oh God," I managed, careening down the tunnel toward release.

He froze.

"Tell me I can have you," he said hurriedly. "Say it."

"Yes," I said, and gasped as his mouth made a trail of urgent, wet kisses to my neck. "Yes. Now."

The storm took us, a frenzy of scraping teeth and fast, desperate touches. He fumbled with the zipper on the back of my dress as I ripped the T-shirt over his head and revealed his broad, sculpted chest, already glistening with sweat. Before my dress was loose enough to pull completely off, he'd tugged it down between our bodies, pinning my arms to my sides with the straps that had sagged down to my biceps. I fought the restraints, desperate to touch him, but his hips pinned me in place. He weighed my breasts with the palms of his hands, a hiss escaping through his teeth, then in a flash, unhooked my sheer black bra and cast it to the side.

The coarse, groomed hair on his chest tantalized my nipples as he adjusted positions and lowered, just enough to hoist me up with his muscled arms. My legs wrapped around his waist, pressing my needy, swollen sex against the rough denim of his jeans. I yanked the dress over my head, hearing the zipper rip just as my sandals clunked to the floor.

"Your cunt's so hot I can feel it through my pants," he growled. "You're going to burn me alive."

Using the door as leverage, he held me in place with one arm while the other hand returned to my breast. He squeezed it, then teased the nipple to a hard point with the rough stroke of his thumb.

I squirmed, throwing my head back, vaguely aware of the pain as it smacked against the door. His mouth skimmed down my chest to my left breast, and he lashed my nipple with his tongue, a series of relentless strikes that made my pussy spasm as the orgasm surged through me.

"Fuck," he said, rotating his hips to help me ride it out. "I can't wait anymore. I'm sorry."

Still pelted by waves of satin heat, I clung to his body, struggling to find my equilibrium as he backed away from the door. He took a few steps and crashed into something, staggered, but caught himself before we plummeted to the ground. When he swore, I kissed him, urging him to hurry as my emptiness became unbearable.

"Alec, please. I need . . ."

"I know," he said. "I know."

He lowered to his knees, keeping one arm locked firmly

around my lower back, the other beneath my rear. And then the wooden floor became my support as he pulled away to remove his pants.

He was mouthwatering. A god. In the fractions of light that sliced across his chest I could see the swell of his muscles, the ripples of his abs, the cut V that lowered beneath his waistband.

His pants were shed, along with his boxer briefs, and his erection, a shaft of smooth steel, bobbed free. He stretched it down with one hand and my breath caught. He was a portrait of masculinity and, watching him, a part of me woke that I hadn't known existed. A part that needed to be claimed. A part of me that needed to claim him as my own.

Then he was tearing the foil off a condom and leaning over me. The look in his eyes made my heart stutter: urgency, need, and a whisper of something else, too, that I didn't understand. I pulled his perfect face down to mine, feasting on his mouth while he pulled on the condom.

Our legs tangled, my nails dug into his shoulders. He placed himself at my entrance and held my gaze. One last breath before the dive.

My body craved him; I couldn't help myself. My heels dug into the floor and my hips thrust up. The head of his penis nudged through my slick lips and a hoarse cry tore from my open mouth.

"You're going to take all of me, Anna," he said tightly. "Every inch. But you have to be still right now. I don't want to hurt you."

He pressed my hips down with one hand, making it clear we would be doing this his way. I wriggled beneath his firm hold. In that moment I would have welcomed the pain if it cured this fever raging through me.

"Fuck me," I demanded. I tried to twist out of his hold, change positions so that I was on top and could get what I needed faster, but his knees parted my thighs, and his cock once again forged through my folds. I tried to open myself as much as I could for his incredible girth, turning my knees out and latching my ankles behind his thighs.

"That's right," he said. "Pull me into that hot, sweet little cunt."

Bearing his weight on his arms, he pushed into me. One inch at a time. Stretching me, filling me, until the pain blended with pleasure and I was nearly blind with lust. His face buried in my hair; the feel of his cheek against mine added a tenderness I didn't expect.

"So tight," he murmured. "God, your body, Anna. It's perfect."

He drew back slowly, fighting for control—I could see the tension spanning his body in every taut muscle. Beads of sweat dripped down his jaw. He pinched his eyes closed in concentration.

More. I needed more. I needed all of him. *Now.*

My nails scratched down his back and he arched, teeth bared. When his eyes shot open, I could see only the pupils.

He drove into me hard, burying himself to the hilt, holding me with his gaze and steely cock. I could feel him all the way to my womb, all the way to my soul as he tore down the barriers I'd carefully guarded for so long. He pushed past my defenses and stripped me bare, and as he found a hard, consistent rhythm, I held tightly to him, afraid of losing myself so quickly.

"Like that," he coaxed. "Squeeze my cock like that."

His words made me so hot.

The pressure was rising again, and as he shifted his weight and his pelvis began rubbing against my clit, I could feel myself beginning to unravel. I thrashed beneath him, straining when his grip slid beneath my shoulders so that he could lock me in place.

He pushed deeper, then traded his measured pace for faster strokes, angling upward. My inner walls clamped down, needing more. Taking more. I became blind to everything but how good he felt.

The sensations were new to me. I could come by my own

hand or another's, but I'd never been able to orgasm during sex. Some past lovers didn't care; others found this a challenge and, to spare their feelings, I occasionally faked it.

I was not faking now. This was real, and more intense than anything I'd ever imagined. The heat spiraled away from a center deep inside of me, a place he rubbed with each thrust. My hips rocked up to meet him, taking everything he gave.

"Feel how deep I am," he said. "I've never been so hard."

Our bodies slid against each other, damp with sweat.

"Alec, *Alec.*"

"Let go, baby," he said. "Come. Now."

I did as he commanded, and when the orgasm tore through me, I screamed. Blinded by white stars, I clawed the wooden floor, shocked as the sensations went on and on.

Swearing sharply, he rose to his knees, grabbed me beneath the thighs and lifted my hips, driving into me in a series of fast, deep strokes.

"Fuck, fuck, fuck," he chanted.

The next orgasm chased the last, just as intense, just as powerful. I couldn't breathe. I couldn't think. And as my muscles contracted, he slammed into me one more time and held. A tight expression crossed his beautiful face. The look sent a new wave of tremors through my body.

"Ah, God, Anna." He collapsed over me, drawing me tightly to his chest as he rolled onto his side.

I don't know how long we lay there; long after our breathing slowed and our hearts stopped hammering. I stayed where he held me, sprawled over his chest with my head resting on his shoulder. He fanned my hair over my back, twisting the ends with his fingertips while his other hand teased down my waist. He was still inside of me, hot and semihard, and as I slid my knee up his side, he gave a soft groan.

"Um . . . wow?" I grinned, unsure what else to say.

"Yes," he said. "Agreed."

I lifted up on my elbows to face him, and for the first time he slid out of me. The ache returned immediately, a soft but anxious throb reminding me how perfectly we'd fit together. He tucked my hair behind my ears.

"Goddamn," he murmured. "You really are beautiful."

Shyness crept over me. It seemed impossible that he could make me feel so many different things in one day.

His hand lowered, thumb skimming the side of my breast. I gave a little gasp. My nipples hardened instantly.

"Are you okay?" he asked, tracing my spine now, and lowering around the curve of my thighs. Whispers of heat remained in the wake of his touch. Already I was becoming aroused again.

"Are you kidding?" I kissed him gently, reveling in the soft feel of his lips. "I'm better than okay."

"I was a little rougher than I meant to be," he admitted. "You were making me crazy in the car."

"You've been making me crazy since I met you," I said. "And how did you mean to be?" I wondered how he'd envisioned our first time together. Whatever *I'd* imagined, reality had left far in the dust.

A slow smile warmed his face. "I'd tell you but then, you know, I'd have to kill you."

"You almost did," I said. "I came three times."

"Just three times?" he asked, a devilish glint in his eyes. "I think we can do better than that."

He rolled over me in a move that made me squeak in surprise. Slowly, he drew my arms over my head and held them in place with one hand while he removed the used condom with the other.

"That's better than anyone else has ever done," I said, feeling that wave of shyness again. "I can't usually get off during sex." I immediately regretted mentioning it when his mouth flattened and a line creased his forehead.

"You can't?"

I shook my head. "That was the first time."

He studied me, as if trying to see if I was telling the truth.

"Things are different with us," he said after a moment.

I nodded, unable to help feeling that he meant in more ways than just the physical.

He kissed my lips, worshipping my mouth with a slow, gentle caress. As his mouth trailed down my throat, my pulse scrambled.

"Do you have a bed?" he asked gruffly.

I giggled. "Of course, I have a bed. You didn't see it?" I lived in a studio apartment, you couldn't *not* see it.

"I was preoccupied." He flexed his hips, and his bare cock, once again erect, pressed against my tender flesh. My breath caught.

"That's right," I said. "I remember now."

He didn't enter me again. Instead he pulled upright, dragging me with him. He stood, tossing me over his shoulder like I weighed no more than a sack of laundry.

"We can do better than three," he said.

Fourteen

I woke just before eight o'clock, roused by a creaking near the front door. The space beside me in bed where Alec had finally collapsed after having his way with me twice more was cool, the pillow still indented in the shape of his head. We'd only slept a couple hours, but I felt invigorated, pleasantly sore, and happy. Too happy.

I opened my eyes, my high plummeting with a sudden sinking dread that I'd made it all up. Every touch, every whisper.

Every mind-blowing orgasm.

Too happy was always a red flag for me. If you climbed too high, you crashed too hard.

I spotted Alec across the room, watching as he carefully positioned the small wire table where I usually left my keys and purse—I vaguely remembered the sound of it tipping over when he'd taken me to the floor last night. He was facing away, wearing only his jeans, and his shoulders, bronze and sculpted, flexed with each movement. His waist narrowed into pants that gave only hints of his perfect ass, which was unfortunate. I would have preferred he stayed as naked as I was.

My stupid grin chased away my wariness. He had a body that could have made the cover of a men's magazine.

As I watched him, a warmth spread from the center of my chest all the way out to my fingertips and toes. Something had happened between us last night, something deep. I didn't know what to think about that, or how it would be between us now in the aftermath.

Because I wasn't ready to deal with any potential awkwardness, I held still, tracking him with my eyes. He picked up a few pieces of our clothing off the floor and placed them over the back of the love seat. His shirt was in the mix, and he pulled it over his head, giving me another impressive view of his back. Then he turned toward the bed, as if he knew I was watching.

My eyelids snapped shut. I tried to look relaxed, which was nearly impossible since I was only halfway covered by the comforter. My naked breasts grew tight and heavy under his gaze. It took everything I had not to close my legs or cover my body with the sheet. Now that the light outside was streaming through the windows, I was painfully aware of my every exposed flaw.

He didn't move for a long while. My skin was heating, and that insatiable need I felt whenever I was close to him was growing once again between my thighs.

When I couldn't stand it any more, I opened my eyes.

Get over here, I nearly said, the smile on my face stretching my sore lips.

But he was facing the other way. And, as I stared silently after him, he grabbed his keys and closed the door softly behind him.

I rose to my elbows, half expecting him to walk back in— laughing, because of course he knew I was awake—and then come back to bed to fuck me mindless.

I waited ten seconds. Twenty. Thirty.

I sat up and pulled the comforter over my shoulders. It felt better to be covered up, even if I was alone.

One minute.

Two.

Five.

He wasn't coming back.

He hadn't even said good-bye.

I rose from the bed. We'd talked about spending the day to-gether, but apparently that was off. Maybe he'd never meant it in the first place.

Whatever hope remained drove me to briefly look for a note— *Thanks for last night*, or *Get back in bed*, or *I'll call you later*— but nothing. Still, I hadn't given him credit before, and he'd found me at that restaurant with Randall. Maybe he was just running home to change clothes or check in at work. I didn't know why I was so quick to doubt him, but it was hard not to when he just disappeared like that.

I locked the door and picked up some of my clothes. My phone was sitting on the table Alec had picked up off the floor. At first it looked like no one had called, but when I opened my inbox, I saw that Amy had left four texts in response to my mes-sage that Alec was busy with another woman, and I was going out with Randall. I knew I hadn't turned off the new message alert, and my stomach sank when I considered that Alec may have seen her responses before me.

WTF is wrong with that guy?

Forget him. You deserve better. Have fun with Dr. Randall.

Do more than have fun. Fuck his brains out. Tie him up to the bed-frame and spank him until he sings 90s boy band music.

Call me when you kick Dr. R out of bed.

I didn't think Alec would have searched through my phone, but he had picked it up and set it here. I rubbed my eyes with the heels of my hands, anxiety tying my stomach in knots. Part of me wanted to call him, but what if he hadn't seen the texts? Then I'd come off as desperate.

Part of me thought it served him right to see them. Especially if he was already on his way out the door.

But what if he hadn't been leaving until he'd seen those?

Dammit Amy.

Drama. Too much drama. I laughed out loud, aware that I had momentarily lapsed into my tortured teenage years. I needed to clear my head and eat some breakfast. Everything else could wait until later.

I went to the bathroom, pulled on a robe, and cringed at my face in the mirror. My eye makeup was smeared, my hair a sexified mess. I looked like a raccoon that had stuck his claw in an electrical socket.

"Yikes," I said. "No wonder he took off."

I turned on the shower and stood in the steam for a few minutes, letting it relax my muscles. I ran my fingertips down my throat, remembering the feel of Alec's mouth devouring me. He'd been so attentive after that first time, watching my reaction to his every touch. He'd practically taken notes. With a careful, gentle exploration, he'd found ways to excite me that even I hadn't known about.

Thinking about it now turned me on all over again.

And made it even worse that he was gone.

I stepped into the shower, one of my favorite features of this old apartment. Spanish tile lined the enclosure from floor to ceiling, roomy enough for the bathtub the previous owners had removed. The water ran in rivulets down my body, rinsing my troubles down the drain. I opened the shampoo and breathed in the strong, relaxing sandalwood scent. As I rubbed it into my scalp, I thought of Alec's fingers, buried in my hair. I'd just rinsed it clean when a creak from the front door made me freeze.

I'd locked the front door, I was sure of it. But someone was undoubtedly in my apartment; I could hear their footsteps rolling across the floor. My brain switched into high gear. Naked and vulnerable, I eased open the glass door and snuck onto the floor. Anything could be used as a weapon if necessary, that was what my dad had taught me. I reached for the first heavy thing I could get my hands on—a blow-dryer—and backed against the wall.

I held it like a gun, the cord dragging on the floor below. Great. I could see the headlines now: Naked Woman Attempts to Shoot Intruder with Blow-Dryer, Killed by Real Gun.

The footsteps outside paused, and then came closer. By the time they were just beyond the door, I was shaking. Water dripped from my hair, my chin, my breasts, making a puddle on the floor. I gripped the blow-dryer even harder and exhaled.

The door opened, and with a screech, I swung upward hard, taking the trespasser by surprise. I connected with the side of his face, and then charged; the only way out was straight through him. He stumbled backward, taking me with him. I was already halfway to my feet when his voice stopped me.

"Jesus Christ, Anna!" Alec was sprawled out on the floor, rubbing his jaw with a stormy look on his face.

He was completely naked.

"Alec!" The blow-dryer clattered to the floor.

I kneeled down beside him, cradling his cheek in my hand. My chosen weapon had left a red mark all the way up to his ear.

"Oh my God, I'm so sorry! I didn't think it was you!"

"Were you expecting someone else?" He opened his mouth wide, wiggled his jaw from side to side.

"I thought you were a robber. How did you get back in? I locked the door." I touched his cheek gently. I probably should have gotten him some ice, but I didn't want to leave his side.

"I had your keys."

I sat back on my heels, glancing up at the door. "My keys?" I'd seen him grab keys before he'd left; I'd just assumed they'd been his.

"Yeah." His gaze lowered down to my breasts, and I became aware of his growing cock, stretching to capacity. "I went to get your car. I got breakfast, too."

"You did?" I was melting. How could I have doubted him? He'd obviously felt that incredible connection between us, too.

"I heard the shower and thought I'd join you." He sat all the way up and blinked as I ran my hands through the silky strands of his hair. "But now that I have a concussion, I'm not sure a slippery surface is the safest place."

"What a baby," I chided. I kissed just below his ear and his shoulders tensed. "You're right. It's probably safest if you lie down."

I eased him back on the floor and straddled him, reveling in the feel of his stiff cock between my legs.

A wicked grin tilted his mouth. "Who am I to argue with a health professional?"

He groaned as I grasped the base of his shaft with one hand, and made a slow circle around the head with my fingertips. A drop of moisture appeared at the tip, and as I gave him a firm squeeze, his abs went rigid.

"Does this mean you're happy to see me?" he asked.

"I thought you weren't coming back," I said, beginning to stroke him. The sounds of the shower in the background faded as I became consumed by the task.

"Why did you think that?"

I hesitated just for a second before continuing. I kept my gaze on my grip, focusing on the engorged flesh and thick vein between my fingers, waiting for the old feelings he'd triggered to dissipate. My baggage wasn't welcome here.

His hand stopped me, and I glanced up at him through my lashes.

"I'm not leaving," he said.

I exhaled, biting my lip so he didn't see how much his words meant to me. I wasn't ready to go there yet.

But maybe someday.

He gave me a gentle tap on the bottom. "And tell your friend the only one getting tied up and spanked is you."

I giggled.

I took his wrists in my hands and pinned them above his

head. He easily could have broken my grasp, but didn't. I think he wanted to see what a girl in charge could do.

"You're not going anywhere now," I told him.

I rose on my knees and seated myself on the tip of his cock, then slowly began to lower, pausing to let my body open for him. He felt harder than before, smoother, and I was slick and ready just from the feel of him against me. My body couldn't get enough.

I gripped his shoulders, watching him watch the place where we connected with a rapidly growing desire. Just the tip nestled inside me, and already I was craving that deep, hard friction. I could feel the need taking over, transforming me into a creature that thirsted for pleasure—a woman I hadn't known until Alec had touched me.

"Wait," he said, just as I'd begun to sink lower. There was a dark, strained look in his eyes. "No condom."

"Do you want one?" I asked. He'd used them last night, but we'd already discussed that both of us were clean.

"I want to feel you," he said. My hands still gripped his wrists, and I reached farther, weaving my fingers through his. When he squeezed, I felt my heart beat harder against my ribs. The move was almost too intimate.

I pushed my hips back slowly, my tender tissue stretching over his hard girth. My eyelids were heavy, and I tried to hold back the groan, but it seeped out between my teeth.

I lowered slowly, until he was completely inside me, deeper than before in this position. I bit my lip, fighting the urge to rise again so soon. I wanted to keep him here, just for a moment, locked inside my body. I didn't understand why. I didn't want to know why. But it felt right and good, and as I rotated my hips, I shuddered, the small spasm in my core just a whisper of what was to come.

His breathing was rough, his grip on my hands almost painful.

"Tell me what it feels like," I whispered.

"Warm," he rasped. "Christ, you're so warm and tight. I can feel every move you make. Every breath."

I moved my hips in a small circle, biting my lip as his pelvis brushed my clit.

"It's too good," I whispered. "It makes me think something's wrong. Nothing's this good." I tried to laugh, but all I could manage was a small gasp.

"Look at me." He released one of my hands so that he could touch my face. His thumb grazed down my cheek. I opened my eyes, instantly lost in his gaze.

"Nothing's wrong," he said. "Let it feel good. Let go."

I didn't know what I was letting go of, but as he said it, that hungry creature inside of me took over. I pushed upright, pulling his hard length against the front walls of my vagina. For a moment I had to remind myself to breathe; the fullness of his cock inside me, the desire in his eyes, and the rigid muscles beneath his smooth, glistening skin were almost too much. My hands dragged down his chest, over his rounded pecs to his hard stomach.

For right now, he belonged to me.

With his hands gripping my hips, I rose slowly, and then settled back down. It was easier to ride him now that he was wet with my desire. His thighs flexed beneath my buttocks. His shaft was rubbing that spot—the one that sent bolts of lightning through every nerve ending every time it was touched. I lifted again, lowered, this time letting my weight carry me down. I adjusted my position, went faster, experimenting with a tempo until I found the right pace.

"That's right," he said. "Let it take you."

My eyes closed again, and my hair, still wet, dripped cold beads down my back and over my breasts. My nipples had grown so tight they'd begun to ache, and as I rose again, I touched myself gently, then pinched the sensitive peaks, something I'd only ever done when I was alone. It made everything hotter knowing he was watching me, feeling how turned on he was in his tightening grip on my waist.

"So good," I murmured. "Too good."

Faster I moved. Faster. Up and down. Again. Again. I slammed myself down on him, my body taking his engorged cock all the way to the base. The muscles in my legs began to quiver. I moaned in beat to my own rhythm. My head tilted back. *I am a porn star,* I thought somewhere in the back of my mind. I'd never felt sexier in my life.

The pressure building in my pelvis shattered apart all at once. Every muscle tightened. I cried out, straining against myself, fighting for more, even as the contact became too much.

"Help me," I cried, falling forward. I needed more. I needed . . . I didn't know what I needed.

He held my hips in place with one hand, fucking me fast, while the other crossed in front to flick over my clit. His thumb rubbed a quick hard circle, making me come again. My sensitive nipples brushed his chest as he thrust into me. I lost control, flexing and writhing, wet with water, wet with sweat and my own slick juices.

Right in the middle, he pulled out.

"No," I gasped, empty when I'd been so deliciously full. My sex contracted as I felt his warm fluid spurt on my back. I arched, aware of his cock between the globes of my ass.

Before I could process what had happened, he'd pulled me forward so that I was straddling his face. Where I'd been empty just a second before, I was filled again with his tongue, spearing into me, and then his fingers as his mouth found my clit. I shouldn't have looked down at him; the pleasure in his face drove me even higher.

I could barely hold my own weight, but his strong arm around my hips propped me up and forced me to take every sweet lashing of his tongue. One gentle suck and I was lost again. My arms were shaking, barely supporting my body as his fingers curved and stroked. The glorious heat pummeled me, taking my body by storm. It was too much.

I collapsed on my side, breathing hard, unable to even open my eyes. My heartbeat pounded in my eardrums as the tremors raced through me, aftershocks of what had just happened.

Without a word, he picked me up, cradling me against his chest, and carried me to the bathroom. Once under the shower's warm water, he set me down, waiting to make sure I could still stand before reaching for the washcloth. Leaning against the wall, I pressed my cheek to the cool tile as he lathered me with soap and gently washed me clean.

I wanted to do the same for him—touch him in the same adoring way—but before I could, the hot water ran out.

Fifteen

"Cold!" I screeched. "Cold, cold, cold, cold . . ." I chanted this until I was successfully able to push past him and crank the handle. The water shut off with a sputter, leaving me covered with goose bumps and dripping from head to toe.

"That," he said, "was definitely the fastest I've ever seen you move. And that's pretty fast, considering you thought someone was breaking in earlier today."

He crossed his arms over his chest, rivulets of water streaming down his bronzed skin. His wet, slick hair was nearly black and had more curls than when it was dry, tempting me to wind it around my fingers and pull his face down to mine—something I would have done had I not been mesmerized by his growing erection.

"I guess the cold doesn't bother you much," I said.

His grin widened. He wasn't the least bit modest.

"Not when I'm naked with a beautiful woman." He stepped forward, and the warmth rekindled low in my belly as he pulled my body against his. "I've thought about seeing you this way since you showed up at the coffee shop with your wet hair." His lips brushed just the corner of my mouth, enough to make my pulse scramble. He moved my hair over my shoulders, and I jumped when he nipped the sensitive skin behind my ear with his teeth. "You smell incredible."

"It's the sandalwood," I murmured, gasping as his fingertips trailed down my breasts. Slowly he began to circle one hardened peak.

"It's you," he murmured. "Everything about you calls to me."

His breath teased my lips as I flattened my hands over his hard chest. His cock twitched against my waist.

"You're trying to kill me, aren't you?" I asked.

He took a step back, brows drawing together. A strange, worried look passed over his face. The separation made me self-conscious, and I covered my chest with my hands.

"Food," he said, his features softening. He reached for my hand, leading me out on the bathroom floor where he wrapped a towel around my shoulders. "You need your strength."

"So you can ravage me again?" As he turned away to dry off, I stared at the winged tips of his shoulders and the lean lines of his waist. Artists made paintings of backs like his.

"If I recall, I was the one being ravaged," he said.

I snorted. "I'd apologize, but I'm not sorry."

"Good."

I put on a short silk robe that was hanging over the door and took a couple minutes to fix myself up. The reflection in the mirror showed a different woman than the raccoon-eyed girl who'd first stepped into the shower. My cheeks were pink and flushed, my lips a little swollen. I didn't bother drying my hair because I knew leaving it wet would drive him crazy.

When I emerged, I found him in the kitchen wearing only his jeans. There was something unbearably sexy in the way they rode low on his hips and left his bare feet peeking out beneath the frayed hems. While he heated something up in the microwave, I sat on a stool at the island, admiring his chest.

He paused, one hand on the microwave door, to narrow his eyes at me.

"If you have to wear clothes, you can wear that," he said.

"Oh, can I?" I twirled the tips of my hair around my fingertip, pleased when I heard the growl rumble in his chest.

"Careful," he said. "You know what happens when you tease me."

My stomach clenched just at the thought of what he could do to me. But there was more to this than mind-blowing sex. I couldn't remember the last time I'd allowed a man to stay this long. Some hadn't wanted to; some I'd just kicked out. Certainly no one had ever brought me breakfast and thought to return my car to the garage. He felt more familiar than anyone I'd ever known—he'd drawn out parts of me I hadn't shared with anyone—and yet he still seemed so much a mystery.

The microwave beeped.

"I hope you like Cuban breakfast sandwiches," he said. He'd already found the plates.

"I've never had one." The scent of eggs, cheese, and pork filled the kitchen. My mouth began to water.

"They're better fresh," he admitted, placing the plate in front of me. "My mom used to make these for my dad."

It occurred to me that this was possibly the first spontaneous thing he'd offered about his past. I wondered if his mother was Cuban—that would explain his naturally bronze skin and dark features—but I didn't want to ask a question I wasn't prepared to answer myself. I didn't know where my ancestors were from. My dad suspected I was a mutt—he always used kinder words, but they meant the same thing.

"Lucky him," I said, noting the way he'd said *my dad*, but not *me*.

Alec snorted. "Right. Lucky him."

Or maybe not so lucky.

"Is she still alive?" I remembered he'd told me he had spent time with Maxim Stein growing up. Maybe the Steins had stepped in when she'd passed.

"Yep."

"Oh," I said. "Does she live very far away?" He appeared to know the area pretty well. It seemed likely that he'd grown up here, or at least lived here for some time.

"Not far enough," he said, elusive once again. I didn't press; his mouth had pulled into a tight frown.

I took a bite, closing my eyes to savor the delicious tastes. "Where'd you get this?"

"There's a great Cuban bakery down the street." He tilted his head at my surprised expression. "You need to get out and explore more."

"You want to play tour guide?" Amy had done some of that, but most of our time had been spent engaging in Paisley-appropriate activities: the aquarium, the water park, Disney World.

"Think you can keep your hands off of me that long?"

"I think I can manage." Maybe.

"I'm not sure I can."

I grinned as his focus turned from his sandwich to my robe, which had slipped off my shoulder.

"If we don't leave now, we're not going to," I said.

His forehead crinkled, as if he was really contemplating this decision. Then, before we could get into trouble, he put his plate in the sink and went to find his shirt.

Half an hour later we were in his Jeep cruising down the side roads toward the bay. I'd chosen sandals and a lime green summer dress, loose enough to be casual but short enough to show off my legs. Despite Alec's protests, I was wearing panties, but once he saw the lacy boy shorts and matching bra, he didn't argue too much.

We took the bridge across the Bay and, when we reached the town of Clearwater, veered south down the coast. There were fewer tourists than there had been during winter break, but still a steady flow of people entered the little beach-front shops and restaurants. He pointed out a few good places to eat, and I thought we might stop and get out, but he continued on.

"Where are you taking me?" I asked suspiciously.

"You'll see."

Leaving the fancy hotels and beach rentals behind, we passed through a residential area, where the gated mansions began to rival Maxim Stein's. Though neither of us talked, there was a quiet comfort between us. The air was still charged with electricity, especially as his fingertips absently began to circle my knee, but it felt less urgent than before.

The mansions gave way to golf courses, and finally to the sandy shores of the Gulf of Mexico. When he stopped at a single-pump gas station for drinks, I remembered to check my phone. Amy had called, and with a wince I quickly called her back.

"What the . . ."

"Sorry, I'm here. I'm alive," I said before she could finish.

"Home visits?" A pot banged in the background and she swore. "I thought you were taking the day off."

"I am," I said. "With Alec."

Pause.

"Alec the ass?"

"Turns out Randall's the ass. And Alec is a sex god."

Pause.

"Go on . . ."

I giggled. "I can't right now. We're out exploring. I'll call you later."

Alec pushed through the door of the gas station, smiling that smile that melted me like butter.

"You can't just . . ."

"I've got to go."

"I hate you."

"I know," I said with a grin. "But I love you."

"Fine," she said grumpily. "Love you, bye."

I shoved the phone back in my purse on the floor as Alec set a paper bag of snacks on the backseat.

"Love?" he asked, one eyebrow quirked. "Should I be worried?"

The butterflies in me recognized the hint of jealousy in his tone and fluttered their wings.

"You should be terrified," I said. "Amy's very protective of me."

He turned the key in the ignition. "I guess that's something she and I have in common."

He said it so matter-of-factly I couldn't help but kiss him. I held his face in my hands, closed my eyes, and breathed him in. He smelled wildly masculine, a scent all his own, and the soft pressure of his lips pulled at my heart just as it stirred something deep in my stomach.

I was falling too fast for him.

"You scare me a little," I admitted.

His hands threaded through my hair, pulling me back for another soft kiss.

"Yeah," he said, kissing the tip of my nose. "I know the feeling."

A little over an hour after we'd left Tampa, we entered Fort De Soto Park. Alec paid the park ranger, and took a right at the historic military fortress, named, he told me, for the explorer Hernando De Soto. We passed long beaches, lined with white sand and sheltered by tangled trees and tall yellow grass, finally parking at the far end of a nearly empty lot.

"This seems private," I noticed.

A salty breeze blew through the car as he opened the door.

"It's quieter than the private beaches," he said. He brought my hand to his lips and bit my knuckles lightly. "I wanted to be alone with you."

My heart stuttered. I was glad when he stepped outside to stretch his legs so I could catch my breath.

"Should I have brought my bathing suit?" I asked when I met him around the back of the car. The air was cool enough that I was glad I'd packed a light sweater. I wasn't sure I could manage a swim.

He shook his head. "I was thinking we could walk."

A walk on the beach? Was this guy for real?

He threw a blanket from the trunk over his shoulder and led me over a short, rickety bridge that crossed the marsh. On the opposite side, the trees opened to a sandy shore and the pristine, blue-green waters of the Gulf. A few people were already there— a different group from those that flocked to the touristy beaches. We passed an older couple in beach chairs, each with a worn paperback. A man teaching his son to fish. A young woman with a purple streak in her hair, who was touching up a painting on an easel.

I kicked off my sandals and carried them in my hand, walking beside him through the surf. The water was cold enough to feel refreshing, and the sand crunched beneath every step. Overhead the sky was clear and blue, but pewter rain clouds gathered over the horizon.

"This is incredible," I said, giving wide berth to a blue heron that watched us from the grass, ten feet away. "I've only been to the beach once since I moved here. Amy and I took her daughter on Christmas."

It had been a hard day; Paisley hadn't said a word to Amy until a man dressed like Santa had waved from his sailboat, just off the shore. That was less than two months ago, and she hadn't said much more since then.

"Did you move here because of Amy?"

I rubbed my arms. The sun was warm, but the breeze was chilly. "Partly. Amy's had it rough since her divorce. It's not easy being a single parent."

"No," he said. "It's not."

I missed a step, caught up.

"So, you . . ."

He laughed. "I was raised by one. There aren't any little Alec Flynns running around."

I wondered if he'd been raised by his father. Earlier he'd said his mother didn't live far enough away. I was just about to ask when he looked over his shoulder at me.

"And the other part? You said Amy was part of why you moved. What else brought you here?"

I twisted my hair into a knot and crossed my arms. "I like to go new places. Try new things."

"But you moved to Florida and have only been to the beach once."

"So?"

"So if you were looking for a new place to experience new things, I'd think you'd make a point of experiencing them. You have a job, an apartment, friends close by. That's what people do when they're trying to set down roots, not just passing through."

My feet had stopped, and I wiggled my heels before I sank in the sand. "Sounds like you've got me all figured out."

"Not *all* figured out." He grinned. "I've got some things figured out."

I put my hands on my hips. "Like what?"

He threw the blanket away from the surf and moved closer to me, gaze sharp and penetrating. "Like being asked personal questions gets under your skin." He moved my hands to his chest, and held my wrists so I couldn't pull away.

I scoffed. "You're one to talk."

"I know you like to keep people at a distance, and I'm guessing there's a reason." I looked down, unable to help it. "I know you like it when my tongue touches you here." He licked the place where my neck met my shoulder. "And here." His thumb trailed down my breast. "And here." His hand slid briefly between my legs.

"Alec," I gasped, then searched the surrounding area for any witnesses. We were alone. For now.

His lips made a slow path across my collarbone. I shivered as his fingertips brushed the strap of my dress off my shoulder.

"I know you close your eyes when you know I'm watching you," he whispered. "And I know you don't trust me."

I stared into his eyes, dark as the ocean and filled with secrets. "Should I?"

"That's up to you."

An alarm rang in my head. *Too close*, it said. I didn't want to sit by, unable to stop him as he slowly stripped down my defenses. I needed to regain my footing, take the upper hand.

"Do you trust me?" I asked.

"I wouldn't be here if I didn't."

My hands lowered down his chest, under his shirt and then back up. My nails raked over his smooth skin—not hard enough to scratch, but enough to remind both of us that I could play this game too.

"What do you want from me?" I asked.

His muscles flexed beneath my touch, and he jerked my hips to his. A small sound of pleasure came from my throat. It was impossible to deny the effect he had on me. Already my temperature was rising, the heat centering at that sensitive point between my legs.

"I want you, Anna." He took my earlobe between his teeth and gave it a light nip. "I want all of you."

All of me. I wasn't sure I could give all of me. But I could give him my body, gladly and willingly, until he grew tired of it. I hoped I could walk away before he did.

His hands lowered around my rear and ground me against him. Fingers roamed, a series of brief, teasing touches. Our kisses became more needy. Our breaths became more ragged. The cold water splashed over our bare feet, and the gentle crash of the waves became our beat. After a while, we were practically having sex with our clothes on.

The ache in my body was starting to take control of my reason. I pulled back suddenly. His hands fell to his sides, then clasped behind his neck. In that position his biceps stretched the thin material of his T-shirt. After a moment he looked up at me, the struggle clear on his face.

"Maybe you shouldn't trust me after all," he said with a strained laugh.

The sand met an outcropping of trees just twenty feet from where we stood. It was sheltered enough to be hidden from those who might walk by, unless they thought to look.

I held out my hand, and he took it. Then I led him up the beach and into the trees.

That night he took me to a nice restaurant downtown that overlooked the water. We drank as we watched the cruise ships come in. And when it came time to order, I asked the waitress for the crème brûlée. She tried to hide her bewilderment and then focused all her energy on Alec. I wondered if she had any idea she was biting her lip while he was speaking to her.

"You don't want dinner?" Alec asked when she had walked away.

"Maybe later," I said. "Life's short. I'm in a fancy restaurant with a gorgeous man, watching the sun set. Dessert seems like the right choice."

"Gorgeous, huh?" he said, a glint of amusement in his eyes.

I hummed. "Our waitress seems to think so."

He reached under the table and pinched the ticklish spot at the top of my knee. I squealed and twisted to get away. The black dress I'd changed into when we'd gone back to my place to shower rode up high on my thighs, and I smoothed it down.

"I like you jealous," he said.

"I'm not jealous."

He smirked and took my hand over the table. Slowly he began kneading the sore muscles at the base of my thumb.

"You have no idea, do you?" he said, keeping his eyes on my

hand. I slipped lower in my chair; it felt incredible. "Every man in here is looking at you, all of them wondering what's under that little black dress. Any of those guys at the bar would leave their dates if they thought they had a chance at taking you home."

I turned slowly to look and, sure enough, caught a couple of them glancing away.

"People want what they can't have," I said.

He rotated my wrist, pressed on the heel of my hand, and I swear my eyes rolled back in my head.

"Why'd you become a masseuse?" he asked.

I focused on our hands, joined over the white tablecloth. "I needed a change. I wanted to do something that made people happy."

"That's why you changed careers. Left child-welfare services."

My eyes shot open.

"Background check," he said with a small wince. "Before Ms. Rowe called to schedule with you, she had me run your name through the system. I probably should have mentioned that earlier."

"Probably. What else did you read about me?" I told myself to relax, but my back was rigid, and I sat up straight in my chair.

He watched me, but continued to rub my hand as if nothing had changed. "Not much besides your employment history. No arrests. A couple speeding tickets." He paused. "Nothing before you're eighteen. Nothing about your family."

The air whooshed from my lungs. My father had had my records sealed when I was child. The adoption, my birth mother, it was all locked away.

"Circus performers," I told him. "I grew up scaling high wires and doing backflips off the trapeze."

He chuckled. "Who'd have thought we'd have so much in common?"

I eased back in my chair, feeling like I'd dodged a bullet but surprised that I wished I hadn't. Part of me did want to let him in. At least a little.

"You're very brave to start over," he said, making me feel as if he knew more than he was letting on.

Brave? It wasn't bravery that pushed me to move on every few months, or that made it so difficult to let people in.

His fingers stroked mine, a whisper of a touch that roused memories of what had happened hours before on the beach.

"It wasn't easy," I said.

"It makes you happy, seeing others happy," he stated.

"Yes."

The memories were becoming clearer. His hands over my hands. The sand sifting between my toes. The rasp of the lace as he'd hurriedly pulled my underwear down my legs. I'd faced the water, staring at the waves while he'd dipped down and entered me from behind.

I could still feel his lips on my neck, and his chest, heavy on my back even through our clothes.

Look at me, he'd said. *I need to see you.* He'd turned me, lifted me, and with my back against the tree, finished us both.

"Does anyone ever get out of line?"

I swallowed, sat up straight. "What's that?"

His mouth twitched, and I could feel the blush rise in my cheeks. Sometimes it honestly felt like he could read my mind.

"I asked if you had any clients who got out of line. I would think it would be difficult for men to keep their hands off you, especially once you're in their house."

He kissed my knuckles tenderly before beginning his glorious assault on my other hand.

"I screen everyone before I meet them in their home. At least, most people—not your boss. But I did a thorough Google search beforehand," I said, remembering the information I'd gathered after Ms. Rowe had made the appointment. "The salon has very rigid rules about sexual harassment. Occasionally someone will cross the line." I cringed as I thought of Melvin Herman and his flagpole beneath the sheets at Rave.

"Anyone I should talk to?"

He kept right on massaging, but his words held a clear promise. My heart beat harder. He *was* protective.

"It's already taken care of," I assured him. "The guy was just lonely. Anyway, he's not allowed back on the premises."

Alec seemed unconvinced.

"Do you carry when you go into someone's house?"

And suddenly he'd turned into my father.

"I carry a massage table," I told him. "And an iPod. And my oils of course."

"Hilarious," he said.

I grinned. "I carry pepper spray. And I'm well trained in self-defense. My dad put me in classes when I was a kid—I took them all the way through high school. In fact, he's the reason I've been doing more home visits these days. Once I save enough, I'll be flying back to Cincinnati to visit him."

"You're close with your dad."

"Yes," I said. "I miss him. My mom died a few years ago, so he's all alone now. I wish I could spend more time with him." I could feel myself frowning. "You're close to Mr. Stein?"

He nodded, serious now. "He's like a father to me."

I couldn't help but think that Alec's real father must have been pretty bad if a man who was cheating his way through wives was his role model.

The waitress returned with the food, asking Alec three times if there was anything else he needed before catching my "get lost" glare.

As expected, the crème brûlée was amazing, and I savored every sweet, succulent bite. I was so happy, I even let him steal the vanilla ice cream that came on the side. The sun had finally disappeared over the water, and the purple sky was growing darker. It had been a perfect day—not counting the earlier hair-dryer incident—and as the minutes wore on, I could feel a sort of regret creeping over me. Days like this were few and far between, and already it was slipping away.

"What is it?" he asked.

I studied him for a moment, wanting to remember him forever just like this. Breathtaking, dangerous, and ultimately heartbreaking. He did something to me I didn't understand. As if I'd been sleepwalking through life, and when I'd found him, some switch had flipped and every sensation had suddenly become a hundred times sharper.

"What happens when this burns out?" I asked.

He tapped his spoon on the white linen tablecloth, his gaze never wavering from mine. "What happens if it doesn't?"

Sixteen

thought about those words a lot over the next week. Whatever was happening between us didn't seem to be cooling off. To the contrary, it just seemed to get hotter. I returned to work the day after our beach trip, and he returned to my bed that night, and the nights after.

I hadn't considered our relationship not ending. Everything ended. And as much as I wanted to live in the moment, I found myself waiting for the other shoe to drop. I still hit a brick wall every time I asked about his life. I'd even asked if we could spend the night at his place, and he'd brushed it off by telling me my apartment was more comfortable.

Sometimes I wondered if he was hiding something.

Worries like these were needling the back of my mind as I laid my hands on Maxim Stein's oiled back and dug my thumbs into his rhomboids.

"There," said Maxim when my fingers slid over a knot in his right shoulder. "Harder."

His words conjured memories of him and Charlotte, and I quickly shook the images from my mind.

I bent forward over him, using my elbow to dig in to the muscle. "How's that?"

He groaned.

Because of the rain, we were in his workout room, the cinnamon scent intensified in the closed space. The lights had been dimmed, and harp music played from the iPod station.

I imagined making love to Alec in this room. The air would smell like sandalwood, and our oiled bodies would slide over each other.

"You are quite talented at what you do," said Maxim as I moved to the other shoulder.

"Thank you." I lowered my voice to maintain the ambience, but Maxim didn't seem to catch on.

"Are you and Alec enjoying each other?"

I stopped, then continued tentatively. "Enjoying each other?"

I remembered that Alec had said Maxim was like a father to him, and wondered what he had said about me.

"Having a good time," Maxim clarified.

"Yes," I said. "I like spending time with him." Something stopped me from saying more. I wanted to like Maxim for Alec, but he didn't exactly have an easy personality to warm up to.

"Good," he said. "He needs a pretty distraction."

My claws began to emerge. Was that all I was? A distraction?

"I'm sure Alec could take his pick of *distractions*."

"Yes, but he chose you."

"I'm honored."

Maxim rose to his elbows, and took a hard look at me. I crossed my arms over my chest.

"I've upset you," he said. "I didn't mean to. You're important to him. Otherwise he would have gotten bored and moved on."

My heart twisted. Alec was a player. How many women, like me, had fallen under his spell? How many had he set aside?

I put on my best smile, but inside I was shaking. "It's a good thing I specialize in entertaining easily bored men."

He smiled. Then laughed. He had no idea he was being offensive.

"You're funny. A good sense of humor will take you far in this world."

He lay back down, and I returned to my work. Full pressure. My knuckles cracked. I'd pay for it later with sore hands, but I didn't care.

When I'd worked my way down to his lower back, Maxim shifted again.

"Let's add another hour on to today's session. Ms. Rowe will reimburse you."

As much as I needed the extra $300 for the plane ticket, I couldn't. June Esposito was waiting for me at her house, and Maxim had already been forty-five minutes late.

"I'm sorry," I said. "I can't stay today. We can reschedule for tomorrow evening if you like."

He rolled over, and I quickly lifted the sheet so it didn't drag under his greasy body.

"She plays hardball," he murmured, eyes closed while I stood behind his head and began to knead my way beneath his neck. "I can appreciate that. How much?"

"It's not a matter of cost, though I'm flattered that you're enjoying your session so much."

"Five hundred dollars?"

I swallowed. Eight hundred dollars for two hours of work. That would pay for the entire ticket.

"You must be really stressed," I said.

"Maybe Alec's not the only one who enjoys your company."

I pulled my hands away. "I think we're done."

"I appreciate two things above all others," he said as I turned away. "Good work and loyalty. I'm willing to pay for both."

My temper flashed. "I appreciate respect. I'm not willing to pay for that, but I deserve it."

He clicked his tongue in his cheek. "You're right. My apologies. I'm used to speaking the language of money."

I stopped and sighed. Alec trusted him, and despite myself I was beginning to trust Alec. Maxim Stein may have been arrogant and condescending, but I could handle him.

"People don't say no to you very often, do they?" I asked.

He smiled and combed his silver mane over his ear. A trademarked move, I'm sure.

Here goes eight hundred bucks, I thought.

"I appreciate the offer," I said. "But I have other plans today. We can reschedule for tomorrow evening if you'd like."

His eyes flashed with such an immediate, intense anger that I took a step back. Then the look was gone. He sat up, pulling the sheet across his lap.

"Tomorrow then," he said. "I look forward to it, Ms. Rossi."

After I'd packed up, I looked for Alec. I hadn't heard from him since he'd left early in the morning. After the way my session had gone, I thought I should probably give him the heads-up that I'd pissed off his boss, but he was nowhere to be found. Instead I ran into Bobby, who met me in the foyer and walked me to the door. He was wearing the same suit I'd seen him in before; the dress shirt could barely button at the top on account of his bulging neck muscles.

"Wandering around again?" he asked with a snide grin. I wasn't sure how Alec could stand working with these people.

"I was just on my way out," I said. He reached for the massage table, but I adjusted it on my shoulder and kept walking.

"So soon?" I glanced over at him. "How about a back rub on the house? We can see where that takes us."

I stopped, turned to face him.

"Sure," I said. "Let me just set up here in the living room."

His brows lifted. "Really?"

"No. Not really." I kept walking, but he stood in front of the door, one hand on the knob. Shivers worked through me. I stood tall, but subtly reached into my bag for the pepper spray.

"I'm just starting to feel left out is all," he pouted, running one finger down my arm. I jerked away. "The boss is getting his, Alec's getting . . ."

"What's Alec getting?" The table clunked on the floor as I spun toward the voice behind me. Alec approached from the kitchen, wearing a neatly tailored black suit. His hands were in his pockets, and there was a fierce look in his stormy eyes.

Relief shimmered through me, along with a hint of arousal. Power came off of him in waves. Bobby may have had more muscle, but I had my money on Alec if it came to a fight.

"Alec," said Bobby, standing upright. "Thought you were taking today off."

I wasn't sure if this was some kind of joke; Alec had told me he was working all day.

"Looks like you were wrong," said Alec. "Go ahead, Bobby, finish what you were saying." His voice was as cold as ice.

Bobby only smiled.

I felt caught between them, stuck between the walls, the front door, and two men quite obviously in the middle of a pissing contest.

"Well," I said. "This is fun, but I've got to get to my next appointment."

Bobby pulled the door open, as if this had been the plan all along. "See you later, Anna."

Alec passed through as well, but not without a long, hard stare at his coworker.

When we were alone outside, I turned on Alec, my temper brimming over. He cut me off before I could start.

"Stay clear of him," he said. "He's . . . trouble."

"Yeah, no kidding," I said. "Do you actually like these people?"

His jaw was still flexed with anger. Without asking, he took the massage table and flung it over his shoulder as if it weighed no more than a bag of feathers.

"It's complicated."

"Complicated," I huffed. We'd reached my car, and I jammed the key into the trunk to unlock it. "You know what else is complicated? Your boss offering me hundreds of dollars for my loyalty, whatever that means. Your coworker asking for a happy ending in the middle of the living room. The fact that you and I have been sleeping together, and I don't know where you live or what you've been doing all day or anything about your past."

"Do you want to tell me about your past, Anna?" He tossed the table inside the back of my car and bent down so that his face was right in front of mine. "You want to tell me why you have a different address every three months?"

"That's not fair," I said. He was throwing the background check in my face, and even though I was fuming, I still felt the pull to slide closer. It was like this man was made of magnets.

"You want to know all about me without giving up anything in return. *That's* not fair." His gaze shot off to the side, and once again I couldn't help but feel like he was hiding something.

I rocked back on my heels. "I'm late to see my next appointment. Call me later if you're not working your way down the list of women your boss so kindly mentioned."

He reached for my arm, but I whipped it back.

"Don't run away," he warned.

His words stopped me momentarily, but before he could see the tears in my eyes I'd retreated into my car.

He didn't try to stop me from leaving.

"Double fudge or salted caramel?" Amy held up two cartons of ice cream from her freezer. I was sitting on her couch, curled up inside a blanket. My phone sat on the cushion beside me. Apart from a quick check-in from my dad, no one else had called.

"Double fudge," I said.

"Uh-oh." Amy brought two spoons and sat beside me on the couch. "Trouble in paradise?"

I couldn't hide the frown anymore, not since Paisley had been put to bed. "How did you guess?"

Amy turned her spoon upside down and stuck it in her mouth. "Because if things were going well, you'd have chosen salted caramel and you'd be dishing about how great he is in the sack. That's the sexy ice cream. Chocolate is for mopey mamas."

I snickered. "I think you've missed your calling."

"Fortune-telling and ice cream readings," she mused. "That's where the money is."

I took another bite. She was right. Chocolate was pity-party ice cream, but that didn't mean I was going to push it away.

"Apparently the money is in massage," I said. When she motioned with her spoon for me to continue, I told her about what had transpired with Maxim Stein earlier in the day, ending with the part where he'd alluded to Alec's man-whoring ways.

"So Alec's had a lot of sex. Look at him. Of course he has."

I took another bite. "That makes me feel so much better, thanks."

"Obviously you've got something special, otherwise he wouldn't be coming back."

Another bite. "I'm not sure he is now." As much as I tried to hold them back, one tear fell free.

Amy reached for my hand. I told her how Alec and I had argued outside of Max's house. It felt good to get it off my chest, but more final in a way, too, like I was sealing our fate.

"Maybe you should call him," she suggested. I looked at my

phone, then kicked it off the couch. "Maybe he's not telling you everything because he's afraid you're going to walk away."

I stared at my phone on the floor. On some level I knew that was true, but I was too busy guarding my own baggage to consider what he was doing with his.

It was after ten when I'd finally gotten home and changed into my comfy clothes—a tank top and boxer shorts. It was impossible to get my mind off Alec; reminders of him were all over my apartment. The comforter on the bed was rumpled; he'd left a cabinet in the kitchen open. Even my shampoo was in a different place from where I normally left it. I'd picked up my phone half a dozen times, but couldn't figure out what to say. Right when I'd settled on a simple *Sorry*, it buzzed with an incoming message.

Remember what I told you at the beach?

I closed my eyes. *I want you, Anna. I want all of you.*

Yes, I responded.

Lock up and come downstairs.

I stood up from where I'd been sitting on the bed and went to the window. Down on the street below, Alec leaned against the hood of his car. He looked up at me, and in that moment I replayed in my mind every romantic movie I'd ever seen where the hero waits outside his girlfriend's house. Time stood still. I could almost hear the sappy love ballad playing in the background.

Excitement, relief, and something else, something more powerful, coursed through me. I didn't know where we were going, so I grabbed my purse and my keys and met him downstairs.

He pushed off his car when he saw me, and I crossed the sidewalk quickly, not caring that I was still in my pajamas or that patrons loitering outside the bar down the street could see me. Alec was here, sexy as ever in his T-shirt and jeans with his thick, messy hair and his thoughtful smile, and I wanted him. Just him. All of him.

When I was close enough to touch, his knuckles skimmed over my cheek and down my arm. The warm feel of his skin was a welcome replacement to the cold air, and when his lips brushed mine, my heart skipped a beat.

"I'm sorry," I whispered.

"You have nothing to be sorry about," he said.

He led me around the hood of the car and opened the passenger side. When I was inside, he shut the door after me.

Twenty minutes later we were alone in the elevator of a ritzy high-rise apartment complex in Bayshore.

"Where are we going?" I asked for the tenth time. A huge grin was plastered across my face. I knew where we were going. Alec was taking me to his place.

"The zoo." He'd given me a different answer every time I'd asked. The movies. New York City. A sex club.

"Uh-uh." I shook my head and stepped into his arms. He lowered to kiss me, and I ran the tip of my nose along the side of his face. "The zoo's closed. The animals have to sleep." I bit his lower lip and he growled.

His hands tightened around my waist and then he lifted me, and I wrapped my legs around his hips. I gave a little gasp as he gripped my buttocks and pulled me closer. He was hot, hard, and ready, and with the mirrored walls of the elevator car, I could see the muscles of his back flex as I raked my fingernails lightly over his scalp.

"Sleeping. Something you and I will not be doing tonight," he promised as the elevator climbed higher. Fifteen, sixteen, seventeen.

"Careful," I said. "This is a nice place. I bet there's a security camera in here. You never know who's watching."

"I know exactly who's watching," he said, nuzzling his face

into my hair. "Max owns the building, and the security guards report to me."

"How convenient."

His tongue skimmed the edge of my earlobe.

Anticipation quickened my pulse, but I wanted him to know that the importance of this move was not lost on me. Tonight, I was going to take care of him, starting right now. I kissed his lower lip, and the corners of his mouth. While he held me, I gripped his strong shoulders and licked his neck just below his ear.

"*Mmm . . .*" I hummed. "You taste good. I wonder if you taste good everywhere." I rolled my hips, increasing the pressure against his rigid shaft. I wasn't normally the type to talk dirty, but the energy crackling between us was enough to draw it out of me.

"Jesus," he muttered.

The elevator climbed past the twenty-first floor.

"Would you like to see me on my knees, Alec?" I bit the base of his neck. He shuddered. His body was one hard, taut muscle.

"Would you like to put your cock in my mouth?" I whispered. He jerked, and pinned me against one of the mirrored walls. His eyes had grown dark, and he readjusted his hands so that he wasn't squeezing my legs quite so hard.

I loved watching him lose control.

Twenty-eight, twenty-nine.

I flexed my thighs, rising an inch, then rubbing back down. Again I moved. I could feel the damp folds of skin swelling, a pressure that would build and build until I found release. I tilted my head back, exposing my neck to his hot breath.

"I want all of you," I murmured.

One raspy breath, and he kissed me, hard enough to bruise my lips. Hard enough to make the fire in my belly rage through my blood. Desperately, our tongues mated. Our teeth scraped. I held his face in my hands and moaned, weightless in his arms and driven by a need that had spiraled out of control.

Somewhere in the back of my mind, I registered the ding of the elevator. Then he was walking, quickly, and when he turned his head to the side, I feasted on his neck.

A door clicked open, slammed behind him.

"Now," I said. "Hurry, Alec."

He set me roughly on a hard surface—a table or a counter. Even though it was dark, I caught a glimpse of cabinets, a refrigerator. Then he was ripping the tank top over my head, freeing my bare breasts. I whimpered as he kneaded the tender flesh, then rolled my nipples between his fingers. His head lowered, and he pulled one hardened tip in his mouth. When his teeth gently teased the end, my hips bucked. All the while his wicked hand continued to massage my other breast.

Though I wanted him inside me, I didn't forget what I'd promised. I needed his cock in my mouth in a primal way. I could already feel my tongue sliding over the smooth skin, and the tender ache in my jaw as he drove himself deeper.

I grabbed the back of his shirt, heard the stitches give way with a pop. A second of separation to discard the stretched material, and then his mouth was back on mine, and his chest was tantalizing my tender front while he nestled himself between my open legs.

He stopped suddenly.

"Shit." His hands cradled my face. "Hold on."

It was like a freight train plowing into a brick wall.

"What?" I managed between breaths.

"Just . . . Don't move. Hold on."

He backed away, leaving me topless and vulnerable. I crossed my arms over my breasts as he pulled his cell phone out of the back pocket.

He had to be kidding.

I looked around for the first time. We were in the kitchen.

The dark wood cabinets were all neatly closed, and the marble countertops were clear.

The screen of his cell phone lit his face with a soft glow as he read through his messages. He looked up at me, then bit his knuckles.

"I'm sorry," he said roughly. "I've got to go."

Seventeen

"What happened?" I slid off the countertop and grabbed my shirt off the floor. "Is everything okay?"

Worry chilled the heat in my veins—in my world, a late-night phone call meant someone I cared about was in trouble—but it wasn't worry that drew his lips into a straight line. It was annoyance.

"Work," he said gruffly. "What perfect fucking timing."

"Work?" I let the tank top I'd been holding to my bare breasts fall to my side. "It's eleven o'clock at night."

When the boss calls, I have to answer. Alec had told me this on our first date.

He was scrubbing his hands over his face.

"I don't exactly keep a traditional nine-to-five."

"What could Mr. Stein possibly need this late?"

His expression turned grave. He opened his mouth. Closed it.

"I can't talk about this now," he finally said.

He wasn't going to tell me. Of course, he wasn't. Silly me to think he might actually clue me in on something in his life.

I started to pull on the tank top, but he grabbed my wrists, holding my arms above my head. For a moment I thought he was going to share what had happened, or even say to hell with the message and take me to bed, but then he released me and stalked out of the kitchen.

Maybe coming here hadn't been such a good idea.

I followed him around the corner and was immediately struck by a stunning view of the Bay through floor-to-ceiling windows. It was black in the night, with only the twinkling lights of a single cruise ship to break the inky water.

"Wow," I said to myself, then took in the rest of the room. One single chocolate leather couch, placed across from a flat-screen television mounted on the wall. There was a dining area, but no dining room table or chairs. No pictures on the walls. The room was spartan to say the least.

I realized why he hadn't brought me here before—he must have just moved in. I felt a little guilty for suspecting he was hiding something.

My bare feet shuffled over the plush carpet as I peeked my head around the corner of his bedroom. The décor was the same in here—a king-size bed on a square mahogany frame with a feather comforter tossed over the mattress, and a single dresser against the wall. There was a sliding door that led out to a patio, but no patio furniture.

Alec was inside the walk-in closet, buttoning up a dress shirt.

"When did you move in?" I asked, leaning against the door-frame.

He didn't look up at me, frustration making his movements hurried and sharp. "Three years ago. Why?"

My brows shot up. "You have less stuff than me, and I've only been in town a couple months."

"I'm used to simple," he said. "Besides, I'm not here very much."

"Where do you usually stay?"

He slipped on his shoes. "I've been at your place the last week."

"And before that?"

He hesitated, and my gaze dropped to the floor. Stupid question. He was used to staying with other women.

"Scratch that," I said. "Never mind."

"It's not what you think," he said.

"It's fine." Not really, but there wasn't anything I could do about it.

He finally looked up at me, and the shadows beneath his eyes reminded me of the picture I'd seen in Maxim's study my first time at the mansion. Something was weighing heavily on him. Secrets he couldn't, or wouldn't, share.

"Pop quiz," I said quietly. "The person you're seeing gets a call in the middle of the night and takes off like a bat out of hell. He's A, a superhero, B, a drug dealer, or C, married."

"Christ, Anna. You think I want to leave?"

I turned away, stung by his tone, but stilled as he came up behind me. Tentatively, his hands came to rest on my waist, and I sagged back against his chest.

"I'll be back as soon as I can," he said. "If you're hungry, there's . . ." He sighed. "Take-out menus in the kitchen."

He clearly didn't want to go. Because it was stupid to punish him for things out of his control, I turned to face him and smoothed down his collar.

"Go," I told him. "I'll be naked in your bed when you get back."

He groaned, and rested his forehead against mine.

"Thanks," he said. And with one very chaste kiss on the cheek, he left.

I searched his bathroom cabinet first, then some of the drawers. It wasn't like I was some creeper, nosing through his stuff, but come on. He sort of asked for it, leaving me here unattended. Any girl would have done the same.

The most exciting find was a box of condoms in his night-stand drawer. It was nearly empty. So not that exciting, actually.

Alec hadn't been lying when he said he was hardly ever here. There were a couple of plates in the kitchen, a box of plastic utensils, and a three-pack of paper towels under the sink. But his bathroom had all the regular toiletries, and his closet was filled with clothes. He obviously used this place for a home base, even if he didn't spend much time here.

I found my red panties—the ones he'd stolen that day at Rave—in the top drawer of his nightstand. He wasn't trying to hide them from anyone who might come looking, so that was something at least.

Still, I couldn't stop wondering what he was doing, what kind of thing his boss might need him for in the middle of the night. I wanted to believe he was telling the truth about working. I liked him, more than I cared to admit. I didn't want to consider the alternatives.

Unsure of when he was coming back, I took off my clothes and curled up in his bed. The sheets were high quality, but crisp, like they hadn't been properly worn in. I liked to think I could help him with that. I wished that they smelled like him, but they didn't. They smelled like clean laundry.

I told myself this was Alec's place. Alec, who I'd spent every free moment of the last week with. Alec, who'd picked me up in the middle of the night, who'd been inside me. But the truth was his apartment was strange and empty, and I was alone. I told my-self I could have left, caught a cab home. I wasn't stranded; it was my choice to be here.

It helped a little.

I kept my cell phone by the bed just in case he called, but as the minutes ticked by, I became more and more drowsy. I told myself to get up and turn on the TV—I wanted to be awake when he got home—but I was already drifting away.

*   *   *

"*You go have fun, understand?*"

Mama picked at a spot on her cheek that was already red and raw. She was scratching at her arms again, too, the way she did after she visited her special friend. She had been pretty once. Long black hair, like I had, and smooth dark skin. Now she was skinnier than me and all scratched up.

When I didn't move, her mouth started to twitch. She was mad again. I'd made her mad. I always *made* her mad.

My stomach started to hurt.

"*What's the matter?*" she said. "*Don't you like to play? What kind of kid doesn't like to play?*" She pointed to the jungle gym and the red tube slide, where a few other kids were laughing and racing around. Even through the glass wall separating the play area from the rest of the restaurant, I could see the smashed French fries on the mat.

I wanted to be a good girl, but I didn't want her to leave. I hated it when she went off with her friends. Sometimes she came back happy. Most times she came back tired, or mean, or bruised up. I didn't want to play. I just wanted to go home.

She pinched my elbow, and I started to cry.

"*You love your mama, don't you? You want to make me happy? Then for God's sake, go play. And don't talk to strangers. The last thing I need is someone snatching you.*"

I wiped my nose on my sleeve, trying to be brave. I looked up at the other parents, scared they might try to kidnap me.

"*Hush, hush,*" she said, and pulled me into her arms. She squeezed too tight, but I didn't want her to let go. "*Mama won't let that happen as long as you're a good girl and you do what she says.*"

She let go and swatted me on the rear as I walked toward the glass door.

"*Oh, and Anna?*"

I looked back, ready to sprint back if she said it was okay. "Don't you run away."

I woke with a start, swallowing the air like I'd been held under water. I thrashed against the covers that bound me, damp with sweat. The room was dark and unfamiliar. I wasn't alone. Someone's hands squeezed my shoulders before I scrambled away.

"Anna," he said. "*Anna*. Baby, wake up."

I inhaled fast and breathed in the warm, familiar scent. I was at Alec's apartment. I'd fallen asleep. The fog in my brain cleared quickly, but my chest ached with the memory.

"Easy," he said. "You're okay. It's me. It's Alec."

I was kneeling, and he was sitting up across from me. Neither of us was wearing clothes. Though the lights were off, the blinds from the sliding glass door were pushed open, and the moonlight cast shadows across his body. I'd pulled the sheets up over my chest, as if the thin material was enough to shield me from my nightmares.

I was cold. Freezing. That's what the past did every time it broke through the barrier. It hollowed me out and chilled me to the bone.

He reached for me slowly, and his gentle touch warmed my cheek. My arms lowered.

"Anna, you're shaking." He moved closer. The concern was clear in his voice.

I didn't want his concern. I wanted his warmth. I wanted to forget my past, my dreams, where he'd been. I wanted him to take away the cold.

I leaned forward and kissed him. He didn't respond at first, so I snaked my fingers through his hair and pulled him closer. I kissed him hard, and when his lips parted, I pressed my tongue into his mouth, shuddering with the heat I found there.

"Anna," he leaned away, searching my eyes for an answer I couldn't give. "What are you . . . ?"

"Please," I said. I laid down, pulling him over me. He hovered over my body, weight on his elbows, knees bent. I wrapped my legs around his hips and pressed our bodies together. He was hard and I was grateful for it; I could feel him nudging at my entrance and prepared myself for a rough entry. I wasn't wet and ready like usual, but there wasn't time for that now. I could already feel the freeze taking me.

"Slow down," he whispered. He tried again to meet my eyes, but I looked away. I reached for his cock, but he stopped my hand.

"Are you crying?" he asked.

"I need this," I said. "Please." I hated that my voice sounded thin enough to break. "I'm . . ."

"What?" he asked, face inches from mine. "Talk to me."

"Cold." I closed my eyes tightly. "Empty."

He was perfectly still; I could feel his gaze on me. I knew he was confused. He was probably wondering how he could back out of this without me going psycho on him.

Desperate, I twisted my hips, so that I was rubbing against him. He faltered, giving a soft groan. His shoulders loosened. His forehead rested on my collarbone.

"Hold on to me," he whispered.

I wrapped my arms around his shoulders, feeling my weakened muscles tremble. I spread my legs to give him room to position himself between them.

"Thank you," I said.

He sat up, pulling me onto his lap. I straddled him, his erection pressed between our stomachs. I held him so tightly I didn't have to see his face; my chin was on his shoulder. Finally, he was going to chase away the darkness.

"Anna, I can't."

I shook harder. My face was wet; there was nothing to wipe my tears on now, and they slid down my cheeks to his back.

"I don't know what's going on," he said. "But I won't do it if you're too scared to look at me. I can't."

My frozen heart was cracking. It *hurt*.

I shivered. "I'm cold."

"Then let me hold you," he said.

His arms were solid, safe, and warm. I wept silently, and he asked no questions, and when the tears were dry, his fingers combed through my hair and ran up and down my spine. An hour or more passed, and when I was strong again, I kissed him, and he responded in the same language—whispers and sighs and soft touches. He made love to me slowly, holding my gaze as he burned away the final bit of ice clinging to my bones. Only at the last moment did he bury his face in my neck and breathe my name.

Afterward, he cleaned us both with a warm towel, and then pulled me back against his chest. It wasn't until his breathing grew heavy and even that I allowed myself to admit the truth: I loved him. I loved him and he would leave me, just like my mom had left my dad. Just like Amy's husband had left Paisley and her. Just like my birth mother had left again and again and again.

The end of us had already begun.

One more night, I promised, and then I'd leave. I had to go before it was too late. Before I couldn't. With that promise echoing in my head, I fell into a deep, dreamless sleep, holding his arm against my chest like a lifeline.

Eighteen

I couldn't break up with him in the morning. It was a blur anyway—I was exhausted, and he had to be back at Mr. Stein's early. We didn't talk about what had happened during the night, and I was grateful for that. He dropped me off at my apartment and promised to call when he had a chance. Part of me wondered if he was feeling the same itch to run that I was.

I was grateful for the distraction at work. As Mr. Stein had requested, I had an appointment this evening with him—the time was sent via text by Ms. Rowe. But until then, I had eight hours to figure out what to do about Alec Flynn.

Ten o'clock found me slumped in Amy's chair, getting my hair twisted into a messy over-the-shoulder braid while I peeled the cardboard sleeve off my coffee.

"Are you going to tell me, or do I get to guess?" Amy finally said.

"I love him," I blurted out, without looking up. "And I'm going to break up with him tonight."

"That's a little confusing." Amy added the finishing touches to my hair, as if I'd just told her it looked like it might rain outside.

"You're telling me."

"If you love him, why are you breaking up with him?"

"Because it's the smart thing to do."

"Oh," she nodded knowingly. "Was that in your horoscope? Bad love in Mercury's ninth house, better break up with the hot guy you're dating."

I gave her a nasty look. "Don't be mean."

"Don't be stupid." She frowned. "Look, I love you, but you can't keep dropping everything every time things start going well. Most people wait until they go bad before doing that."

"I'm not most people," I said.

She wrapped her arms around my shoulders. "I know. But sooner or later you're going to get tired of running."

I pondered this as I made my way toward the front desk to greet my first client. Derrick, looking very fierce in his retro black boots and striped tee, informed me I had been double-booked at eleven, but that one of my clients could come back during lunch if I was willing to skip my break, which I was. The busier I was, the better.

"Now that that's settled," he said, pulling me off to the side. "I saw your sexy client last night."

I groaned, taking this for one of Derrick's sarcastic jokes. "Melvin Herman came here?"

"No." Derrick shook his head emphatically. "Not Melvin. The other guy. Tall, hair like an Abercrombie model, perfect teeth."

I swallowed. Alec did have perfect teeth.

"Alec Flynn," I said.

"That's it. Shame he isn't gay; he was getting cozy with some redhead."

"He was, was he?" I muttered.

I realized Charlotte wasn't the only redhead in the world, but it seemed a little too coincidental they'd be out together after the last time I saw them at Mr. Stein's house.

I busied myself straightening the comment cards. "Where did you see him?"

"At Peaches, down on the waterfront. Shady place, not my usual scene, but I like the bartender. We met last week at . . ."

"What time?" I asked.

"Oh God." Derrick scratched his temple. "Late. I don't know, it was after midnight. Maybe one? Why?"

I had a sinking feeling in my gut, and was almost glad for it. This definitely made my decision easier.

"No reason," I said as my client arrived.

So maybe I'd planned on walking away from him anyway, but I would be damned if he was going to humiliate me.

Alec Flynn was a dead man.

By the time I pulled into Mr. Stein's estate I was ready to rock. The hurt I'd felt when talking with Derrick had been squashed by anger—anger that had festered all afternoon until I was counting down the minutes until I could see Alec in person. I knew I should just cut my losses and walk away, but I couldn't. Not when he'd made it abundantly clear that we were exclusive and Charlotte was only work.

He'd texted twice, but I hadn't responded. I couldn't without sounding pissed off, and I didn't want to give him a chance to come up with an excuse. I wanted to see his face when he found out I knew he was a liar.

But as I walked up to the house, I faltered. I thought of how I'd met him on the street outside these walls, and how we'd had this unreal, intense sexual chemistry right from the beginning. I remembered the first time we'd been together, and how he'd made me feel things I hadn't thought possible. I stopped before I made it to the front steps, feeling like the massage table over my shoulder weighed a thousand pounds.

"What am I doing here?" I murmured.

My skin prickled with the awareness that someone was watching me. I turned my head quickly and saw Bobby leaning against the black SUV parked on the opposite side of the fountain. He didn't move, just continued to stare at me in that way that made me wish I was wearing a hooded parka and snow pants instead of my thin black yoga pants and fitted T-shirt.

"Creep," I said quietly, and climbed the steps.

Ms. Rowe checked me off her electronic schedule and ushered me upstairs to the balcony. Alec wasn't there, but as I finished setting up, I eyed the security cameras and wondered if he could see me.

Mr. Stein's massage went by excruciatingly slowly. He didn't speak. I should have been glad for that after yesterday's session, but instead the silence made me antsy. Part of me wanted to ask about Charlotte, but I figured that wasn't exactly professional.

I was almost finished when the balcony door opened and Alec appeared.

Seeing him made my chest hurt. He was painfully gorgeous, and with that dark possessive look in his eyes it was impossible not to feel drawn to him. I almost felt bad for us. We were good together when I wasn't weighed down with baggage and he wasn't being a lying, cheating man-whore.

As he watched me slide my hands over Maxim Stein's back, his fists bunched and then deliberately opened, making my anger rekindle. He didn't get to be jealous after he'd left me naked in the middle of the night to be with another woman.

I focused on Mr. Stein's neck and tried to act like Alec wasn't there.

After a few moments, he cleared his throat. "Sorry to interrupt, boss."

Mr. Stein turned his head so he was facing Alec, but motioned me to continue with one hand.

"Is everything ready?" he asked Alec.

I moved down Mr. Stein's oil-slicked back, watching Alec from under my eyelashes. His gaze was flicking between the balcony and us, and through his crisp, button-up shirt I could see that his shoulder muscles were tense. His discomfort wasn't about me, I realized, but Stein. I could almost feel the strain in the space between them. Strange, considering Alec had said the man was like a father to him. It occurred to me I'd never seen them together.

Alec nodded. "You sure you don't want your nephew on this one?"

"If I'd wanted him on it, he'd be on it. I need this to go smoothly."

I didn't know who Stein's nephew was, but it didn't sound like the boss had much faith in him. As I moved around to the other side of the table, he caught my forearm.

Alec stepped forward, eyes on where Stein and I made contact. For the first time I met his gaze, saw his jaw twitch and his eyes narrow, and then the way his expression smoothed to become unreadable.

"Stay on that side," Stein said, oblivious to Alec's concern. "I liked what you were doing there."

"*Please,*" I reminded him, removing my arm from his grip.

Stein smirked.

"Please," he repeated. "I'll say this much, Alec, your girl isn't afraid to say what's on her mind."

"No, she's not," Alec agreed. It baffled me that Stein couldn't sense Alec's discomfort. The air felt thin enough to snap in half.

"And she gives one hell of a massage."

"I wouldn't know," muttered Alec.

I wasn't sure if that was meant to make me feel guilty or not.

"Keep me updated," Stein told him, an obvious dismissal. "I'll see you in a few days when you get back."

I tried not to let my surprise show. Alec hadn't told me he was going away. But he hadn't told me he was going to a bar with Charlotte, either.

He seemed torn on whether to stay or to go. Finally, he left the way he'd come, leaving us to finish.

The second Mr. Stein had cleared the balcony after his massage, Alec returned.

I was kneeling on the floor, gathering my supplies, and he reached under the center of the massage table to undo the latches so it would collapse in half. It bothered me that he was helping, that he was going to try to pretend everything was normal.

"If Max wasn't the boss, I might've had to kick his ass back there," he grumbled.

"It's my job," I said sharply.

"Even so, it's not going down as one of my favorite moments."

I threw the water basin into my duffle, where it made a satisfying clank against the wooden deck of the balcony, and then I stood and rounded on him.

"Was last night one of your favorite moments?"

One of his brows cocked. "Which part?"

I shook my head, snatching the table from him as best I could. It was big and clunky, though, and ended up tipping over onto the deck. I was so steamed I could have kicked it.

"Let's see," I hissed. "The part after you almost screwed me, but before you actually screwed me."

He moved toward me quickly, making my breath catch in my throat. Before I knew it, he'd backed me into the balcony railing, and I was gripping his biceps, dizzy from the height.

"I don't remember us screwing last night," he said quietly. "That was something else. And if I recall, you didn't seem to mind."

I couldn't look at him.

He leaned forward, lips brushing along my temple. My breath came faster against my will.

"If you want to know what I was doing with Charlotte, just say so."

I pushed him back, throat burning. "You're not even going to deny you were with her."

He gave me a dangerous smirk. "Did you want me to?"

"No." I frowned. Crossed my arms over my chest. "Yes. Shit. I don't know. What were you doing with Charlotte?"

"I can't tell you that."

I threw my hands up and laughed coldly.

"Of course, you can't," I said. "You know, I actually believe that you don't want to share me. But the same rules don't apply to you, do they? You can have me all for yourself, but the second you see some hot cougar you're all over it."

His jaw flexed. "I told you, my relationship with her is strictly professional."

I planted my heels and glared at him. "I don't believe you."

"Careful," he warned. "You know what it does to me when you get all worked up."

My skin flushed, and I felt that deep, familiar ache inside of me. I turned my back on him before I did something stupid like kiss him. "This is fun for you, isn't it?"

I heard him approach behind me, and when his hands slid down my arms, my muscles warmed, and relaxed. His voice was quiet when he spoke.

"I told you I'm not with anyone else. You'll just have to trust me."

"How am I supposed to trust you when you don't tell me anything?"

He glanced up at the overhang. A security camera rested there and was pointed directly at us.

"We can't talk about this here," he said.

I took a step back and picked up my duffle bag, holding it in front of me like a shield. If Alec was with me, either I was being taped or someone else—probably Bobby—was watching.

"I'll walk you out," he said.

I let him escort me to my car, but even then I didn't feel as if our conversation was private. Dark emotions swirled inside me. I couldn't be so close to him without my heart hurting, but he was wrong for me in so many ways. He couldn't even be honest about what he was doing with another woman in the middle of the night.

In silence he loaded my car, and before I was in the front seat, he took my hand and brought it to his lips.

"There are things I want to tell you," he said. "Some I will, someday. Some I may never be able to. I'm not asking for you to wait forever; I'm just asking for you to trust me right now. I haven't been with another woman since I first saw you, and I won't be until we're over."

My stomach twisted. He sounded so sincere.

"What if we're already over?" I asked.

"We're not. We're just getting started." He said it with so much confidence, I almost believed him.

He opened my car door, and I sat inside.

"I'm coming over as soon as I'm done here," he told me. "We're going to talk about what happens when you doubt me."

He shut the door and walked away, leaving me annoyed, confused, and ultimately curious.

Nineteen

He worked quickly, I would give him that. By the time I got back to my apartment, there was a package on my doorstep. A green box tied with an elaborate copper bow. On the top was a small typed note that just said, *Anna, I'm sorry. See you soon.*

"You're damn right, you're sorry," I muttered, unlocking the dead bolt and pushing inside. I flipped on the lights and took the box to the kitchen, searching for the scissors to cut the ribbon. They weren't in the usual junk drawer where I kept pens and notepads; Alec had probably gone looking for them and put them back in the wrong place. I found them where I kept the knives and I cut off the ribbon. If he thought a gift could fix what had happened, he had another think coming. But as I opened the box, I wavered a little.

Chocolate, really good chocolate—handmade truffles on some ridiculous white satin pillow. It was a cheap shot to say the least.

I popped one into my mouth—I deserved it after the day I'd had—and groaned out loud. Delicious. But that didn't address the issues at hand. Alec had railroaded me back at Stein's house. I'd walked in expecting a good-bye, and left with the opposite. I probably should have felt weak about my lack of resolve, but instead I felt relieved. Maybe Amy was right; I had been being stupid. Alec didn't want to let me go, and that had to count for something.

Still, I was just prolonging my heartbreak. Each day that we got closer would make it harder to back away.

I told myself this as I lit a few candles, brushed my teeth, reapplied my lipstick, and put on a black satin thong.

The knock came at the door an hour later. It was almost seven, so I thought he might want to talk over dinner, but that didn't appear to be the case. There was a predatory look about him, a sharp hunger in his eyes and a coiled tension in his muscles that had me taking a step back.

"Stand by the bed," he ordered, stalking toward me.

"You can't just . . ."

"Now." He removed his jacket, folded it in half, and laid it over the back of the love seat.

Irritation stoked through me, but the rumble in his voice excited me.

"Fine." I walked to the bed. He sat on the end, facing me, and leaned back on straight arms. The position made his shirt pull across his body, giving a mouthwatering view of his pecs.

"Take off your clothes," he said.

I had changed into leggings and a peasant top, but hesitated before doing what he asked. I'd imagined doing this, but not at his command. Still, his tone had me pulling at the strings that closed the collar of my shirt.

"Slowly," he said.

I told myself it was part of the show, but I turned away because of the sudden dose of nerves that had boiled over in my belly. With my back to him, I twisted my hair over one shoulder and pushed the soft cotton down my arm, letting the wide neck give a broader view of my upper back. I became aware of every sensation: the brush of the material, the tickle of my hair against my neck and chest, his stare, moving over me like a physical touch.

I glanced over my shoulder and found him unmoved, except for the obvious erection straining against his pants.

"Keep going," he said.

The nerves in my belly turned to water. Anything that had happened earlier was forgotten. All that existed now was the rising need between us.

I slid my thumbs into the waistband of my pants, already feeling the breath rasp my throat. He was just feet away, but he could have been stroking my back with his fingertips, lowering his mouth to my neck. I closed my eyes, knowing he could see the rise and fall of my shoulders. There was a creak in the bed as he sat up.

I bent at the waist and leaned forward, slowly sliding the skintight fabric down my smooth legs. He made a small noise of appreciation at the view of my behind, but made no move to rise or come closer.

I stepped out of the pants, one leg at a time. I turned now and faced him, suddenly brave and reckless. He gripped the comforter, and his jaw twitched as I reached for the hem of my shirt and pulled it over my head. I never once broke his gaze.

I stood before him in only my bra and underwear, a matching satin set by La Perla that I'd blown half a check on a few months back. I'd never actually worn it until tonight.

"Your bra first," he said, strained.

I reached behind and unfastened it, then slid the straps down my shoulders. My breasts fell free, heavy, peaked, and ready for his hard caress. I shuddered as the cool air made contact with my flushed skin.

Heart hammering, I awaited my next command. He stared at me for several long beats, gaze rising, lowering. Hand moving over his pants to adjust his cock.

"Finish it," he said.

Adrenaline raced through my veins. With trembling hands I lowered the sides of the thong, one at a time, over my hips, down my thighs, over my calves. I stepped free, completely naked.

"Fucking gorgeous," he said, rubbing a hand absently over his chest. And right then, in that moment, I felt more beautiful than ever before.

"Come here," he finally said and, as if I were walking through a dream, I complied. I reached for him, but he grasped my wrists and directed me to the bed.

I let him put me where he wanted me, which was on all fours, facing the headboard. He hadn't taken off his clothes, didn't seem to want to yet.

"Clasp your hands and rest your cheek on them."

I did as he said, attempting to lie on my stomach, but he held my hips in place so that my knees were bent and my buttocks lifted. In this position, my damp folds were exposed, swollen and ready for his touch. Displaying myself in this manner made me a little self-conscious, but he seemed to like what he saw. I wanted to please him; I wanted to drive him crazy.

He laid his hand on my lower back, sending shivers straight to my loins. Up and down his fingertips stroked, lowering over the back of my thigh and then skimming back to where they started. He kneeled beside me, placing his other hand on my shoulders.

"When you came to the house tonight, you thought I'd been with another woman."

My heart ached, one hard pang.

I didn't move.

He continued to trail his fingers over my skin.

"You didn't answer my texts today for the same reason."

I still didn't respond, but my muscles were beginning to quiver in anticipation.

His fingers slid between the globes of my ass, gently prodding, then skimming lower, over my center. My back arched involuntarily, giving him more access. One finger circled my clit, never actually touching it.

We're going to talk about what happens when you doubt me.

I should have known he didn't intend to talk. He intended to punish, with a sweet torture that would drive me insane.

His fingers rose to my back, then lowered down around to the bend of one knee. My muscles flexed everywhere he touched.

"Why would you think that, when you know what you do to me?" He asked calmly. It was rhetorical, so I didn't answer. "Did you think I would touch her like this?"

I bit my lip, fighting not to break so easily.

"Did you think I would put my fingers inside of her?"

His index fingers traced my slit, and then pushed, painstakingly slowly, inside. My muscles contracted involuntarily, and I tried to push up on my forearms, but he held me down.

"Did you imagine me fucking her, Anna?" He added a finger, and began to slide in and out. In and out. "It's okay. Answer me, baby."

Eyes pinched closed, I nodded, cheek still pressed against my knuckles.

He removed his hand, making me gasp. My inner walls squeezed together, missing him. Needing him.

His hand slapped down on one buttock, not hard enough to hurt me, but enough to sting. My eyes shot open. The breath huffed from my lungs. Then, as if it had never happened, he returned to his gentle caress. Up and down. Up and down. Soothing the heated skin.

"You think I could be inside another woman when I had this waiting for me in my own bed?"

He spanked me again, cupped hand breezing off my flesh in an upward motion. The vibration of my body struck my center, making my pussy clench. He had caught me by surprise, but as he returned to his soft touches, I stayed taut and ready.

"Do you still believe I could?"

I wanted to tell him no so that he might finally take off his pants and finish me. I needed him to fill me, to rub that place inside of me that would break the tension and erase the images of him in another woman's bed.

But I nodded yes.

He sighed. "I thought so."

Easy strokes, grazing my now soaked folds. I wanted to weep, I was so tied up in knots.

"I don't like it when you doubt me, Anna."

Another slap, this one a bit harder but still not painful. He blew across the skin to cool it, holding my shoulders down. He had to feel me trembling now; the whole mattress was practically quaking.

He spanked me again and again, each time stroking upward. I'd never been touched like this; it had never sounded like something I would have liked. But as he continued, a fever took control of my body, and the pleasure turned to something else, something more carnal.

"This body is mine," he said, drawing a feral groan from my lips as his hand moved inward, and he began to pat his flat palm against my very slick center. The wet rhythmic sound should have embarrassed me, but it just made me that much hotter.

He alternated pressured spanks against my bottom, with lighter pats between my legs. He spread my knees wide, and then rubbed my labia, and tapped my clit with his middle finger. Just when I became used to the assault he would switch course.

I could hardly hold myself up. I squirmed, muscles trembling.

"Do you still doubt me?"

I cried out as his fingers thrust into my vagina. Deeply they reached, until his knuckles were flush against my outer lips.

"Damn you," I muttered. I was on the verge of spinning out of control.

He finger-fucked me hard, and then suddenly emptied me. Before I could object, he'd reached beneath my hips and dragged me to him, then bent down and began to tongue me. His palm rubbed against my clit, a strong, relentless friction. My hips rotated, giving him more room to turn his head. As he scraped his teeth lightly over one lip, then the other, I lost what little control I had left.

I came hard, gasping for breath. My legs shot straight back, pushing him away. My hands fisted the sheets as I buried my face in the pillow. My muscles spasmed in waves—unending, unyielding waves.

He flipped me onto my back, discarding his clothes like they were on fire.

"I crave the taste of you," he said, burying his face in my pussy again. He licked frantically, spearing me with his tongue, spreading the surface wide and then swirling around my clit. I arched back, fisting his hair to pull him away.

"Too much," I managed. "Too much."

"Not enough," he said, rearing back and then driving his cock into me in one claiming stroke.

I gripped his shoulders and hung on while he thrust fast and deep. My body shook with the impact, nipples aching as my breasts jostled. He lifted my knees, pulled them together against his chest to find a different angle. The pressure squeezed the bundle of nerves between my legs, dragging me up the ridge of a tidal wave, bucking, reaching desperately for something to cling to before he sent me careening over the edge into oblivion, crying his name.

He held still, lodged deep while I clenched around him, while I went blind and began to seize in pleasure. It went on, hot tendrils pulsing through my cunt, forcing me to swallow him deeper into my tender flesh. Then he pulled out, leaving just the head of his monstrous erection inside.

"My body belongs to you," I heard him say through the ringing in my ears. "I am yours just as much as you are mine."

There was no reprieve. As soon as I could open my eyes, my gaze became trapped in his—in the deep blue of his irises and his pupils, dilated and filled with emotion. Perspiration had dewed on his brow. He slipped out and back in, enticing me with his tip, bringing a new layer of sensitivity to that small, hungry mouth.

His muscles clenched, but before I could prepare myself, he drove in hard, all the way to the base. Slowly, he withdrew. A shallow stroke, a deep stroke. He varied, just as he had with the spanking. And as I felt myself rising again, he pulled out completely, and lowered down my body, kissing my breasts, my belly button. Forcing my thighs apart and then sucking my clit into his mouth while his fingers pushed me up and over the edge.

It was too much. Too good. I was lost on some plane beyond reality, where there was nothing but sensation. Thoughts ceased to exist. There was just him around me, against me, inside of me. The ridges of his abdominals, the hard tips of his shoulders, the slippery sweat on his back. His toes sliding up my instep, his knees spreading mine farther apart.

He rose, kissed me as his cock slid inside me again. His hand cupped my breast, massaged it with just enough pressure to urge little gasps from my throat. He took my earlobe between his teeth.

"What are you doing to me?" I panted.

He seated himself deep. "Showing you."

Showing me what? What I'd be missing if I walked away? The very thought of it seemed impossible now.

It began again. He withdrew an inch, pushed back in. He stayed close that way, keeping the tempo slow and intimate.

"Do you doubt me?" he whispered between strokes.

"Alec."

He lifted my legs, tossed one over his shoulder. He pushed in all the way, turned his hips and held, searing me with a pleasured pain that compressed my organs.

"Feel how deep I am." He slid out, buried himself again.

My head thrashed against the pillow. "Yes."

"Feel how much I need you."

"Yes."

"All for you, Anna."

"*Yes.*" Tears streamed down my face.

"This is real, baby."

I was rising again, impossible as it seemed. It was starting in the center of my core, sending bolts down every nerve ending. My feet flexed. My fingers numbly reached for him.

"Alec," I panted.

He released my legs, leaned over me, and held me tightly as he hammered home.

"I'm yours, Anna."

He was close; his thrusts became jerky and uneven, his arms began to tremble. With my last bit of focus, I wrapped my arms around his neck and whispered, "Stay inside me."

And then I broke. My fear, my trepidation—it shattered as I fell to pieces in his arms.

"Mine," I murmured. "Mine. Mine. Mine."

One last thrust and he was lost.

Twenty

The bass from the clubs up the street created a rhythm for the faraway sirens and the clatter of pans from the Chinese restaurant downstairs. It was the music of Ybor City, a song all its own, made richer by the steady beat of Alec's heart beneath my ear.

Candlelight flickered from the nightstand and the windowsills, leaving the rest of the apartment bathed in shadows. A peace had settled over us, warm as any blanket. Our bare legs were twisted together. I wrapped my arms tighter around his chest, wishing there was a way to stay in this moment forever.

"Come with me tomorrow," he said quietly, combing his fingers through my hair.

I lifted my head and wove my fingers over his chest, resting my chin on my knuckles.

"Where are you going?"

"New York."

I laughed. "I've never been to New York."

He sat up a little, folding a pillow under his head. "So come with me. After I'm done working, we'll take a look around." He smirked. "Or we'll stay in. Either way."

I searched his face for the truth. "We'd just hop on a plane and spend the weekend in New York."

His lips rose on one side. "Is that hard to believe?"

No one had ever asked me to do anything like that before. It sounded amazing—fun, exciting. *Serious.* We had only been dating a little while, and just hours before I'd been prepared to call it quits.

But we were serious. Our bodies knew it, and so did my heart, even if his didn't.

"Wow," I said, trying to keep things light. "First chocolates and now a trip to New York? You're definitely racking up the points."

"What do you mean?" His grin faded, and his eyes became serious.

I sat back on my heels. "What's next? Mind-blowing sex? Oh wait, you did that, too . . ."

"What about the chocolate?"

"Oh." I smiled. "Exquisite. Marvelous. Orgasmic."

He sat all the way up. "I didn't bring you any chocolate."

I gave him a puzzled look. "Of course you did. You sent it. The box was right outside when I got home."

I began to feel a little lightheaded watching Alec's expression turn grim. If he hadn't delivered chocolates to my doorstep, then someone else had. Amy wouldn't have sent an apology, and my father would have called to make sure I was home to get the delivery.

I thought of Randall, but I'd never brought him home, and either way Alec had made it clear he wouldn't try to contact me again. If he had, he was in for a world of hurt—Alec would make sure of it.

Another man's words echoed through my head: *I brought a box of chocolates—for everyone. I thought maybe you all might enjoy them.*

Melvin Herman.

I pushed off the bed, grabbing my silk robe hanging over the couch on my way to the kitchen. Alec pulled on his pants and met me there, taking the note when I passed it to him.

I couldn't be sure it was Melvin, but if it was, he knew where I lived. I hadn't considered him much of a threat before, but following me home took on a whole new level of stalkerhood.

"Any idea who this is from?" Alec asked, looking through the box. The frown on his face was etching deeper.

"I have an idea." I sat on the stool, head in my hands. "I'm not certain though."

I described Melvin with as much detail as I could remember, while Alec placed the chocolates in a plastic bag from my pantry. I mentioned Randall, too, but Alec had already considered him.

"How many did you eat?" he asked.

"One." I lied. "Two. Okay, three." I regretted that now.

"How do you feel?"

I considered this, moved by the way he took my hands in his. Despite recent developments, my muscles were loose and my whole body felt like it was glowing.

"Satisfied?" I offered.

"Anna."

"Starving?" I shrugged. "You wore me out."

"Aside from that."

Concern was starting to needle at my temples. I rubbed at them impatiently.

"Fine."

"Not tired? No fuzzy memory? Not buzzed?"

"If it is Melvin, I don't think he's the type to mess with my chocolate," I said. "If he thought that was going to win me over, he's sadly mistaken. Anyone who knows me would know that's an unforgivable sin."

"Nothing else has been off lately? The locks haven't been tampered with, none of your things are missing?"

I shook my head. "You're starting to freak me out."

He stepped closer and pulled my arms around his back.

"There's nothing to worry about. I'm not going to let anything happen to you."

I closed my eyes, warmed by his words, but my gut sank all the same.

"I couldn't find my scissors earlier," I said. "You didn't move them, did you?"

He took a step back. For the next few minutes, I walked him through everything that had been off over the past week—things I hadn't worried about, because I thought he'd done them. He made me show him where the scissors had been left, what cabinets had been opened, the different place in my shower where I'd found the shampoo.

"I probably just misplaced some things," I said, wrapping my arms around my waist. "I've been a little preoccupied with everything lately." I motioned to his half-naked sex-god body.

He kissed my forehead. "Why don't you call your boss at the salon and see if Herman's stopped by while you've been off."

I checked the clock; it was almost ten. Derrick would just be closing up.

"That's a good idea," I said, feeling heavy.

I found my phone on the table by the door and made the call. Derrick picked up on the last ring. When I told him what had happened, he got very quiet.

"You're sure it couldn't be someone else?" he finally asked.

"I don't know," I said. "It could be." I hugged the robe tighter around me. Alec was making his own call and speaking quietly enough that I couldn't tell what he was saying. He'd already checked the dead bolt on the front door and was now inspecting the windows. I looked at my things, my furniture, and wished they made me feel safer.

Derrick sighed. "You better stay home tomorrow. In fact, take a few days." The *click-click-click* of computer keys came over the line. "I'll find someone to cover your clients. File a restraining order first thing in the morning."

"You really don't have to do this." I bit my thumbnail. I was making a nice supplemental income through my home visits, but that didn't mean I could just skip a few days of work. I'd have to pull money from my trip-to-visit-Dad fund to pay bills.

"I do," he said. "You do good work, and I want you to keep working for me. You can't do that if you're afraid of your clients."

"I don't know for sure it's him," I argued weakly.

"Let the police decide what to do then," he said. "I'll call you if Mr. Herman shows up. Stay safe, Anna. I'll see you soon."

I thanked him, and, since Alec was still on the phone, called Amy.

"By any chance did you send me chocolates?" I asked when she picked up, groggy.

"Depends. What kind?"

"The really expensive kind that comes with a note that says *I'm sorry.*"

She hesitated. "Sure. What was I apologizing for again?"

"Nothing," I said. Alec had finished his call and tossed his phone on my bed. "I'll call you tomorrow. Bye."

I hung up and met him in front of my dresser. "Who was that?"

"A guy that works for me," he said. "He's going to look into it."

I wasn't sure what that meant, but I was too unsettled to ask. "Doesn't that seem a little extreme? Maybe I should try to find Melvin and Randall. Ask some questions."

The whole situation irritated me. If either had been to my house, they had crossed a line, and I needed to make sure they wouldn't do it again.

"It's already taken care of," Alec said, and when he registered my shock, he added. "Neither will know he's being followed unless he does something stupid. Now pack a bag. We're staying at my place tonight. We'll fly to New York first thing in the morning."

I planted one fist on my hip, feeling my mouth tighten.

"I can take care of myself, you know."

"I have no doubt," said Alec, opening drawers and tossing random pieces of clothing onto my bed. "But right now you're going to let me do it."

I faltered—half-loving him for being protective, half-wanting to throttle him for being a caveman. But in the end, reason won. Tracking down a potential stalker, even one as seemingly benign as Melvin or Randall, was a stupid thing to do. And as confident as I felt defending myself, the thought of staying here alone right now made me nervous.

"So," I said. "How's the weather in New York?"

That night we ordered pizza and curled up on his couch to watch a movie. We didn't talk any more about who had delivered the chocolates, though he kept his phone near him and left the room twice to check his messages. He seemed intent on keeping me distracted; I don't think he wanted to scare me, but I kept hoping he would come back with answers.

Despite that, there was something romantic about those hours. The passion had been temporarily put on hold, and I was reminded how much I liked Alec, not just for the things he could do to my body, but the way he made me feel when I was with him. He smiled easily, and laughed as we recited lines from the movie. When I told him I wanted a Hawaiian pizza with extra pineapple, he told me it was a shame we wouldn't last. And when I groaned because I had forgotten my toothbrush, he revealed that he'd picked one up for me earlier that day at the drugstore. He even acted shy when I noticed it was the same exact one I had at home.

Later, after he'd packed, we lay in bed, me in one of his T-shirts and him in his boxers, both staring out the window at the night sky. His thumb grazed absently over my stomach, and I could feel his warm breath in my hair. His touch was hypnotizing, and with his warm body spooned behind me, my eyelids started to droop.

"Anna," he said quietly. "What are your dreams about?"

When I stiffened, he pulled me closer.

"What happened to you?" he asked.

I was quiet for a long time. My chest had begun to ache, a dull, consistent throb, but the chill stayed away. Maybe it was because he was so warm that I told him. Maybe it was because I trusted him. Either way, when I opened my mouth, my voice was as thin as glass.

"My birth mother used to party when I was little. Hard stuff. She did whatever she could for it. It was that way as long as I could remember."

I closed my eyes, seeing the pockmarks on her face and that crazed look in her eyes. "She was really pretty once; she used to tell me that's how she met my father. He picked her out of a crowd at a concert. She didn't even remember what concert it was. I guess it was fitting—she didn't remember his name, either."

I took a deep breath. "She used to set me up at the fast-food playgrounds while she went to find a date. They were always crowded enough that no one noticed I was alone. Sometimes she was gone an hour, sometimes longer. I was six the first time she didn't come back. After a while I got scared and went looking for her. Child protective services found me first. They brought me home and gave her a slap on the wrist."

"How?" he asked. His hand had gone still on my belly. "Why did they bring you back?"

"She put on a good show," I said. "Our cupboards were never empty. I never had any bruises or marks. And I never, ever ratted her out. I became a social worker because I thought I'd be able to see through all that bullshit, that I'd be able to tell when people were lying. I could. But as long as they said all the right things, there was nothing I could do about it. I wasn't any more effective than the workers who'd returned me that day."

"That's why you left the job," he said.

"I did what I could," I said. "But in the end that wasn't enough."

He considered this a moment.

"What did your mom do when they brought you back?"

I snuggled closer to him. "She was furious that I'd run away. She told me the social workers would feed me to the rats if they caught me again." I tried to laugh, but it was a hollow, weak sound. "She locked me in her closet for the rest of the night."

"Did she . . ." His grip tightened, then deliberately relaxed. "Did any of her dates . . ."

"Touch me?" I murmured. "Not that I can remember."

He was quiet, waiting for me to continue. My throat was thick, and the words were hard to find.

"When I was eight, she left me for good. I waited all day—nine hours. The cashiers noticed me and said they were going to call my parents, but I said she'd be right back. After a while they called the police. One cop car came. Then a bunch more." I rubbed the heel of my hand into my forehead.

He turned me to face him, sheltered me in his arms. "You don't have to say . . ."

"She was dead in some john's car in the parking lot." I was unable to stop now. It was flooding from me like water from a broken pipe. "I waited all day for her to come, and she was right there, thirty feet away. Heroin overdose. I didn't find that out until later. This cop sat with me until the manager locked up. He was the one who finally convinced me to leave. Benjamin Rossi. He came to visit me in foster care that week, then the next week he brought his wife."

"They adopted you," said Alec, filling in the blanks.

"Later that year. My mom—Katie, my real mom—she died a few years ago from cancer, so it's just Dad and me now." I took a deep breath, surprised by how much lighter I felt. "And now that I'm missing these next few days, I probably won't get to see him for a little while longer."

For a long time we said nothing. I could tell he was working through what I'd said; his heart beat quickly, and the thumb of his free hand tapped against his leg. I began to wonder if maybe I'd said too much and scared him off.

"My mom left us too," he said quietly. "I'm not like that. I won't leave. Not until you tell me to go."

For the first time since I'd begun to tell the story, tears filled my eyes. My heart felt so full I couldn't speak. And then, marking the end of the conversation, he wrapped me tightly in his arms and said good night.

Twenty-one

It turned out Alec was crazy. There was no other reason for him to wake before dawn and go down to the building's gym to exercise. He seemed nervous about the day, like he needed to burn off steam. And though I didn't know what kind of work he had to do in New York, I wasn't alert enough to ask. While he burned, I slept, and an hour later he was practically rolling me out of bed.

Just after six a.m. we were headed toward the airport down side roads. I was wearing black jeans and a bright pink halter and had dug a sweater out of my Baltimore box in anticipation of the cold weather. I glared at him across the car, clean-shaven and gorgeous in his tailored suit, and silently cursed people who didn't need caffeine to form coherent sentences before noon.

When we reached the airport, he drove behind the terminals, in through a back gate where he had to show his ID, and then on a narrow road that cut across a runway. Before us, giant dome-shaped hangars had been opened to reveal jets of various sizes and schematics. Some were silver, others black. The wings on some fanned up at the ends, while others had broader bodies and round noses.

"We're taking one of those?" I asked, no longer in need of coffee. I was definitely awake now.

"Have you ever been on a private jet?"

I turned to look at him. "Aside from the last time I went to Tahiti for the weekend, no. Normally I stick to travel by Kia."

I expected him to laugh, but instead he exhaled, shoulders falling an inch. I hadn't realized he was so tense. Maybe there was more to that morning sweat session than I'd thought.

We passed a black limo, parked right beside a sleek silver plane, and a man in a suit opening the door for two women.

"Celebrities?" I asked, wishing he'd slow down.

"Probably not," he said. "These planes are all owned privately. The ones down there," he pointed down the row, "are chartered by individuals and corporations for events."

"Rent-a-jets," I said. He chuckled. "Are these all owned by Mr. Stein?"

A serious look came over him. "No, these are our competitors'."

We passed three more hangars with sleek silver planes inside. They may have been smaller than the rest, but they looked fast and powerful.

"Private aviation is cutthroat right now," he said. "Manufacturing was expensive even before the price of oil went sky-high. A lot of U.S. clients have turned to commercial travel to cut costs. Some of these people would pay a lot of money to bring down Force Enterprises."

The underground world of plane wars. I imagined men in thousand-dollar suits sneaking around with shiny silver guns like James Bond.

"Do they want to buy the company?"

"Or steal it."

"Is that what your meeting is about today?"

His head jerked in my direction.

"Is the company in trouble?" I clarified. "You said you're losing clients." That would explain the tension.

"No," he answered quickly. "A lot of our biggest clients are oil manufacturers. As long as planes need gas to fly, we're in good shape."

"What else would they use?" I asked. "Fairy dust?"

He smiled tightly.

"So what *is* this meeting about?" I wondered if he was being purposely vague.

"I'm checking in with one of Max's lawyers."

I waited for more, but he was obviously preoccupied. According to Ms. Rowe, Maxim's wife stayed in New York; maybe he'd sent Alec to negotiate his next divorce.

A small plane facing the opposite direction accelerated down the runway beside us. The sound of the engine was loud enough to make me clap my hands over my ears.

Alec shifted in his seat, keeping his eyes on the road. His thumb had begun to tap the steering wheel. It became clear to me then what the problem was, the source of his anxiety.

The man who worked for a company that built jets was afraid of flying.

Curiously, I examined him as he pulled into the next hangar, one that boasted a large sign over the entrance, ten feet in diameter, of a jet flying through a black circle. Alec was definitely pale, and though he leaned back in his seat, a thin line of perspiration had dewed on his hairline.

Well, this is going to be interesting.

Before us was a white jet, sleek and powerful with its twin engines and nearly eighty-foot wingspan. Six oval windows lined the body of the aircraft, and the tail fanned like that of a whale. The door to the cabin was already open, and a male pilot in a blue suit waved from the steps that unfolded to the ground. Max returned a curt nod.

"It's a Force 250," he said as he parked near the edge of the large steel garage. "Max's personal jet. It can travel from here to

India without refueling." He didn't sound particularly enthusi-
astic about this statistic.

"It looks fast."

He took a deep breath. "Mach .88."

"Okay. That's fast."

We admired it from the safety of his car for one more moment,
listening to the powerful thrum of the boosters. The plane
appeared to be all ready to go. I assumed all the pilot was waiting on was the passengers.

"Does Max know you're afraid of flying?" I asked.

He glanced at me, then back to the plane. After a moment he
laughed dryly and raked a hand over his skull.

"No, I don't suppose he does."

If there had been an option to drive, I was certain Alec would
have explored it. Clearly, since we were still here, we were getting on the plane. I felt a little guilty for my excitement, knowing
how Alec felt about it. Without another word, he got out and
carried our bags from the car—my suitcase, his duffle bag, and a
leather briefcase that added a sexy nerd appeal to his animal
magnetism.

I followed Alec up the stairs of the plane and smiled as he introduced me to the pilot—Jim, a thin man in his fifties with a sun-
burned nose. He took our bags and retreated to the cockpit, and I
took a look around the cabin. On one side stretched a long beige
leather couch. On the other, matching recliners faced each other.
Small wooden tables were fixed to the walls, and the windows
were adorned with curtains—real curtains, not the pull-down
screens like on commercial flights. Even the floor was carpeted.

"This is nicer than my apartment," I said.

A woman in her thirties wearing a short black sleeveless dress
emerged from the back. Her blonde hair was neatly fastened behind her neck, and when she saw me with Alec, her smile faltered, just for a second.

"Good morning, Alec. I didn't realize you'd have company today." Her gaze lingered on his mouth, and her tongue wet her lips.

A sudden urge to claim him reared up inside of me. I didn't know how well they knew each other, but I didn't like the way she was looking at him. I placed my hand on his shoulder, and slid it down the smooth material of his suit coat and the muscles beneath.

Alec never faltered. "Jennifer, this is my girlfriend, Anna."

Her mouth pinched at the corners. I hesitated before shaking her outstretched hand; it was the first time he'd made a public declaration about our relationship status. It surprised me how much I liked it.

"Can I get you a bourbon?" Jennifer asked him.

I laughed. "It's seven o'clock in the morning."

Her chin tilted in my direction.

"Nothing for me right now, thanks," Alec told her.

She looked surprised. "Anything for you, Anna?"

"Coffee," I said. "Alec practically had to drag me out of bed this morning."

"I can think of worse things," she said smoothly. "Espresso all right? I can have it ready by the time we're airborne."

"Sure. That'll be fine." Espresso on a private jet? Amy was going to flip out. I made a mental note to call her. When Derrick told her why I wasn't at work, she was going to worry.

Jim's voice came over the intercom: "Once we're all settled in, we're good to go. Should have smooth sailing today. Estimated flight time is just under two hours."

As Jennifer latched the heavy metal door, Alec led me to a seat, one of the two that faced each other. He reached between the cushions for his seat belt and closed the open curtains.

"Did you sleep with her?" I whispered.

His brows lifted. "Not that I can remember."

I kicked him.

"No," he said, rubbing his knee. "Why?"

I gave my best pouty look. "I didn't realize you'd have company today," I mimicked.

His eyes took on a wicked gleam. "Keep it up and I'll spank you again."

The memory of his hand stroking my blushing skin jolted through me like lightning, but a scowl tightened Alec's features as the engine began to rumble. Jim eased out of the garage, taking us into the early morning light.

"Flight attendant, please take your seat," Jim said over the speaker. "Please turn off all electronic devices until we're up in the air."

I snagged my phone from my purse and, before I turned it off, sent a quick text to Amy: Going on a business trip to NY with Alec. Call u when we land. I clicked the phone off.

Reluctantly, Jennifer departed to the front of the plane, closing the door to the pilot's cabin behind her, and leaving us completely alone.

"It really isn't fair what you do to women," I told him, watching her go. "She's all tied up in knots over you."

The crease between his brows deepened. "You should put on your seat belt."

I leaned forward across the space between us.

"Air travel is safer than driving a car," I told him.

"I'm driving the car," he muttered. "I'm not flying the plane."

I put my hands on his knees, stilling his right heel from tapping a hole through the floorboards. "So it's about control."

"It's about 75,000 pounds of metal floating 45,000 feet above the ground."

The poor guy took off his jacket and tossed it haphazardly on the couch across the aisle. He loosened his tie and unbuttoned the top of his shirt.

"What happens when you fly with other people?" I inquired.

He glanced out the window quickly, as if to check the status of the wing, and then reclosed the curtain.

"I drink. Heavily."

That explained the bourbon offer. "But not today?"

"This meeting's important," he said.

I felt terrible for him. I wished there was something I could do to take away some of his anxiety.

There was *something* I could do.

I slid out of the chair and kneeled on the floor.

"What are you doing?" he asked sharply. "Get back in your seat."

The intercom clicked on. "We've been cleared for takeoff. Please make sure your seat belts are fastened until we reach our cruising altitude."

"Did you hear that?" Alec asked. I almost giggled. The guy who played by no one's rules was suddenly very concerned about my seat belt.

"Is Jim a good pilot?" I asked.

"The best."

"Good," I said. "Then I have nothing to worry about."

He started to object, but I reached for his belt. I didn't get far; he stopped my hands with his hard grip. His heel resumed its tapping as the plane turned down one of the runways.

"The key is focusing on something else." I rotated my wrists and his hold loosened slightly. "Let me distract you."

"Anna . . ."

I worked myself free and unbuckled his belt. I knew Jennifer was just behind a door, ten feet away, and would come out as soon as the plane leveled in the sky. I also knew it wasn't safe to mess around in the middle of takeoff, but it only added to the thrill. I could feel the recklessness beginning to pump through my veins as I unbuttoned the top of his pants and lowered the zipper one click at a time.

The engine roared as the plane picked up speed. Since I was facing the back of the cabin, the pressure pushed me forward into his lap. I braced my knees against the seat, leaning my elbows on his thighs. As I skimmed my knuckles over his erection, still tucked within his navy boxer briefs, his hands gripped the armrests, flexing then fisting.

His breath came out in a stutter.

"Have you ever tried this before? On a plane, I mean." I slipped my hand up his shirt, spreading my fingers over his rigid abs. I loved his body. I worshipped it.

He shook his head.

I looked up at him through my lashes, and then peeled his palm from his knee and placed it on my cheek. Slowly, I drew one of his fingers into my mouth, sucking it, feeling it with my tongue, scraping it lightly with my teeth.

His lips parted as his chest began to rise and fall. His eyes grew dark and hungry. Outside the wind began to rush by as the nose of the plane lifted off the ground. His gaze shot to the window, then back to me.

Focus on me.

"I'm going to put your cock in my mouth, Alec."

His Adam's apple bobbed.

"Do you want that?" I asked, slipping my fingertips into the waistband of his briefs and inching them down slowly. He lifted his hips to help.

The wheels rose off the ground. We were airborne.

"Look at me," I snapped, jerking the fabric the rest of the way down and setting his cock free. It stood from his body, thick and glorious, skin stretched taut. The head was swollen and deep red, and moisture dewed from the tip. Just looking at it made my body clench in need. What I would have given to crawl into his lap, straddle his hips, and ride him straight into the mile-high club.

But first, I wanted this.

"So hard," I murmured, running my fingertips down his length. "I want to taste it. I've fantasized about you like this."

I licked him from stem to tip, one long pull with the back of my tongue.

He stared down at me, lust in his eyes, and I knew I had him.

I wrapped my fingers around the base of his shaft, giving him a hard squeeze before massaging his balls in my other hand. There wasn't enough time to make this last like I wanted, but that didn't mean I wouldn't give him every ounce of pleasure I could.

With the tip of my tongue, I swirled around the head, tasting the slippery, musky liquid. The response it evoked was instantaneous. My eyes drifted closed. My stomach tightened. The plane hit a bump, and for a split second it felt as if we were cresting the top of a roller coaster. His breath caught, and I pulled him into my mouth, nestled the smooth head of his penis over the back of my tongue, and sucked.

"Jesus fuck," he muttered. His hands fisted in my hair.

I went wild, forgetting everything but the feel and taste of him. I pulled him deeper inside my mouth, sliding my hand over his length while I pressed my thumb behind his scrotum. My cheeks drew in while I licked him, drawing more of his salty flavor into my mouth. He was so big I couldn't take all of him, but I took as much as I could.

I rose on my knees, aware of his rasping breath and the groan that vibrated through his stomach. Both my hands became dedicated to jacking him off, squeezing as I rose up and down his cock, now slick with my saliva. I twisted my grip, spread my fingers, then closed them. All the while I rubbed the smooth spot of flesh beneath his head with my tongue.

His thighs quivered, hard as a rock. His grip fisted in my hair, forcing my chin to tilt up. I stared into his eyes, defiant and shameless, while his lips drew back in a tight grimace.

"Anna."

I sucked him deeper, wanting him to fill me here as he'd filled my cunt. Wanting to erase any other thought from his brain, to scar him with a pleasure he would never forget.

"*Anna.*"

His cock hit the back of my throat. I swallowed. I gripped him tighter, moved faster.

"I'm going to come."

I would take everything he offered. It was as necessary in that moment as breathing.

He came in hot, salty spurts that filled my throat and made me press my thighs together to contain the heat pooling there. I held him as he grabbed the back of my head, seeking control as he fucked my mouth, and when he was done, I rocked back on my heels, and licked my lips.

He stared at me for one awed moment, then fixed his pants and pulled me into his lap. He held my face in his hands as he kissed me passionately, his tongue beckoning mine into his mouth.

"I can taste us," he murmured.

I thought that might have bothered him, but his cock stirred beneath my hip.

We stayed that way—in an in-between place, burning like embers without an open flame—until Jim signaled it was time for our descent. It wasn't until then that I turned around and saw that my coffee sat on one of the side tables, cold.

A private car met us at the airport and took us to a swanky hotel a few blocks away from Times Square. Seeing images of New York City in pictures and movies did not do the city justice. The lights were dazzling; bright billboards with advertisements for Broadway shows stretched overhead, and news tickers gave the latest reports while huge televisions played commercials. Steam puffed from the subways where people swarmed in and out. The streets were crowded with men and women in black suits, families taking pictures, and vendors selling hot dogs and souvenirs. It was both awesome and overwhelming at the same time.

The hotel had a bellman in a long red jacket who took our bags and ushered us out of the chilled air into the lobby. Five minutes later we were standing in our room, a suite, with heavy antique furniture and a view of Central Park.

"I'm not sure how long I'll be," Alec called from the bathroom, where he was fixing his tie. "Why don't you order room service? Get something I can lick off you when I get back."

I grinned, making my way to the briefcase he'd set on the king-size bed. I ran my hand up the smooth wood of one of the four posts that made up the frame.

"Maybe you should pick up some rope while you're out," I said. "I always wondered what it would be like blindfolded and tied to a bed like this."

He went quiet, and my smile widened when I heard him mutter a series of swear words and something about not being able to concentrate through his meeting.

His briefcase was open, and out of curiosity I lifted the edge of the slim gray folder within. Immediately I recognized the logo—a slim emerald leaf. Beneath, in small block print were the words *GREEN FUSION*.

The image spurred a memory from my first night working for Mr. Stein. When I'd been hiding in his office, I'd seen a set of blueprints on his desk for a plane engine. I pulled the folder open the rest of the way, finding the same documents here.

Beneath the folder was a black handgun.

"What are you doing?" Alec stood in the doorway, the light behind him darkening his features. His tie was in a perfect Windsor knot, his suit jacket lapels smooth over his chest. He strode over to me and snapped the briefcase shut.

"Nothing," I said, taken aback by his obvious irritation. "I'm sorry, I . . ."

"Why were you looking at that?"

"Why do you need a gun for your meeting?"

"I always have it," he snapped. "Answer the question."

"Take it easy," I told him, flipping my hair over my shoulder. "I've seen the blueprints before."

His eye twitched. "I asked you what you'd seen. You said nothing."

The first night we'd went out for burgers he'd asked me this. It had pissed me off then, and it pissed me off now.

"I didn't remember until I saw the logo."

"That's convenient."

My eyes widened. "Is it?"

We faced each other, too stubborn to break until I finally threw my hands up.

"Not that I care, but is this what your meeting is about?" I asked. "Green Fusion? What is it, some clean green alternative to a gas engine?"

He flinched.

A lot of our biggest clients are oil manufacturers, he had said. *As long as planes need gas to fly, we're in good shape.*

If Force's biggest clients were in the oil business, why was Mr. Stein looking at a Green Fusion engine? If his planes didn't need gas—or at least as much gas—to fly, that would put him in a position to upset his existing patrons.

"Did you tell anyone about this?" Alec grabbed the briefcase, gaze cold.

"No."

"You're sure, Anna?"

"Yes, okay? I'm sure. I haven't said a word."

He shook his head as if he was disappointed. "Good. Keep it that way."

With that he headed toward the door.

"That's it?" I followed after him. "You're just going to leave like that?"

"Stay here." He didn't even turn around as he strode out, shutting the door behind him.

For a full minute I stared at the brass doorknob. What had just happened? One second we'd been flirting, the next he was as cold as ice, taking off without even saying good-bye. This was not the same protective, dedicated man who'd insisted I come to New York. This Alec clearly had issues.

Stay here, he'd told me. What was I, his lapdog?

"To hell with that," I said aloud. I grabbed my coat off the back of the desk chair where I'd left it, snagged my purse, and made for the elevator.

I decided to walk through Central Park. I wasn't in the mood for fighting the crowds of Times Square, and besides, I needed to walk off some anger. It was chilly enough that I could see the breath in front of my face as I chugged down the paths that cut through the yellowed grass. Winter had stripped the trees of their leaves and left skeleton branches that revealed the bridges and statues down the way. It was beautiful and would have been a whole lot more romantic if I'd been here with Alec.

I still didn't understand why he'd been so defensive, or what the big deal was about Green Fusion. Surely he knew I didn't care, I wasn't going to tell anyone about his business, and I certainly wasn't going to do anything to hurt the company.

"I'm just the masseuse for Christ's sake," I said, scaring away some watchful squirrels.

My cell phone vibrated, and I fished it out.

"Hey, Amy."

"Are you okay? Derrick just told me you think Melvin Herman is stalking you!"

I found the nearest park bench and told her what had happened with the chocolate and the little changes around my apartment.

"I'm probably just being paranoid," I said. "My locks weren't broken. No one's been in my apartment but Alec and me." At least, I hoped.

"Well, if I see him, I'll kick his skinny ass," she said. "And Randall's on my schedule for tomorrow, so I'll see what I can find out from him, too."

"Thanks," I said.

"Now, are you seriously in New York?"

I snorted. "I am seriously in Central Park, right now."

"Holy cow."

I wanted to tell her about the private jet and the cold espresso, but I didn't have the heart.

"Can I call you when I get back?" I asked. "Kind of busy here." I hated lying to her.

"Sure." She hesitated. "Be careful, all right?"

"Of course," I said. "I'm okay, Alec's looking into the chocolate thing."

"I mean with him. Be careful with Alec. I'm glad you're into him, but honestly Anna, you haven't known him all that long. Taking a trip to New York is a big deal."

"What happened to taking chances and not pushing him away?"

"That was before you decided to elope in New York."

"We're not getting married." I forced a laugh, but she'd hit closer to the mark than I cared to admit. Sometimes I felt as if I knew Alec better than anyone. Sometimes I felt as if I didn't know him at all.

It was afternoon by the time I made my way back to the hotel. My mood was lighter, thanks to some delicious kettle corn and hot chocolate I'd picked up at a cart in the park. I thanked the bellman and headed upstairs, only to find the door propped open and Alec pacing within, talking on his cell phone.

When he saw me, he said a quick good-bye and hung up. The sleeves of his white dress shirt had been rolled up past his elbows, the jacket and tie discarded on the chaise longue. The apprehension that tightened his body socked me with guilt.

"Where the hell have you been?"

"Walking," I said, trying to play calm. "How was your meeting?"

He stared at me. "I told you not to leave."

"You don't get to tell me what to do," I said evenly.

"I called you. You didn't answer."

I shifted. I didn't know he'd called. I must have accidentally turned the volume off on my cell phone after talking to Amy.

"You've never been to New York. I thought you were lost. Someone could have . . ." He shook his head. "Forget it. We're leaving."

"That's not exactly the nicest way to ask me to dinner."

"We're not going to dinner. We're going home."

I balked, amazed by his audacity, and at the same time worried that the meeting he'd gone to had gone terribly wrong. It didn't seem possible that he'd fly us home early just because he was mad at me, but then, as Amy had said, I hadn't known him very long.

"Alec."

He was already in the bedroom gathering the things I hadn't even had a chance to spread out. I caught a flash of the gun as he moved it from the back of his waistband to his duffle bag. The briefcase, I noticed, was missing.

"We should talk about this," I said.

"There's nothing to talk about," he said.

I followed him to the elevator, the silence between us so thick it might have been a wall. The car ride wasn't much better. And when we boarded the plane, perky little Jennifer was oh-so-happy to serve Alec the bourbon she'd assumed he'd wanted this morning. He downed two shots before we even took off, and with me on the couch and him facing away in one of the seats, we climbed through the atmosphere.

My resolve was past wavering, but I didn't know what to say to him. It was enough that we were on thin ice without me stating the obvious. As I closed my eyes, the simple truth nestled itself in my ribcage. I'd waited too long. He was going to leave first.

It was going to break my heart.

* * *

Sometime later, Alec nudged me awake. I rubbed my eyes, remembering what had happened in New York, and averted my gaze as I followed him off the plane into the hangar. I wanted to be strong when he walked away, and that meant I needed to be more alert. But right now I was groggy and my insides were all twisted up.

I slid into the back of a black Lincoln, and he sat on the other side leaving the center space between us. I placed my bag there like a shield and checked my phone, scrolling through pictures Amy had sent of Paisley, telling myself I'd survive Alec Flynn.

It was dark out now, and I didn't look out the tinted windows until the car slowed and we entered a neighborhood. I was suddenly jarred by my surroundings—this wasn't Tampa, there wasn't a palm tree in sight. We weren't even in Alec's Jeep, which we'd driven to the airport less than ten hours ago. I couldn't believe I'd been so focused on myself that I'd failed to notice where we were.

But I knew where we were. I knew *exactly* where we were.

As the car pulled to a stop in front of the one-story brick house, my throat grew thick and hot, and I blinked back tears.

Alec had brought me home to see my dad.

Twenty-two

I turned to face him, hand over my mouth to stifle my bubbling laughter, and then gave up and launched myself across the seat. I threw my arms around him, kissing his face everywhere I could. He pulled me closer, arms around my waist, and tucked his chin against my neck.

"I'm sorry," he murmured.

Whatever we'd fought about was in the past; I wanted to forget it. I pulled back, holding his cheeks in my hands. The apology in his gaze captured me, and I ran my thumbs over the rough stubble on his jaw.

"How did you do this?" I asked. "How did you even know where we lived?"

"Your background check had your previous addresses," he said. "It wasn't hard to find out if your family still lived here."

"Was this your plan the whole time?" I couldn't believe I'd almost screwed everything up.

His mouth turned down. "It came into play a little sooner than I expected."

"Your meeting didn't go well," I inferred. A chill worked its

way down my spine when I remembered the gun in his briefcase—
the briefcase I hadn't seen him bring back to the jet.

He glanced at the house, avoiding my gaze. "It went exactly
as planned."

I had a bad feeling about what that meant, but something
stopped me from asking more. This was Alec, and I felt safe with
him, regardless of what secrets he kept.

"Does my dad know we're here?"

Alec scratched a hand down his jaw. "No."

My smile returned. "Let's go."

He hesitated. I'd completely forgotten a driver was in the
front seat until he cleared his throat.

"Come on," I said. "You're not scared, are you?"

"I'm not . . ." His gaze darted to the side. "I'm not exactly the
guy you bring home."

My chest constricted not just at his words, but his tone. He
was more than nervous, he was honestly worried he wouldn't be
good enough.

"It's too late to get out of this," I said.

His jaw worked back and forth.

"Yeah," he muttered. "I was afraid of that."

With that, we left the car, and I practically pulled Alec up the
walkway behind me. I had a key, but my dad had a gun, and
since he wasn't expecting me I figured it was better to announce
my presence with the doorbell.

On the third ring, Ben Rossi opened the door. He was wearing navy sweatpants and a worn gray T-shirt, and had a dish
towel tossed over his shoulder. Even though it had only been five
months since I'd seen him last, his hair looked a little lighter, and
there were more lines around his eyes and mouth. He was still
handsome, but losing Mom was taking its toll.

"Anna?" His open mouth warped into a shocked smile.

I crossed the threshold and hugged him, hating how skinny
he'd gotten this past year. I needed to come home more often.

"Surprise!" I was jostled to the side as a giant black dog cut between us and slobbered all over my shirt. "Thanks, Mug." The Great Dane's tongue lolled out of his mouth as he jumped up. With his enormous paws on my shoulders, he was almost taller than me.

"What are you doing here? Is everything okay?" Dad asked, pulling Mug down by the collar.

"Everything's fine." Telling him how Alec had arranged for us to come here in a private jet could wait until he'd had a chance to adjust. "Dad, this is Alec. Alec, Ben Rossi."

Alec was still outside, but at the introduction stepped into the threshold. Mug immediately greeted him with a nose to the crotch. It took most of my strength to pull the dog back.

"It's nice to meet you, sir." Alec stretched out his hand, which my father took only after a moment's appraisal.

"Alec, huh? You got a last name?"

"Dad," I warned. *Here we go.*

"It's Flynn."

Their hands were still clasped, but they'd stopped shaking.

"Is that your car out there, Alec Flynn?" He nodded over Alec's shoulder to where the Lincoln was still idling. I was sure he had already committed the license plate number to memory.

"It's a company car," said Alec.

"Fancy." My dad clicked his tongue inside his cheek. "So what brings you here, Alec Flynn?"

Alec forced a smile. "Anna talks a lot about you. I wanted to introduce myself."

"You did," he said. "How long have you and Anna been talking? I haven't heard a word about you."

"*Dad.*" Unbelievable. It was like I was still sixteen years old.

"What?" he shrugged.

"Just a couple weeks," answered Alec. I had to hand it to him; he'd yet to wither beneath my dad's policeman stare.

"Interesting," said my dad. "And she hasn't kicked you to the curb yet?"

Alec inhaled, and it occurred to me that he was taller and more built than my father. Apparently no one had told my dad this.

"It surprises me, too, sir," Alec answered.

"Okay," I said, pushing my dad's arm back to break their death grip. "It's kind of cold outside, and I'm hungry, so maybe we could recommence with the shakedown in the kitchen."

"I should get going," said Alec, laying a hand on my lower back. "Leave you two to catch up."

"All right," said my dad.

"I can pick you up tomorrow morning, Anna?"

I glared at Alec. "You're staying." I turned to my dad. "Be nice." He raised his hands in surrender. "And just so we're all on the same page, I love both of you, so you just better get used to it."

They both stared at me for a full second as the weight of what I'd said sank in. Alec's lips parted. The color rose in my dad's cheeks. They each looked equally mortified. I couldn't believe I'd let that slip. But since there was no going back now, I backed out of the entryway and escaped to the kitchen.

I was rooting through the pantry when Alec appeared behind me. I didn't know where my dad was, but the kitchen smelled like a TV dinner, and the microwave door was open.

"Hey," he said quietly. He moved close enough that I could feel the warmth from his body through my clothes. He was too big for this tiny kitchen, too high-class with his private jets and fancy New York hotel rooms for linoleum floors and a water-stained sink. He didn't want to be here, and I'd been stupid to make him come in.

I grabbed a can of diced tomatoes and a dusty box of lasagna noodles. The expiration date said July—yep, still good.

"By some miracle there's hamburger in the fridge," I said. "I just need some cheese and I can make lasagna."

"Anna."

I couldn't face him, couldn't stand to hear that regret already thick in his tone. I shouldn't have said I loved him. That was stupid. And it was a hundred *thousand* times stupider to throw it out publicly in front of my dad. Maybe Alec should have gotten a hotel. He might not survive the night now.

"Maybe the neighbors have cheese," I said, dumping the supplies on the counter. "I'll go ask."

Alec put his hand on my arm, freezing me in place with his touch. This place was thick with memories and full of love; it clearly made me too comfortable, made me think I could open my big fat mouth and say anything.

My eyes focused on an old picture framed on the counter of my mom and dad at the annual police Christmas party. It was years before I'd come to live with them. She was wearing a frilly black dress and sitting on his lap, and they were looking at each other like they had no idea there were other people around.

"What was that back there?" Alec asked.

I took a deep breath.

My dad walked in and saved me before I could say anything else. He looked back and forth between us, eyes narrow.

"I need mozzarella," I blurted.

"Alec and I will go get some," Dad offered.

I shot him a hard look. "Why does that sound like a bad idea?"

"I don't know. Sounds like a great idea to me." My dad grabbed his keys from a hook off the wall. "Come on, Alec. Let's go through the garage. I'll show you my gun collection."

Alec followed him, but before he reached the door, he glanced over his shoulder and sent a smirk my way.

That damn smile knocked me on my ass every single time.

*   *   *

I don't know what happened at the store, but Alec and my dad returned in a very different place than when they'd left. I didn't even realize they were home until I called my dad's cell and heard it ringing in the garage.

I opened the garage door, ready to rescue Alec from my father's interrogation, but instead found them elbow to elbow beneath the hood of the candy-apple red '67 Chevelle my dad had picked up at auction a few years ago. Rebuilding the engine had been one of his favorite pastimes, though he'd been neglecting it since my mom had gotten sick. It was nice to see his interest piqued again.

"I added headers for better exhaust flow," my dad was saying, "and swapped in a hotter cam to speed up the gas intake."

"And exhaust expulsion," added Alec. When Dad looked impressed, Alec shrugged. "The camshaft profile. Some early plane engines used similar principles."

Now I was impressed. I knew Alec managed some of Force's business, but I wasn't aware he knew much about the mechanics behind it. He was just full of surprises.

"Male bonding?" I asked.

They both stood up at the sound of my voice. Alec reached for a beer that apparently they'd already opened, and my dad grabbed the grocery bag off his workbench. He brought it over to me with a twinkle in his eye.

"You know cheese typically has to stay refrigerated, right?" I said.

He kissed me on the temple, then threw one arm over my shoulder. "Anna knows a thing or two about cars as well. Helped me restore a '69 Mustang."

He squeezed me a little tighter against his side. We both knew that project—the first project we'd done together as father and daughter—was more about rebuilding something that was broken than it was about cars. Either way, he was so proud I couldn't help but puff my chest out.

"I can't claim to know much about cars," said Alec. "Just engines."

Like Green Fusion engines. His words spurred the memory of the blueprints I'd seen in his now-missing briefcase. He must have been thinking the same thing because the carefree expression on his face turned serious, and he hid it in a long pull of his beer. Again I wondered what had happened at his meeting in New York.

"Dinner will be ready in a few," I said. "I just need to grate the mozzarella."

"I'll do it," Dad offered. "And you can sit at the counter and tell me all about this stalker you must have forgotten to mention the last time you called."

I wilted, giving Alec a look of betrayal. "You told him. Thanks for that."

He didn't look particularly sorry. "Your dad has some contacts in Tampa PD that might come in use."

Just then Alec's phone buzzed, and he removed it from his pocket, quickly scanned through the text message, and placed it back inside. I tried to read his expression to see what that was about, but he seemed to be deliberately avoiding my gaze.

"Turns out Alec and I are on the same page when it comes to your safety." My father grabbed his beer off a stool and frowned at it. "I guess I should be happy about that."

With that he headed inside, and I followed, wondering what else Alec had thought to mention in my absence.

Dinner went better than expected, considering I had two security-trained, overprotective men reviewing the details of my safety. I learned that Alec had received two calls from his associate in Tampa, and both had led nowhere. Randall had spent the night at a woman's house in the suburbs, and Melvin Herman was on vacation in the Keys—or at least that's what the secretary at his accounting firm had said. There had been no movement around my apartment, which had apparently been equipped with a security system in my absence. I didn't like that Alec had done that without consulting me first, but with my father on his side, the chances of winning an argument about it were slim to none.

I put a halt to the conversation when they started talking about installing a tracer in my phone.

We laughed about my dad's adventures on the retired-cop bowling team over seconds of homemade lasagna. After, while Dad was taking the dishes in to the kitchen, I felt Alec's gaze and became aware of the heat rising in my cheeks. Now that we were alone, I hoped he wasn't going to ask me about the whole I-love-you debacle again.

"You've been holding out on me," he said. "I didn't know you could cook."

I couldn't help but grin. "My mom taught me how."

"She must have been very good."

"She was." I took a deep breath. "I'm glad you stayed. I know this probably isn't what you're used to." I motioned around the small dining room. The walls were lined with pictures—most of me, many of my mother—and the old oak cabinet on the far wall held her grandmother's china.

"Why do you say that?" he asked, reaching for my hand. He watched where our fingers wove together, and I sighed softly as his thumb made a half-moon arc around the base of my wrist.

I lifted my gaze, lost for a moment in the curve of his lips, and his wavy brown hair, and that thin scar over the bridge of his nose. He'd discarded the suit jacket, and his dress shirt was unbuttoned at the collar, giving just a hint of the swell of muscles at the base of his neck. I had the sudden urge to lick him there. Nip him with my teeth. He liked it when I got a little rough with him.

"Private jets," I said, clearing my throat. "Fancy hotels. Drivers.

I wasn't apologizing—I love this life . . ." And there I went with the
L word again. It wasn't lost on him, his brows arched and his
thumb stilled on the heel of my hand. "I don't want you to think
I'm after your money or something," I finished lamely.

His mouth gaped open, and then he threw his head back and
laughed. It was too bad I didn't have any more ice water left to
drown myself in.

"If you're after my money, you're going to be disappointed,"
he said. "How much do you think I make?"

I bit my thumbnail. "I don't know. Six figures at least."

"Wrong," he said. "It's all smoke and mirrors, baby. Max is
the one with the money. I just get the perks."

I thought of his bay-front apartment in the high-rise Maxim
owned. Those were some nice perks.

"Damn," I said. "I went after the wrong guy."

Beneath the table, his hand closed around my knee and
squeezed. He knew it was one of my ticklish spots; I nearly
jumped out of my seat. I tried to push him away, but his hand
rose higher, fingers spanning over the inside of my thigh. My
breath caught. Behind me, I could still hear my dad whistling
while he washed the dishes.

"What if I'm the wrong guy?" he asked quietly. There was a
difference in him now, a change in the energy between us. It
made my head ring with warning bells just as it made my body
ache for his touch.

"What if I'm the bad guy?" His fingers reached higher, still
only mid-thigh but close enough to my center to trigger a memory
of more, a promise for later. My eyelids grew heavy, and I found
it hard to concentrate on the worry thickening in my lungs.

"You're not the bad guy," I said.

"How do you know?" He was whispering now, using the
same voice he used when he came over me, slid inside me, told
me how beautiful I was.

I clung to his gaze, to the desire I saw burning in his deep blue eyes.

"Because you brought me home," I said. "Because you moved my car and bought me breakfast. Because you want to keep me safe, and you eat take-out pizza and drink cheap beer, and you're funny, and you're scared of flying, but you do it anyway because someone important to you asked you to." I swallowed. "Because of the way you touch me and the things you say when we're together."

It came out like a confession, and maybe I was mesmerized by his strong, steady stare, but I wasn't embarrassed or ashamed. I was relieved. For once I was an open book, and he was free to see me for all of my insecurities, strengths, and faults.

He leaned back in his seat, releasing my hand.

"You give me too much credit," he said.

There was a heaviness hovering just above my shoulders, threatening to drop down and flatten me. Did this mean he didn't care for me as deeply as I did him? Or was he scared, as I was?

"You shouldn't love me, Anna."

"What did you think was going to happen?" I murmured, feeling the weight now, pound by pound, pressing me into the worn carpet beneath my socked feet.

And yet he had the nerve to look as though *I* was the one breaking *his* heart.

The water in the kitchen shut off. My dad appeared a moment later, carrying a square box in one hand and a stack of paper plates in the other.

"Who wants apple pie?"

Twenty-three

That night I stared at the ceiling, counting the glow-in-the-dark stars Amy and I had painstakingly placed in the shape of actual constellations across the plaster when we were fifteen. A few were missing now, leaving irritating gaps in an otherwise complete image.

There were pieces of Alec I didn't know, crucial pieces, things I wouldn't have minded taking time to learn but that he was deliberately holding back. He was the master of changing the subject, throwing up a brick wall, deflecting, deflecting, deflecting until you were so twisted around you didn't remember what you'd asked in the first place.

Dammit. He was me, only ten times better.

So what was he hiding?

Fed up, I rolled off the inch of my bed I'd managed to steal from the giant beast of a dog and froze, waiting until Mug sighed and continued his efforts to soak my pillow in his sleep drool. When he was still, I tiptoed to the door and gently eased it back. The door to my dad's room down the hall was wide open. No surprise there. It wasn't enough that he'd relegated Alec to the couch; he had to keep watch on me as well. Luckily, soft, consistent snores were coming from the dark room, so I snuck by, avoiding the creaks in the floorboards, just as I'd done when I was sixteen.

My eyes were already adjusted to the dark, and as I stepped through the dining room into the living room I was surprised to see Alec sitting up on the couch. The blanket was still neatly folded next to him, the pillow atop it.

For one fearful moment I thought he might have planned on leaving, but it was two in the morning, and besides that, he'd changed into a white undershirt and boxer shorts. He held a framed picture in his hand—one of the many on the end table—and when he heard me, his chin shot up and his gaze locked on mine.

"I push people away because my birth mother was a junkie and a prostitute," I said quietly. "What's your excuse?"

He placed the picture back on the table. It was one of Amy and me at my high school graduation. I'd had terrible layers in my hair then, and she was wearing black lipstick, but we were smiling like we'd just won a lifetime supply of cupcakes.

"What?" He gave me a puzzled look, and then sat straight up. "Wait. Your dad made it very clear that if I touched you, he'd deprive me of some of my favorite parts."

"So don't touch me," I challenged.

He grimaced. "It's been over a day since I had you naked, Anna. You're underestimating my will power."

Deflection.

"Why do you think you're the bad guy?"

I moved closer. His thumb began to tap on his thigh.

"We should leave. Get a hotel. We'll be back before dawn, I promise."

Deflection.

"Why won't you let me in?"

My knees prodded his open. He glanced away, eyes glinting in reflection of a streetlight outside.

"I'm having very vivid memories of this morning's plane ride."

I kneeled before him, hands on his thighs. Though he was the one looking down on me, I was in control.

"That doesn't help," he added, voice deeper.

"I keep people at a comfortable distance, that's what Amy says anyway. And if they get too close, I run." I wrapped my hands around his calves, flexing beneath my grip. "You're like me, Alec, you just don't run."

It was a bold move and I knew it. If someone had cornered me before I was ready, before I trusted them with my deepest secrets, I would have hit the road in five seconds flat. But Alec had become a statue. It was as if my words had locked him in place.

His hand ran down his throat, like the words were caught there. After a moment he slid down to the floor, so that we were face-to-face. Something was eating him up—his features tightened, then twisted, as if he were in pain.

"Some things are hard to talk about," I said. "I get that . . ."

"The truth," he said in a quiet voice. "That's my excuse."

His thumb grazed my lower lip, his eyes focusing there. The darkness settled around us, wrapping us in a cocoon far from my father and my childhood home.

"What truth?" I asked.

My knees made a hushing sound against the carpet as I scooted closer between his legs. His pride was growing thin; I could feel the vulnerability just beneath it. Gently, he tugged at the hem of my tank top.

He finally looked up at my eyes.

"That I'm not good enough for you," he murmured. "Not by a long shot."

A lump was growing in my throat. My brain said to push deeper, but my body wanted nothing more than to soothe him, take away his hurt.

"Why?" I asked. "How could you even say that?"

His lips were a breath away. It was like he wanted to kiss me but couldn't, so I moved closer, crawling into his lap where I could straddle his hips. Too many clothes were between us, separating his chest from my heavy breasts, his hot, hard cock from its place inside me. It frightened me how acute our need was, and how powerless I was against it. Even now, with our fear just beneath the surface, I couldn't help but press closer.

"I've done bad things," he said.

"What kinds of things?"

He shook his head, hair falling forward over his eyes. "I've hurt people."

"Who?"

"A better man would walk away."

My insides were twisting, pulling everything too tight. And yet, despite our words, our bodies connected on a different level. It was as if they were having a conversation of their own. His hips lifted, mine pressed back. His breath grew rough, mine shallow. I rotated my pelvis, just to feel his erection grind against my soft parts, and he hissed in response.

"You promised you wouldn't leave," I said, reminding him of what he'd told me in his apartment before New York. "Not unless I told you to go."

His arms wrapped around my waist, fingers spreading over my back. My hands threaded through his hair, pushing to the back of his skull and drawing his face to mine. He turned before giving me the kiss I craved, and ran the tip of his nose from the soft, sensitive skin below my ear down my neck. I rose up on my knees as his forehead came to rest on my heart.

"You will soon enough," he said, so softly I could barely hear him.

My cheek nuzzled against his silky hair. "Please."

I didn't know which voice spoke louder, my mouth or my body, but his grip hardened on my hips and he crushed me back down against him so that nothing but some damp fabric existed between us. He held me against his chest, and I gasped at the strength in his arms and the relief in my tender breasts. He could feel my heart beat, I was sure of it. I knew I could feel his.

Still, he didn't kiss me. His lips skimmed up the cords of my neck, and my arms and knees gripped him tightly.

"I'll tell you everything soon," he said in my hair. "I promise. Just give me a few more days."

"Alec."

"I need you, Anna. Just a few more days."

He was asking for my trust, and though it scared me to think about learning the truth after the weight he'd put on it, I had to agree. Because I trusted him. Because I loved him.

"Okay," I said.

Our bodies took over again, feeling each other, teasing each other. Showing that trust was there between us, we just needed to speak it. Our breath quickened, our movements became more rushed, and when his hips began their slow rhythm, I moaned softly. Even with our clothes on, I was losing my mind.

He clamped a hand over my mouth, muffling my sound of pleasure.

"Fuck me," he muttered. "You need to go."

I blinked.

"Go," he said again, pushing me back. He winced as he adjusted his erection. "Go before I can't stop."

"Who said anything about stopping?"

"Your dad's right down the hall."

I bit my lip to hide the giggle. Oh yeah. Dad.

"So we'll be quiet. I can be quiet."

He swore again. "No, you can't. And even if you could, I wouldn't want you to be."

He lifted me off his lap and then returned to the couch, bending over his knees and vigorously scratching his nails over his skull.

I stood, both shocked and endeared by him. And more than a

little frustrated. My arms crossed over my chest, hiding my painfully hard nipples.

"You really are scared of him, aren't you?"

"I respect him," he grunted. "Now go."

His cell phone buzzed, and we both looked over to the end table, where the white screen lit a straight beam to the ceiling. He snatched it quickly, reading the incoming text.

"Everything okay?"

"My balls feel like they might actually explode, so no." He pointed down the hall. "Go."

I turned, making sure he watched me walk away, but my insides were churning. What was Alec Flynn hiding?

My dad made breakfast in the morning. Pancakes and eggs he'd bought when he'd gone to the store with Alec. While he cooked, I sat on a stool next to the counter, spinning right, then left, then right again.

Alec was in the backyard, pacing beside the covered barbeque. The deck was covered with a thin sheet of frost that had yet to melt away, but he seemed not to have noticed the cold yet. I bit my lower lip, still thinking about what he'd meant last night—that he'd done bad things, hurt people. I didn't know why he was making me wait before telling me what was going on, but I couldn't believe he'd done something so terrible that I wouldn't want to be with him.

"I miss you, Anna," Dad said, grinning as my knees clunked against the cabinets. I spun the other way. *Clunk*. "I was thinking about taking a trip down to see you soon. Maybe this weekend."

I snorted. "And this would have nothing to do with what Alec told you about the possible, though highly unlikely, stalker situation?"

"Of course not," he said. "It has everything to do with my tan."

"Or lack thereof." My father's skin was naturally pale, and five minutes in the sun practically gave him third-degree burns.

"Exactly," he said. "I haven't seen where you live yet. And I haven't seen Amy in years."

I smiled at this. He'd like Paisley. If anyone could make her talk, he could. He was good with troubled kids.

"And if you happen to pay a visit to your friend in the Tampa PD and ask him to poke around my business?"

"Then that would be a totally normal part of any cop vacation," he finished. He tapped the spatula against the frying pan, following my gaze out the window to Alec. He rolled his shoulders back, as if to release some tension.

"How well do you know Alec, sweetheart?"

My shoulders tightened. "Dad . . ."

"I had my buddy run him through the system last night . . ."

"Dad!"

He pointed the spatula at me, comically serious in my mom's red apron. "It's my job to look out for you, Anna."

I huffed. "It's your job to teach me to look out for myself. Which you've done."

"There are a lot of dangerous men out there. I just wanted to make sure he wasn't a known felon."

"And?" I glared at him.

My father sighed, then wiped his nose, smearing dry pancake mix across his cheek. "He's got a record."

I tried not to let my surprise show.

"Mostly juvenile stuff," he continued. "But it's fairly serious. Assault. Possession. Trafficking. He was arrested a dozen times before he was fifteen."

Cold, sharp claws unfurled inside of me. I'd avoided people who did drugs since my birth mother had left me for the last time. I could usually pick up when someone was using; if Alec was an addict, I'd know.

"And after fifteen?" I asked.

"A couple arrests over the years, but all charges dropped. That kind of pattern usually indicates a lot of money and a sleazy lawyer."

Money like Maxim Stein could provide. A lawyer like the one Alec just supposedly visited in New York.

I focused on braiding my hair over my shoulder.

He took a long, slow breath. "One of the people who dropped the charges was a woman, Anna."

I paused. Forced my fingers to continue braiding. Alec would never hit a woman. It wasn't possible.

I've hurt people.

He returned to the pancakes, and I was reminded of Ben Rossi, the detective. The calm, cool-tempered man who never jumped to conclusions without a thorough investigation.

"I know money puts a target on your back. That's the only reason why I haven't kicked his ass out of my house," he said. "That, and the fear that you might go with him."

My heart clenched. He wasn't going to make me choose.

"He told me everything," I lied. "I trust him."

My dad nodded slowly. "Just be careful. He cares about you, but that doesn't necessarily make him a good guy."

What if I'm the bad guy?

I shook my head. "You saying you don't like him?"

My dad sighed, then clicked off the stove. "I'm withholding judgment."

"Oh?" I faked a smile.

"This whole you-in-love thing is new to me. Go easy."

I rose and crossed the kitchen to him. He folded me under his arm and I hugged him. It hadn't always been easy to do this, but it was now.

"Dad?"

"Yeah, sweetheart?"

"Would you do it again? If you knew Mom was going to get sick. If you knew how it was going to be in the end." *When she*

cried all the time, and then was so stoned on pain meds that she
couldn't even remember who you were.

He hugged me closer.

"I'd do it a hundred times over," he said. "And then if I got another chance, I'd do it again. The things that are the hardest are usually the things most worth doing."

Super-helpful Jennifer the flight attendant claimed that her safety belt in the pilot's cabin was broken, so she spent the flight back to Tampa sitting in the front of our cabin. Which meant Alec managed his anxiety with alcohol, and I didn't feel comfortable enough to bring up what my dad had told me.

I reminded myself that Alec had said he would tell me everything soon enough, but now I was dreading it. He was a good man, loyal and kind. Not the type to hit a woman, and not the type to avoid responsibility if he'd been at fault. Whatever charges had been brought against him as an adult had been dropped, that was what I needed to focus on.

That didn't make me feel a whole lot better.

Unfortunately, he was called in to work as soon as we arrived home. He tried to convince me to stay at his place, but I objected. I needed to go back to my apartment and face the music. Before he left, he showed me how to use the security system installed while we were gone, which he claimed my landlord didn't have a problem with, as long as he had access to the code. Alec checked my place himself. When he was satisfied, he kissed me quickly and departed.

Nothing was out of place. All my stuff was right where it should have been. I'd overreacted before. The chocolates were one thing, but thinking someone had broken into my apartment had just been paranoia. With that settled, my mind turned back to Alec, but thinking about his police record and whatever had happened in New York just made me crazy.

I cleaned a little, got my schedule in order for the next few days, checked in with my dad, and called Amy. She told me that Randall had canceled his appointment with her and that she didn't expect him to reschedule. I was sorry she'd lost a client on my behalf, but she didn't seem too worried.

I was glad to be going back to work tomorrow.

Late in the afternoon, my phone rang.

"Hey," I answered.

"Everything all right?" Alec asked, undoubtedly hearing the tension in my voice.

"Everything's fine." *Except for the assault and drug record you keep neglecting to mention.* "You?"

He hesitated. "Do you need me to come over?"

I inhaled. Exhaled. This was Alec, the same man I'd known yesterday and the day before. "No, I'm fine, really. Just bored. I don't sit still well."

Another hesitation. "I've got to work tonight."

My stomach sank. As concerned as I was, I was still disappointed not to see him.

"Just come over when you're done."

He sighed. "It'll be late."

"I don't care."

I could feel his smile. "Keep the bed warm for me."

The warmth that flooded through me didn't make the doubt disappear.

"I will."

Twenty-four

I woke up alone.

Alec hadn't come, nor had he called, and he didn't text until ten o'clock the next morning when I was on my way to Rave.

Still held up, he wrote. Sorry about last night.

No problem, I texted back. Called my backup lover to come satisfy me.

I grinned at my own wit, but the truth was, I was itching for release. Alec had turned something on inside me that couldn't be shut off. I craved his touch, and now two days without it seemed almost unbearable.

"The first step is admitting you have a problem," I mumbled to myself.

I had a problem. I just didn't know how big a problem yet.

My cell buzzed with an incoming message.

Careful.

I felt the frown pull at my lips. He was joking. Teasing me. He was probably smirking that sexy smirk of his. But doubt had rooted itself deep in my gut, and I couldn't shake the feeling that

I'd gotten in too deep, too fast, and the intensity I'd become addicted to was somehow dangerous.

I slipped my phone into my purse without responding.

Work was a welcome diversion, and the scents of the oils and the soft music relaxed me some. Amy and I had sushi down the street for lunch, but though she was my best friend, I held back from telling her what was going on. I needed to hear the truth from Alec before I made any decisions, and I didn't want to say anything I'd have to take back later.

Alec didn't come that night, either, and by the time I went to bed I was pissed.

How could he possibly think it was okay to hide his past from me when I'd spilled my guts in his arms? Did he think I was just one of his flings who wouldn't ask questions? Who didn't care? It was infuriating. And his vague texts that he was still busy and worse, that he *missed* me, just did more to fuel the fire.

The next day I finished at five. I walked home, my way lit by the bright lights of the bars and restaurants, and picked up Chinese take-out before heading up the stairs to my apartment. I had home visits the next day and had big exciting plans to oil and clean my table before then.

The anger, the fear, the disappointment over Alec's behavior made my heels stick to each step as I kicked off my shoes and collapsed on the couch. I hadn't taken him for a coward, and yet I couldn't help but feel that this was his good-bye. Who knew, maybe meeting my dad had freaked him out. Maybe it was my saying I loved him. Either way, he hadn't texted since the previous night.

The knock on the door came just after seven p.m.

I was wearing a T-shirt and pajama shorts, and my hands smelled like cleaning products. I rose from the floor, where I'd been wiping down the undercarriage of the massage table, and pattered to the door. Before I opened it, I hesitated, one hand on the knob.

I had to get these damn butterflies under control. They were in complete defiance of common sense.

But when I opened the door and saw Alec standing there with his hands in his pockets, my heart throbbed. My skin tingled. The weight I'd been carrying around disappeared. He was here.

He'd come back.

And he looked awful. He was in the same clothes I'd last seen him in; the pants and the shirt were wrinkled. His face was un-shaven, and there were bruised rings under his eyes from lack of sleep. Voices from the past whispered to me, conjured by the record my dad had looked up. I found myself looking at Alec's hands and arms for injection sites or track marks, at his skin for that high flush or signs of scratching. He looked okay, but that didn't mean he couldn't hide it. He was hiding quite a bit after all.

He stood on my welcome mat, staring at me in a way that made me feel as if I'd just pulled him from a sinking ship. That look shredded me, so I reached for his hand and pulled him inside.

"Don't take this the wrong way," I said. "But you look like hell."

He chuckled, but there was no happiness in the sound. "Long hours. Not a lot of sleep."

"*Any* sleep?"

He rubbed his chin. "I can't remember."

"Alec." I forced myself to look in his eyes. "Have you been using anything?"

He stopped, chin pulled in indignantly. "What? Why would you say that?"

There was no need for me to explain; I'd already told him about my mother.

"No," he said. "I used to, but it's been a long time."

Okay, at least he wasn't going to lie about his past when asked directly.

"Sit down. Let me get you something to eat." I led him to the couch.

"I'm not hungry."

He sat, and spread his knees so that he could pull me between his legs. I couldn't sit. I had to do something. Get him food, a drink, something.

"What do you need?" I asked, covering his hands on my hips.

"You," he said quietly.

He looked up at me, and I saw that same staggering vulnerability in his eyes that I'd seen late in the night at my father's house. I melted into him, sitting across his lap. He buried his face in my hair, and held me close, and as the seconds passed, I could feel his breathing slow.

I wanted to ask him what had happened, but I couldn't rush him. Something told me to proceed with caution. His shoulders stayed tense, and as I ran my fingers down his neck, the muscles jumped beneath them. He was wound so tight, he was about to snap.

"Alec, I want you to do something for me." I sat back and ran my thumb down his temple. His eye twitched at the pressure; he clearly had a headache.

"Hm?"

"Take a shower."

His mouth quirked. "That bad, huh?"

He complied. I had to turn on the water myself, and he nearly dragged me under the spray completely clothed when I made it clear I would not be joining him, but he did it.

By the time he emerged, towel wrapped around his waist and body still shiny with a thin layer of moisture, I was ready. The massage table was covered with fresh sheets, the candles were lit. I even had the sandalwood oil ready.

He stopped short, surveying the scene as if unsure what to make of it. He didn't look particularly excited, and that brought a new wave of nervousness crashing over me.

"Anna . . ." He raked a hand through his wet hair.

"Lie facedown," I said, stretching my hands. "Please," I added, when he didn't move.

Slowly, he made his way to the table. "You don't have to . . ."

The look on his face stung me; he was clearly uncomfortable, but more than that, he looked as though he didn't want to put me out.

"You've done this all day," he said, confirming my suspicions. "You're probably tired."

"I'm not tired." I'd never felt more awake.

My fingers skimmed down his pecs, tracing his perfect abs. He shuddered beneath my touch, lips parting. I placed a kiss on his shoulder, smiling as the goose bumps rose on his skin. Then the center of his chest, where the short wiry hairs tickled my lips. My body was already warming, readying for him, but it would have to wait. Right now, I needed him to relax.

My pointer fingers slid beneath the towel and pulled it free. It fell to the floor, leaving him gloriously naked before me. I glanced down at the dark, engorged head of his penis, already stretched to capacity, and swallowed. My fingertips slid over his perfect buttocks, feeling them flex beneath my grasp.

"Anna." He stepped closer, his hard length pressing against my stomach. His face tilted down, but I only allowed our lips to touch for the briefest moment. If I let it go too far, I'd lose my focus, and I really, really wanted to do this.

His gaze darted to the table, then back to me. He rubbed the line that had creased between his brows.

He was clearly out of his element.

"Have you ever had a massage, Alec?"

His silence was enough of an answer. For some reason, this surprised me.

"I don't know what's going on with you," I said quietly. "But I want to help. This is the only way I know how." Our bodies connected on a different level, beyond words, beyond the sizzling sexual attraction. Maybe this was a place where we could find trust.

"You can't help me," he said.

I siphoned in a determined breath.

"Let me try."

I pulled back the sheet so he could lie down, face in the head-rest. He tentatively sat, then turned on his belly. I covered him with a sheet, regretting that it hid his perfect ass from my view, and hoped that this worked. That this gesture calmed him and showed him I was here, unafraid of the demons that haunted him.

Before starting, I flattened my hands over the sheet on the strong planes of his shoulders, then down lower, on either side of his back. Slowly I moved to the tense, flat muscles of his latissi-mus dorsi, then the base of his spine, and finally to his buttocks, transferring my warmth and energy into his body.

"Is this how it starts for everyone?" His muffled voice came from beneath the headrest.

"You get special privileges." I smirked. "Or maybe I get spe-cial privileges." I spanked him lightly and was relieved to see the chuckle roll through him.

Before getting to work, I rubbed the sandalwood oil over both hands and held it under the headrest.

"Breathe in deeply," I said.

He did. And then I went to work.

I started with his upper back, moving one strong arm, then the other so that I could reach the deep-set muscles beneath his shoulder blades. Though the oil made his skin slick, the muscles beneath were hard and nearly unforgiving. The tension rose in knots. He was a mess; clearly someone who feigned calm while the stress racked his body. It broke my heart to feel how much he locked away.

I took my time, working diligently, tirelessly. When he sighed, I felt some of my own anxiety strip away. And as I worked my way down his back, he readjusted his position and sighed again.

"Feel all right?" I whispered.

"Yes," was all he said.

It didn't matter if I'd done this a million times, knowing it was Alec beneath my fingers did something to me. I poured every bit of care into each touch, kneading away his pain, replacing it with a soothing pleasure. He was so beautiful in those quiet moments. All hard steel, bending at my will. With the candlelight flickering over him, and the heady scent of spice thick in the air, the rush of my own blood became more insistent. My body yearned for more. To slide over his slick skin. To feel his slippery hands wick away as they tried to grip my hips.

I kissed his shoulder blade, letting a little of my hair tickle his back. He stilled, but then relaxed as I moved lower. I kissed him again just below his ribs, where a particularly hard knot had been. Then again on his side, when he flinched as my fingers feathered over him.

I rubbed his strong biceps and triceps, enjoying the thrill that it took both hands to wrap around the girth of his upper arms. I closed my eyes as the groan slipped from him, feeling the sound rumble straight through my core. As I worked, his wrist turned, and his fingertips found the outside of my thigh. They pushed my shorts up, skimming the surface of my skin. Just that small touch was enough to make me tremble.

My mouth was growing dry, my sex beginning to pulse. I needed to focus on what I was doing, but it was becoming more difficult every second I slid my hands down his oiled skin.

I told myself it was just because I was working so hard that I was getting hot. That that was why I slipped silently out of my shirt and shorts.

And bra and panties.

I kept one hand moving over him the entire time. He didn't notice until I rounded the other side and my hardened nipple grazed the back of his arm as I leaned over him.

I couldn't hide my gasp.

It was a foolish move; the second he felt my breast, his body went rigid, and all the muscles I'd worked so hard to loosen clamped down. Since it was too late to turn back, I stretched over his length, pulling my thumbs hard enough down either side of his spine to leave red marks. I felt the muscles give way one fiber at a time, and closed my eyes, relishing in the feel of my aching breasts against his warm, slick back.

"Enough," he ground out, pushing up.

His legs swung off the table, and he pushed to a stand, body moving with a predatory grace that made me feel like a wide-eyed doe. The sheet slipped off the table, exposing his hardness and every lean, powerful inch of him. His hair, still damp, fell in pieces across his cheekbones, and his eyes burned with a need so urgent it stole my breath.

"What do you want, Anna?" There was an edge to his voice that had my arms hugging my chest to cover my bare breasts. It wasn't fear he conjured, but submission. Moments ago I'd had him beneath my hands, but now there was no mistaking who was in charge.

He took a step closer and lifted my chin with the back of one knuckle so that I was forced to meet his gaze. The heat radiated off of him, and I knew his touch, whenever it came, would scald me. His head lowered, but his lips stayed a breath away. My chest had begun to rise and fall with each breath.

"This wasn't meant to be a trade," I said quickly. "I didn't expect something in return."

He flinched.

"What do you want?" It was a raspy whisper this time, a plea. He needed an answer as much as I needed his touch.

"You," I told him, just as I'd told him the first time his fingers had been inside of me. "I want you."

Twenty-five

Alec closed his eyes. The quake started in my heels, rising up my body. The tension between us was sizzling, and I yearned for it to finally break. His hands moved over my shoulders, down my arms, but never touched my skin. It was like being trapped behind glass.

His eyes opened. "What do you want me to do?"

"Touch me."

"Where?"

I wet my lips, then pressed my index finger against them.

The kiss came with bruising force. His lips found mine, parted. His tongue pushed past my teeth, thrusting into my mouth and tangling with my own. My knees turned to water, my hands gripped his shoulders for support. Something profound was happening; it was as if his soul had entered my body. I could feel him inside my chest, burning me, consuming me. And when I recognized it, I gave back every ounce of passion so he could feel the same.

His mouth lowered then, burning a trail down my neck to the base, where his tongue scraped the soft, sensitive skin. At some time while he'd been kissing me senseless, his arms had slipped around my waist and were holding most of my weight.

"Where?" he demanded.

My eyelids fluttered open. I reached for one of his hands, sliding it up my side to my breast. The oil made the path slippery, and his burning hands ignited it, creating flames to lick my skin.

He bent his knees, and to gain leverage he pushed me back, hoisting me up just in time to soften my fall to the couch. The air fled from my lungs as I hit the soft cushions. He hovered over me, pinning my legs closed against the padded armrest as his mouth found my right breast.

His tongue swirled over the sensitive bud, and as he sucked it into his mouth, a hoarse shout tore from my lips. His thumb worked the other hard peak, flicking it gently, then circling the areola. He knew exactly how to touch me, every move that drove me crazy. He'd taken the time to learn all of me, and I was at his mercy. My knees struggled to bend so I could open myself to his weight, but his free hand lowered and held my pelvis still.

My fingers laced through his hair, holding his head to me one second, then trying to push him away the next as the pleasure became too intense. Sparks shot across the floor of my pelvis, coming faster and faster as he worshipped my other breast.

"Alec." I reached for something to anchor me and found his shoulders, but the oil made him too slippery to hold. "*Alec.*"

The explosion came with shocking force, causing my legs to scissor in order to create some friction to relieve my pulsing sex. The pressure there was sharp, demanding. It hit me again, and again, pummeling my body with heat. My sounds seemed to make him wild, and his hands dove beneath my arching back, pulling me deeper into his mouth. I didn't know if the first orgasm ended before the second began; all I knew was that the sensations suddenly doubled in strength, and I stretched straight and tight, crying his name.

And he had yet to be inside of me.

Finally I succeeded in dragging his head up, but he didn't kiss me. Still, the hunger in his face was clearer than ever.

"Where?" he demanded. And when I could only pant, one hand slipped behind my neck and forced my gaze to his. "Where do you want me to touch you?"

"Everywhere," I gasped. "Everywhere."

His hands raced down my belly, spreading the oil over my hips, beneath my buttocks. And then he was spreading my legs, lifting me, plunging his fingers into my vagina with a force my body demanded of him. I was already wet; my inner thighs were slick from what he'd done to me. Urgently he stroked, rubbing my inner walls. My cleft was swollen and needy, and my small muscles clenched, pulling him deeper.

"Feel me," he rasped. "I need you to feel me." The look in his eyes was that of desperation.

His fingers twisted, and the wave hit me by surprise. There was no chance for breath. It wrapped me in hot velvet, turning me to liquid in his hands. While I was still spinning, his mouth found my swollen clit, and began a slow, tortuous lapping, scraping his teeth against it every few moments to heighten the sensation.

I was gasping for oxygen, fumbling for his hair to push him away, but my fingers had gone numb. My knees attempted to close, lock him out, but he held me wide open with his elbows and feasted. His tongue was everywhere. His fingers everywhere. Touching me. Fucking me. Teasing me to the point of insanity. I lost myself, became a riot of colors and heat, a never-ending pulse of pleasure. When I thought I could take no more, he tilted my pelvis up and pressed my knees open wide. The cool air on my wet skin brought a chill, which he dissipated with long, lapping strokes that circled my center.

His tongue prodded inside of me, but it was too shallow. Not enough. If he was going to push me to the line, I wanted us to cross it together.

"You." My voice was small, the words difficult to find. "I need you."

"Not yet," he said.

"Now," I begged. "Now. I need you, Alec."

He lowered my hips, and wiped my juices off his lips with the back of his hand. He was primal now, hedonistic, and I drank in the sight of him. Bronzed body, slick with oil and perspiration. Heaving chest. Thick, defined arms. Cock jutting out, heavy and veined and so huge it sent a shiver of panic through me.

I'd taken him before, and I would again now.

The speculative look on his face caught me off guard. But before I could think clearly enough to make sense of it, he crawled over me, pulling me lengthwise on the couch beneath him.

I felt him at my opening, prodding gently through the soaked lips, letting my still spasming muscles adjust to his broad girth. My heels hooked around his calves. My hands reached for him, but he stopped me, and pinned them against the pillow over my head.

I knew something was wrong. A cold feeling seeped into my lungs, spreading silently, reaching for my racing heart. But I couldn't concentrate on it, because he was still entering me. That delicious contact I'd craved was happening at last. Inch by inch he claimed me, until my insides compressed to accommodate him, and the spark of pain blended with the searing pleasure. I could feel his pelvis against mine, his balls brushing against my ass.

I exhaled. *Finally.*

With his jaw flush against my cheek, his face was hidden from me. I could feel the sweat on his brow, feel the tips of his wet hair tickle my ear. His mouth pressed to my neck, to the scrambling pulse that beat within.

"Anna," he breathed. The broken way he said it brought a pang to my heart, and again I felt that coldness inside my chest.

I hated that he was constricting my hands. I needed to hold

him. *He* needed me to hold him. An awareness filtered through my trembling body: I'd wanted the truth, and this was it. His body was trying to tell me what his mouth couldn't.

I was a masseuse; it was my job to listen to people's bodies.

I closed my eyes and focused on the clenching of his thighs between mine, on his flexing biceps and his ragged breaths. On his hard body as he rotated his hips to rub the deepest part of me. On his heart, as it hammered through his ribs against my breast.

He rolled his pelvis, then again, allowing no friction but increasing the pressure all the same. Another roll and I was coming, losing my focus on him for timeless moments as I crested the peak.

"I can feel you," he said into my hair. "Your hungry little cunt gripping my dick."

His words made me cry for more, and soon he was sliding in and out, angling at just the right place to keep me soaring. His strokes quickened, grew harder.

"Come again, baby," he demanded. But I twisted my head into the pillow, and I was unable to tell him that it hadn't stopped. It kept going and going, even as the sweat soaked my hair and ran in rivulets between my breasts. I was dying.

And just as I thought he would join me, he stopped.

Arms shaking, he released my wrists at last and rose, pressing his forehead to mine just for a moment before rising on his knees, and pulling my hips around his. We never broke contact as he began hammering into me from above. His eyes fixed on my breasts, which I held in place against my chest.

Again the pressure increased.

And again he stopped.

He turned me over, and though I tried to help, I was so weak I could barely hold my weight on my forearms as he took me from behind. He couldn't come, or he wasn't letting himself. I didn't understand; he'd never done this before. Tears streamed down my nose as he reached around and massaged my aching clit.

When I groaned, he went faster, driving every sound he could from me. He was close, now. I could feel his fingers tighten around my hips. His strokes lost their rhythm.

I sobbed his name, needing him to come with me.

But he pulled back again.

"Stop," I said.

He froze.

"Alec, stop," I said again.

As if I'd struck him, he jerked back, leaving me empty. I was so sensitive, I gave a stunted cry, but before I could turn around, he'd sat me up, and was kneeling on the floor below me.

My hands were in his, and the look on his face was that of horror.

"Are you okay?" He brushed the hair out of my face. "Anna? Baby, did I hurt you?"

I was crying. He had hurt me, but not in the way he was thinking. Physically I was fine—exhausted, satiated, maybe a little sore, but fine. But the cold inside had taken over and was spreading down my limbs.

He had fucked me. Like I'd asked him to. But unlike every other time he'd been inside of me, we'd been out of sync. He hadn't felt that same connection I'd felt. He'd never been so far away.

"Anna? God, I'm sorry. I'm so sorry." His thumbs traced my cheeks to wipe away the tears. "I fucked up. What can I do? What do you need?"

"You!" I shouted, the rage taking hold of me.

His hands dropped, and he fell back so he was seated on the floor.

"I don't . . ."

"You're such an idiot!" I yelled, the moisture in my eyes blinding me now.

"Yes," he agreed.

"Shut up!"

"Okay."

I hunched over, elbows on my knees, the heels of my hands pressing against my eyes to stop the tears. When I had myself back under control, I looked up again, only to find him staring at me worriedly.

"Where are you?" I asked. "Because you're not here with me."

His mouth opened, but no sound came out. One hand dragged down his jaw, the other fisted on his knee.

"I thought . . ." I shook my head. "I thought you felt it."

He looked as though I was cutting his heart out.

"Felt what, Anna?"

I hugged myself, wishing I had a blanket. "*Me.* I thought you felt me." I forced myself to breathe. "I don't just want your body, or your fancy apartment, or your body."

His mouth quirked, though his eyes stayed sad. "You said that already."

"I thought you needed me as much as I need you. But you don't."

I recognized the cold then. It had morphed into something more intimate, but its origin was the same. My own mother hadn't needed me, and Alec didn't either.

"How can you say that?" Anger hardened his features. He touched me then, hands cupping my calves. I glanced down and saw that he was still rock hard. It looked like it must have been painful.

"You just tried to orgasm me to death," I said, exasperated. "But you didn't feel anything."

"You have no idea what I feel."

"Because you don't tell me! You're a complete fucking mess, and you won't share any of it with me. You told me I don't trust you, but you're the one who doesn't trust—"

Before I could finish, he'd jerked me down to the floor. I steadied myself on his shoulders, while his mouth frantically sought mine. He pulled me into his lap, hands on my face, then in my hair. His arms circled my back and smashed me to his chest. My knees slid open, and hit against the floor as our hips came together. Between us, his hard cock was pressed, still slick from being inside of me.

"You think I don't need you?" he growled, lifting me and then sliding into me. I cried out as my nerves went haywire.

"You're everything, Anna." His lips crushed mine. "Everything." His hips began to move and I helped, lost by the sudden passion pouring off him. "I can't breathe without you." His movements became more insistent, and I held his face in my hands while he stared into my eyes.

"Your body is fucking paradise." He lifted me. Lowered me. Not enough to ride his full length, only enough so that we stayed deeply joined. "When I'm inside you, nothing else matters."

His thighs were solid beneath me. My breasts stayed pressed against his flexed chest. He was chasing the cold away, one word at a time. One stroke at a time. And finally, finally, I was full.

"I would die for you," he said through gritted teeth.

He moved faster, and I held him close, even as his gaze flicked to the side.

"Stay with me," I murmured, forcing him to look at me. His eyes were breathtaking, infinitely deep.

"I don't want it to end," he confessed. I realized in the back of my mind that this was what he'd been doing before. Prolonging what we had. Making it last as long as possible.

"Stay with me," I begged.

Beads of sweat rolled down his temples. I felt it again, the melding of his soul with mine, that undeniable connection. Only now I knew he felt it, too.

"Anna."

"Alec. *Alec*." I held him against me, feeling the tension swell, and swell, until it became hard to breathe.

"Anna," his forehead fell against my shoulder. "I love you." His thrusts turned hard. His abdominals clenched. "I love you."

The separation between us was severed; there was no he and I, only us. I no longer felt where he ended and I began.

He loved me.

He *loved* me.

I broke with a sob as my body finally gave its last, and he followed, filling me with all his could offer.

When he was finished, he lifted me gently and carried me to the couch. He kissed my brow tenderly, then my lips. I couldn't keep my eyes open.

I heard his feet on the hardwood floor as he made his way to the bathroom, but I was drifting in and out of consciousness. When I opened my eyes, he was standing close, fully clothed. That same twisted expression was back on his face, and at the sight of it, I was filled with dread.

"I'm sorry," he whispered. And with that, he left.

He walked right out the door.

I scrambled up, cracking my knees on the floor when they gave way. Adrenaline shot through me, giving me strength. No. He couldn't leave. Not after that. He loved me.

I snagged my robe and stumbled toward the door, but already I could hear the car engine turning over in the street below. I ran for the window, looking down as Alec's Jeep pulled away. My hands banged on the glass. I didn't understand what had happened, what I'd done.

The dark street was filled with patrons, making their way to the restaurants and bars, but Alec did not return.

Over the ringing in my ears, I heard the buzz of a cell phone. I turned numbly, finding it on the kitchen counter. It was his; he must have left it when he'd taken off. I lifted it, and pressed the button to light the screen.

Sender: Charlotte

Need to see u right now. Can't wait any longer.

There were two previous messages that had come earlier.

Where r u? Said you would b here.

Not going to wait all night.

I threw the phone across the room, watching as it hit the wall and shattered pieces of glass and plastic across the floor.

Twenty-six

For a long time I sat on the couch. It was still damp from our lovemaking and smelled like oil. After a while I couldn't stand it, so I moved to the bed. We'd lain together there too, though, and the soft bedspread and rumpled sheets did nothing but remind me of the last time he'd spent the night. I couldn't even shower because it made me think of him.

Alec loved me.

Alec had been missing for two days.

Alec was on his way to another woman.

He had a record—drugs, which he claimed not to have used in a long time, and assault, one count against a woman who had dropped the charges. I didn't know that person. He wasn't my Alec.

But then again, apparently Alec wasn't even my Alec.

I stripped the sheets off the massage table and put them in the hamper. Gaining speed, I cleaned up the oils, put away my materials, and blew out the candles. I turned on the lights and sprayed air freshener to kill the sandalwood scent still heavy in the air. I put on sweatpants and a T-shirt—nothing I'd ever worn around him. I swept up the pieces of his cell phone and dumped them in the trash.

Alec loved me.

Alec was a liar.

The constant voices in my head would not shut up, so I turned on the small TV in the corner. I didn't have cable and only got four channels. One was a Mexican soap opera, but kissing was the last thing I wanted to see, so I flipped to the news.

As we had made love, Alec said he didn't want it to end. He'd already known he was leaving. He'd come to say good-bye. That's why he'd looked like hell. That's why he'd objected to me giving him a massage. He didn't want my kindness, because he was there to end our relationship.

He had already chosen Charlotte over me.

I was the biggest idiot in the world. The proof had been right there—phone calls in the middle of the night, unexplainable disappearances, Derrick had even seen them together—and still I'd believed Alec.

I glanced at the clock. It was just past midnight. Alec had been gone hours already. Was he back in Charlotte's bed yet? Was he fucking her, the way I'd seen Maxim Stein fuck her?

Sick bastards, passing around women like they were possessions.

I wanted to throw up. I found a sweatshirt, but even that didn't stave off the cold. I grabbed my phone and opened the Internet. So Florida had a chill, but Southern California didn't. Maybe it was time for a trip to the West Coast. I'd never been to L.A. Maybe I could be a masseuse for movie stars.

". . . breaking news coming across my desk . . ."

I glanced up, distracted by the pretty Asian reporter with a graduated bob.

"A fatal car crash has blocked both lanes of traffic on the Sunshine Skyway between Terra Ceia and St. Petersburg. At approximately ten thirty p.m., the driver of a red sports car lost control of the vehicle, knocked down the median, and drove off the bridge into the water. Rescue crews on site have recovered the body of Charlotte MacAfee."

The picture of a woman with orange hair and flawless white skin appeared in the corner of the screen. The photo was clearly professional, and she was smiling and wearing a charcoal suit jacket.

"Holy shit," I said.

"Police are still trying to identify if there was anyone else in the vehicle, investigating a broken passenger-side window, but at the present time, no other bodies have been recovered. The late Ms. MacAfee was the president of Green Fusion, an alternative-energy company on the verge of declaring bankruptcy, according to the *Times*. The cause of the crash is not yet known. In other news, cat fever is hitting the Tampa Bay area tomorrow . . ."

Charlotte MacAfee—Maxim Stein's mistress, Alec's girl-friend, the *president of Green Fusion*—was dead. And another person may have been in the car.

My brain was sprinting a mile a minute. Alec had left around nine. Charlotte was in the crash around ten thirty. That was enough time for them to have been together.

I hurriedly dialed his number and swore when it went to voice mail. Of course, he wouldn't answer. He couldn't. I'd smashed the hell out of his phone.

The phone that may have had Charlotte's last communication with him.

Pacing, I scrolled through other numbers. My pulse was thumping in my eardrums. It felt as if there were ropes tighten-ing around my chest. Finally, I came to Ms. Rowe's number, from when she'd called last to schedule Maxim's massage, and pressed Send.

Only Ms. Rowe didn't answer.

"Force Enterprises," came a creepy male voice.

"Bobby?" I said. "Bobby, it's Anna. The masseuse."

"Okay," he said after a moment.

"I saw the news about Charlotte . . . I know this is probably crazy . . ." I pulled my hair back out of my face and forced myself to take a breath. "Do you know where Alec is?"

A pause.

"What about Charlotte?"

"Nothing," I said. "I mean, I just heard that she died on the Skyway."

"You did," he said slowly.

"*Alec,*" I said. "He might have been with her. I need to find him."

I closed my eyes, imagining what Charlotte must have seen in her last moments. The dark drive, the lights from the bridge. The crash as she hit the cement median and then swerved off the bridge. Had Alec been with her? Was he still alive?

"He has a cell phone."

Dammit.

"I know. I know he does, only he left it with me, and I was thinking that maybe you knew another way to reach him."

"Why would he leave it with you?"

My jaw clenched. Bobby probably thought Alec and Charlotte were together. There would be no reason for him to leave his phone with me.

"It doesn't matter," I said quickly. "I just need to talk to him. Is he there?"

Please. Please let him be there.

"Hello?" My voice broke.

The line went dead.

Bobby had hung up on me.

"Goddammit!" I nearly threw my phone, too, but thought better of it. With shaking hands I found the non-emergency police number.

"My name is Anna Rossi," I said when a woman answered. "I'm looking for information on the Sunshine Skyway accident. There was a woman who drove her car . . ."

"Are you family, ma'am?"

"No, but my friend may have been—"

"Did you witness the accident?"

"No . . ."

"All information will be available to the public as we receive it. At the present time we have nothing new to report."

I punched my thigh in frustration. "Listen, I know you're very busy . . ."

"Ma'am, if you're not family of the deceased, there's nothing I can do."

"You can tell me if they found a man in the car with her!" I shouted.

She was quiet. "Ma'am, I'm going to ask you to lower your voice."

"You're a huge fucking help, thanks." I hung up, and dialed my father, hoping his connection in the Tampa police department might have some friends working the accident, but after four rings, my call went to voice mail.

"Where are you?" I demanded as his greeting played.

Bowling. I dug my thumb into my temple. It was bowling night. Did he always stay out so late when he was out with the guys? Rattling off a message that I needed to talk ASAP, I slipped on my sandals and grabbed my keys. I couldn't sit by and do nothing. Bobby was clearly awake, and if anyone had the clout to find Alec, it was Maxim Stein.

At the front door I paused, forcing myself to take one second to think. If I showed up frantic in the middle of the night looking for my non-boyfriend, I was going to lose my position there. Hell, I might not even get through the gate.

Alec had chosen Charlotte over me. If he had been in the crash, he had been with his girlfriend. I was nothing to him.

But I loved him, and betrayed as I felt, imagining him dead hit me like a punch straight through the chest.

I turned on the security system—the precaution Alec had

insisted on—and ran down the stairs and through the parking
garage to my car. The drive took far too long, and I prayed that
there was no law enforcement to pull me over as I drove thirty
miles over the speed limit.

How had Charlotte lost control of the car? The news had said
her company, Green Fusion, was bankrupt. Had she tried to kill
herself? Taken Alec with her?

No. I couldn't think that way. I would get to Maxim's house,
and they'd tell me Alec was alive and well and I had nothing to
worry about.

And then I could hate him for breaking my heart.

My tires squealed as I tore through the ritzy neighborhood
like a drag racer. When I reached the front gate of Maxim's estate, I slammed on the brakes.

The gate was open. It was never open.

I rolled inside, nerves raw. The property was still, though well
lit by the security lights that bathed the circle around the fountain in an eerie yellow hue. I didn't go all the way to my usual
spot; it was too dark in that direction to tell if any other cars
were there. Instead I parked behind the black SUV directly in
front of the main entry. My eyes were drawn to a long scrape
down the side panel. Apparently someone had had a hard time
parking.

I climbed the steps on weak legs, doused by a sudden terror.
I'd hoped Maxim would help me get information about Alec, but
what if he already had the information? He might already know
that Alec was dead.

"Please be alive." I knocked on the door.

No one answered. I moved to the window and looked inside,
but the interior of the house was dark. There was a high likeli-
hood that Maxim wasn't even here—he could have been anywhere in the world.

Voices drifted toward me on the breeze. I recognized Bobby's,
though I couldn't tell what he was saying. Making the split-second

decision to take my chances getting arrested, tazed, or, worse, shot by Maxim's security, I crept around the far end of the house, keeping my steps as quiet as possible.

The manicured grass gave way to the stone path that led to the guesthouse, the same place I'd found myself trapped my first time here. I snuck toward the lights that glowed in the window, listening for news I wasn't sure I wanted to hear, much like before. The irony of the situation was certainly not lost on me.

I reached the wraparound deck and plodded along the floorboards, telling myself I should stand and walk to the office door. Knock, like a normal person. Instead I found myself crouched below the same window, scarcely breathing so that I could hear what was being said.

"It's not my fault she drives like a bat out of hell. It was an accident—don't look so fucking glum. Now we don't have to keep watching our backs." I recognized Bobby's voice.

"A woman's dead," came Maxim Stein's low rumble. "A woman I had relations with. You don't think someone will look into this?"

Bobby stammered. "There's no chance of a kickback. I swear. Not on the redhead's end anyway."

"What's that supposed to mean?"

"There may be a problem on Alec's side."

"What kind of problem?"

Maxim's demand was met with a period of silence, then a third voice entered the conversation.

"I don't know what he's talking about."

Alec.

Alec was alive.

Alec was here.

I sobbed, and then silenced it in my shirt sleeve. I should have left; I had the information I'd come here for. But I couldn't bring myself to stand. I'd been so afraid he was dead, I just needed to hear his voice one more time.

"She called here, asshole," said Bobby. "Your assignment. The *masseuse*."

My ears perked up.

"When did she call?" asked Maxim. "What was said?"

"She said she knew about Charlotte and needed to talk to Alec," said Bobby. "It was about an hour after I got back."

"What did you tell her, Alec?" Maxim demanded.

"Nothing," said Alec. "She doesn't know anything."

"You took her to New York," insisted Bobby.

"How was I supposed to keep eyes on her if I was out of the state?" Alec shot back.

My spine zipped straight.

"Why would she call here?" asked Maxim.

"She said he left his cell at her place." Bobby cleared his throat. "Maybe if he wasn't so busy fucking her, he might have paid more attention."

Something smashed against the interior wall of the office directly behind me, hard enough to send reverberations through the window above my head. Surprised, I jumped, and straightened one leg out on the deck. It had to be visible from the window above if someone was looking. As fast as I could, I pulled it back to my body.

"Knock it off!" shouted Maxim.

"Fuck!" Bobby's voice was muffled now.

"She doesn't know anything," Alec said again. His tone was cold as ice.

An overwhelming need to run kicked through my body. I crawled across the deck in the direction I'd come, and when I was clear of the office lights, I ran down the path, hard breaths louder than my footsteps. The sinister shadows of the foliage reached toward me. The uneven stones threw me off balance. Before I reached the driveway, I fumbled with my keys and dropped them. It was so dark I had to get on my hands and knees to feel across the ground.

"Shit," I hissed.

Hurry, hurry, hurry chanted through my brain.

Finally, my fingers closed around metal. I rose. My car was ten feet away, clear of the looming shadow of the main house.

A second later someone grabbed me from behind, and a hand clamped over my mouth to stifle my scream.

Twenty-seven

"I'm going to let go, but you have to be quiet. Nod if you understand."

I nodded, recognizing Alec's voice, but not comforted by it like I had been in the past. He released me slowly, and as soon as his hands had loosened, I swung back hard with my elbow and cracked him in the side of his head. He staggered right, and though I should have run, I spun to face him and slapped him as hard as I could.

"Fuck me," he muttered. "You got me the first time."

"Just wanted to make sure you understood," I spat.

He stooped to pick up my keys off the ground where I'd dropped them again, and thrust them into my hand. Fear skittered through me as he straightened to his full height, forcing me to look up at him. There was cold fury in his face, hardening his features, making his throat jump with his pulse. His hair was a mess—the oil he had yet to wash out from the massage had made it greasy, and he shoved it behind his ears.

And still, despite everything, I was relieved he was alive.

"What are you doing here?" he demanded.

"Oh, you know," I said, my voice shaking. "A little breaking and entering, a little sneaking around. It's what I do for fun when the insomnia kicks in."

"This isn't a joke," he said. "I saw you on the video feed. You need to get out of here. Now."

"No problem."

He glanced behind him. "Go home. I'll come by later."

"Why don't you go to hell instead?"

I had turned, but he grabbed my arm. "What did you hear?"

"Get your hands off of me," I said between my teeth. "You don't get to touch me. Not ever again, all right?"

He let go, eyes flaring with panic. "Anna . . ."

"Enough," I snapped, continuing on to my car. "I heard enough, okay? So why don't you go back in and put your feet up because this *assignment* is over." If I didn't get out of there fast, I was going to break down.

"You don't understand," he said quickly. "I can explain."

"But you won't," I said. "Because you never do."

I opened the car door but stopped before getting in.

"I know about the woman you assaulted," I said, staring down at the seat. "And I know about the drugs. I didn't believe it, but now I'm not so sure."

"Anna . . ."

"You're not the only one who can do a background check," I added. Technically my dad had done it, but he didn't need to know that.

I lifted my chin. One last time I faced him, feeling as though my ribs were snapping, one by one.

"I thought you were dead," I whispered. "I knew you had left me for her, and when I saw what had happened on the news . . ."

I covered my mouth with my hand to stop myself from saying any more. He was already wavering in my vision, his beautiful, tortured expression swimming in my tears.

I got in the car and drove away, leaving him standing in the driveway the same way I'd left him in the street the first time I'd met him.

It was almost two in the morning by the time I got home. I ripped my suitcase out of the closet and began haphazardly stuffing my clothes into it. The apartment had been fully furnished when I came in, but I had accented it with knickknacks I'd picked up here and there. I gathered those things together now; a few pictures off the wall, the small wire table where I left my keys. A set of bowls in the kitchen that had been my mom's. I took out my cosmetic case and threw all my makeup into it. The blow-dryer and shampoo were tossed into the sink—I'd find somewhere to put them soon.

It was time to move on; I'd stayed too long. With my smartphone, I'd be able to find a place to stay while I was driving. Southern California sounded nice.

Amy.

The thought of leaving my best friend—my only friend, really—hit me hard enough to slow me down. I glanced at the clock in the kitchen. It was still nighttime, not even four a.m.

I sent her a text.

Awake?

Three minutes later I got a response.

U ok?

I held my breath, pushing down the tension in my throat.

No.

Come over. Door will be open.

I left everything where it was and drove to Amy's.

She had the coffee on when I got there. It warmed my body and settled my stomach, but did nothing to patch the hole in my chest. I told her as much as I could before it became too hard to speak, and when I cried, she cried with me.

I'd fallen for a man who not only had another girlfriend, but was only dating me because his boss had told him to. It didn't get much more twisted. I'd been played fifty ways from Sunday, and I'd been too lovesick to see it.

Sometimes I wondered if there was something really wrong with me. Maybe the damage my birth mother had done was irreversible.

Just after dawn, I called in sick to Rave and crashed in Amy's bed. My sleep was plagued by nightmares; I was stuck in a glass box while Alec watched from the outside. No matter how hard I beat my fists against the glass, I could not break free.

I woke to Amy's raised voice at the front door.

"I told you, I'm calling the cops if you don't leave. She's not here."

I sat bolt upright, rubbing my throbbing head. The shades were still drawn in Amy's room, but there was no light sifting through. I glanced at the clock. It was almost nine p.m. I'd slept all day.

"I know she's here. Her car is here." Alec's voice was like a vise, squeezing my lungs. He sounded hoarse, exhausted.

"So you're a detective now?" snapped Amy. I couldn't see her, but I could imagine her jutting her chin out, the way she did when she was really pissed. "How's this for a clue?"

I closed my eyes, fairly certain she was flipping him off.

"Believe me," he said flatly. "You can't hate me more than I do right now."

Amy sighed. "Look, I don't know what to tell you . . ."

"Tell her I'll wait," he said. "I'll wait as long as it takes. I have to talk to her before she leaves town."

I scooted to the edge of the bed. He must have been in my apartment—he had the security code—and seen that I'd started packing.

I may have forgotten to mention that part to Amy.

"Go," said Amy after a moment. "If she wants to see you, she knows how to reach you. If she doesn't, do the right thing and leave her alone. She's survived losing people before. She'll do it again."

The door closed with a click.

Amy appeared in the bedroom a few moments later. She sat beside me silently and stared straight forward.

"Your dad called again. I told him you have the flu and I'm taking care of you."

"Thanks," I croaked, throat dry.

She nodded. "Alec looks like shit."

I picked at my thumbnails.

"So do you," she added.

I looked away.

"Was that true?" she asked. "Are you leaving town?"

A tear rolled down my cheek, and I hastily wiped it away. I'd cried enough in the past two days to last a lifetime.

"I can't stay here anymore," I said.

She looked at me. "You can. You just don't want to."

"Amy . . ."

She stood up. "Where will you go when you've been to every city in the U.S., Anna? Canada? Where then? Greenland? Assholes are everywhere, but people that love you, really love you, aren't."

Amy could sure twist the knife when she wanted to.

She took a deep breath. "Don't make the same mistakes your mom made."

I put my head in my hands, feeling about a zillion times worse than I had two minutes ago. I didn't want to make my mother's mistakes, I didn't want to leave Amy and Paisley, but I couldn't stay waiting for someone else to hurt me. I had to get back in front, keep ahead of the pain. That was how I survived.

"Okay," I said. "I'll stay for a while, but I'm not making any promises."

Though I couldn't see her, I could feel her victorious smirk.

"Now get your ass in the shower. I bought new flavors of pity-party ice cream."

The next day I went back to Rave. I parked at my place and walked, grateful for a couple minutes without Amy looking at me like I might spontaneously combust. I skipped my apartment, still not ready to face the reminders of Alec or my own half-packed belongings, which ended up being fine since Amy had played human Barbie doll with me before I'd left. She'd loaned me one of her black sheath dresses and a pair of open-toe pumps, and experimented with a darker, more sultry color palate. Unfortunately, the dress was her size—three smaller than mine—so it clung to my curves like it was made of latex, not satin.

Good thing I mostly worked in low lighting.

When I arrived, I cut straight through the salon to the spa area, hoping to sneak by unnoticed. Though no one besides Amy, and maybe Derrick, knew that Alec and I had been together, it felt painfully obvious that I'd recently been chewed up and spit out.

Somehow, I got through my morning without breaking down. I focused on each massage like I had in the weeks after I'd gotten out of school—naming each muscle to myself, diligently attending to each zone I worked through. I stripped the sheets, started laundry, and began again. Each hour that passed, it became easier. Nobody noticed that my smiling face was only a mask.

Just after two, I went on break. I wasn't hungry—I hadn't had anything but a few bites of ice cream since yesterday—but thought I'd walk to Javaz and get some coffee.

I had just reached into my cubby to get my purse when the door shut behind me. I turned, expecting to find one of my coworkers, but instead came face-to-face with one of my previous clients.

"Anna."

"Melvin," I said, my shock twisting to wariness. "What are you doing here? You can't be back here."

I looked behind him, to where he was blocking the door. Urgently I scanned the rest of the room. The wall behind me was lined with lockers and cubbies, the opposite side of the room had been converted into a kitchenette with a refrigerator, sink, and microwave on the counter. A black square table sat in the middle of the room, surrounded by three folding chairs.

He'd taken some care with his appearance; his face was clean-shaven, and he was even wearing a tweed suit. It had to have been terribly hot, and lines of sweat ran down the sides of his face. Or maybe that was just the anxiety of stepping foot on a property that he'd clearly been barred from reentering.

"I'm so glad you're here," he said. "I've been waiting since this morning to see you."

My ears began to ring. I should have taken Derrick's advice and taken out a restraining order. Another stupid trust-Alec move.

"Here?" I asked. Surely someone would have noticed him hiding in our break room.

"Outside, in the back. You asked me to leave that way once."

"I remember," I said.

He smiled broadly and pushed his round glasses up his nose. "From the window on the back door, you can see people come in and out of the break room. Since your boss sent me that letter saying I can't go through the front . . ." He laughed. "This probably sounds a little weird."

"You're right."

He took a step closer. "It's so good to see you."

I stepped back, hitting the lockers. "I'm afraid I can't say the same."

With a deep sigh, he shoved his hands in his pockets. "You're mad about what happened last time. I understand. I was too forward. I should have asked you out to dinner first."

Slowly, I reached into my purse for my keys. Without making any sudden moves, I wrapped my fingers around the pepper spray.

"Melvin, you need to leave."

"You got the chocolates I sent to your apartment, right? Did you like them? The man at the candy shop picked them out when I described the kinds of things you like."

Okay. This was bad.

"You don't know me, Melvin," I said slowly. "And you shouldn't have gone to my apartment without my permission."

His cheeks turned red. He looked down, and I could see his throat bobbing as he worked to swallow. "Why would you say that?"

"You broke into my place," I said. "You moved some of my things."

"Why would you say that?" he demanded again, making me jump. His gaze shot up, and the anger in it brought a slow drip of fear down my spine. I needed to get around him to the door, but he was still blocking the way. Slowly, I inched behind the table, placing a blockade between us.

"I didn't break in. I respect you, Anna."

"You're right," I said, realizing I needed to play into his delusion if I was going to get out of there anytime soon. "I shouldn't have accused you."

"You were being stupid." He stood straight upright and moved toward me, scratching the side of his head vigorously. "I'm sorry, that was cruel. I don't mean to be cruel. I love you. Let's just forget about this little fight."

"Love?" I asked, unable to keep the shock out of my voice.

In a burst of speed, he grabbed the back of one of the chairs, lifted it, and then slammed it down on the floor. It didn't break, just made a loud noise. Straight as a board, I dropped my purse and pulled out my pepper spray, holding it out before me. Melvin didn't seem to notice. He was busy fitting the back of the chair under the doorknob so the door couldn't be opened.

Somewhere down the hall I heard a door open, then slam shut. Then another. Someone was coming. I *hoped* someone was coming.

I looked at him, seeing longing so evident in his every feature. He did believe he loved me. Pity slashed through the fear. He needed help.

"Melvin, open the door," I said, voice softer. "I was stupid earlier. Let's just go have lunch and we can forget about it."

"You think I can forget about it?" he asked. "It's as if you don't want us to be together. I just have to show you, then you'll see."

He took off his jacket.

"Take it easy, Melvin." A jolt of strength ripped through me. My back was to the wall. There was no way out but through him.

When he reached for me, I pressed down to release the pepper spray into his face. He covered his eyes, howling like a dying animal. Quickly, I skirted around the table, but he blocked my path, eyes bright red and streaming tears. Blindly, he swung, hitting me in the shoulder and taking me to my knees. Keys still in my hand, I jabbed them down above his knee, and he cried out in pain as the fabric of his pants ripped.

The door thudded, the chair beneath it holding steady.

"Anna!" came a voice from the hallway.

Alec. He was close, just outside the door. Other people were there, too. I could hear them shouting.

"Help!" I screamed as Melvin's long body folded over mine. My dress ripped around the thigh then straight up the bodice as I scrambled to get out from underneath him.

"Hold still," Melvin was saying. "Hold still! I just want to show you!"

Remembering the self-defense courses my dad had sent me to, I focused on soft spots. First I jammed a thumb in his eye, then I hit him in the ear with my knuckle. When he rolled back, I kneed him in the groin and jolted to my feet.

The door thudded again. Again. The wood splintered as it broke open, and in my attempt to escape I ran straight into Alec's hard chest.

Twenty-eight

For one split second, I pressed my cheek against his chest, feeling safe and warm and unafraid, and then Alec shoved me behind him into Amy's outstretched arms. He was on Melvin an instant later, shoving him facedown on the floor.

"Stupid son of a bitch," he muttered, blocking my view with his broad shoulders. "Stay down," he ordered.

"Wait," Melvin was saying. "Wait, wait. This is a misunderstanding."

"Anna? You all right?" Alec asked. Amy's bright eyes were round with shock. She rubbed my trembling arms and pulled me away from the door.

"Fine." My voice cracked over the word.

"Jesus Christ, you can't have that in here!" Derrick was suddenly in the middle of the hall, arms lifted as though he wasn't sure if he should defend himself or throw a punch.

For one terrifying moment, I thought Melvin might have had a weapon I hadn't seen. He'd said he'd wanted to show me something, but I'd sprayed him with pepper spray before he could.

Frantically, I wedged between the doorway and Derrick, staring down at the whimpering man on his knees.

It was Alec who was holding the gun.

He aimed a black pistol, the same I'd seen in the briefcase in New York, between Melvin's shoulder blades. A twitch in his eye was the only evidence of his thinly veiled fury.

"Clear the area," Derrick was saying. "Amy, get these people back into the salon. I want everybody out!"

"Easy!" I shouted at Alec as he jerked Melvin's arm at an awkward angle behind his back. "He's not well. He needs help."

Alec barely glanced at me. He fitted Melvin's wrists together with a plastic zip tie.

"Call the police," he told Derrick.

"Oh, I already did," Derrick responded sharply. "Right after you tore by reception and started busting in on every private room."

"He what?" I asked.

"My pocket," Melvin said. "Please. She needs to see."

"I got a call tracing Herman's location to your work," Alec explained, hauling Melvin into the chair. "When his car was empty, I suspected he'd cornered you in a room."

"There were clients in those rooms!" Derrick roared. Over the speakers, soothing harp music played.

Alec glared at Derrick. "They'll live."

Derrick looked at me for the first time. "You're right. *Shit.*" He grimaced, then put his hands on my shoulders. "Anna, are you okay?"

My gaze darted away from his, unable to hold still. My senses seemed impossibly focused. The music seemed too loud; it grated on my raw nerves. The scent of massage oils and hot wax from the aesthetician's parlor clashed with smells of nail polish and hair product. I could see the vein throbbing in Alec's neck as his gaze lowered down my body, pausing on my waist. I didn't remember my dress was torn until his eyes narrowed.

He shrugged out of his suit jacket and tossed it to me. Gratefully, I wrapped it tightly around myself.

"My pocket!" Melvin said again.

Alec had already patted him down, but now reached into the right hip pocket, where Melvin was motioning with his chin. He removed a folded piece of paper, and as he read over the contents, he sighed.

"What is it?" I asked.

He folded it back up, and tossed it to me.

A love poem. For me. There was even a bit about my eyes.

"Shit," I muttered.

Melvin Herman relaxed in his chair, a small, relieved smile on his face.

"It's all true," he said.

The police arrived a few minutes later. They took Melvin into custody, but told us he would be taken to a psychiatric hospital for assessment prior to booking. I hoped he was going to get the help he needed.

Derrick closed Rave down for the rest of the day. After I was done giving my statement, I offered to help him cancel clients, but he told me to go home.

I sensed a certain finality in his tone.

"I'm sorry this happened," I told him.

He groaned and dug the heels of his hands into his eyes, smearing the silver-tipped eye shadow he'd been sporting today.

"What happened with Melvin Herman isn't your fault," he said, sounding exhausted. "I'm glad everyone is fine. But I can't ignore the fact that your boyfriend . . ."

"He's not my boyfriend," I said quickly.

"Even better," said Derrick, flattening one hand on the front desk. "That yet another man who *thinks* he's your boyfriend, showed up at my business, scared the hell out of half a dozen clients, and then pulled out a gun in the middle of the hallway. Anna, I adore you, you know that, but this is my life. Small businesses don't rebound well from this kind of thing."

I hugged Alec's jacket closer around my body, hating that my belly clenched at the dark masculine scent that drifted up from the collar. Even now it was impossible not to want him.

I looked for him, but he wasn't in sight. I felt his absence sharply, but he'd left as soon as the police had taken his statement and private-security-license information. What he'd been doing here at all confused me. Was his boss somehow invested in keeping me safe? Was that Alec's assignment? If so, why?

"I know," I told Derrick. "I'm sorry. What can I do?"

"You can go home," he said.

Amy had come up behind me and pulled me away before I could say more. Outside, it had begun to rain. Just a drizzle, but a roar of thunder that shook the building all the way to the foundation promised more.

"I'm driving you to my place," she said gently. "I'll come back and finish up here later after we get Paisley."

"I can walk home," I said, heading toward the entrance. "I'm fine now. Really." I held my hands out, showing her that the shakes were gone.

I paused at the door. Across the street, Alec leaned against his Jeep. Just the sight of him made my heart leap in my chest. He was like a striking, sad piece of artwork. His head was tilted forward, and his white shirt was already soaked and see-through, clinging to his sculpted shoulders. The wind picked up, bringing the rain in sheets, but he didn't move.

"It's pouring," said Amy, following my gaze with a frown. "In five minutes it will be a torrential downpour. You're not walking. Especially not in my Jimmy Choos."

"Knock-off Jimmy Choos," I said absently, watching Alec squeeze the water out of his hair the same way he was squeezing my heart, right now.

Her eyes narrowed. "You wouldn't know that if I hadn't told you." She tried to block my view of Alec. "Come on. Let's go."

"I need to talk to him," I said.

"You don't. He finished with the police. He's got no business staying here."

"He came for me," I said simply. "He thought I was in danger, and he came." I didn't understand the rest of it, but I believed that much was true.

"His boss probably paid him to," she said, and then bit her top lip when she saw me flinch.

She was probably right. I had no reason to believe he'd come of his own free will, not after what I'd overheard at Maxim's house. But I still had to know why he'd done it.

"I'll be okay," I told her. "I just need to talk to him."

After a while, she nodded and handed me a closed umbrella standing in the box by the front door, a courtesy for clients so the weather wouldn't mess up their styled hair. I took it and pushed through the open door, crossing the street with my purse hanging from my opposite hand.

When he saw me, he pushed off the car, water dripping down his face, his ears, the tips of his hair that always curled a little more when wet.

"It's raining," I said, pointing up at the sky. "I don't know if you noticed."

He gave me a small smile. "If only I had a jacket."

I shrugged out of his coat, feeling the cold air bite at the exposed skin along the ripped seams of my dress. It didn't matter to me if I was standing naked in the middle of the street. Things couldn't get much worse than they already were.

I thrust the coat in his direction, out from under the shelter of the umbrella, but he didn't take it. As the water saturated the expensive fabric, it grew heavier, weighing my arm down.

"Take it," I said. "You waited long enough to get it back."

"I was waiting for you," he said. God, he looked tragic. Like

a boxer making one last stand in the ring. It pulled at my soul,
seeing him such a mess. As much as I wanted to hate him, it hurt
to see him like this.

Another blast of rain hit us, threatening to flip the umbrella
inside out. I gave up and closed it, and within seconds I was
soaked straight to the bone. His shirt pressed flat against his
chest, revealing a white undershirt underneath. His pants stuck
to the strong, lean muscles of his thighs. My gaze lingered there,
unable to tear away. The rain had somehow made him a hundred
times sexier.

"Well, you saw me," I said before I melted in a hot, steamy
puddle. "Thank you for coming. I'm sure it was probably part of
your job or something . . ."

"Anna." The broken way he said my name made me want to
curl into his arms and punch him in the face all at the same time.

"Why?" I demanded. "Why are you here? Why did Bobby
call me an assignment? Why did you say you have to keep an eye
on me? Why did you say you loved me, and why the holy fuck
did you choose Charlotte?"

I swallowed a deep breath, still fuming. Saying the words out
loud had made the actions behind them that much more painful.
He stared at me while the rain pelted him, a hundred emotions
playing across his face.

"I didn't choose Charlotte," he said. "I chose you."

His phone rang—a new phone apparently, since I'd broken
the last one. Even through the rain I could hear it. He pressed a
button to send the call to voice mail.

"But you left me for her. I saw the messages on your phone."
Guilt took a bite out of my rage. He'd cared for her, and now she
was gone.

"Will you come with me?"

I hesitated.

"An hour," he said. "Just an hour."

"Will you talk to me?"

He nodded. "Yes."

His phone rang again. He silenced it.

I glanced down the street in the direction of my apartment. I knew what waited for me there—half-packed bags and an option to leave town with my tail between my legs. But here, right in front of me, was the possibility for truth. It scared me to death.

He held open the car door, and as I moved past him I could feel the heat from his body through the rain. It seemed to sizzle between us as he took the umbrella so I could slip inside.

When he was in the driver's seat he reached into the back and grabbed a T-shirt to wipe off his face. It only helped a little. The water still dripped from his hair and off his shirtsleeves. I began to shiver and hugged my chest as he turned on the heat and pointed the vents in my direction.

The windows fogged. It wasn't exactly the way I'd imagined steaming things up before, but things had changed. When he was finally able to see, he drove away from Rave.

His jaw was flexing, as if he were chewing on the words.

"I'm sorry about Charlotte," I said to break the silence.

"Yeah, me too."

Tap, tap, tap. His thumb kept tapping against the wheel. The sound was torturous, like a never-ending supply of water dripping on the center of my forehead.

"Stop that," I said. "You're making me nervous."

He froze. Readjusted his position in the seat.

"Sorry," he said without looking over. "It's hard not . . ." He motioned my direction.

"What?"

"Touching you," he said finally. "It's hard not to touch you."

I swallowed. It was hard to keep my hands off him as well.

"I never hit that woman," he said bluntly, his scowl etching deeper. "I would never hit a woman."

Hearing him say so made me feel minutely better.

"But you would sell drugs."

"That was a long time ago."

His phone rang again.

"The man can't make a sandwich without letting you know," I said, miffed at the constant interruptions. Not that we were really talking anyway, but still.

"It's not Max," said Alec, annoyed.

I realized what was happening a moment later. It wasn't his boss. It was another woman. He didn't want to answer it in front of me.

"Wow," I said. "Amy was right. This was a bad idea."

"It's not what you think."

"Just take me back to the salon. I can walk home."

"You said an hour."

I sank back in the seat, exhausted.

As if making a last-minute decision, he suddenly veered across the lanes and took a right out of the historical district. Through the splashes of water thrown by his windshield wipers, I made out a group of men huddled on the corner under a bus stop awning. Behind them was a stone building with the windows boarded up. As we continued on, the neighborhoods became progressively worse. Graffiti and barred windows. People glaring at us from their front stoops as we drove by. Not exactly the kind of place I wanted to find myself alone after dark.

We came to a decrepit-looking two-story apartment complex. The streets here were empty and looked like they had been for some time. He pulled up to the curb and killed the engine.

"Five minutes," he said. "Then I promise I'll explain everything."

He reached for my hand, but I pulled it away. As much as I wanted to fall into him and forget everything, I couldn't. I didn't know what was going on. I didn't even know what he was doing here.

With that, he left the car, jogging through the rain up a set of concrete stairs. I didn't see him enter the apartment, but the window facing the street suddenly brightened to reveal the silhouette of an elderly man, thin, and hunched over.

What are you doing, Alec? I said to myself.

I don't know if it was because I was worried for Alec or for the old man, or if I was just tired of all the secrets. But before I thought twice, I was out of the car, running in my torn dress and knock-off heels over the patchy grass toward the stairs. I took them one at a time, shoving my hair back. At the top of the stairs were two doors, the paint peeling off both. Light peeked from beneath the one on the left.

I stood before it, gathering my courage. From inside came a man's voice, older than Alec's, and tired.

"For Christ's sake, just make it stop."

I should have gone back to the car, but a morbid curiosity had been piqued. I had to know what kind of man Alec Flynn was.

With a shimmer of fear, I inched open the door.

Twenty-nine

The bell that rang overhead made me jump. I glanced up, cringing. It was fastened to the doorframe above the entry, triggered to sound every time the door was opened. So much for being stealthy.

A second later, a dog began to bark.

The old man yelled a command I couldn't distinguish just as a white-faced golden retriever came barreling around the corner.

"Who is it, boy?" asked the man. "Who's there?"

Well, there was no going back now.

I leaned around the corner, peering into the narrow kitchen that dead-ended at a small dining room. Right in the center of my view was Alec, shirtless and mouthwatering, standing on a chair. He was reaching overhead into a small white plastic box, showcasing every glorious section of his abs.

A mechanical chirp came from the smoke detector, then a long, piercing beep.

"Alec, who is it?"

The old man appeared between us and, apart from being thin and walking with a slight hunch, he was undeniably handsome.

His thick coffee-colored hair was highlighted with strands of white and gray, and curled down past his ears. But it was his eyes that caught me. They were light blue, nearly translucent, and he stared at some point in the distance, unfocused.

The dog immediately took his place beside him.

Alec was replacing the batteries in a blind man's smoke detector. I'd wanted to see what kind of man he was. I guess this answered that question.

"Hey," Alec said to me, concern flashing over his face. "Just one second, all right?"

"A woman?" said the man.

Alec snorted. "How can you tell?"

"Behind this handsome face is a brilliant, deductive mind." He scratched a hand over his broad, familiar cheekbones and a square jaw, covered by a layer of scruff. A flannel shirt covered a worn green tee, and he smoothed it down, standing a little taller.

"I'm sorry to barge in," I said, feeling like the world's biggest idiot. "I'll wait in the car."

"Oh my," said the man with a smirk I'd recognize anywhere. "She sounds lovely."

"Take it easy." Alec closed the box and stepped down to the floor.

"You're Alec's father," I said, slightly baffled. He'd made it sound as if he didn't know his father, that Maxim Stein had filled that role in his life.

"Thomas Flynn." Alec's father reached out his hand, and I crossed the kitchen and took it, wishing I'd thought to dry off a little before coming into the apartment. His grip was warm and steady, and took away some of my chill.

"And this is my dog," he added.

I glanced down. The golden retriever was seated politely beside his owner in a very un-Mug-like manner.

"Does he have a name?" I asked.

"Ask 'em," said Thomas. Behind him, Alec muttered something I couldn't make out.

"*Umm.*" The retriever looked up at me expectantly. "What's your name?"

The dog's tongue lolled out the side of his mouth.

Thomas threw his head back and laughed, bringing a blush to my cheeks.

"The fool named his dog Askem," explained Alec, "just for moments like this."

"It never gets old," said Thomas. He raised my hand to his lips and left a long, lingering kiss there. I shook my head, and couldn't help but smile.

"Jesus," said Alec. "She gets the point." He wedged between us in the narrow kitchen and pulled me back a step. "Dad, this is Anna."

"Anna," said Thomas with a dazzling smile. "You're very beautiful, I can tell."

"Thank you," I said. "I like a man who can appreciate a woman without any teeth."

Thomas's brows shot up.

"She's fucking with you," Alec said. "She's gorgeous." He turned away to grab a dish towel off the oven rack and handed it to me without meeting my eyes.

Thomas barked out a laugh. "I see how it is."

"You started it," I said.

"I'm making dinner," said Thomas. "We're celebrating."

"Oh," I glanced at Alec. "I can't stay."

"Nonsense," said Thomas. "It's my birthday."

I winced.

"It's not his birthday," said Alec.

"It's Alec's birthday."

"Nope," said Alec. "That's not right either."

"You're really something," I told Thomas.

"You're the first woman he's brought home," said Thomas. "So we're celebrating."

"Sure. Whatever you say," I said.

Thomas smiled. Alec inhaled, pushing his hands into his pockets. Side by side, they were clearly cut from the same mold. The same mold, apparently, as Greek gods and the male models that graced the covers of romance novels.

"Wait," I said. "Is that true?"

"We can't stay, Dad."

"I am sort of hungry," I said. It was true; I hadn't eaten anything other than last night's ice cream and was starting to feel a little light-headed. But more than that, maybe if we stayed, Thomas would let me in on a few more secrets about his son. It occurred to me that Alec may have asked me to stay in the car for this exact reason.

"You want to stay?" Alec asked, as if I were joking.

I shivered. The A/C was blasting from a vent directly overhead.

"Sure," I said. "Why not?"

"Come on." Alec pulled me out of the kitchen to a short hallway. As soon as we were around the tight corner, he released my forearm, breaking our brief contact. I rubbed my arm, feeling the traces of heat fade away.

The apartment was small, the floors clean, the walls bare. Simple, like he'd told me he was used to the first night I'd stayed in his place. From what I could tell, there was one bathroom and two bedrooms. Alec pushed through the door into a small space with a single bed against the wall and a simple oak desk in the corner. Above it was a bulletin board smattered with a few papers. I wandered in that direction while he dug through the sparse closet, and I was wondering how he could let his father stay in such a sketchy area when he lived in a bay-view high-rise.

A photograph caught my eye first. It was the same picture I'd

seen framed in Maxim Stein's office. A young Alec, with that secretive expression, and Maxim, his arm over Alec's shoulders.

Just below it was a college diploma from Florida State. It
wasn't framed, but simply tacked to the board.

Alec Flynn had a bachelor of science in engineering.

"Here." Alec was standing behind me, holding a dry T-shirt
and a pair of sweatpants. He had another shirt for himself and
pulled it over his head. I would have been lying if I said I wasn't
sad to see him cover up.

"Who are you?" I looked back at the degree.

He took a deep breath. "You're shaking. Put on some clothes
before you freeze."

I faced him, aware of how close the walls were, and how he'd
shut the door behind me. We were alone, and the tension had become a heavy, palpable thing between us. I shivered. My skin
alighted with goose bumps. My nipples were so tight, they were
painful. Every part of me was straining to move closer to him, to
share some of his warmth.

"Tell me something real," I said. "At this point, I don't even
care what it is."

He stepped back until his calves hit the bedframe, then sat on
the worn denim comforter, elbows on his knees. Fatigue weighed
him down.

"I grew up in this neighborhood," he said. "Just my dad and
I. He wasn't always blind—he has macular degeneration. It was
diagnosed early when he was in his twenties. He'd been working
in maintenance at the airfield, but when he lost his sight, he lost
his job. A hiccup in insurance and just like that, he was on the
street."

I turned away, intrigued by Alec's past, but feeling suddenly
self-conscious changing in front of him. It wasn't like he hadn't
seen me naked before, but something about right then made me
nervous. Facing the wall, I kicked off the ruined shoes and pulled
down the zipper on the back of Amy's tattered dress.

"Keep going," I prompted.

"I . . ."

I turned around and caught him blinking, then rubbing his jaw. He didn't look away as I stepped out of the dress. By now he would have seen I wasn't wearing a bra—the dress had been so formfitting I hadn't needed one. I pulled his T-shirt over my head, feeling the soft cotton brush against my nipples.

"Focus, Alec."

"Right." He cleared his throat. "One of the men my father had done work for heard what had happened and paid the deposit on an apartment, then hired a nurse to get him back on his feet. That man was Gregory Stein, Max's father."

Since my panties were soaked as well, I slipped them off as discreetly as I could and kicked them under the dress. Then I pulled on his sweatpants. They were huge, and I rolled them up at the ankles.

"Okay," I said.

"The nurse was married with three kids, and my dad, well . . . you've met him."

I smiled. "Incorrigible?"

"She ended up pregnant," he said flatly. I moved to the bed and sat beside him, far enough away that I could keep my brain working. I leaned back against the wall and hugged my knees against my chest.

"Her husband gave her an ultimatum. She left the baby—me—with my dad and moved with her real family to Miami."

Her absence bothered Alec; I remembered he'd told me he wouldn't leave the way she had.

"Have you ever met her?"

"She sent a card on my birthday each year. When I was four-teen, I caught a ride down to Miami and looked her up. She wasn't exactly thrilled. I didn't get a lot of cards after that."

"I'm sorry."

He shrugged. "Dad and I didn't get along so well when I was

growing up. He drank away his disability checks, and I figured out fast that selling drugs was a pretty effective way to supplement an income. I fell in with some guys I probably shouldn't have, and he was too drunk to notice." Alec faced me, holding my gaze. "I sold whatever they gave me, took whatever I could skim, and got picked up more than a few times. I didn't want to tell you after you told me about your mom."

I nodded, chest hurting for the boy who was forced to make ends meet. Part of me wanted to tell him it was okay, I understood, but the other part didn't want to slow his momentum. He'd told me more in the last five minutes than he had in our entire relationship.

"When I was fifteen, Dad got evicted while I was in juvie, and I didn't have enough money to get the apartment back. He'd told me about Gregory Stein, so I went to look for him, to see if he could fix things. It ended up he'd died a few years before, but his son Max had taken over the business. He told me he'd help me out on one condition: I get clean and work for him."

It was difficult to imagine the Maxim Stein I knew offering to help a boy from the wrong side of town. He must have seen something in Alec, even then.

"He showed me my first plane, a Force 170, and it blew my mind. I'd never seen anything like it." He smiled down at his open hands. "I wanted to know how it worked, what made a twenty-ton piece of metal stay up in the air." When he hesitated, I glanced at his degree. Was this why he'd majored in engineering?

"Max set me up to learn the business along with his nephew—the heir to Force. Robert Calloway. *Bobby.*" He sighed. "In exchange, Max paid me enough to get our apartment back."

Bobby was Maxim's nephew—who Alec had thought should replace him in New York when we'd gone. I hadn't gotten the impression at the time that Maxim thought too highly of his nephew. Not that I blamed him. I wouldn't trust Bobby as far as I could throw him.

"Max paid for a tutor to get me through high school. Then he paid for college. I respected him, followed his rules. No drugs, no selling. I helped Dad find a sponsor, and he got cleaned up. Things were good."

"And then?" I prompted, sensing this wasn't all.

Alec put one hand on my foot. I didn't know if he was even aware he'd done it, but he kept it there, running his thumb over my instep as if he needed the contact.

"I was nineteen the first time he sent me to collect on some debts. I didn't think anything of it until the guy pulled a gun on me. I was quick enough to get out, but Max was shocked I hadn't finished the job. I went back with Bobby, who showed me how it was done. The man filed a report in the hospital." His thumb began to tap on my foot. "I hadn't touched him, but Max asked that I fess up. He said his lawyer would get me out."

"You took the fall," I realized.

"I took the fall. It was just the beginning. There was still the legit business, but there was another side too. Competitors began backing out if Maxim entered negotiations. I didn't have to do much more than show up."

I looked at where we connected. "The woman who charged you with assault?"

"I never touched her," he said. "Bobby picked her up at some club. I found her at the house after he was done with her and took her to the ER. Next thing I know, Max's lawyer is there, and she's saying I'm the one who hit her. The charges weren't dropped until the next day."

I shook my head, remembering Bobby crowding me at the door near the house. How defensive Alec had been.

"What an asshole," I said. "You should have turned him in."

Alec huffed. "Sure. Like anyone's going to believe me over Maxim Stein's nephew."

He had a point. The Steins had money and powerful attorneys, and Alec already had a track record with the police.

"Why didn't you leave?" I asked.

His finger stroked up my big toe, sending a shimmer of heat up my leg.

"Max dug us out of a hole. I owed it to him to take a few hits."

"No," I said. "You're the one who dug you out of the hole. He used you."

Alec was scowling. "I didn't see it that way at first."

The betrayal was evident in his voice. In exchange for his loyalty, he'd been thrown under the bus.

"What happened with Charlotte?" I asked. "And why was I your assignment?"

"Anna," he said quietly, rubbing his temple with his other hand. "If Max knew I was telling you this . . ."

"Tell me," I said. "If it's about me, I have a right to know."

He took a deep breath and turned to face me, a grave expression on his face. He reached for my hands, holding both of them together within his and then pulling me forward to press them against his chest. I could feel his heart beating there, hard and heavy.

"I never meant to hurt you," he said, gaze truthful and soul deep. "If I could take any of this back I would. You're going to hate me after what I'm about to say, but I can't let you go. Not yet. It's not safe."

Thirty

I pulled back and wrapped my arms around myself, trying to stave off the shudder that had nothing to do with cold. My mouth was dry, and a persistent throb had begun at the base of my skull.

"Dinner!" called Thomas from the kitchen.

Alec glanced at the door.

"What do you mean, it's not safe?" I pressed.

"I slaved over a hot stove!" called Thomas as the microwave began to beep.

"Am I in trouble?" The dread coiled in my stomach. My head was beginning to spin.

"You look pale." Alec was shutting down, the light dimming behind his eyes.

"Wait. You can't stop there." I jolted to my feet. Too fast; the room began to spin, and I caught myself on his shoulder before falling.

In a flash he was up, supporting my weight with his hand beneath my elbows.

"Anna," he said, inspecting me closely. "When did you eat last?"

I shook my head, clearing my vision. I felt weak, but how was I supposed to eat when Alec had said I wasn't safe?

"A while ago," I answered. "Yesterday maybe."

He grit his teeth. "Eat and I'll tell you what I can."

"No!" I shouted, pushing away. I rocked back on my heels, blinking rapidly as my stomach did a slow roll.

"I'm tired of this," I said. "You'll tell me everything. If you ever cared about me at all, you'll tell me."

His mouth tightened.

"All right," he said. "After you eat."

Stubborn mule. I let him lead me back to the living room, where Thomas had put a glass pan of pulled pork on a scratched coffee table in front of his small couch. The cushions had popped a couple stitches, and when I sat I had to readjust my position to avoid some well-placed springs, but the scent of barbecue sauce was enough to make me salivate.

Thomas moved comfortably around the room as if he had perfect vision and then sat beside me, maybe a little too close. He handed me a plate, and the distance by which he overshot my reach reminded me of his blindness.

"Thank you for dinner," I said tensely. "It smells incredible."

"The sauce is a secret," he said, passing a plate to Alec, who had opened a bag of hamburger buns.

"It's such a secret even he doesn't know it," mumbled Alec.

Thomas grinned. "Caught. My sponsor believes food is a suitable replacement for booze."

With Alec watching me closely, I took the first bite. Despite the stress, my body melted into the couch. Apparently I was famished.

"Your sponsor's right," I said. "This is delicious."

"I'll let Mac know," said Thomas. It took a moment for me to place the name, but when I did, I blushed. He'd been the owner of the burger place Alec had taken me on our first date. The same place Alec and I had nearly ravaged each other in the parking lot, right in front of an audience. I remembered Mac saying he would stop by the house when we left. He must have meant this house.

It wasn't hard to eat fast, and when we were done, my body felt better, even if my brain was still racing. Alec cleaned up while Thomas walked me out to the front entryway, closing the door behind him. Askem the dog plopped down on the cement beside his calf.

"Thanks for having me," I said. "I know it was unexpected."

"I live for the unexpected." He gripped the railing, staring out into the night, and I gave in to the sudden urge to squeeze his hand. With a smile, he tucked my still cold fingers in the crook of his elbow.

"Alec's always trying to get me to move out of this place," he said. "But this is my home. It's important to have a home. Somewhere you can put down roots."

I wouldn't know.

"My son's a good man," he said. "Loyal. Sometimes *too* loyal. For him to tell you all that history, you must be very important to him."

"You were listening?" Why didn't that surprise me?

"I have impeccable hearing." He smiled. "It's not my business what he's done to wrong you, but I know this much. Alec will love one woman all his life. He's like me in that way. I wasn't sure it would happen for him, but I'm glad it has."

I wasn't sure how to respond; his statement was like an arrow in the back. I hadn't seen it coming, and it hurt like hell.

Inside, the water at the kitchen sink shut off.

"I think he's like you in a lot of ways," I said quietly. "Good ways."

Thomas pulled me close and kissed my cheek. "That's the best news I've heard all week."

* * *

"I need to show you something," Alec said when we were back in his car. I was still wearing his clothes, and I was glad for the extra warmth now that it was dark outside.

"You promised you'd tell me what Maxim meant."

"I will," he said.

Silently, he drove in the direction of my apartment. I watched him carefully, mind still reeling with the previously hidden details of his life. Things appeared to be good with his father now, but they hadn't always been. I tried to imagine the lost boy who'd been abandoned by his mother and left alone by his father, who'd turned to drugs for escape and sold them to survive. A boy who had trusted a man who'd taken advantage of him. It reminded me of my days working in child protective services, and for the first time in a long while I had the urge to go back. I was certain I could have helped the kid that Alec had been.

I wasn't sure if I could help him now.

Less than a half hour later he was parking on the street across from the Chinese restaurant below my place. The rain had lightened, but it was still misting. As soon as he shut off the car, the window clouded with a million tiny droplets.

I met him outside on the sidewalk, feeling a little ridiculous in Amy's heels and Alec's baggy clothes.

"I don't understand," I said, looking up to my dark second-floor windows.

Sorting through his keys, he led me in the direction opposite from my apartment, down a narrow dark alley between the steak house and bar across the street from my place. The path was empty, and dingy with the walls' weathered bricks and the trash that gathered at our feet. My senses became more attuned as my nerves heightened. Bass thumped from a club behind us, the scents from the restaurants mingled with the pungent smell of garbage. I kept glancing behind me to make sure no one was coming.

"Don't be afraid," he said, sensing my hesitation.

I moved closer to him, just in case.

We came to a metal door near the back of the lot, and he opened it with one of his keys. Inside was a stairwell, and I followed him up in silence, wishing for more visibility than the square, rain-stained skylight overhead could provide. At the top of the second-floor landing was another door, and through that a large open room, the same size as the restaurant floor below, spread out before us. The floor was intricately designed with Spanish tile, and wires hung from the ceiling panels where lights should have been. Despite its haphazard shape, the room looked as though it had been recently cleaned.

Floor-to-ceiling windows made up the wall facing my apartment—a straight view into my place.

"What is this?" I asked.

"It's a property Max is looking at renovating for a high-end nightclub."

"So much for keeping my windows open," I muttered.

Alec leaned back against a pillar in the center of the room, arms crossed over his chest.

"Charlotte MacAfee was the owner and president of Green Fusion. I knew her in college—she guest lectured in some of my classes. She and her brother were working in secret to build an engine powered by high-grade ethanol—corn fuel—a renewable, cleaner energy source. Her plane-engine design was the first out there; the flight industry has had a history with big oil since planes first started using jet fuel. This would have changed things. In a big way."

I faced the window, looking across the street through my open curtains. I could make out my dresser, the edge of my bed-frame. If the lights were on, you'd be able to see everything.

"Force's biggest clients are oil manufacturers. You told me that before," I said.

"Yes," he said. "Charlotte knew I worked for Max—for

Force. We'd talked a few times after I graduated, but just casually. She approached me last year to tell me her design was nearly complete, but that it had taken everything they had. She was broke and couldn't finish it."

"The news said she was on the verge of declaring bankruptcy."

He nodded. "I told her I'd talk to Max and see what he could do. She was looking for investors to fund the rest of the project and help her pay back an enormous amount of debt. He agreed to help."

"And they started sleeping together."

"They were both using each other. She needed his money, and he needed her design. He convinced her to show him the plans before she filed a patent. I guess she thought it would impress him enough that he'd agree to invest. You saw those plans on his desk the first time you were at the house."

Out of nervous habit, I began to braid my damp hair down my back.

"I wasn't supposed to see them."

"No," he said. "And neither was he. Without a patent, the work was unprotected. She didn't even have him sign a nondisclosure form—maybe she couldn't afford the lawyer, I don't know. He could have filed documents saying the design was his own, and reaped the rewards."

"But?"

"There is no *but*," he said. "That's exactly what he was planning to do. Steal the design, file it under Force's name. And then stop production."

"Stop production?" I asked. "Why not build the engine himself? He has the money. He could change the plane industry, like you said."

"And go broke in the process," Alec explained. "Our biggest clients are in oil, remember? Piss them off and there goes three-quarters of our revenue. No, Max wanted to claim the design as his own and then sit on it, making sure no one could build an engine to compete with his. That way he stays rich and our clients stay happy."

"Wow," I said. "My opinion of him is rising higher by the second."

"There were two problems," Alec continued. "One, Charlotte couldn't find out that he'd stolen the design until after he'd filed the patent under his name, and two, you'd seen the plans. If you wanted to, you could have sold those plans to a competing industry."

"Or gone to the police," I said.

"You signed a waiver when you first got there saying everything you saw in that house was confidential. If you'd gone to the cops, he would have ruined you. Taken every penny. Anything you made from now until retirement would go to your legal fees."

The power Maxim had over both our lives loomed heavily over me. I remembered that waiver well. I'd thought it was offensive at the time. I'd felt like Ms. Rowe had been questioning my professionalism—like I was going to steal a cereal bowl from the kitchen or something. I'd had no idea what was at stake.

I kicked off my heels so I could pace more effectively, and the tile floor was cold under my bare feet. "I couldn't go to the cops, but if I'd taken it to a competitor, they could do the same thing Maxim was trying to do—claim the patent as their own and make all the money. Or sit on it."

"Right," he said. "One of us had to follow Charlotte and make sure she didn't catch on or go to the cops. The other had to follow you. I made sure I was the one to follow you."

I turned back to the window, wishing I didn't feel so small.

"Why?" I asked. "You knew Charlotte. She wouldn't have suspected anything if she'd seen you hanging around. You barely knew me."

"I didn't like the way Bobby was looking at you," he said.

I softened a little, but couldn't look at him.

I tried to put myself in Alec's shoes. It couldn't have been easy convincing Max that he should follow me when he already had a previous relationship with Charlotte.

"And so you were assigned." It was impossible to hide the prickle in my voice.

He looked up at me, shadows hiding his expression. "Yes."

His shoe made a scuffing noise across the floor. "Max came to me with the design and said I had to get to one of his high-powered patent attorneys to file it as soon as possible. It had to be me, that way if anything happened, Force would be clean. Max would have plausible deniability while I'd go down for corporate espionage—but, of course, his lawyer would get me off."

"Oh God," I said, beginning to hate Maxim Stein for all he'd put Alec through. A moment later a heavy realization weighed down on my shoulders.

"You did it," I said quietly. "That's why we went to New York."

He was quiet long enough to let the full effect of his actions sink in. I closed my eyes, burying my face in my hands. He'd done something awful and was totally screwed. It didn't seem possible that even the best lawyer in the world could help him now.

"I told Charlotte," he said. "After I met with her, she showed up at Max's house ready to burn the place down."

That was the first time I'd seen her—with her clothes on at least. Ms. Rowe had shoved her off, saying Maxim was with his wife. Alec had barely acknowledged me, he'd been so intent on getting Charlotte out.

"I remember," I said.

"I had tried to get her to file the patent first, but she insisted on going to the press. Exposing Max. She knew Bobby was tailing her. He scared her, I think. Before she drove off the bridge they'd gotten in a fight outside her house. From the sounds of it, it wasn't pretty." His voice had grown thin, angry.

I was back near the window and leaned against the glass, letting it hold my weight.

"The reporter had mentioned that the passenger window had been smashed. That was why they thought there'd been another person in the car," I said quietly. "I was afraid it was you."

He pushed off the pillar and walked to the window beside me, staring at my apartment.

"I'm sorry I left the way I did. It killed me to leave."

There was such raw honesty in his voice that it was impossible not to believe him.

"I called," I said, dropping down yet another step in this slow motion tumble to the truth. "When I knew you didn't have your cell, I called Maxim's house looking for you. They thought you'd told me about the patent."

He nodded.

The pieces were falling into place one by one. "Bobby must have just gotten back from Charlotte's."

"If I'd gotten to her faster . . ." He shook his head. "We weren't supposed to meet until later that night. I was going to take her to the police. I told her not to leave her house without me. She didn't know what Bobby was capable of."

Like assaulting a woman and leaving her at his uncle's house for Alec to clean up.

"If you'd gone to the police with her . . ." I twisted the hem of my shirt. "If they'd taken Maxim into custody, he would've thrown you under the bus. You would go to jail, Alec."

He was still. Stone still. Still enough to tell me he'd already considered this.

He had been trying to make things right and would still be punished for it. I thought of the wreck he'd been when he'd shown up to my apartment. I'd been correct—he had come to say good-bye, but not because he was leaving me for Charlotte. Because he was going to jail.

Despite the bad things he'd done, he was a good man. This was clearly eating him alive.

I moved closer to him, put a hand on his arm. The muscles beneath clenched, then relaxed.

"What happened to Charlotte isn't your fault." I paused, a deeper fear clawing up my spine. "Do you think Bobby had something to do with her driving off the bridge?"

He scratched a hand over his jaw, still staring forward.

"I watched you," he said absently. "The first night after I met you, I came here and looked through this window, and saw you undressing. You'd done something to me at the house. I couldn't explain it. I'd never felt that way about anyone."

I swallowed, throat hot as he turned to me and moved closer, a dark heat in his eyes.

"It's my stalker magnet." I laughed weakly.

"Something changed that night," he continued. "The thought of Bobby laying a hand on you, or Max fucking with you . . . I couldn't let it happen. I couldn't let them near you."

He was closer, caging me against the window. He didn't touch me, but I could feel his warm breath on my lips, his chest inches from mine. A flush heated my skin. My body yearned for contact. A rhythm had begun pulsing in my sex, keeping beat with my accelerating heart. Behind me, the window was hard and cold, but in front of me was fluid fire.

"I couldn't look away," he whispered tightly. "Your back was against the window, just like this, and you began to move. Just a little. I had to watch closely to make sure I'd seen it at all."

I was trapped in place, mesmerized by the growl in his voice. I was afraid of what he'd done, afraid for him and for myself as well, but the fear only heightened my arousal.

"Your fingertips skimmed your shoulder." He showed me how, just a light brush of his thumb down my neck to my collarbone and out. My pulse beat wildly. Automatically, my head tilted to the side, exposing more flesh to his caress.

"I wanted to kiss you there," he admitted.

His lips ghosted a trail down the same path, never once touching my skin. Staying a breath away.

"Your face turned to the side, like it does when I make you come."

I was breathing hard now, and my hands were fisting in the baggy sweatpants that hung off my hips.

"Did you touch yourself and think of me?" he murmured. "It drove me crazy wondering."

I shuddered with the memory of the first time I'd wanted to be with him. Moisture dewed on my hairline. My sex clenched. Without my panties, I was acutely aware of the dampness between my thighs.

"Alec." My heart hurt, but my body still wanted him. I couldn't give in to the need without the rest of me feeling whole.

"Anna," he said roughly. "I knew then I had to have you. All of you. Not for Max, not just for one night. For good. I needed to be someone you'd want. Someone worthy."

His hand lowered over my waist, and my abdominals quivered in anticipation. Still, he didn't touch me.

I did want him. I wanted him so badly it hurt.

His face tilted, and his lips brushed gently over mine.

"Before I saw the lawyer in New York, I made copies of everything and took them to the FBI," he said. "Very soon Force will crumble, and Maxim Stein with it."

Thirty-one

"You . . ." I blinked. "You what?" I put a hand on his solid chest and pushed him back. My body was still humming with need. The blood was pounding in my ears. Either my brain was about to explode, or I was going to tear his clothes off. It could have gone either way.

As if searching for something to grasp, his hands clawed through his hair, then wove behind his neck. Then shoved into his pockets.

"I'm turning Max in," he said. "Too many people have been hurt. *You* could've been hurt. And Charlotte . . ." He turned away, shoulders tensing as a shudder raked through him. "Whatever loyalty I've shown Max won't mean jack if he gets in a bind. I always knew it. I just didn't care until I met you."

I was still trying to catch up and couldn't think of anything to say in response.

"That night you came to Max's house, the FBI had put a wire on me," he said. "I think Bobby may have had more to do with Charlotte's death than he's saying, but they needed him to admit it on tape. My fists were just about to convince him to talk when I saw you on the monitor."

The wall I'd been leaning against outside Maxim's office shook as Alec had rammed Bobby into it—I remembered the way the window overhead had rattled.

"What did you do?" I finally managed.

He turned, streetlights gleaming in his eyes.

"The right thing. It just took me a while to get there."

"What did you do?" I said again, feeling the tremor start in my heels and work its way up my legs. Higher it went, through my core. Higher, into my chest.

"Anna—"

"Stupid man!" I shouted, covering my mouth. The words came out anyway. "You stupid . . . crazy . . . *stupid* man!"

I lunged at him and grabbed his shirt in my trembling fists. His hands wrapped around my wrists while I tried to shake some sense into him. His brows came together, his mouth made a tight straight line. I kicked him in the shin and he hissed in pain.

"They're going to kill you!" I yelled.

"Anna, they're going to protect me."

"Not the FBI!" I shook free of his grasp and pummeled his chest. "Maxim Stein. Bobby. They probably got rid of Charlotte, and when they find out what you've done, they're going to get rid of you and me next."

"Anna." He wrapped me in a bear hug, so tightly I could barely breathe. One of his strong arms latched behind my shoulders, the other crossed my lower back. He held me until the shaking finally stopped.

"Baby," he said in a hard, quiet voice I'd never heard before. "They're not going to touch you. I'll die before they hurt you, understand?"

I closed my eyes, burying my face in his chest.

"You can't die," I said. "I won't let you."

That broke him. He chuckled softly. The sound made me that much more afraid. How he could be so calm right now was beyond me.

I pushed back, and reluctantly, he let me go.

"You hid all of this from me."

This wasn't a simple omission. He was tangled up in the FBI now, and playing a very dangerous game that could mean jail or worse. After everything I'd heard tonight, I had no doubts Maxim Stein was capable of really hurting him—*us*. How could I trust Alec after this?

"I wanted to keep you out of it. If you had found out, you'd be culpable." He cleared his throat. "I never wanted you to have to carry my burden."

He didn't apologize for being protective, and somehow this smoothed some of the sharp emotions raging through me. His concern was staggering. There was no question in my mind that he wanted to keep me safe.

"You didn't even give me the choice."

He nodded slowly. "The truth is I couldn't let you go. I love you, Anna. You're it for me. I knew I was done the moment I saw you in your car outside Max's house."

I stood before him, unable to move. The room was too quiet, my thoughts, too loud. He loved me. He'd hidden the truth to protect me, hidden his past because he was afraid I would turn him away. Alec Flynn was a good man in a bad place, fighting to change the course of his life because he loved me.

"Who said anything about letting me go?" I asked.

One brow arched. "What?"

I took a step back, then another, slowly stretching the space between us until my heel hit the tinted glass wall that faced my apartment across the street. I leaned against it, the way I had leaned against my window the night I'd met him.

My thumb skimmed inside the waistband of my borrowed sweatpants. Ten feet away, his fingers began drumming against his thigh.

"Is there anything else?" I asked. "Any other life-changing bits of information I should know about?"

"I . . ." His gaze lowered to my mouth, leading me to lick my lips. "I love vanilla ice cream," he said. "And you're the sexiest woman I've ever seen."

I smiled. He took a step closer.

He wasn't smiling.

"No more lies," I told him.

His movements were graceful. Strong. He moved with a confidence contrary to the uncertainty in his eyes. He didn't believe that I would still love him, want him, after what he'd told me.

But I did.

"No more lies," he agreed.

"You hurt me," I said. "And you scared me. And worst of all, you left me wondering what had happened to you. You can't do that to me."

"I'll spend every day making up for it," he said. "I swear to you, Anna."

I believed him.

"What happens now?" The heat was rising in my veins.

Another step. Another.

"I can think of a few things."

I longed for his touch. My whole body burned for it.

"It was you," I whispered. "I was fantasizing about you the night you watched me."

He was close now. His hands slid beneath my T-shirt and closed on either side of my waist, fingers spanning over my ribs. I felt small in his grasp, delicate, but powerful too, because there was no hiding the desire that tightened his features.

"Tell me what I was doing," he said. "How did I touch you?"

We shouldn't have been doing this. Not now when so much was happening. Alec should have been with the FBI, and maybe I should have been there with him. But one look at him, and I knew that would have to wait.

My hips pushed forward, moved by an uncontrollable need to be closer. I closed my eyes. With him touching me, everything else faded into the background. Charlotte. Bobby and Maxim. A curtain slid over them, hiding them from view.

"You wanted me so badly," I said. "No one had ever wanted me so much."

His breath came in one hard rush, and then his mouth was on my neck, his tongue rasping over my skin. His hands dipped below the elastic waistband, curving around my bare bottom and crushing me to him. I rode his muscular thigh, the pressure teasing my sex. His cock twitched against my stomach, hard and heavy.

"Tell me," he growled.

"You touched me."

"How?" When I hesitated, he lifted me higher on his thigh. My hips writhed uncontrollably. *"How?"* he demanded.

"You put your fingers inside of me." I turned my head away. "You spread my legs wide, and while you touched me, your mouth was here." I rubbed my tight nipples. "Then here." I lowered my hand between my breasts to my now very wet center.

His hand rose up my chest, weighed one breast, then circled the peak with the rough pad of his thumb. I groaned.

"Alec."

"Keep going." He stretched the collar of my T-shirt, revealing my shoulder. His teeth scraped the top of my breast, making me jump.

"You made me crazy." I panted.

I clung to the window as he pushed me back. My feet flattened on the cold floor. A moment later he was easing down my sweatpants, exposing my damp skin to the cool air. My muscles quivered as a flash of heat seared through my belly.

He kneeled before me, and the sight of him there, looking up at me with such devotion made my knees buckle. He caught me, steadied me against the window, while he planted one tender kiss below my belly button. Then another lower, and another below that, until he was gently spreading my legs and worshipping me with long, leisurely strokes of his tongue.

My cheek turned against the cool glass, and though the windows were tinted, someone outside looking in could have been able to see us the way Alec had seen me that first night. He was living out his fantasy, just as I was living out mine, and the realization of this made me that much more desperate for him.

The slow pace became torturous. I longed for speed, the flash of fire. But like always, he was perfectly in tune with what my body needed. With one firm suction from his mouth on my clit, I fell off the cliff I hadn't even seen coming, landing in a churning pool of sensation. The current pulled at me, lashed at me, had me gasping while my fingers fisted his hair. The only things holding me up were the hard glass and his fingers, still deep inside me.

As the world righted itself, he stood, still massaging my tender inner flesh.

"What else did I do?" His voice was no more than a rough whisper.

My breathing had yet to slow. "You fucked me up against the window."

I heard his pants unzip.

"Slow at first," I said. "And deep. Like . . ." I gasped as his hard cock came to rest on my thigh. "Like you couldn't get close enough."

He moved my arms around his neck. Pressed my body against the window with his. I was soft in all the places he was hard, and we fit together like two pieces of a puzzle.

"I need you," he murmured. "I'm not whole without you."

"You went faster. I came with you inside of me," I said, flushed and ready. "I'd never felt that before, but you knew what to do."

"Because your body was made for me," he said. "Because I was made for you."

"Yes." I finally opened my eyes, and kissed him with everything I had, everything that had been building up over the last hours. Our lips crushed against each other. He devoured me. Claimed me, just as I claimed him.

My heart was beating hard, beating for him, and I was desperate to fill the hole he'd left there.

He lowered, and his cock grazed over my tender skin as he slid into position. I could feel his hot, steely head nudging at my entrance, and his heart hammering against mine. Nothing was more right than this.

"I missed you," I said.

He lifted me, and I clung to him, ready for that glorious impalement. The stretch, the fire, and our mutual destruction.

"I love you, Anna."

I blinked, needing to watch his face as he filled me. But something changed in his eyes. A glint of light, a reflection, that tore him away from me. His gaze was fixed on something beyond the glass. It was so intent I turned my head to see what he was looking at.

A light in my apartment had come on.

Thirty-two

In a flash, he'd jerked me away from the glass. I was still wrapped around him, hoisted off the ground, although his grip around my hips and back had ratcheted so tight I could barely breathe.

"Melvin?" I asked. Would he seriously come back to my place after all that had happened?

"Still in the hospital," Alec answered quickly. For a fraction of a second I wondered how he could know that, but I dismissed the thought as fast as it had come. He'd known the moment Melvin Herman had shown up at my work. Of course he was keeping tabs on him now.

Alec set me down, then tucked himself back into his pants and swiped my sweats off the floor. He kept me behind him, in the shadows.

A dark figure moved across the apartment, making me bite back a scream. It was hard to see details—the only light on was the lamp near the front door. Crouching low, I strained my eyes across the distance, feeling a bolt of anger as my dresser was knocked on its side.

"Son of a bitch," I said. I searched for my phone to call the police but realized I'd left it in my purse in the car.

"Stay here," said Alec.

I stared at him incredulously. "You're not going over there."

My bed was overturned. The mattress slapped against the glass and then disappeared from view.

"Stay away from the window," he said. "I'll be back soon."

"No." I grabbed his arm, panic prickling up my spine. "Wait. What if it's Bobby? He's dangerous, Alec."

"He's not the only one."

His teeth glinted in the reflection of the streetlights. It was the kind of smirk that made me nervous in all the wrong ways.

"We need to call the police!"

Alec was already striding toward the stairs. "Even if they arrest him, he'll be out by the end of the night."

"And if it's not him?"

"Then it's your landlord," Alec said. "Your alarm's programmed to send an alert to my cell phone if someone tries to break in. Only the three of us know your entry code."

I pictured my landlord, an old Spanish man with long silver hair. No, this was definitely not him.

Alec registered the concern on my face and kissed me on the brow.

"I'm going to get what I need to end this," he said.

A confession. If Bobby said he'd had more to do with Charlotte's death, then this would be over. I didn't know if he had the FBI wire, but he didn't seem concerned about it.

He kissed me once more on the mouth and then ran to the stairwell. Heart racing, I sprinted to the darkest corner of the window where I wouldn't be seen and knelt on the tile, peering across the way. A moment later Alec appeared on the street. He stopped at his car, opened the passenger-side door and leaned in. A silver handgun caught the light as he tucked it into the back of his waistband.

"Shit," I hissed.

Alec ran across the street, and by the time he'd disappeared inside the stairwell beside the Chinese restaurant, I'd chewed my thumbnail down to the quick.

"Come on, Alec," I said. "Get in and get out."

A noise behind me drew my attention. It was probably just somebody downstairs in the restaurant. They were in full swing now; I could see the hostess greeting patrons who walked through the oversize front doors.

I turned back to the window. Someone was still inside my apartment, but the light had turned off. Had Alec done that? Was he trying to catch the intruder by surprise?

Another noise behind me—a clang on the stairs. Someone was coming up. I jumped to my feet and cursed the open room. There was nowhere to hide but the restrooms on the opposite wall near the exit.

It could have been Alec—he might have thought better about his plan and come back, slipping across the street when I'd been distracted by the first noise—but I couldn't take any chances. Barefoot, I ran for the restrooms, trying to keep my steps quiet. But before I'd reached my destination, the hallway door swung open to reveal a muscular man in a black hooded sweatshirt and jeans. He pushed the hood of his sweatshirt back, showing his buzzed hair and sharp features.

My gaze dropped to the gun in his right hand.

"Anna," said Bobby. "I'd say I'm surprised to see you here, but that wouldn't be true."

I took a step back, a cold fire coursing through me. Was Alec still across the street? Would he realize Bobby was here when he found my apartment empty?

"Are those your clothes?" He assessed the borrowed T-shirt and sweats Alec had given me with a look of disappointment. "I've got to say, you've looked hotter."

"What do you want?" I asked.

"I'm glad you asked that." He moved toward me with a little too much pep in his step. "I'm here for you, Anna. It's time you and I spent a little quality time together."

"How'd you know I was here?" I had to keep him talking. That was one of the things my dad had always told me. Keep them talking, get them to lower their guard, then strike when they least expect it.

I sidestepped, trying to keep my moves subtle in hopes that I could skirt past him. He juked in front of me, more agile than I ever would have expected for a slab of meat.

"I was waiting for you to come home," he said. "You two sure took your sweet time."

"Well, you know," I said. "Places to go. People to see."

He laughed. Deliberately, he cradled the gun, and started flicking his thumb over the safety.

"We have to go," he said. "There are things we need to do, and this isn't the place for it."

I shivered. It was now or never.

I whipped my head to the side, as if I'd heard something to my right. Bobby followed my gaze and in that instant I bolted for the door. With a grunt, he swung back in my direction and snagged my arm. It threw me off balance and sent me careening into a stone pillar. I fell to my knees, the pain ricocheting up my thighs. Before I could rise, he'd hit me on the side of the head with his fist.

The world spun. I blinked, and the decorative tiles made a kaleidoscope pattern before my eyes. A searing pain lit up the back of my skull as he lifted me by my braided hair. I siphoned in a quick breath and kicked out as hard as I could, aiming for his balls. Instead, I got his knee, and with a grunt of pain he wheeled back and slapped me.

I fell to the floor in a heap, black spots taking over my vision. I tasted blood. My cheek felt as though it had instantly swollen an inch off the bone.

"Yes!" Bobby cheered, air-boxing like he'd just won a champion's belt. "You've got some moves. I get why he likes you." When I could finally look up through my knotted hair, he was grinning from ear to ear.

"Fuck you," I said.

He laughed again. And then his laugh stopped abruptly. He held the gun out before him and aimed it at my face.

I stared straight down the barrel, the fear turning to ice inside my belly.

Alec, where are you?

Still training the gun at my head, Bobby pulled a cell phone out of his pocket and dialed three numbers.

"Yes, it's an emergency!" he said when the attendant answered. "Someone broke into my neighbor's apartment. There's a woman there, her name's Anna. I think she's in trouble, I just heard her scream."

Frantically, I tried to make sense of what he was doing. He'd clearly called 911 and seemed to be reporting his own break-in.

"I think it's this guy she used to date—Alec something. He's about six three, dark hair, sort of shaggy. She's scared to death of him. He broke into her work earlier today. She said he has a gun." He rattled off my address.

"Stop," I said, but Bobby moved closer and pressed the gun flush against my cheek. I locked my jaw to stop the shaking and focused on the bruises and scabs that covered his knuckles.

"Hurry! I'm going to try to go over there. I've got to do something!"

He hung up, grinning broadly.

"You're sending the police after Alec," I said. "Too bad he's going to be gone by the time they get there."

"I doubt it," said Bobby. "My associate should be keeping him busy."

A surge of fury took me at the prospect of someone hurting Alec. I was going to claw Bobby's eyes out the second I got the chance.

"Your associate," I repeated.

Bobby's mouth pulled into a tight frown. "I'll admit, if he'd just grabbed you earlier at the salon, this would all be a lot cleaner now. *And* I wouldn't have had to pay hospital security to let him go."

"Earlier?" It felt like someone was jabbing an ice pick into my temple. "Melvin Herman works for you? He's . . . sick." The last time I'd seen him, he'd been red-faced from pepper spray and begging for me to read a love letter.

"He's as sick as I pay him to be," Bobby scoffed. "Come on, you didn't think we'd put together a backup plan when Alec jumped in the sack with you? It became clear pretty fast he wasn't going to do his job effectively."

"But . . ." I shook my head. "I've known Melvin for months."

"Which is exactly why I recruited him," replied Bobby, as though I should have known this already. "He was really pissed that you had him kicked out of the salon. When I offered him a chance to get you back, he was . . . eager, to say the least."

I wasn't sure who I wanted to strangle more—Melvin or Bobby.

"Alec's going to kill Melvin," I said.

"No, he won't. He'll knock Melvin around a little, but he won't be able to leave him there, and then the police will come and wrap everything up."

Bobby was on a roll now. I had to keep him talking, get him to lower his guard again. There was still a chance I could escape.

"The police will arrest Melvin," I said. "He's the one who broke in."

"First of all, he didn't break in," said Bobby. "He told your landlord he was your brother and had forgotten the code to your security system—nice touch by the way. That had to be Alec's doing." He scratched his chin. "Second, he was just there to apologize for what had happened earlier. At the most, he's going to get carted back to the hospital. Alec's the one who went apeshit and tore up your place. Lucky you weren't there. He does have a history of beating up women."

"That's not the way I heard it," I countered, but the dread was already sinking in. Alec had assault charges on his record. Even if they'd been dropped, it looked as though he had a capacity for violence.

Bobby shook his head. "Wow. You've really got him by the balls, haven't you? He told you everything."

I glared at him. "Melvin's going to rat you out once the police question him."

"He better not," said Bobby. "Otherwise he won't get the second installment of a very nice paycheck."

From down the street came the sounds of sirens. The police were on their way. I just needed to get their attention.

"Get up," Bobby said. "We're going for a ride."

He hauled me up by the arm and pulled me against his side. My head was throbbing now, and I spit a mouthful of saliva and blood onto his sweatshirt.

"Really?" he asked, clearly disgusted. "That's unhygienic." He wiped it off with his sleeve.

"Let me go." I thrashed as best I could, but my knee had twisted in the fall, and it felt like someone was digging a knife into it every time I moved.

"Soon," he said. "First we're going downstairs. You're going to be a good girl and keep quiet, otherwise I'm going to shoot you."

"You can't," I argued as he dragged me down the first of the stairs. I let my body go limp and made him carry me. "Even your big-shot lawyer wouldn't be able to save you from prison after that."

Bobby frowned. He was so strong it barely hindered him to pull me down the second flight of stairs.

"You've got a point. I guess I could just have your favorite stalker kill Alec." He opened the door at the bottom of the stairwell and backed us through. I could hear people talking twenty yards away, but no one passed by.

I tensed, and he pulled me upright. "He wouldn't." *He hasn't yet.*

"For enough money, some people would do just about anything." He opened the door at the bottom of the stairwell. "It would tie things up nicely if Melvin shot Alec with that pistol I gave him. Jealous lovers battle to the death. Poetic, isn't it? Just one call and I can make it happen."

"You can't buy everyone." Melvin may have been under Bobby's spell, but that didn't mean he would kill someone.

"Yes," said Bobby. "But you can buy some people."

A cold silence crept through me. Alec was close, maybe hurt, and Bobby claimed he could have him killed if I didn't play along.

"I don't believe you," I said. I didn't believe Melvin could better Alec—Alec outweighed him in fifty pounds of muscle alone. And if Bobby wanted me dead, he would have done it already.

Rule number one of self-defense: If you can run, do it.

Barefoot, and on a twisted knee, I spun and clawed Bobby's face. When his hold loosened, I pushed back and sprinted in the direction of the street.

"Goddammit!" I heard Bobby shout behind me.

Twenty feet and I was free. Bobby wouldn't dare take me down in full view of the restaurant.

Fifteen.

He got the back of my shirt. I powered on, feeling the fabric strain then rip. My breath was harsh in my ears. Gravel dug into the pads of my feet. I opened my mouth to scream; it had to be loud enough to rise over the bass from the clubs.

His forearm latched around my throat. I dug my chin in, scratching at his wrist. I struggled, fought with everything I had.

The air in my lungs was dwindling. The pounding of my heart echoed through my head. I turned my cheek, tried to bite, but my jaw closed on his sweatshirt alone. My throat was on fire.

A black frame surrounded my vision. I couldn't pass out. I had to keep fighting.

"That's it." I heard Bobby's voice as if he was calling from the end of a long tunnel. "That's it. Go to sleep."

The street before me faded, and went dark.

Thirty-three

The first things I registered were a pounding in my head and a sharp pain in my wrists. I opened my eyes, groaning, then immediately squeezed them shut as another hard throb slammed through the back of my skull. Gradually, a consistent whirring sound filtered through the headache. My cheek rested against a strap of some kind. A seat belt. My eyes shot back open. I was in a car. *My* car.

Another rule of self-defense: Never get in a car with the bad guy. Once he's got you there, you're not getting back out.

"Good morning, sunshine. Or I should say, good evening."

I turned to find Bobby in the driver's seat. He looked huge in my small car. Four long, pink scratches stretched from his eye down his jaw, lit by the glowing gauges in the dashboard. The gun rested in his lap. It was so dark outside I could barely make out the road ahead in the high beams.

My wrists, resting on my lap, were bound together by a bungee cord so tight my fingers prickled. My ankles were bound as well.

The last events I could remember came crashing to the forefront of my mind.

"Where's Alec?" My voice was scratchy. How long had we been driving? The clock on the dash said 10:14 p.m. Almost three hours had passed since Alec and I had left his father's.

"Probably in jail by now, where he's going to be for a long time," said Bobby. "Did you know he stole the design for a plane engine from Green Fusion and tried to get a patent on it? That's a serious offense." He had the audacity to try to sound shocked.

My throat was dry and aching. I wished for water, but wouldn't have trusted it coming from Bobby even if he offered.

"Where are you taking me?"

I twisted my wrists a little, stretching the cord. There had to be some way to loosen its hold. I kept working them from side to side, searching for a weak point as we drove into the night.

"Somewhere quiet," he said.

Dread coiled in my stomach. My teeth began to chatter.

"You're going to kill me." I meant to ask it as a question, but it came out as a statement.

Bobby sighed. He tapped the handgun against the driver's-side window.

"You're what we call a loose end," he said. "You've seen a little too much. And now with Alec going away, I really don't have the time to keep tabs on you."

I glanced at the key in the ignition. It was my spare key—the one I kept in the junk drawer in my kitchen. Dangling from it was the cheesy flip-flop key chain I'd bought at a gas station my first week in Florida.

Bobby had been in my apartment—that had been why my things were out of place. The thought of his thick fingers on my stuff made me ill.

"Why didn't you just do it back at the restaurant?"

"And do what with the body? Carry it across the street in front of everyone? Or leave it? That would go well. Max wants to develop that property. It's bad business if one of his previous employees ended up dead there."

Being referred to as a dead body made the bile rise in my throat.

"Is this what you did to Charlotte?" I asked, unable to hide the tremor in my voice.

He glanced my direction. "Worried you won't be able to swim with your hands tied together?"

He was going to push me over the edge. Drown me. My ankles worked back and forth, the cord making my skin raw. I tried to be subtle so he wouldn't hear.

He sighed loudly. "The thing about Charlotte is she had a hard time listening. I asked her nicely to get her ass out of her car, but she didn't." He flexed his hand over the steering wheel, showcasing its crisscrossed scabs.

"You punched a hole through her window."

"She's a redhead," he explained. "Stubborn, you know? She liked to taunt. Said she was going to talk to a reporter and send us all to jail. So we raced to see who could get there first. It wasn't my fault she couldn't control her own car."

"You drove her off the road."

"She drove herself off the road," he said, making a clear distinction. "I just gave her a little push."

The scratches on the side of the black SUV I'd seen at Maxim's house came to mind. Bobby must have sideswiped her while they were driving. I wished I'd had Alec's wire from the FBI so that I could have recorded our conversation. It worried me that Bobby was talking so freely. The only reason for him to do that was because he knew for a fact I wouldn't, or couldn't, repeat what he'd said.

"Someone had to see," I said. "Bridges have surveillance cameras." My father had once told me the cops had used the footage off a bridge in Cincinnati to catch a murder suspect. I was grasping at straws now, trying to cling to any hope that his actions would be discovered.

"Did you know just one lonely employee works at the transportation authority after hours?" Bobby asked. "I paid him a little visit after Charlotte and I went our separate ways. That footage is long gone, and if he's smart he's not going to say a word about it."

I had to hand it to him; Bobby wasn't as stupid as he looked. But the fact that he'd known just what to do made me wonder how much thought he'd put into this ahead of time, or if he'd done something like this before.

A small pop, and the binding around my ankle loosened. I checked on Bobby in my peripheral vision, but he didn't seem to have heard it. I began working the ties more vigorously. Ahead in the distance was an arcing line of streetlamps. A bridge.

"Where are we?" I asked, desperate to tell someone—the police, my father, Amy, *Alec*, though there was nothing he could do now to help me.

Bobby ignored me.

I wished I had my regular keys and the pepper spray attached to them. Immediately I started a mental inventory of what I could use to defend myself. There wasn't much. I could unlock the door and jump from the car, but we were going too fast. With my arms and legs bound I'd probably break my neck. I didn't see his cell phone—it was probably in his pocket. Not that I had time to call the cops anyway. My glove compartment was filled with registration papers and condiment packages. No help there. The back-seats were laid flat to accommodate my clunky massage table and my duffle bag filled with oils. There was a silver basin farther back that I might be able to swing if I could get my hands on it.

In the rearview mirror I caught sight of headlights, the first I'd seen since I'd come around. Someone was a few miles behind us, driving fast enough to catch up. If I could turn on the interior lights when they approached, I might be able to wave them down for help.

"You don't have to do this," I said.

Bobby wiped his nose with the back of his hand. "People

really do say that, don't they? I thought it was just in the movies. *You don't have to do this.*" He finished with a sniveling face.

"Well, you don't," I said. "You could be, I don't know, a decent human being and let me go."

"But what then?" he asked. "You sit at home for a couple days, then start thinking about it—how Bobby and Max fucked everything up for you, and how they should pay for it, and next thing we know, you're trying to file a statement with the police and I'm right back in the same situation."

My ankles were free. I'd slipped them out of the stretchy cord. I kept my legs pinned together so he couldn't tell. I focused on my hands, keeping them low and in the shadows so as not to attract Bobby's attention. The urgency was beating through my veins. I had to break free by the time we got to the bridge, otherwise I was going into the water.

"I did think about letting you go," he said after a moment. "This was Max's idea. If it helps, he was conflicted about it."

"Yeah, I bet," I said, hating that I'd once lathered him up with oil and rubbed his tense muscles.

"He was. You don't understand how upset he is that Alec was going to turn him in. Max loved him. Like a son. Or a really good dog." *Tap, tap, tap* went the gun against the window. "He needed a suitable punishment for that betrayal, and your death just happens to be it."

I focused on Bobby's words. He'd said that Alec was *going* to turn him in, not that Alec *had* turned him in. It was possible Maxim Stein didn't know Alec had gone to the FBI, that Alec still might have a case against him.

I hoped Stein was going to rot in some dark dungeon for what he'd done.

"How did your uncle find out about that?"

The car behind was closer now—a couple miles back. But we were only a few miles from the bridge. I turned away to hide my wrists in the shadows and began pulling the cords apart with a new desperation.

"Charlotte told me they were going to the police before she went for a swim," he said. "She was practically bragging about it."

My wrists weren't coming loose. The bridge was in sight now, and though there was a stop sign at the base, Bobby didn't show any signs of slowing.

"You're not ever going to run the company," I said. "One day someone's going to find out everything you've done and you'll get what you deserve."

He laughed. "Can I tell you something?"

"What is this, confession?"

"I don't even want Force," he said. "I still can't believe that with five wives and a hundred side dishes, Max doesn't have his own kid to pass it on to. I like my life as is."

"Being someone's henchman."

"It sounds sexy when you say it like that."

I snorted. "You man the gate. You're one step above mall security."

"You didn't seem to mind that Alec did the same."

Bobby looked down at my legs and I froze, thinking he'd seen that I'd freed my ankles. Instead, his gaze lingered, and I scooted against the passenger-side door to put more distance between us.

"I know you aren't wearing panties," he said in a quiet, creepy voice. "Or a bra. You're normally not my type, but those tits may have changed my mind."

Unable to help myself, I curled into the door. The thought of him fondling me when I was passed out was too much to handle. What else had he done? I pinched my legs together, trying not to think of it.

"Don't get so uptight," he said with a laugh. "I prefer active participants in the bedroom."

That came as a relief, but only a small one.

I wasn't going to make it to the other side of this bridge. I didn't know if Bobby planned on throwing me over, shooting me, or both, but I wasn't about to find out.

In a burst, I lunged across the divide, grabbed the wheel, and jerked it as hard as I could toward me. I saw the cement barrier marking the edge of the bridge one second before we slammed into it.

Thirty-four

The airbags deployed like an explosion, and I was only just able to block my face with my forearms. My head slammed against the headrest, and for several dizzy moments, time seemed to stand still.

Bobby's face gradually came back into focus. The airbag had broken his nose; it was already bruising, and blood poured from both nostrils. I started to pull at the bindings around my wrists only to find that the crash had dislodged the cord. As I found my breath, I searched for his gun, but it wasn't on his lap any longer. It must have been on the floor.

I didn't have time to look. I needed to run.

Shaking the cord free, I reached for the door handle and gave it a jerk. It was stuck. I tried again and again, but the door didn't budge. Panic flooded me. I was trapped in a car with a man who wanted me dead. My time had run out.

"What the fuck . . ." Bobby touched his face, looked at the blood on his hands. In a matter of seconds he would realize what I'd done. I needed to hurry.

Abandoning the door handle, I looked up. The windshield

had cracked but was still in place. Behind me, the table had slid forward in the impact and my duffle bag was now within reach.

I scooted down in the seat, wedged my shoulders against the cushion, and kicked at the windshield with my bare feet. My twisted knee sent a jolt of pain up my leg as I gritted my teeth and kicked it again.

"You crashed us?" Bobby asked.

He was staring at me, blinking. And as a light from behind the car drew closer, a bright reflection off the broken rearview mirror shone on his face, and I could see that his eyes were out of focus.

Frantically, I reached between the seats and snagged the first thing I could get my hand on in the duffle bag—the box of massage oils. They'd broken in the crash and the sharp scents of peppermint and cinnamon invaded my senses.

Survival instincts took over. I backhanded him in the face with the box. He swore again and clutched his nose.

"You stupid little bitch," he said.

The windshield had popped out in the corner. One more kick and I had my exit.

Outside, the lights were blinding. The driver who had been following us was finally here, but I couldn't wait for a rescue. I had to keep fighting.

I had to get back to Alec.

Bobby grabbed my hair, and I hit him again. The box opened, and the shards of glass rained down over his sweatshirt. I snatched one of the larger pieces and drove it into the hand that restrained me, making him howl in pain. At that moment his car door ripped open and he was dragged from the vehicle. The distraction was all I needed to dislodge the window. I scrambled up over the swollen airbag onto the hood and down the crunched metal with only one broken headlight to guide the way.

Falling gracelessly to the ground, I crawled as fast as I could over the asphalt toward the car that had followed us. I paused when a grunt and the distinctive crunch of fists striking flesh came from behind me.

I glanced back, shocked to find Alec on top of Bobby, pummeling him in the face.

"Alec!"

Bobby wasn't moving.

"Alec!"

As if waking from a dream, Alec stopped. He rose, and dragged Bobby by the shoulders to his Jeep—the car that had been behind us. There, he removed a set of plastic zip-tie cuffs, the same kind he'd used on Melvin Herman at the salon, and bound Bobby's hands behind his back.

From far away came the haunting wail of sirens. I turned and could just make out the blue and red flashing lights of two patrol cars a few miles behind us.

"You're a dead man, Alec." Bobby's voice was muffled. "Both of you. You're dead. When Max finds out . . ."

Alec kicked him hard in the gut. He didn't say much after that.

He left Bobby there on the street and headed to where I was, still on my knees near the Jeep's tailgate. There was something different about him, wild and animalistic. His body moved with a fluid, dangerous power and his fists were clenched and covered with blood. I could see the muscles of his neck standing taut, and a flash of white teeth.

This was not a man you wanted to mess with.

I crab-walked back a few steps, still shaking with adrenaline. Moving because my body demanded it, not because I was afraid. Alec would never hurt me. And because I knew this, it baffled me when he stopped and lowered to a crouch a few feet away.

"Anna," he said softly. "It's okay. You're safe now."

He reached out a hand, and after a moment I took it. He didn't move fast; maybe he knew it would have fried my last nerve. Instead we stayed that way—him holding my hand, rubbing his thumb over my knuckles, while my heartbeat slowed one beat at a time.

"You came." My voice cracked.

"As fast as I could."

"How'd you find me?"

He gave me a guilty smile. "Remember that GPS tracking device I put in your car?"

I most certainly did not.

"Wait," I said, recalling a joke he'd made after he'd found me at a restaurant with Randall. "I thought you were kidding about that."

For some reason this was suddenly hilarious to me, and my tear-drenched laugh broke through the tension.

"I'm coming closer," he said. A little while ago he'd been terrifying, but now his touch soothed me, and his voice was calm and steady.

I nodded. He scooped me up off the ground, cradling me against his chest. I closed my eyes and breathed him in, savoring his dark, heady scent and the steady beat of his heart. He carried me to the passenger side of his Jeep and gently set me down on the seat. It was too soon; I could have stayed in his arms for the rest of my life and been happy.

Carefully, Alec tucked my hair back behind my ears and examined my face. His eyes narrowed as his thumb brushed over my cheek and cracked lip. I jerked as his other hand came to rest on my sprained knee.

"I'm going to kill him," he said, jaw flexing. For a flash I feared what he was capable of.

"No," I said. "Stay with me."

The sirens were closer now, their volume deafening as the patrol cars blocked the road.

I held his face in my hands and forced him to look at me. After a moment he nodded, and then he held me as tightly as he allowed himself to while the shudder raked through his body.

"It's over," he said. And I nestled my face against his shoulder and finally let myself cry.

The police came to the car soon after, and a Latino man with salt-and-pepper hair and a short goatee introduced himself as Terrance Benitez, a friend of my father's.

"You called it." He shook Alec's hand. "You were right about Herman, too. He broke when he realized no one was going to come bail him out. He'll be going away for some time."

"Thanks for the help." Alec's hand came to rest on my lower back, a move that made me feel safe and strong all at once. "I got in a jam at your apartment. I'm not sure asking your dad to call in a favor with his friend at the Tampa PD earned me a lot of points." He sighed.

"You called my dad?" It was probably a death sentence, but for some reason I found this endearing.

"Bobby set me up. He had Melvin trash the place, and then, when the cops showed up, blamed it on me. They would have carted me away if Terry hadn't been there."

Once again, I had to hand it to Bobby. Things had played out just as he had anticipated. I looked up as he was shoved into the back of a patrol car. He was repeating the same line over and over: "Do you know who my uncle is?"

Pretty soon the whole country would know who his uncle was.

"Your dad called me about the stalker issue and asked that I keep an eye on you," said Terry. "When your name came up on the screen, I hightailed it over to your apartment, only to find this guy swearing up and down that you'd been abducted." He stuck a thumb out in Alec's direction.

"Melvin let that slip just before the police took off your door. Cocky bastard." Alec mumbled something about taking it too easy on him.

"Where was the FBI?" I asked. "Why didn't they vouch for you?"

"They were busy." Alec grinned. "Raiding Max's house. It's really over, Anna."

The weight I'd been carrying on my shoulders suddenly felt lighter. Maxim Stein couldn't hurt Alec anymore, Bobby was going to jail, and we were safe. There was just one more piece.

"Bobby ran Charlotte off the road," I said. "He confessed the whole thing to me. He threatened her, ran her down, and then destroyed the bridge footage to cover his tracks."

Terry scratched his chin. "We'll look into it. We have enough, between the white-collar crimes and the abduction charge, to hold him for long enough to wrangle a murder confession out of him, don't worry."

I breathed in slowly and tucked myself against Alec's side. My cheek rested against his warm chest, and my arms circled his waist. This really was over, and now Alec and I could move forward, together.

A shared look passed between him and Terry, and then Alec pulled me even closer. Something was still wrong, I could feel it. I pulled back and looked up at him, seeing my suspicions confirmed in his scowl.

"Terry, can you give us a few minutes?" he asked.

Terry hesitated, then nodded toward where Bobby was still shouting for his uncle from the backseat of a cop car.

"I'll have my hands tied with this asshole for a while. Maybe we can finish our business back at the station. Eight a.m. sounds like a good time."

Alec shook his hand again. "I'll be there."

"You'd better be."

I stared at Alec, searching for some hint as to what was going on, but Terry patted my shoulder. "Call your dad," he said. "He wanted to let you know he'll be flying in first thing tomorrow."

"Great," I said, but couldn't blame him. Dad would have to see I was in one piece for himself—anyone else's word, including my own, wouldn't matter. I could only imagine how he and Alec were going to get along now. I hoped that he'd be grateful Alec had come after me, but I doubted it would be that simple.

"Come on," said Alec. "I'll take you home."

Thirty-five

After a short visit with the EMT, Alec drove us toward home in his Jeep. I refused to go anywhere in an ambulance and insisted that Alec would take me to a hospital immediately, should I show any signs of concussion. We left my car as part of the crime scene, and Terry agreed, as a friend of my father's, to take my statement about what had happened the following morning.

I was still ramped up, but at least I wasn't afraid. What peace of mind Bobby had stolen from me Alec had replaced, just by staying close. He didn't say much while he drove, but I could feel him watching me. It still brought the same rush as it had the first time I'd met him, even if it came from a place of worry, not lust.

My forearms had minor burns from the airbag, and I blew on them to take away some of the sting. I felt like I was coming down from three pots of coffee—a little buzzed, a little twitchy—and when the jitters made it hard to stay still, my heels began to tap the floor mat.

"Can we stop?" I asked. We were still an hour away from the city, and I couldn't sit any longer.

"Sure." Immediately he cut across the empty lanes toward an exit.

"Is there a motel or something close by? There has to be, right? This is Florida."

He glanced over at me. "I'll find one."

"I just want to take a shower," I explained. I twisted my hair around my finger. "I know it sounds crazy. I just need to clean up. I'd settle for a hose at a car wash at this point." I wanted the memories of Bobby's hands and fists on me scrubbed away as soon as possible.

"Of course."

I eyed him across the car. "You're being awfully agreeable."

At the end of the off-ramp, he stopped, and turned to me.

"I'll do whatever you need tonight." His eyes fell to my lips, and a sudden wave of heat stole my breath. I wanted him to kiss me senseless, make these last hours disappear. I wanted his mouth to race over me while he made love to me like he couldn't restrain himself, but instead he was so calm and controlled. It made me even more antsy.

"You're not going to tell me we're only an hour away from Tampa?"

He shook his head, the darkness hiding his expression.

"If you say you want to stop and take a shower, we'll stop. If you say you want dessert for dinner, we'll get you dessert. I'm not in the business of telling the woman I love no."

My heart seemed to stop, then restart, doubling up on beats to make up for the skip. I wasn't sure I'd ever get used to hearing him say that he loved me. When I was with Bobby, the thought had crossed my mind that I'd never hear it again. It was what had driven me to crash my own car, kick out a windshield, fight for my life.

Alec leaned toward me, as if to kiss me. He was a few inches away when he hesitated, and lifted his thumb to trace the cut Bobby had left on my lip. It stopped him short, and he shoved back in his seat, then pulled out his smartphone and waited for the map program to pick up our location. That simple, dismissive move made me feel a hundred times grimier. A minute later we were back on the road.

We couldn't stop soon enough.

He found a pretty beach motel, and after a quick exchange with the night manager, we were headed to a second-floor room. It was small but cozy, with a view of the Gulf and a king-size bed. The walls were the color of lilacs, and there were white sand dollars lined up on a bookcase filled with worn paperbacks.

While he stood on the balcony and stared out over the dark waves, I retreated to the bathroom. The shower was pristine white and surprisingly large. While the water began to steam up the room, I took off my ripped, dirty T-shirt and sweatpants, and examined myself in the mirror.

My cheek was still red from Bobby's fist, and my lip was a little swollen. The seat belt had bruised my shoulder, and my hands and feet were scratched and dirty. I could clean myself up, but I would probably look worse tomorrow.

The door creaked open, and the steam dissipated. Framed in the entry stood Alec, still wearing a faded red T-shirt and jeans. His hands were now clean of Bobby's blood and hung loosely by his sides. I stared at them, wishing they were holding me, making me feel good, and then I crossed my own arms over my breasts because I'd never in my life felt as vulnerable as I did in that moment.

He took a step forward. "Can I wash you?"

Just the words were enough to send shimmers through me. I nodded slowly and lowered my hands. Gingerly, I stepped into the water and waited for him to come in behind me. Knowing his eyes were traveling down my back, over my naked body, sent a hard contraction through my core.

I heard his shoes click against the tile. The water soaked through my hair and made a river between my shoulder blades. The warmth did nothing to relax the growing tension in my breasts. The hard peaks began to ache as the seconds passed.

He entered the shower behind me and I held still, waiting for him to make the first move. After a moment, the gentle pressure of a washcloth skimmed over my shoulder. It lowered down my back, and then returned to clean my other side. The soap smelled fresh, like the ocean.

Unable to stand the distance between us, I glanced over my shoulder, surprised to find him still wearing his clothes. The water splashed off my body, peppering his T-shirt, and soaked the worn cuffs around his bare feet.

"I think you forgot something," I said.

He continued his slow, tender work, moving over my bottom and down my legs, where he washed one foot, then the other. He was so careful where Bobby had been so brutal that it brought tears to my eyes. When he rose, I turned to face him, watching the way his features tightened as his eyes lowered. His hair was responding to the dampness and curling around his ears.

"Did he hurt you, Anna?" he asked in a quiet voice.

My breathing hitched. He applied more soap to the washcloth and wove it through my fingers, careful to avoid the bandages on my knuckles from the EMT.

He wasn't talking about Bobby hitting me; he was asking if Bobby had tried to rape me.

"No," I said, suddenly angry. "Would it matter if he had?"

He froze, leveled me with his gaze. "Of course it would matter."

I couldn't stand his soft voice or his gentle touch any longer. I didn't want his pity, I wanted his love.

"I'm not broken." I'd begun to shake again. "Stop acting like I'm broken!"

He stepped forward, pushing me farther into the water. It soaked his shirt, making the fabric cling to his chest.

"You're not," he said. "Look at you. You're anything but broken."

I buried my face in my hands, frustrated because he wouldn't give me what I needed.

"I thought you were gone, Anna." His voice was rough with emotion. "I followed your position on my GPS for an hour, losing my mind with what was happening to you. And then you stopped." He twisted the washcloth so vigorously his knuckles turned white. "Christ. I thought I'd never see you again."

I felt his fear then. It was bright and toxic, big enough to swallow us both.

"I couldn't let that happen," I said.

"You were there because of me. What I'd done."

"I was there because Bobby's a psycho, and his uncle is a rich, maniacal fuck."

"Goddammit, Anna. You could have died because of me!" He threw the washcloth down. "A better man would leave."

"So go!" I pushed him back. "If you want to go so bad, do it!"

He lunged forward and kissed me, hard enough to sting my bruised lip. His hands rose to my face, cupped my cheeks, and pulled me closer. His tongue plunged into my mouth, claiming me with hard, frantic licks. The emotions were surging through us, clashing at every point we connected.

Thrown off-balance, my front rasped against his wet T-shirt, and twin bolts of electricity shot from my nipples straight into my sex. With a desperate cry, I arched into him, the desire to feel his skin more acute than the need to breathe. I tugged at his shirt, shoved it up his stomach, and felt the groan rumble through his chest as my breasts smashed against him.

"Tell me to stop." His hands flew over my shoulders and down my back, pulling me hard against him. "Tell me it's wrong to want you like this right now." His hands slid between us, and my nails dug into his shoulders as he tugged at one nipple. "Tell me if you're scared."

"I'm not scared. I need you." My knee traveled up his thigh, and he gripped it and ground his hips against me. His eyes, deep and mesmerizing, locked on mine, and in them at last was the need I'd been longing to see.

"Make me forget," I said.

He swallowed. Nodded once.

His shirt came over his head and was discarded on the shower floor, and then he was kissing me again. I winced as his teeth grazed the cut on my lip, and his shoulders bunched in response.

"Don't stop," I begged. "Don't stop."

He swore sharply. "I love you, Anna. I'm sorry. I love you so damn much." He lowered, drawing one nipple in his mouth while the other hand dragged down my wet stomach. His fingers slid through my slit, finding it slippery and hungry for his touch.

I fumbled with his belt, the need to be filled overwhelming. His jeans were stiff from the water and hard to remove, so he threaded my fingers behind his neck and did it himself. The zipper lowered, and as he tugged the fabric down his hips, his cock, dark and engorged, came free. I gasped at the sight of it, at the physical proof of his desire. Before he could disrobe completely, he bent his knees, and drove into me in one stroke. The breath expelled from my lungs in a huff. I was on my toes, holding on to his slick, wet shoulders for support as he flattened my back against the cold shower wall.

Before he could withdraw and thrust again I was coming. It was like no other orgasm he'd ever given me. It was hard, and punishing, and it slashed through the fear that had pooled inside of me. I cried in relief, tears streaming from the corners of my eyes as he tucked his face against my shoulder. He buried himself again and again, destroying any hold this night might have had on us. It was fast and urgent, and with his teeth scraping my neck and his hands gripping the soft flesh of my thighs, he followed my lead, filling me with every ounce of his love.

"Anna," he murmured against my neck.

"More," was all I could respond. His cock twitched inside of me, making my muscles bear down on him. He shuddered.

He carried me from the bathroom to the bed, his hard length still embedded deep in my body. Throwing aside the comforter, he laid me down on the sheets, placing feather-soft kisses on my cheek and lips. My hips beckoned him on, but he slowly withdrew, and I threw back my head in protest.

As quickly as he could, he maneuvered out of his wet jeans and underwear and soon was sliding over me again. I could feel the thick weight of him on my thigh, but though his head pressed against my tender opening, he had yet to push inside.

"Please," I said as his tongue stroked my nipple. "Make me yours."

His hand slipped under my lower back as his mouth rose up my neck to my ear. I wound my legs around him, crossing them at the ankles.

"You're already mine, Anna," he said, a clear possession in his tone. "But now, you need to do this. Everything I am belongs to you."

His words sang through my veins, making me strong. I stared into his eyes, seeing his intent as clear as any truth. My power had been stolen from me, and now he was giving it back.

In one fluid move, he flipped us over, and I hovered over him, savoring that last step off the ledge. His hands rode up my thighs to my hips, and I grabbed them and moved them to my breasts. My heavy lids drifted closed as he began his gentle kneading, and I squeezed his grip, showing him the firm pressure I needed.

"Make me yours, baby," he said, voice husky.

I adjusted my hips so that he was pressing against me, and then I lowered. I was still slippery with our combined juices, but though he slid into my body, his substantial size stretched my flesh, burning my muscles with the impact. I moaned, unable to hold still, and swiveled my hips the way he did when he made love to me. His thighs tensed, and the growl that slipped through his lips spurred me on. I rotated my hips again, until he was nestled in the perfect place.

Then I rode him harder than I ever had.

When my muscles began to quiver, I leaned forward, and he

moved his hands down to my hips, but still did not help me. I did it all myself, taking from him what I needed, while he whispered in my ear about my beautiful body, and my strength, and his love for me.

"Come with me," I cried just before I let go. And he did, holding me tight against his chest as he emptied his very soul into me.

We stayed that way for some time, and as the tremors passed, I grew drowsy. Before I could sleep, he lifted my chin to kiss me tenderly on the lips.

"Whatever happens in the morning, remember this," he said.

Sensing his sadness, I rose on my elbows.

"I remember all of it," I said. "Every second with you."

He kissed me again and rolled onto his side so I could rest my cheek on his biceps. I traced the rise and fall of his abs with one finger while he dragged my knee up over his hip.

"What is it?" I asked.

His brows pulled together, and I smoothed them with my thumb, wishing I could fix what was bothering him.

"I have to go away for a while," he said. His eyes moved over my face, as if memorizing every feature.

I wondered if he was still worried about Max and Bobby.

"I'll go with you," I said.

He gave me a small smile, but his expression grew serious once again. "The district attorney agreed to work with the FBI, but she couldn't let me off with nothing. I . . ." He cleared his throat. "I have to serve three months in prison, then six months parole."

I sat up. "No." I shook my head emphatically. "You did the right thing. They can't punish you for that!"

He pushed himself up so that his back was against the headboard, and drew me onto his lap. I couldn't believe this was happening. We'd fought to be together, and now we couldn't be?

"I did a lot of wrong things to get to that right thing," he said, nuzzling his face against my neck. "Terry told me earlier. I have to check in at the station in a few hours."

Maybe we can finish our business back at the station, Terry had said. *Eight a.m. sounds like a good time.*

"No," I repeated. I shoved off his lap and stood. Sure I was naked, but that didn't mean I wasn't ready to take on the entire FBI. "Tell them it's not an option. You're free now. You're mine now."

"Anna." He swung his legs off the bed. "I'm yours regardless."

From the look in his eyes, he'd already accepted his fate. And though I fought it, I knew it was a losing battle.

"Let's run away," I said. "Canada. Or maybe Mexico. I've never been to Mexico."

He smiled. "If it's possible, I think I love you even more for saying that."

"I mean it."

"I know." He reached for my hands, drew me closer. I sat on his lap, and with his fingertips skimming down my spine, I slouched and let the gravity of the situation weigh me down.

"I know it's not fair to ask you to wait," he started, but I cut him off.

"Shut up," I said. "I'm not going anywhere."

I'd never felt such a strong urge to stay in one place as I did with his arms around me. Right then, I knew that my days of moving on were over.

He chuckled. "I don't deserve you."

"You're right," I grumbled. His hand slipped between my knees and began its slow ascent up my inner thighs. I could feel his cock stiffen against my hip, and I couldn't help but soften.

"You could stay at my place if you wanted," he said. My breath caught as his thumb reached my center and teased a slow line up to my clit.

"I've got a place," I said, but the butterflies had already begun to come alive in my belly. My head tilted back, giving him easier access to my neck, where he licked a slow, sensual line to my jaw.

"It's a wreck," he said. "And your landlord blew it when he

gave away your security code." I reached between us, rubbing my thumb over the swollen head of his penis. He instantly became rock hard.

"You could put up some things," he said, his voice more strained. "Some of your things."

"Are you asking me to move in, Alec?" I asked.

He caught my earlobe in his teeth. "Take it easy. I just wanted to know if you'd house-sit."

I elbowed him in the ribs and pushed him onto his back. Crawling over him, I ran my nails up his chest and grabbed his steel-hard cock with both hands.

"What are you doing to me?" he asked quietly.

"I'd think that was obvious," I said.

I was giving him something to remember.

Epilogue

I was rolling up my yoga mat in Alec's apartment when my cell phone buzzed. It was a text from Amy, telling me to turn on the news immediately.

I did as she said, falling back on the leather couch. As I found the channel, my bare feet rubbed along the soft cushions. I was going to make love to Alec on this couch when he got out. He would be sitting, and I would straddle him. Dig my knees into his hips as I rode the hard, satin length of his cock.

It was one of the many plans I'd been concocting since he'd been shipped away to a white-collar prison in Pennsylvania two weeks ago.

Feeling the pang in my chest that came whenever I thought of him—which was constantly, now that I was staying here—I chewed my nails, but froze when a familiar face appeared in the left corner of the screen.

Maxim Stein.

I had to say, he looked like shit in orange. The prison uniform did nothing to complement his smooth, perfect hair or his dark, calculating eyes. Too bad for him.

The reporter said he was going away for about a million years once all the conspiracy and corporate espionage charges were added up. There was new information coming to the table, too; apparently his nephew Robert, also in custody, had confessed that Max had ordered the death of Ms. Charlotte MacAfee, the former president of Green Fusion.

I wished more than anything that Alec could have seen this.

But he would know soon enough. I knew the district attorney was still using him as a key witness in the case, and besides that, I was going to write him a long letter about it. Just as soon as I found some paper that didn't have a take-out menu printed on one side.

As I rose and made my way to the balcony window, I again made a mental count of the days until he'd be out. Ten weeks seemed like a long time, but Derrick had agreed to take me back at the salon. And I was always welcome at Amy's after work. I still had to move the bulk of my things into a little place I'd found on Westshore Boulevard; I wasn't ready to completely invade Alec's life, even if I was spending most of my nights here. And besides that, my dad was making another trip out to check on me next weekend. I was going to be busy.

That didn't mean I didn't miss Alec like crazy.

I leaned back against the window and smiled, imagining him on the other side watching me.

He'd better be ready to rock when he got home.